ONLY THE GRASS SUFFERS

ONLY THE GRASS SUFFERS

A Novel

DALE MOLL

LUMINARE PRESS
WWW.LUMINAREPRESS.COM

Only the Grass Suffers: A Novel
Copyright © 2021 by Dale Moll

All rights reserved. This book or any portion thereof may not be reproduced or used in any manner whatsoever without the express written permission of the publisher, except for the use of brief quotations in a book review.

Printed in the United States of America

Luminare Press
442 Charnelton St.
Eugene, OR 97401
www.luminarepress.com

LCCN: 2021916512
ISBN: 978-1-64388-785-2

for Barbara

*"When two bulls fight,
it is only the grass that suffers."*

—an old African saying

Chapter 1

PRELUDE TO A REUNION

The sun had stretched its path across an aqua sky until a now late afternoon warmed the quiet Wisconsin town. The summer of 2018 was still yet new, so gentle breezes chilled the blue nights and golden sunlight offered refreshment to the heart of Cottage Grove after a long harsh winter. The warmth felt good and you could almost smell it in the air.

On the west side of the square stood the archaic theater where Jack Llewellyn worked as the projectionist. The January-Wabash Theater. Marked by ornate and somewhat gaudy murals and wood carvings, the theater was a piece of history in the otherwise culturally limited town. Built three-quarters of a century ago, the theater served as a picture window to everything that Cottage Grove was not. It brought dancing lights and flourishing colors and resonant voices to an oftentimes vanilla existence. It was the town's robust splash of visual art and not many in the Grove realized even that condition.

The second story flat of Jack Llewellyn was just a few short blocks away from the January-Wabash. The town was only quietly alive as he slowly shuffled to the front of the movie house. Stopping in front of the newspaper stand,

Llewellyn looked for any familiar faces that were usually present around the city square, a square around which most of Cottage Grove's more prosperous merchants were located. He pushed four quarters in the newspaper vending machine and pulled a copy of the *Journal Scene*. With his paper tucked under his arm he unlocked the main entrance doors and strolled into the lobby of the theater.

Although it was late afternoon and the films were not scheduled until 7:00 p. m., Llewellyn had varied duties beyond the projection room. Equipment maintenance, janitorial labor, beverage and food preparation also needed his attention. Along with longtime proprietor Santosh Pulvermacher, Jack had a half-day's worth of work before the feature film rolled and made its snake-like journey through two different 35mm projectors.

Together the two old men ran the theater and welcomed the community on a daily basis featuring one or two second-run movies for its viewing pleasure. With the help of a handful of high school students manning the ticket booth and the concessions, they provided a consistent and welcomed motion picture experience.

On a rare occasion, Llewellyn dusted off his doctorate in Film Study and gave a two-minute preamble to a noteworthy movie before a sparse crowd at show time. It was never lost on either Pulvermacher or Llewellyn that the latter's academic expertise in film art and history was redirected to a more practical, if not mechanical, application – that of a projectionist. There was an almost ironic amusement in the encore career that Llewellyn selected upon his retirement from the university.

The lobby was spacious with a large square concession counter that claimed the middle of the lushly carpeted room. The area was intentionally large to accommodate the gathering of people around all four sides before the inner doors were opened to the theater proper. The space also gave ample elbow room for haphazard lines to form at each side of the concessions.

The theater itself afforded two separate aisles and three well-defined seating areas. But, because the theater was not grand, there was no balcony. Floor lights dimly illuminated the two walkways and a stage raised the level of the massive white screen so a view was never a problem for any seat in the house. An emergency exit door was located both stage left and stage right at the forward corners of the house.

Although the back wall was nondescript, both side walls were impressively ornate using a baroque motif in which columns and wall coverings were famous by extravagance and flamboyance. Varied styles of patterns and swirling colors characterized the ornateness to the extent of a borderline gaudiness.

By early evening, Pulvermacher had finally arrived with unusual lateness. Llewellyn heard his movements from the anteroom that separated the theater house from the lobby. He had just finished vacuuming the carpet and was rolling up the machine's long soft cord when he observed his boss.

Santosh wore a pale blue collared shirt and khaki trousers that were supported by wide navy blue suspenders. The gray hair was thinning terribly and was destined to be short-lived in the coming years. He was heavy-set with a full face and an affable manner. After all the years, he was still one of the Grove's leading personalities.

Alongside Pulvermacher was the distinguished police chief of Cottage Grove. Dressed in a crisp white shirt crowned with four stars on each shoulder and a large shiny-silver five-point star over his heart, the city's number one law enforcer stood somberly with hat held in hand and gun and telephone at his waist.

"Good evening, Sandy. Thanks for coming in," he teased his late-arriving boss. But there was silence and a grim expression of the owner's face as he moved toward his old friend.

Llewellyn turned to the uniformed officer with measured hesitancy.

"Hello, Chief," he said slowly.

"Jack, I have some terrible news for you," Santosh started, stopped and continued on with a slow dread. "Early this morning, the police chief called to tell me that Julia had died. He wanted to talk to you as soon as possible."

Although Julia and he had been divorced for a good number of years, Llewellyn still loved her and acquiesced to doing favors for her often and with careful attention. His old enemy, Michael Carlisle, continued a lengthy affair with Julia and that long ago ended their marriage but not his love for her.

There was not only silence in the theater anteroom, there was a deafening stillness that consumed the air that Llewellyn breathed. The three men stood and said nothing for a short while, then the old projectionist spoke.

"How did she die? When?"

The distinguished-looking police chief made his report with both efficiency and compassion. Like most people, he, too, liked and respected Llewellyn.

"Jack, she committed suicide in her condo… she hung herself… with the cloth belt of her bathrobe… in the bedroom closet," he pressed quietly. "The coroner guesses that she died a few days ago. The maintenance lead at the condo was responding to a neighbor's complaint of a disagreeable odor and he gained entrance into her home after making several attempts to contact her."

The chief watched the face of Llewellyn as the ghastly method of death sunk in and the information was registered onto the projectionist's brain. Llewellyn stood frozen with despair and slowly, mechanically, completed the task of rolling up the vacuum's extension cord. All that he could think was that he still loved her, even after all of the years of sheer betrayal, humiliation and consequent divorce.

Now, there was no hope of whatever slim chance ever existed for reconciliation. Julia was dead and he did not know why. In a way, he really had no right knowing. They were no longer husband and wife and had not been for many years. Llewellyn thought that his old swarmy nemesis, Michael Carlisle, had more right to know about Julia than he did. After all, it was he who came between them and cultivated a love affair for years in the sublime betrayal of a bad wife.

"There was no suicide note but we found anti-depressant drugs in the bathroom," the policeman continued. "Do you know why she was taking these drugs? Do you know why she was depressed?"

"No, Chief, I haven't talked to Julia for a number of weeks. Have you contacted Michael Carlisle? He would know better than me."

"Not yet, but we will get around to that. We understand he was close to her, as well." The police chief shifted his weight slightly because the conversation took a naturally uncomfortable turn.

After another painful pause Llewellyn finally acquiesced to his new world. "I guess I had better call David and let him know what has happened. What a sad thing it is to call one's son and inform him of his mother's death."

Pulvermacher and the police chief stood in silence and subsequently placed their hands on the shoulders of the old projectionist. There was very little else to say other than the sharing of logistical details.

"After the autopsy, the coroner will send Julia's body to Riedelsheimer Funeral Home," whispered Pulvermacher. "Because of the circumstances surrounding her death, there has to be an autopsy."

"Of course," replied Llewelyn slowly.

"Take off a few days, Jack. We can make it well enough while you're gone. Take as much time as you need."

"Thank you, Sandy."

Llewellyn collected a few of his things and left the building without further comment. His quiet movements and glazed expression reminded Pulvermacher very much of a man who was walking away purely on automatic.

IN THE SMALL KITCHEN OF HIS LODGINGS THE OLD MAN'S hands were wrapped around a warm cup of coffee. The cracked and crusty fingers separated and closed and separated, and finally rubbed themselves into solace and contentment. He thoughtfully lifted his coffee to his mouth. He slurped slowly, repeatedly. His nostrils flared as they searched for that comforting aroma of warmth and home. Jack was thinking. He sat his coffee down on the wooden table. Because his flat was chilly even on early summer afternoons, his coffee sent steam across his thickened glasses as he sat before his bologna sandwich. Taking out his white handkerchief to gently rub his bifocals, he got up for another cup of coffee.

Only the Grass Suffers

In recent years and since being divorced, it had always been the same. His routine consisted of work to sustain a physical existence and contemplation to sustain enduring memories and undying grudges. His only recreation was long walks along Sweetwater Creek and the occasional reading of a good book. And with the singular exception of his modest profession, he had only a handful of ties to an indifferent world.

What was always in the back of his mind was the unsettling knowledge that his fiercest enemy had profoundly and adversely altered his life - twice, but Jack never offered any indication to a curious public of its effects. Even so, he was always a thoughtful man. More than that, he was also a very patient man. It is said that the longest odds in the world are those of getting even. Time would tell if that tiresome axiom still held true throughout the autumn of his life.

The cup once again filled with black water was carried back to the kitchen table and the projectionist sat again. He had lived in his flat for almost three years.

Before that he lived with his son and his daughter-in-law, but moved out after a long-standing disagreement concerning his personal habits. Mostly the conflict was related to his sweet and sour disposition and his tendency to leave about the rooms of the house sundry quantities of peelings and rinds of fruits. In the mornings he was a veritable bear before his customary pot of coffee, but by midday he was congenial and forthcoming. In a way, coffee grounds and fruit peelings ended what could have been a very comfortable existence. His friends called him Jack, sometimes J. D., but his full name was John David Llewellyn.

His preoccupation was surviving in his apartment, keeping his job, and entertaining himself with gossip. He was simply a man who was not much afraid of old age, dying, or even loneliness. The world had changed dramatically in front of his eyes that sometimes felt ancient to him. Throughout it all, he remained constant and there was no real misunderstanding of the world around him. He had lived long enough to anticipate and appreciate the motives of people and the natural order of change even in a small town. From the political chicanery of academia from which he once negotiated to the quiet parochial setting of a farming community, Llewellyn took care of his work and personal life without troubling the waters.

On this day he sat for a while and thought about Julia, what she had meant to him, and now her untimely and self-inflicted death. In the end, he thought about his son, David. He would have to be told as soon as possible and as gently as possible. There was no longer any use crying for or about Julia, she was gone forever. Now there was only David to consider. But he wanted to give him the news in person. He made a telephone call and headed back to the theater. There was nothing else left for him to do.

THEY ARRIVED INTO TOWN DURING THE LATE EVENING. He was with his wife, Jana, but his thoughts were re-examining a once upon a time of which she had only little knowledge. Their Ford Explorer hummed along Highway 61 as he reached the outskirts of Cottage Grove. Off the interstate highway now, they were no longer cruising. Now, the engine had throttled down to the casual speed of local traffic.

David M. Llewellyn reached up to turn down the music volume. Listening to the lively piano sonatas of Domenico

Scarlatti gave him a good measure of comfort while in transit. Jana did not object in the least. It was not a long trip from the Milwaukee area to Cottage Grove, so they enjoyed whatever time they had to relax in an atmosphere of lively classical music.

The town looked familiar to him, though he had been gone a very long time. Oh, there were changes, to be sure. But the basic landmark buildings still stood alongside new businesses as a reminder of the past in marriage with the present. It was just a small-time small town. Charming at first glance but slow in progress and that was by design. The city fathers were wise enough to know that enlarging a population, in and of itself, was not always the best course. Growth and municipal expansion must be done thoughtfully and with great care. And if they erred, it was on the side of caution.

Although the Grove was not the county seat, there did exist a working courthouse and the companion, if not obligatory, square that anchored the downtown. It was an old building that one could see from most any part of town. Naturally, the four-faced clock did not work and always the hands rested at five o'clock. Someday, when the time was right, the city fathers would generate a fund raiser to fix that clock. Unfortunately, the time was never right.

As a small mid-western town Cottage Grove is rather commonplace. With a population just over six thousand, its one weekly newspaper serves as a careful gauge for the more important events. Entertainment is restricted to a dance hall, a movie theater and a small community park. There is a bowling alley and a handful of eating joints. The local high school provides some concert or play or sports event every now and then.

Commerce is very much present in the form of a shoe factory, a cereal plant, a slaughter-house and a myriad of small dairy farms speckled throughout the county. There are a few small businesses ran rather prosperously in the town. Just a few miles off the interstate highway, Cottage Grove has access to neither railroad nor airport. It is a small conservative community concerned with its own world, its own existence, its own way of life. Only on occasion does the town acknowledge the importance of the outside world.

Jack Llewellyn's son was coming back to his hometown to meet with his father. He received an urgent summons to the Grove by virtue of an early afternoon telephone voice message from his father insisting that Jana and he travel to the Grove as soon as possible. He would not deny his father anything that could be accomplished because in the early years the consideration had always been given to the son. The son was determined to return the in-kind favor.

So, they packed their travel bags and brought along coffee and cookies. His construction business would be fine for a couple of days and would easily continue on without disruption until his return. In the short miles that he had to travel he had much to think about. His work challenged him and he found that exhilarating.

Of course, growing up in Cottage Grove, there was much history for the younger Llewellyn. Driving back to his origins gave him reason to reminisce. It had been a long time since he had been home and there was much to consider about the people he had grown up with and others with whom he still retained an acquaintance, albeit long-distance. Across the miles and subsequent years, David still remembered the faces and feelings that remained part of him. Sometimes there lingered a softened bitterness to the memories… the adultery of his mother and the consequent tempestuous time leading to marital divorce, as well as the prolonged but uneventful mutual flirtation with the now married, and somewhat older, Mikaela Rhea.

Still, the love for his mother and Mikaela persisted even after all the recriminations involving the former and the uncertainty that accompanied the latter. The problem is that such disquieting relationships sometimes have no remedy, but only a continued soreness. To tempt fate, as it were, by further interaction was indeed rolling the dice. There was always a chance for closure, but the smart money was on increased turmoil for the heart. Really, the odds of something fulfilling happening in either relationship were not all that good. Opening old wounds was not what David Llewellyn was looking to accomplish.

From his mother he was estranged for some months now for reasons he kept from his father and even his wife. And though he always found Mikaela very beautiful, he did not find himself attracted to her in a romantic way. She had been a good friend growing up together, but there was always something awry that prevented a romantic relationship with her.

And so the SUV moved on through town and toward the downtown area by way of St. Joseph Street. Finally, he reached the town square. The courthouse loomed in majesty across the way and he circled the square as to weigh the parking options before deciding to stop in front of one of the local taverns. Adjacent to the theater, it was most convenient for his father to frequent after the last picture show of the night. While his father was not technically an alcoholic, he drank too much for his own good and too frequently, at that.

Out of the Explorer, David instinctively locked their SUV – no local resident in the Grove would ever bother to do the same – but an out-of-towner always did. The front door of the January-Wabash was unlocked and the lobby was as vacant as it was still beautifully ornate, even after all of the years. The concession counter still resided in the middle of the lobby and was well stocked with candy, treats and sundries under glass on all four sides and quite inviting for purchase. The popcorn machine stood like a sentry in one corner of the concession stand, whistle clean and ready for service.

Once through the lobby doors and into the corridor that adjoins the theater proper, David and Jana made a left turn and up the stairs they climbed. They passed the old, dingy and somewhat forbidding restrooms and walked toward the projection room where he heard the distant hum and clicking of a 35 mm projector gliding film through its bowels. Finally reaching the doorway to the projection room, the good son and his wife looked in to see the aging father concentrating on the whirling film reels atop the arms of the projector.

"Dad, hello. How the heck are you?"

The old man looked up from his labor. "Hey, hello, David, Jana. Please come in. Just let me finish setting up this reel and I will be right with you." The hands worked quickly now, threading and lacing the celluloid through the last few inches of the projector and onto the second reel. The hands were still limber but slightly puffy. Although flexible enough to still do the work required of a projectionist, his fingers were like crusty sausages. Before the varied weekly matinees and featured movies he manipulated film and sprockets with seeming legerdemain.

Only the Grass Suffers

There was no arthritis to worry about. Years of teaching did no damage to his hands or body. Now that he was retired, he was still in good physical condition to work a second career – as a movie theater projectionist. His sense of humor devoured the fact that for thirty years he taught Film Study at the university in Madison. Now, he had become part of the physical movie industry by way of his second career. With the task completed, Llewellyn turned to his son and furnished a warm hug and kiss on the right upper cheek.

"Thanks for coming, David," he began. "Let's go get something to drink. It's pretty warm in this projection room and I could stand a cold beer." Llewellyn smiled warmly at his son as he walked across the room and turned off the overhead. Together they walked down the second floor corridor, past the dank bathrooms and down the steps into the theater lobby.

"Did you have a good trip?" the father asked as they went through the front doors and out into the warm sun.

"Sure, Dad, it's a pleasant and easy enough drive to the Grove – it's only windshield time. Actually, it's kind of nice to get away." He continued, "Business has been good as of late and I have been working longer hours than I like – not that I am complaining about business being good."

It was only a short distance to The Devil's Elbow – just a couple of doors down on the same side of the street as the January-Wabash Theater. It was a convenience that Jack Llewellyn really appreciated. The large front window, colorfully and stylishly etched with "The Devil's Elbow Tavern" on it, was adjacent to a heavy wooden front door that opened outward and was kept that way all summer so that only the companion screen door separated the watering hole from the square. Now, the door was open and only the screen door remained as a weak obstacle between troubles and refreshment. The smell of long-ago spilled beer aging on the wooden floorboards of the entryway greeted the Llewellyns as they pushed the handle of the screen door.

The older man went in first and looked over his shoulder to his son, "Let's grab a booth and have a cold one." After the long morning drive, David was more than amenable to idea of refreshment. Jana was not.

Behind the long bar a rather unkempt employee of thirty-three years waited for the three new customers to seat themselves. Virgil "Shadow" Pleasance was unusually handsome in spite of his deportment and dress. He was clumsy and uncollected in his locomotion and there was upheaval and disarray in the wearing of his sweatshirt and blue jeans, but there was also eagerness in his demeanor and easiness in his grin.

After a few minutes the man-boy known as Shadow came up to them with a knowing look. "Say, boss, what's your drink?"

"Virgil, I want you to meet someone." Now, looking at David and Jana, Llewellyn said, "David, Jana, this is Virgil Pleasance. People in the Ford call him Shadow, but I like his Christian name well enough. Virgil, this is my son, David and his lovely wife, Jana."

Still grinning from ear to ear, Shadow pumped with hurried enthusiasm the outstretched right hand of David Llewellyn. He repeated the ardent salutation with Jana. He was ecstatic to receive the son and daughter-in-law of such a good friend as Mr. Llewellyn. But he did not say a word – he just kept grinning and shaking the hand of Jana – and he did it with such passion.

Finally, David said, "We're glad to meet you, Virgil." And eventually he had to pry Jana's hand out of Shadow's – but he did it gingerly and with good humor so that Shadow would not be slighted.

"Virgil, would you please bring us two Genuine Drafts and a glass of iced tea?" Llewellyn asked. "We have a powerful thirst and we want some satisfaction."

"Coming right up, Boss," Shadow responded dutifully. And he went away for a while until the Llewellyns heard him rummaging through the beer cooler underneath the bar for two Genuine Drafts. Although the tavern was not altogether empty, only a couple of regulars sat at the bar and a middle-aged pot-bellied couple sat in a darkened corner on the other side of the room. David decided that the overweight couple worked the second shift at the cereal plant – they wore white shirts and white trousers – and the two burly guys at the bar were either farmers or unemployed. He decided that they were unemployed. Farmers got busy again in the spring. If it had been winter, it would have been a tougher call.

Llewellyn paused at length to stare down at his hands – blistered, but still pliable. He continued to stare at them. Shadow arrived quietly and deftly placed the two beer bottles and companion glasses on the table in front of each Llewellyn, grinned whole-heartedly and walked away, proud of the accomplishment of another completed task. He forgot the iced tea for Julia. She let it go and said nothing.

Llewellyn hesitated, took a slug of beer from the bottle and returned it to the table. He looked at his son intently. "First, let me just state the obvious. I loved your mother more than words can express. But right now, I have to tell you these are hard times, Son."

Jack paused to look down at his beer bottle and began peeling off the paper label. Then, he rubbed his hands together as he often did. They were only slightly dirty from his handling the cans of 35mm film and lacing the contents through the projector. The beer bottle still felt cold to the touch and his hands were soothed by its temperature. "It all makes me extremely uncertain, maybe even a little fearful, so I want to proceed slowly and thoughtfully. This sort of thing is way out of bounds for me."

David finished his beer and he, too, began peeling off the paper label on his beer bottle. There was an uneasy quiet for a while and then Llewellyn began, "David, yesterday afternoon the police informed me that your mother died a few days ago…"

THE SUN MOVED ACROSS THE ROOF OF THE OLD BUILDINGS on the west side of the square. The glare on the front windows evaporated and a new coolness permeated the tavern and the three stem-mounted ceiling fans whirled away.

The father took out a canvas-colored notebook from his back pocket and began to write. After a brief moment he tore the paper from the booklet and set it on the table between his son and his beer.

David looked away for a moment – toward the middle-aged pot-bellied couple in the far corner of the tavern – and then returned his focus to his father. Jana held the right arm of her husband tightly and throughout the announcement of death had kept silent. Her hands gripped tighter as her father-in-law explained the gruesome details of the self-hanging. The old man took one last swig and set down the bottle as if to punctuate this last narrative.

"Your mother's body will be at Riedelsheimer Funeral Home sometime tomorrow. They have to do an autopsy because she did not die naturally."

He pushed the ripped page across the table closer to his son. The paper bore funeral related tasks that had been conveyed by telephone from Alan Riedelsheimer earlier in the day.

"How awful," lamented Jana.

The response gave no relief to Llewellyn. If anything, he seemed stoic about it, as if it was only the first of many steps to be completed before some desired conclusion could be realized. "I wanted to tell you in person, David, face to face – not just over the telephone," he continued and looked at both of them. "Thank you for allowing me to do that much."

The three departed from each other's company. David got up first, then Jana. They nodded respectfully and walked out the front door. Llewellyn watched him go and said nothing. In truth, the father and son did not like each other all that much. They were different... and the same... but they did love each other. Both reminded themselves of this from time to time.

Jack looked over at Shadow who was behind the bar day-dreaming. "Virgil," he called, "one more beer, if you please." Awakened from his musing, Shadow smiled and dutifully brought over another beer for the old man. A few beers later, the afternoon ended and the evening came again, bringing an immeasurable loneliness to him.

DURING THE EARLY EVENING DAVID WAS COMMISSIONED by his father to make further funeral arrangements and charge final expenses to the senior Llewellyn. After that being accomplished, the son insisted that Jana rest alone at the hotel room. She acquiesced because she was tired and she knew that a hot bath would refresh her body and spirits after a day of travel and emotional upheaval. After all, Jana much admired Julia Llewellyn in spite of her notorious flaws.

Chapter 2

THE MORTICIAN'S ASSISTANT

It was quiet on the square with very little pedestrian traffic moving from store to store. Older automobiles and pick-up trucks were scattered pell-mell in parking spaces and their owners fed shiny quarters into parking meter pedestals, just as their fathers and mothers had done a generation earlier and beyond. It was early afternoon and most people had already accomplished their shopping tasks.

A little girl of ten years with auburn hair and chocolate eyes approached the tavern on the square. Slowly opening the screen door her diminutive hands pushed in determined fashion against the warped and wood-framed screen door. Unfortunately, they were not as effective pushing away the eternally sour smell of the watering hole.

The Devil's Elbow Tavern boasted a high archaic metal ceiling with a pattern of two-foot by two-foot floral panels imprinted throughout the space. It supported three large paddle fans that circulated both air and sound so that customers enjoyed the slight movement of both while quenching a common thirst.

The tables at the large front window were the most desirable location for they gave access to a view of the town square while maintaining a good spot to oversee the attendance of the tavern. Inside patrons could select a booth, a table, or sit at the bar and eat cold-cut sandwiches that Shadow hurriedly prepared, while Cash poured the beer and mixed a variety of high-balls.

Every table suggested a vintage metallic 1940s motif and every chair and bar stool was manufactured with a thick heavy red vinyl cover. The walls were decorated with lighted mirrors and hand-painted with beer advertisements. Sporting posters of hunters and fisherman and game that were framed cluttered the remaining vertical spaces.

The long, dark and imposing bar itself was pure mahogany. It covered three-fourths of the north wall and was complemented by the bas-relief of a full width mirror. The saloon's panoramic reflection was seemingly guarded by a hundred bottles of various bourbons, scotches, gins, vodkas, rums and ryes. The kegs of various beers were hidden directly underneath and on the back-side of the bar adjacent to two stainless steel sinks and between cupboards and coolers.

All through any given night and in any of the four seasons, the cash register sang a happy tune for the watering hole. A small screen television at each end of the bar's ceiling kept customers amused should their liquid conversation stop abruptly. It was a place of unchallenged merriment for those in attendance as a general rule. On a cold winter's night there was no better place to be and in the heat of summer the saloon was an obvious oasis for any thirsty working stiff.

Once inside, Lauren stepped to the end stool at the bar and seated herself comfortably onto it. She licked her left thumb in business-like form and planted a printed four-by-six card on the massive mahogany bar. The bartender clinked a couple of just-cleaned glasses together and placed them neatly against the back-mirrored wall. He smiled at the little girl and at her industry in working for the mortician.

"Uh, let's see who died today," said the bartender, picking up the card that lay before him.

"Good morning, Mr. McDermott. Could I have a cherry coke, please? I'm awfully thirsty. I've gotten awfully warm delivering the notices today." said the little girl.

"Hey, Shadow," he yelled to his assistant in the back room. "Come here, will you?"

He was a short-spoken, hard-scrabble of a man, married and divorced three times over three decades. Cash McDermott had endured a life of disquiet in his personal relationships and had seen pretty much everything else in the course of his work in the tavern.

Older now, heavy-set and balding, he was forced to wear suspenders – a leather belt no longer supported his stomach. A flannel shirt and blue jeans sufficed as his work clothes and dated Red Ball Jets provided comfort while tending bar during long days and late nights.

Although rough-shaven and born with a naturally cranky disposition, McDermott was ever congenial and conciliatory to his patrons. McDermott furnished booze, beer, and a discreet ear on a daily basis. Virgil Pleasance and he manned the saloon every day without vacation and without exception.

From somewhere in the back room there came a crash and through the doorway staggered the rather unkempt man-boy called Shadow. He collected himself as much as possible in the wake of his scrimmage with the beer kegs and crates. Immediately upon seeing his boss his mind was set on high alert and when he recognized the presence of the mortician's assistant, he focused on what next assignment Cash might announce.

"This young lady would like a cherry coke. Get it for her, will you please? And, by the way, what the hell are you doing back there?"

"Uh, yes boss, uh, nothing boss, just straightening up a little," said Shadow.

He began preparing the cherry coke in quick motions in order to accommodate Lauren. He was efficient in completing his work, but a little haphazard in the execution of it. His task completed, he gingerly delivered the goods to his favorite customer.

"Thanks, Shadow," she said with a remarkably engaging smile.

"Well, Cash, did you know the man that died?" asked Shadow.

McDermott surveyed the four-by-six card on which the announcement of death was printed. Name, date of birth and death, and funeral arrangements were all there encircled by a floral design. Usually, there was an accompanying picture in color placed at the upper left-hand corner. This time was no exception. The postage-stamp size photograph of a strikingly attractive but older brunette laid adjacent to the vital statistics of a lost human life.

"It wasn't a man that died. It's a woman. My God, it's Jack Llewellyn's ex-wife. Lord Baltimore!" He announced in hushed voice, "Julia Llewellyn."

There remained a quiet for just a moment to let the announcement linger and take its toll on the bartender. The employee and the young customer looked on with anticipatory patience for Cash to continue but he just stared at the funeral card.

After a second moment longer, Shadow wiped his grimy hands on a gray towel and proceeded to carefully prepare the cola for the little girl.

"Okay, Cash, here she is for you," said Shadow.

"It's for the kid, just give it to her."

Peering down and from behind the bar with gruff demeanor McDermott offered the cherry coke gratis.

"It's on the house, kid. I guess you're a working stiff just like the rest of us."

"Thanks, Mr. McDermott," she said, and gulped at the frosty glass.

After a while, Shadow said, "I remember Mrs. Llewellyn, you know." He continued, "She was very nice to me. Once she let me kiss her and that really felt good. She was a good kisser. It was back in the alley one time when it happened. But I don't remember exactly when."

"You lying dog," yelled Cash. "What are you talking about?

Why would a high-class, good-looking woman like Julia Llewellyn kiss you?"

Shadow dropped his head and slowly backed away out of the immediate and threatening reach of Cash McDermott. But he did remember Julia Llewellyn well enough. Again, in the back-storage room amid empty beer kegs and cases of whiskey, he reminisced to himself the once-upon-a-time when he fell in love with Mrs. Llewellyn.

"I know it was a long time ago," he said out loud to himself, "but I remember frost on the ground." He paused and stared at the shiny empty beer kegs and visualized how it was in a dark alley long ago. "It must have been springtime," he continued aloud and to himself and with slowness and certainty. "I was straightening the trash cans in the back alley. I didn't see her until she touched my shoulder. I turned around to look at her and…"

Shadow had to stop for a moment to sigh and shift the balance of his weight to the other leg. The shiny beer kegs kept his focus on the memory.

"Now I know she opened her dark coat for me and surrounded me with her arms. And, then she kissed me right on my lips." He stopped to think about that for a good length of time. "I just about died seeing her without no clothes on underneath that coat. I sure do remember that night. But that was a long time ago," he concluded, "she sure was a very nice woman."

After a while, he escaped his reverie and went back into the saloon to continue his duties.

Cash McDermott, the proprietor and bartender at The Devil's Elbow Tavern, gave Virgil "Shadow" Pleasance a job as stock boy and janitor a couple of years ago during a weak moment. And although Shadow has done every rotten job imaginable for those two years, Cash always viewed him more as a necessary nuisance than anything else. After all, he was incredibly cheap labor.

"Thanks for the cherry coke, Virgil," Lauren said, smiling at Shadow and inviting him into the conversation. But he just stared at her and shrugged his shoulder and turned his eyes toward the floor in shy retreat.

"I wonder how she died," quietly queried the bartender. But there was no reply from either the bar assistant or the little girl. While the silence went unnoticed the room filled with the regret of lost treasure emanating from both Cash and Shadow. Over the years Julia Llewellyn had become an occasional but pleasant fixture in their small world.

The mortician's assistant finished her cola in a deliberate workmanlike fashion and laid three shiny quarters on the bar in payment full. She was a working girl and could afford the refreshment.

"Thanks, Mr. McDermott, I really needed that," she breathed heavily. The child picked up the balance of her notices and slid off the bar stool effortlessly. And with a quick smile she turned toward the screen door and pulled its wooden frame. Lauren Rhea was gone but her magic lingered a little after and McDermott grinned his admiration for her. A moment later, a crash could be heard coming from the back-storage room.

Once out the door her sweatshirt and faded blue jeans worked in concert with the morning sun to give comfort and warmth. That was good because she had a lot of work to do. Around the square to each shop and then three blocks in each direction to outlying stores before she could call it a day. It was Saturday, that meant warm cookies and cold milk by mid-afternoon if she was lucky and her mom was in good humor.

But the girl miscalculated the time of deliveries and there was no way to get home in time for a Saturday snack. Later, the cookies would be cold, but still good. It was only a mild sacrifice to advance her business interests.

Already her hands were blackened with cheap ink that rubbed off as she dispensed the funeral notices. It was her first real job and she was very efficient and most reliable. Of course, the store owners loved her and her industry and her dedication to her work. But, generally, what they liked was her business-like approach, although it was a plus that she was cute. In any case, they hoped that she was paid commensurate with her service, but somehow most people doubted it.

Upon request Lauren would present her new business card, also made with the same cheap ink. It read, "Lauren Rhea – Mortician's Assistant." And while it suggested her modest credentials, it did validate her membership in the town's workforce and authorized her to conduct weekend business activity with admiring adults. It also made her the envy of every Fourth Grader at St. Boniface Grade School.

Her mother taught at the same parochial elementary school and her father was a lawyer. Together they made a very good living. This summer she was to begin piano lessons – her mother had promised and her dad had agreed to the financial commitment of a new piano after an unspecified time had proven that "Lauren would stick with it." As was her custom, Lauren Rhea determined to apply herself to the piano and compel her father to make the purchase.

But all of that was a ways away and presently she was focused on applying her trade in a necessary, if unpalatable, service industry. Although not seriously considering a career in funeral services – after all, she was only ten years old – she could see the advantages of having a job with little possibility of running out of clients. Job security was what her parent talked about often enough at the dinner table. Still, a concert pianist probably would not have time to deliver death notices. Either profession had its merits, she would have to decide later.

SHE ARRIVED HOME IN THE LATE AFTERNOON WITH ONLY a handful of cards still in her pocket. Lauren was done with her deliveries and the extra notices could be thrown away. She climbed the stairs to the front veranda of her house and sat on the top step for a moment to reflect on the day's deliveries and to catch her breath. She was hungry now because she worked through lunch and soon she had to go to the bathroom, so she didn't stay on the steps very long.

The mid-morning cookies and milk were history hours ago and her mother would be worried because she was gone until now this afternoon. Although the little girl had no wish to upset her mother, there was work to be done and she had to take care of her business. Surely, her mother would understand and respect that much.

After a while, Lauren Rhea went inside and headed for the kitchen. Her mother was coming up from the basement laundry room with a basket of towels. "Oh, Lauren! Where have you been all of this time?" she asked.

"It took longer than I thought to deliver the notices." She continued, "Can I have something to eat?"

"Of course, sit right down. I'll fix you something," her mother said.

Lauren placed her left-over cards in the waste basket underneath the kitchen sink and left the room to use the bathroom. She was glad that her mother was in good spirits and not cross because of her tardy return home. Five minutes later, she came back into the kitchen and sat at the table. A chicken salad sandwich and two chocolate chip cookies were in front of her waiting to be consumed. It was both a late lunch and early dinner. Sometimes the Rhea household on Scuppernong Drive flexed its adaptability and adjusted its mealtime to suit their varied schedules. Lauren's father would be home late from an out-of-town conference, so Mikaela did not have to worry about timing Vincent's arrival with a formal dinner.

Her mother sat next to her and the two of them smiled at each other. Lauren Rhea enjoyed her sandwich and cookies and cold milk and, most of all, the company of her mother.

With her elbows on the table and chin cupped in both her hands, Mikaela watched her daughter for just a short while before getting up to straighten around the kitchen. As she did so, they began to recite silly songs together and, every now and then, Mikaela teased her daughter about boys in the neighborhood.

Satisfied with her Saturday's late lunch, Lauren inexplicably felt adventurous in probing the soft spots in her mother's emotional make-up. "Mom, tell me more about when you were born," she suggested.

It was a sensitive subject for her mother because she did not know her parents, but rather, she had grown up with a kind, but not altogether loving, aunt. For Mikaela, her aunt always held back something, there existed some emotional incompleteness to their relationship. That persistent lacking made all the difference for a little girl growing up without real parents. She was always provided for, but there was always some unknown ingredient that was missing in their relationship. Mikaela had never gotten over that.

"Well, there really isn't that much to tell. Aunt Helen was very good to me, she raised me from the day that I was born until I married your father."

Mikaela poured herself a cup of coffee and sat down again at the kitchen table next to her daughter.

"But, where were your parents, Mom?' Lauren asked. "I never really knew about that part."

There was a certain sadness that washed across the face of the mother. But it only lasted for a moment and then it was gone. Then, a sigh of practicality yielded the familiar refrain, "Well, my mother died when I was born and I never knew my father." She spoke quietly, "We have been all through this before – why ask again, dear?"

Lauren reflected for a while, and then, "I don't know. I just like talking about you when you were a little girl. It all seems so mysterious," she replied with a measure of wonderment.

The story goes that her mother died at childbirth and her father's whereabouts were unknown. The details of her mother's death were sketchy at best because Mikaela was born in a small settlement called Gills Rock which sits atop the Wisconsin peninsula that is Door County. There were rumors, of course, but the mystery surrounding Mikaela's entrance into the world remained for a number of years. In any case, there was an investigation into her mother's death and the upshot was that the mother died at childbirth and the doctor is no longer practicing medicine.

So, the baby went to live in a foster home and was adopted by a middle-aged widow in a rather diminutive and run-down Cape Cod house on the outskirts of the Grove. It wasn't an ideal situation, but she was the only available and local foster care option at that time. Helen Quesnell was around and she was semi-retired, so she could make things work out. County Social Services was inclined to allow the abbreviated family to stay together indefinitely. And, really, they did quite well for themselves in taking care of each other despite the modest home.

Quesnell was once married to a man who was both onerous and slovenly. When he died, Cottage Grove noticed that both Helen's demeanor and skin complexion improved noticeably. The house was kept neat and clean and the widow's good spirits were indelibly ingrained in Mikaela for a lifetime of good use.

And it really was a good home, but her "aunt" always maintained a slight emotional distance from Mikaela as she grew up and there was never enough money. The girl adapted to the aunt and allowed that Aunt Helen's disposition was a loving one, but that the old woman was sister to Michael Carlisle, so the shared family trait of measured love was given. For the family Carlisle, there was only so much love to be given and received. She learned to love her aunt out of gratitude as much as anything else. It can be said that they gave to each other what they could and, as the years passed, their bond became stronger. Although Quesnell had adopted Mikaela, it was an interesting feature of their relationship that the young girl growing up still referred to her as "Aunt Helen."

Her husband's employer knew the story very well – why should he not, he invented it, orchestrated its development and paid for its execution. All accomplished in great secrecy. Michael Carlisle knew a lot of people and he could make things happen, even within the medical community of Gills Rock and the workings of County Social Services.

Mikaela finished her coffee and punctuated the conversation's end with a genuine smile for her daughter. The mother got up and placed her cup in the sink and walked toward the dining room to gather the mail. As she did, she noticed through the front window the black Mercedes parked across the street. It was the same car that she had seen there before every now and then since they had moved to Scuppernong Drive. The motor was not running and there was a man looking through the driver's side window. It was Michael Carlisle, her husband's employer.

She wondered what he was doing there and why he did not come to the door. The young mother walked gingerly toward the dining room's picture window. Her hand slowly pushed aside the lace curtain to reveal the full presence of the street.

"Michael, what are you doing there?" she asked herself. Suddenly, the black sedan's engine started and Michael Carlisle drove away without acknowledging the young woman that he surely understood saw him parked across the way.

As this was not the first time such an occurrence met her observation, Mikaela was beginning to be concerned about the curious behavior of her husband's employer. Of course, it would mean a conversation with Carlisle, preferably without her husband's initial knowledge. Maybe, after some delicate inquiry, there would be less strangeness than she thought. It was not a conversation to which she looked forward. Her family owed so much to the old lawyer. Their entire way of life came from his generosity and genuine affection for as long as she could remember.

After a stream-lined academic career and an eminently successful law school performance, Vincent Rhea was ready for big-time corporate law in Chicago. If it was not love at first sight, it may as well have been. After deciding to forego Chicago in favor of Cottage Grove where he grew as a boy, his time was spent concentrating on a long-distance relationship with the beauty from Gills Rock. After a while he opened a small law office at the edge of town. Young, handsome, educated and eminently capable, clients slowly materialized during his first year of practice.

Eventually, Michael Carlisle invited him to join his law firm. It became incorporated in the state of Wisconsin as Carlisle & Rhea, SC. He accepted the position as full partner on the condition that the old man would approve of an extended holiday in order to marry Mikaela Quesnell. The bargain being made, Carlisle had a partner and Vincent had a wife. Neither man looked back, but Mikaela did. Her beginnings were not so crisp and clear, but rather murky, even to her young daughter. All of her adult life there existed a pronounced uneasiness to her self-worth, but having a husband and daughter who loved her was immensely comforting.

For some time, Vincent had worked with and for Carlisle in their successful law practice. Although it was a joint venture, it was the old man who had all the connections and held the majority of stock in their service corporation. Since their marriage, the old man had been eminently generous to Vincent and especially kind to Mikaela. At times, it seemed that Carlisle was more than an employer – he was family to the Rheas. As time went by, he seemed to be more and more a part of their personal lives. He was an influential man who was like a father to Vincent and Mikaela and possessed a grandfatherly gentleness toward Lauren.

AFTER A LENGTHY, WARM BATH THAT REFRESHED THE little girl, she spent the remainder of the day helping with light chores and playing in the backyard with temporary and imaginary friends. A child of ten does that. She has to because she does not have built-in playmates in the presence of brothers and sisters. The mortician's assistant and possible future concert pianist mastered the art of play by using her imagination and talking to herself with detailed explanations of how and why things were the way they were. It gave Lauren Rhea a playmate unto herself. More than that, it gave her mother another reason to smile from time to time as Mikaela listened secretly to what her daughter was saying aloud to herself privately.

Only the Grass Suffers

When the day was done and after business was conducted and household chores completed and playtime enjoyed and bath taken and dinner eaten and television watched, she slept the sleep of contentment. Altogether speaking, she really was having a pretty good summer.

Chapter 3

THE BREAKFAST CLUB

The Danbury Café had existed for over fifty years in the heart of Cottage Grove. Passing through the ownership of a dozen families, the café was soul of the Grove because of its longevity and most importantly because it was the place where people met, analyzed, discussed, disagreed, reconciled and got to know one another on a personal level.

It offered a full menu from an old-fashioned breakfast of biscuits and gravy to lunch specials to greasy plate dinners – all of which were delicious and literally to die for. The tables gave the impression of a rather large diner as waitresses ran pell-mell with coffee pots and food trays from the kitchen to customers.

Behind the counter and companion stools were cabinets with glass sliding doors that displayed homemade pie wedges and pastries. Beneath a new clock and poster advertisements was located a rectangular window into the kitchen through which a cook passed plates of food to be delivered to the proper patron.

In short, it was a place to meet and eat and being on the town square it was conveniently located. Unfortunately, it was always crowded and noisy during peak times. Because of this, people talked louder so the joint got even louder until the crowd dissipated toward mid-morning or mid-afternoon or late night.

In the far corner sat three men around the most popular table in Danbury's. It was a café table in which a daily breakfast club met and long-standing civic icons gossiped and lied to one another. It was a fraternity of sorts in which men who had known one another for decades could hash out their daily affairs. And they could do it over breakfast and bottomless cups of coffee.

From out of the cool early summer sunrise Michael Carlisle pushed through the heavy glass door and into the restaurant. Thoughtfully, he shuffled over to the table and the others made room for his chair.

Dressed in a stylish gray suit with a Phi Beta Kappa key dangling from his right vest pocket, the lawyer slowly walked toward the pre-eminent table in Danbury's. It was a first – Carlisle had never been an ex-officio member of the breakfast club. His circle was of a higher order and the rank and file were not so familiar to him.

Of medium height and frame, Michael Carlisle carried himself with dignity and stately deportment. His gray hair at the temples gave him that certain distinguished and almost scholarly aura that worked well in the courtroom and out in upscale restaurants. His baritone voice signaled meaning and importance to every argument that he ever made in front of a jury and mesmerized a singular married woman as he made love to her on an intermittent basis. His suits were always hand made in Chicago by an Italian tailor of some measured fame and he always arrived in a Mercedes-Benz luxury sedan.

While Carlisle was ruthless in his legal cases, he did possess a softer side on the personal level. Perhaps he understood the value of family more than others because he had none that was truly his own.

He had no wife and his daughter was unaware of their consanguinity by his own singular and hidden efforts. What family he could have had was forfeited long ago, placed on a nearby shelf and kept secret only to him. Carlisle lost both his lover who he never married and a family who was never aware of his intermittent involvement. All of these terms were accepted in deference to his former prestigious judgeship and a current lucrative law practice in a relatively small fish bowl.

But none of this was for public consumption; otherwise, the judgeship and law practice would have been doomed from the get-go in a small town. And Michael Carlisle was a small-town boy. He was considered the best that Cottage Grove could construct and it was his intention to keep that idea alive and well.

Beyond the career accomplishments the old lawyer engaged in a prolonged love affair with another man's wife and ruined their marriage in the process. Thus, profound hatred existed between Jack Llewellyn and Michael Carlisle. And although the public knew of the latter relationship, it did not know of the former – an earlier love triangle that involved the same two men and produced a baby girl. No one did except his sister who moved from Gills Rock two hundred miles away to Cottage Grove. This relocation was necessary so the lawyer could handle the finances and monitor the lives of Helen and especially Mikaela.

As in most professions, timing in a legal career is everything. The public would not tolerate a young lawyer getting a girl pregnant and then asking for personal confidentiality in a family law practice or sitting on a judicial district bench. But, in later years and within an established career, a seasoned and tenacious legal mind with questionable morals might be considered an almost attractive trait in corporate law. So the lawyer's reputation was safe and he could conduct business anywhere anytime in Cottage Grove, even during early morning breakfast at the Danbury Café.

Although his attendance was unusual, he was a recognized city father that commanded a good measure of respect. Moreover, it was always wise to stay on the sunny side of a potentially malevolent and historically vindictive man. Besides, they were an agreeable bunch of men with very few axes to grind. Life was tough enough, they might have offered; there is no reason to make it any harder than it has to be. This is a philosophy that is not universally shared. But on an early summer's morning in the cozy confines of this café and among the present company, it was the basis of good conversation and a welcoming attitude.

"Good morning, gentlemen," Carlisle began, "May I join you?"

"Yeah, sure, have a seat," Dan Joda invited. He was the general manager at the shoe factory and the Coppaway Shoe Company was an important corporate client of Carlisle. He was an eager middle-aged man, physically fit and with an obvious intelligence about him. He had been working at the factory, learning the ropes, for over a decade. Last year, he was promoted to run operations. The consensus was that because of his attitude he would secure the shoe factory's presence in Cottage Grove for years to come.

Besides Joda and Shubel Terhune, who drove a rendering truck for the county, there was only *The Journal Scene* editor Tom Pfefferkorn, pipe stuck in his shirt pocket and notepad sticking out of his back left trouser pocket. He was an older, graying man, a little weary looking from trying to keep his paper afloat at a time when businesses were cutting back on advertising.

There were other members of the breakfast club, but today it was a limited attendance. Sometimes it was just like that. Maybe, someone's wife had car trouble that morning, or maybe some chore needed to be done before work that day – it really didn't matter that much. Tomorrow, there would be a larger assembly of iconic brethren. The number could reach as high as eight on any given weekday.

Carlisle scraped his chair back to seat himself and signaled to the cute blonde behind the counter for service.

"Good morning, Mr. Carlisle," said a slender, but strong, young man in a plaid flannel shirt and khaki pants. And then he slurped his coffee.

"Good morning, Shubel."

He continued his acknowledgement by nodding for the lawyer to take a chair as he signaled the waitress for service. The other men gave brief but silent acknowledgment, as well. This discreet salutation was standard behavior by the others because they were well into a pointed discussion concerning the Green Bay Packers off-season acquisitions.

Negotiating her way across the café and through the collection of small tables, the waitress carefully walked with coffee pot in hand. She was beautiful in every way. What you noticed first was her long blonde hair. She had a delicate walk, a smooth gait, if you will. And she was so lovely with her powder blue uniform fitting snugly around her body. All the men noticed Wish McGuire. And every man would have loved to have her for at least one night. But Wish was only nineteen and her father was generally known to have a terrible temper and so, by and large, she was safe from the man-handling that would surely have been present without the reputation of her father.

Wish arrived with coffee cup in one hand and a full pot in the other. She placed the cup in front of Carlisle and began to pour. As she did, she brushed her arm against that of Terhune and he blushed with profound love. But Carlisle gave only peripheral notice to Wish McGuire, rather he stared at young Shubel and his chemical reaction to the waitress and envied his raw youth and untapped potential in what love might eventually bring him.

"May I help you, Mr. Carlisle," she inquired in a warm but business-like fashion.

"Yes, I'd like some biscuits and gravy, the small plate. Thanks for the coffee."

"Coming right up, Mr. Carlisle," she said. As she walked away all eyes momentarily focused on the sweet body that moved with such suggestive motion. Even Carlisle had to watch as the young girl walked back into the kitchen area of the café.

She leaned upward to impale the breakfast order onto the ticket pick that was stationed atop the kitchen's window ledge. Carlisle and Shubel watched her closely, admiring her long blonde hair and her marvelous young body. They watched her as her dress pulled up some to reveal her slip and a good portion more of her legs. Shubel always would have like to sit at the counter to eat breakfast, but the others preferred their usual table. In any case and for all concerned, it was an extra benefit for breakfasting at the Danbury Café. One could eat his biscuits and gravy and gossip and admire the beauty of Wish McGuire.

"God, when she reaches for the food at the serving window I fall in love with her all over again," Shubel silently admitted to himself as he wiped gravy from the corner of his mouth. He continued to stare at Wish so long that even the all-business Carlisle noticed his preoccupation with the counter area.

"You know, Shubel, Dirk McGuire is very protective of his daughter under all circumstances and with all potential young men."

"Yeah, but not even old man McGuire can prevent his daughter from dating someday."

But Michael Carlisle was unconvinced about what Shubel could do to move out of the way such an imposing obstacle as big, mean Dirk McGuire. Besides, long ago, Carlisle decided that Shubel, though eminently rough around the edges, was so much bluster in the presence of others but thoughtful and reserved in his own company. He had seen this on more than one occasion when Shubel was unaware that he was being observed. The odds of Shubel Terhune mustering enough spit to ask Wish McGuire for a date constituted a statistical monstrosity. And his odds were slightly better than those of Wish accepting the invitation.

For nearly a year Shubel Terhune had been a driver of a county garbage and rendering truck. Twice a week he worked his section of Cottage Grove collecting garbage and trash while on Saturdays the same truck traveled the out-lying county highways to collect any animal road kill. Because the county had more money than Cottage Grove, it had taken over trash collection long ago. In both cases, the work was filthy but the county paid well and offered good benefits.

With long flowing black hair nearly down to his shoulders and with grease spots from his truck maintenance and garbage collection, Shubel lead both a dirty and smelly existence. His hands were perpetually marred and stained and the red cap that he wore was stationed atop his head for as long as anyone could remember.

Always seen with and engaging grin, he was sociable to any resident of Cottage Grove. He meant no harm and he was eager for friendships. Shubel was smart, but formally uneducated. Generally, though, people warmed up to him in spite of his rough appearance and inevitable occupational and unfortunate scent of trash.

After a while, the fat cook tapped the small bell to signal that the order was ready to be picked up. Wish whirled around and gingerly picked up the mud platter that was the lawyer's biscuits and gravy breakfast special. She carefully negotiated her way to the far corner table and delivered the goods to the waiting Carlisle.

"Here you are, Mr. Carlisle. Will there be anything else?"

"No thanks."

She stood next to Shubel and paused for a moment as if for effect or that she might say something, but didn't. She looked at him for briefly as if to announce that she acknowledged his presence. It was a silent greeting of sorts without words. Then she smiled almost imperceptibly. Terhune looked up at her, but nothing came to mind quickly enough for him to react. And then she was gone. He sipped his ice water in order to recover from the encounter.

With breakfast served Carlisle was ready to conduct business even if the conversation was aimed at only one other man seated at the table. The local small talk was of no interest to the lawyer, only his client meant anything to him.

"Dan, would it be okay if I drop by your office in the next few days? We should go over some of the language in the proposed union contract before too much longer."

"All right, is the middle of next week good for you, Mike?" answered Joda.

"Perfect. I will have Cosie, my secretary, call you later today to confirm a day and time." At that moment, his breakfast became a business expense and, therefore, was tax deductible. Carlisle enjoyed his profession – and took good advantage of it – on every occasion that came his way.

"You know, Michael, I've had some closed-door meetings with the union rep of Local 555, Dirk McGuire," Joda announced. "But between the two of us, we haven't accomplished anything."

"Dan, let's discuss that later in your office." The lawyer cautioned, "I don't think you want to say anything in public just now."

"The only thing I want to say publicly, counselor, is that Dirk McGuire is one stubborn bastard who is going to single-handedly shut down the shoe factory if he's not careful"

In a hurried hoarse whisper, Carlisle responded, "Dan, please keep it down. Your waitress happens to be the daughter of that 'stubborn bastard' and she doesn't need to hear that." And then, "Again, this discussion needs to be behind closed doors in your office."

"Mr. Joda, I'm sure Mr. McGuire is a very fine man," countered Terhune with a defensive tone of voice. "If I were you, I would not be speaking so poorly of Wish's dad." Terhune said it slowly and Joda could tell that he meant the words.

The shoe factory manager poured a last gulp of coffee down his throat and laid cash on the table before him. "I'll talk to you later, Michael." He pushed his chair back with an intentional scraping of metal legs on the tiled floor and left the café with hurried steps.

With Joda absent, Terhune steamed, "He shouldn't talk like that about Wish's dad, you know. It ain't right."

"Let it go, Shubel. It doesn't mean anything," said Tom Pfefferkorn, as he pulled out a pen and notepad from his shirt pocket and scribbled something onto it.

"Now, Tom, anything Dan Joda says about shoe factory and union negotiations is strictly off the record and unofficial," claimed Carlisle.

"It may be unofficial, Michael, but it is definitely on the record," came Pfefferkorn's retort. "Dan Joda knows who's sitting at this table and he knows that I work at the *Journal Scene*.

"Listen, Tom, let me meet with Dan later this week and I will give you a real update on the negotiations," pleaded Carlisle. "You can wait another issue or two and then provide your readers with real news instead of idle speculation. What do you say?"

The editor thought for a moment and was persuaded to wait for something more concrete from the lawyer. "Okay, Michael, I'll wait," and then the caveat, "but not too long."

With the business portion of breakfast concluded the lawyer ate quietly and without further personal interaction. There was much to do that day and there was always some legal angle on his mind, so he was pretty much unaware of the conversation taking place around him. With a final slurp of his coffee, he got up to go as Wish handed him his check. A modest tip left behind on the table, he walked over to the cash register to pay his bill.

His massive leather billfold held cash and credit cards and, as he reached for it, he observed the standard four by six death notice atop the glass candy case adjacent to the check-out area. There, with floral design and an accompanying small color photograph, was the announcement of death of Julia Llewellyn. Dates of birth and death and funeral details were all listed for public information and use.

For one brief undeniable moment there seemed to be neither sound nor movement in the café. There were no people talking and laughing, there was no clattering of plates and dishes and cups and glasses, and there was no life beyond the pressured mind of Michael Carlisle as he stared at the name of Julia Llewellyn on a four by six funeral notice that a little girl had placed on the glass counter the day before.

After a while he mechanically completed his payment for his breakfast and began his payment for loving another man's wife for the better part of their marriage and consequent years of divorce. Michael Carlisle was without hope of ever fulfilling his love for Julia. There would never be a marriage now. No reconciliation for Jack Llewellyn, but more importantly no legal contract between Julia and the lawyer who had effectually stolen her years ago. She was his, yet she never belonged to him.

Carlisle slipped the funeral card into the right pocket of his suit as he walked out of the café and toward his Mercedes. All sounds and movements of the café resurfaced as he exited. Life continued on as it always does, but the Grove icon was flattened by the news and his drive to the office was trance-like. The surreality of Julia's death would remain until he saw for himself her body laid in a casket. Even then, he would roar with outrage and bitterness.

JUST OFF THE SQUARE THE LAW OFFICE OF CARLISLE & Rhea presented a stylishly quaint façade for clients to enjoy as they approached the old two-story building. The upstairs was used for storage only of both legal papers and discarded office furniture. On the ground level, large glass windows with painted lettering invited clients as they entered through aged and heavy double doors with brass knobs.

Inside a matronly legal secretary sat at her desk in the front office to welcome visitors while typing away at any number of legal briefs or pointed correspondence to other law firms on behalf of Carlisle & Rhea clients. Naturally, she was both overworked and invaluable to both attorneys. Cosette was eminently capable and efficient and relentlessly impatient with the foolishness of other law firms and the general public. Without peer, she was the consummate office manager. Generally, Carlisle and Rhea handled her with kid gloves out of much respect and a little fear.

That morning Vincent was already in his office as Carlisle entered through the back way of the building. The old lawyer sat down his briefcase on his desk and lumbered toward the front reception area. He waved a weak hand to his partner as he walked the narrow corridor that led to Cosette's desk.

"Good morning, Cosie," was the salutation, "Are there any messages?"

"Good morning, Michael. No messages."

"Cosie, would you please set up a meeting next week with Dan Joda at the shoe factory? Later in the week is better," he continued, "Also, you will need to send a flower arrangement to Riedelsheimer's this morning. Julia Llewellyn died."

That was all he said and removed himself from the front office as Cosie opened her mouth with shock but no words came out. In business-like form, she telephoned for the flowers first and then continued with her managerial duties.

Carlisle knocked on the office entrance of Vincent's doorway and entered. From his suit pocket he pulled out the funeral card of Julia and laid it on Vincent's desk.

"Apparently, she died two or three days ago," Carlisle said as he slowly sat on one of the two leather chairs before the large desk of the young lawyer.

Vincent inspected the card and quickly looked up at his senior partner. "I am so sorry, Mike. I know how much she meant to you."

There was a natural and lengthy silence for a while and then, "How did she die, Mike?"

"Vincent, I don't know. I just found out about it as I was leaving Danbury's this morning," he moaned. "That card that you have in your hand is all I know at this point." And, finally, "But I intend to find out why it happened and why I had to find out about her death in this fashion."

His fierce pain and resentment were clear to Rhea and the young lawyer knew that Carlisle's determination and tenacity was legendary. There would be hell to pay for Julia's death as well as the oversight of not properly informing the old man of it. People in Cottage Grove knew of their relationship and the authorities simply handled things far too carelessly.

Returning to his office at building's backside, Carlisle reached for the telephone land line and slowly punched Cosie's extension. "Cosie, would you please contact the police department and ask the chief to give me a call as soon as possible?"

"Yes, sir, right away," was the response over the wire.

Carlisle was compelled to wait for the chief's call. It would be a brisk conversation with direct reproach of the chief's omission in not informing him of Julia's death.

Over the years the lawyer was becoming weary of constant confrontation; but this was personal. He had as much right to know what happened as soon as it happened as anyone else – including the projectionist, his long-time antagonist.

But his enmity toward Llewelllyn was always unfulfilling. And now because of his profound loss for a woman in which mutual passion, but not commitment, had lasted for years… This was what Carlisle dwelled upon as he sat in his stylishly impressive leather chair in his stylishly impressive office.

It was all true that Julia and he had discarded long ago the feelings of Jack Llewellyn in preference to their own desires. But not even her infidelity and his wanting her trumped their knowing that they were two strong people more in love with themselves than with each other. A marriage would not last a month, but an affair could last years. So, they chose the latter over the former and both found it satisfying enough.

His reverie was broken by the ringing of his desk telephone. He placed the receiver to his ear in anticipation.

"The chief is on line one, Mike," the secretary reported.

"Thank you, Cosie."

Carlisle pushed the line's speaker phone button and began his inquiry.

"Chief, tell me about Julia Llewellyn and why I was not informed."

From his office across and down the corridor Vincent Rhea could hear the animated one-way conversation of his law partner. He got up and closed his office door for the sake of Carlisle's privacy and in deference to his own embarrassment.

It would be a bad day for a lot of good people in Cottage Grove.

Chapter 4

MORNING AT THE MCGUIRES

The young girl wanted to sleep late that morning because she had gone to a friend's beer party from work the night before. By six o'clock her father decided that he should wake her before she slept the day away. He had made himself breakfast and the dishes were waiting for washing. He wanted some company on a warm early Monday morning. There were chores to be done and he wanted his daughter to return to consciousness.

Dirk McGuire loved his daughter as much as a man could love another human being. She was his world and everyone else was only scenery to him. His wife died instantly in a car crash years ago as glass and chrome metal rippled across her body at lightning speed. It was an ending in which a will to live and promises to keep proved worthless.

He grew up in Crown Point, Indiana, and was known to be a hardscrabble brawler in every watering hole south of the Illinois-Indiana border. He was intelligent and tough, but his heart was soft and pliable when it came to his daughter. Because of that, the gruff and gritty tradesman spoke with a vocal kindness reserved only for Kathryn. Moreover, in Cottage Grove it was well advertised that he did not like the nickname "Wish" for his daughter. To Dirk McGuire it implied an improper attitude toward his uncommonly beautiful daughter.

For the past few years McGuire worked for the Coppaway Shoe Company at their lone factory in Cottage Grove and rose to the rank of business manager for the Boot & Shoe Workers Union Local 555. He was well regarded by the three hundred men and women who relied on his resoluteness and negotiating skills in the face of opposition from Coppaway management and its lawyers.

"Kathryn, Kathryn," he said with some resolve, "Rise and shine, hit the deck, up and at 'em. It's a brand-new day, girl!" he shouted with exuberance. After all, he had been up since 4:30 and he loved early summer mornings, especially when he, himself, had not been drinking the night before.

From her rubbery sleep and with a dull slowness caused by her throbbing headache, she managed to slip off the sheet and blanket that covered her. Turning toward the edge of the bed, she positioned her body in a such a way that the floor accepted her bare feet and she sat for a while before she dared to stand.

"Good morning, Dad. What time is it?" she moaned because she did not feel well. The aftertaste of the beer formed what seemed like cobwebs inside her mouth and the damn headache would not subside.

"It's early, Kathryn," he replied with amusement and affection. "But its time to begin your day." He paused to smile at her transition from glorious sleep to the acceptance of another day. "What time did you get in last night, young lady," he asked quietly because he knew that she was not quite herself yet.

"Oh, Dad, far too late I'm afraid," she muttered. "But it was a champion party."

"Yes, well. Now you must pay the piper," he replied without sympathy. "Rise and shine!"

He tapped her upper back for encouragement and she responded with throwing off her covers and slowly walking into the bathroom like a tradesman's daughter methodically completing the work at hand. In this case, the task was preparing for the day with efficiency and, most importantly, in silent solitude.

At the breakfast table McGuire finished his last cup of coffee as his daughter entered the kitchen. As she poured herself her first cup, he got up from the table and rinsed his mug and sat it down into the sink before him.

"Have you given any more thought about going to the junior college, Kathryn?" he asked with some hesitation.

"Yes, Dad, I'll look into it this morning. There has to be something more to life than being a waitress," she said. "I'm going to sign up for a couple of classes today for the fall semester." She continued, "Since my grades were pretty good in high school, I'd like to take some business and art courses. Maybe someday I can open up a flower shop."

"Good, I'm glad you feel that way. I'll talk to you about it tonight. Right now, I have to get to the factory."

"I had a dream last night," she said while sitting down at the table. "I dreamt that I was married and he was kind to me, but he was just a vague image"

"Well, I guess that's natural enough, Blondie. Of course, you don't know who you'll marry yet."

Kathryn looked up at her father standing at the kitchen sink and who was looking back at her. Then, a certain sadness changed her face and she sighed, "Dreams don't always come true, do they, Dad?"

"No, Kathryn. Sometimes dreams don't come true… but sometimes they do, you know."

She stood there to wonder about her life with her father. "I guess when Mom died that was the end of your dream," she offered.

"Yeah, I guess so, but then I got a new dream. It was for you to find someone and live a happy life with him. That's my dream now, love."

She smiled.

Then he returned to the immediate problem at hand. "I have to prepare for a meeting later this morning with Gordon Coppaway. He's the owner of the plant, you know. We're going to walk the building together and discuss all of the improvements that he's paid for this year." With what his daughter thought was a slight sign of resignation, he said, "I guess he wants me to know how much he's invested in the future. So, now he'll want his employees to make some big-time concessions."

"Do you think they'll be a strike, Dad?"

"I don't know," he replied slowly with reflection. "I hope not. But Gordon Coppaway is a mean old bastard who cares only for his business, which he built with his bare hands and hard work. And I respect him for that. But he does not care about his company, which is the people who work for him. It is a fine difference, you know, but I don't know how else to explain it."

With some hesitation he expanded his answer, "I meet with our lawyers later on tonight to go over our strategy and list of demands. Hopefully, they can help us negotiate a solid contract with Coppaway. Actually, I hired them to partner with our union local because a long time ago they did some good things in Crown Point when I lived there. They are serious people with some bad attitudes. You definitely want them on your side in any kind of legal fight."

"What's the name of their law firm, Dad?"

"Fedoryshyn and Davis. I don't know Davis, but Tony Fedoryshyn grew up on the south side of Chicago. He moved to Crown Point to give his family a better environment while practicing law. He did me some favors and I threw some business his way. We became very good friends."

He gathered up his lunch box and thermos bottle and placed his old lambskin briefcase under his left arm and started to leave.

"Dad, do you know Shubel Terhune? He works for the county," she inquired.

He stopped in front of the door and turned to face his daughter. "Yeah, I've seen him around every now and then. What about him?"

"Well, he comes into the café regularly and he watches me a lot of the time while I'm working. I don't mind, though. He is kinda cute." She concluded, "I think he's going to ask me out on a date eventually.

"Well, just so you know, I've been thinking about going on a date with him, that's all."

He smiled.

Chapter 5

THE WAKE OF JULIA

T he death of his ex-wife came as a shock to Jack Llewellyn. Although it had been months since they had seen one another, he had heard that she was well, socially active, and living a very comfortable life.

It had been a bitter and gut-wrenching divorce years ago with salvos of intimate hurtfulness and public recriminations hurled back and forth until even the lawyers became weary. However, it was not a contested divorce. That is, ultimately and without contest Jack Llewellyn allowed Julia virtually all material possessions with the exception of his social security benefits and the hard-bound books that he had collected over the years. While Julia had better lawyers, she did not need them. Jack did not fight for the assets with any exuberance. After all, although he hated her, he still loved her, too.

In the end, he filed for Dissolution of Marriage based on "irreconcilable differences." But, in the main, it was her intermittent affair and recognizable indiscretions through the years with Michael Carlisle that crushed their marriage and his heart.

What surprised Jack was how Julia died – an apparent suicide by hanging herself in her bedroom closet with bathrobe belt. It never occurred to Llewellyn that Julia might have been unhappy or otherwise dissatisfied with her life. That just never occurred to him. It was his intention to pay for her final expenses out of respect for his love for her and their years of marriage. Now, most importantly, he wanted to show David that his mother was loved and held in the highest regard in spite of her long-endured indiscretions with Michael Carlisle.

Still, the projectionist was hurt by Julia in life and horrified by her in death. He found a small measure of comfort at the bottom of a rum bottle by early evening. In the funeral parlor his demeanor did not advertise his drunkenness and he was able to sit quietly for some time if left alone. He could smile and shake the extended hands of well-wishers, but generally, he neglected to look at anyone in the eyes, only staring forward without facial expression. David and Jana could see clearly that Jack was indisposed and very much not himself for the duration of the evening. Still, they pushed on out of respect for the memory of David's mother.

THE FUNERAL OF JULIA LLEWELLYN WAS A CLASSIC SOCIAL event for Cottage Grove. It required the attendance and participation of anyone who was anyone in the village. The Riedelsheimer Funeral Home was ill-prepared for the turnout as family, friends and the general public compressed their way into the largest chapel that was available for the wake.

Because of the circumstances of her death, the casket remained closed. It was said that she was clothed in a yellow cotton dress with buttons lined down the middle of the front to the waist and requisite rosary about her hands. She had led a zestful life that came to a turbulent conclusion. That was the end of it and there was not much else to say.

Only the Grass Suffers

Enveloped in the stringent and overwhelming aroma of lilies, Jack and his son, David with his wife Jana, sat in the front row and accepted condolences from all who filed by in single-line formation. The chapel was brimming with flowers of all varieties but the lilies championed the number of arrangements and consequently left a compelling fragrance.

Amid the whispers of shared stories of intimacy with the deceased there was a sense of surprise that Julia's death was of her own making. Moreover, the underlying question was a natural and high-pitched "Why?" Even at this moment in time there was no answer and this exasperated the shock that accompanied her violent and untimely death.

MICHAEL CARLISLE CAME THROUGH THE CHAPEL'S entrance at about 8:00 p. m. He was alone as usual and apparently had just come from the Devil's Elbow to Riedelsheimer's. An invisible cloud of alcoholic foulness accompanied him as he entered through the doorway. He was recognized and acknowledged by Vincent and Mikaela Rhea. Lauren did not look up to observe the old lawyer. Instead, she kept her focus on the small prayer book that Father Timothy O'Halloran had given her a while ago. It was a gift from one kindred spirit to another.

On the inside cover of the booklet O'Halloran had written a brief excerpt from an Emily Dickinson poem:

> *Finite – to fail, but infinite to Venture –*
> *For the one ship that struts the shore*
> *Many's the gallant – overwhelmed Creature*
> *Nodding in Navies nevermore –*

When the little girl had approached her mother for its meaning, Mikaela struggled with an explanation for someone so young. Once explained, the words had inspired Lauren to believe in herself and her ability to accomplish what her imagination would require. Although not entirely friends with Miss Dickinson, she would take these words to heart. Thus, her employment at Riedelsheimer became her first victory over the difference between what was expected of her and what she could accomplish.

As Carlisle reached the Rheas seated at the rear of the chapel, Mikaela sighed with some measure of relief at his successful arrival in front of an empty chair. Vincent felt a blend of aggravation and amusement. He was not sure which emotion would prevail, but he thought, really, no one likes a drunk. As much as he liked his boss, the drunken stupor was really inexcusable. Most likely, this would mean he would have to drive the old man home after the wake while sending Mikaela and Lauren home by themselves.

"Have you been here long?" loudly slurrred Carlisle, as he collapsed onto the padded chapel chair.

"No, we arrived just a few minutes ago," Mikaela returned in whisper.

And so they sat silently for a while, not talking and only looking straight ahead at the crowd. The large gathering seemed to relax and became chattier and, eventually, morphed into a rather spirited social gathering as wakes can sometimes become.

At about 8:30 p. m., Carlisle decided it was time to officially pay his respects to Julia by praying for her at her casket in front of the chapel's population. Llewellyn would not like it, but neither man could prevent the inevitable social expectation of paying one's respects to an ex-lover.

The old lawyer had reasoned that the gesture must occur or people would think less of him as her long-time lover. That romantic indiscretion was outed long ago during the Llewellyns' divorce. It was just as well to complete the role of home-wrecker and former lover.

The lawyer shuffled slowly up to the casket to view Julia. It had not occurred to him that Julia's wake would be a closed-casket affair. There was a moment that passed before it struck him that she was found dead a couple of days after she hung herself, so her beauty was very much tarnished. And so the viewing of Julia Llewellyn was not possible.

At last, he prayed to God for whatever it was worth to God and to the public in attendance. Although Carlisle was sincere, it still made good theater and his reputation did not suffer for it.

After an appropriate amount of time, he turned away from the casket and flowers and moved toward David Llewellyn still stationed on his chair in the front row. The old man wavered some but kept his walk deliberate and finally extended his hand.

"I am so sorry for your loss, David," he began with difficulty, "Your mother was a very special person." His gaze was glassy and his words were louder than usual so as to maintain clarity of pronunciation.

The son said only, "Thank you, Mr. Carlisle." And then he looked at Jana and then he looked down at his own slightly scuffed shoes. Jana held David's arm tightly as if to brace him for the uncomfortable exchange. Sitting on the other side of him was his father who became red-faced with alcoholic outrage at the presumption that Carlisle's condolences would be welcomed.

IN VIOLENT RAGE, LLEWELLYN STOOD AND STEPPED IN front of his son's chair to grab at the throat of Carlisle. "Dad! Don't!" shouted David, but it was too late. Llewellyn had wrapped two strong hands around the throat of Carlisle. A moment later David was alert enough to hold his father back and stepped between the two antagonists. Both were drunk so they were both easily manhandled, Llewellyn by his son and Carlisle by Vincent Rhea, who wisely and quietly followed his partner to the front of the chapel.

"I've had enough of you," roared Llewellyn as he clawed at the lawyer.

His first instinct was to cower, but then Carlisle rushed back into the hungry clenches of the projectionist and the interference of David and Vincent was required once again. Eventually, and with order restored, Jack was back onto his chair, ruffled and red-faced. The old lawyer stood collecting himself while unruffling his suit and tie.

"I have as much right to be here as you do, Llewellyn," he cried. "You aren't married to her any more than I am."

"Rot in hell, you bastard," was the projectionist's retort.

"We both loved her," the attorney countered. "The only difference is that she loved me back." Entirely stunned by the salvo's audacity, the chapel congregation was spellbound into a stillness as that before a violent storm.

Unsure as to what to do next, and with the release of Vincent's hold, Carlisle walked up to the casket once again and appeared to pray. Then, quicker than Vincent thought possible Michael slashed back to the seated Jack and began pummeling the old film professor with a flurry of fists.

Instinctively, David grabbed at the old lawyer and yanked

cruelly at his shirt and suit collars and hurled his mother's lover across the room and through a large floral arrangement against the chapel wall. Dazed, Carlisle quickly bounced up and rushed David and shoved him backwards against the ornate casket of Julia. In a violent motion the funeral closure twisted and turned on its side edge, slid off its metallic tubular stand, and then landed flat and upright upon the floor.

Jack laid against his overturned chair in semi-consciousness until Carlisle attacked again beating on his face in encore. The two were eventually separated by well-wishers from the second row. Eventually, shock, horror, and confusion gave way to a returned sense of reason and proportion. But all propriety and decorum and civility and sensitivity that ever existed in funeral lore flew out the window and headed for the trees.

Alan Riedelsheimer and two colleagues set the casket right side up and back onto its silver stand, then wheeled it out of the chapel and into the adjacent room. They opened its lid and rearranged Julia's body as quickly and quietly as possible. Upon reclosing, the morticians pushed Julia's remains back into the chapel while the wake visitors settled in and restored their lost composure as much as the circumstances would allow.

EXCEPT, OF COURSE, THAT IS NOT WHAT HAPPENED.

It occurred with crystal clarity in the mind of Jack Llewellyn – but only in his drunken daydreaming. The skirmish and its aftermath were imaginary because civility and decorum would not allow such horror regardless of their history and untimely loss. Llewellyn's revengeful reverie would have to suffice for comfort.

Still standing in front of David, the old lawyer stared momentarily at the projectionist and they exchanged glances of hatred but maintained a respectful silence in deference to the gathering. It was brutally awkward for those in attendance, especially for David who was the only physical barrier between the two enemies.

"We will now recite the Rosary," Riedelsheimer signaled to the gathering, "This will conclude this evening's visitation." There was to be a brief private burial the following morning, he indicated, "Family only, please."

Father O'Halloran stepped forward to lead the Rosary before the murmuring congregation. By mid-Rosary, people were able to breathe again and there returned at least a thin veneer of propriety as one would expect even at the wake of a convict.

As the prayers were recited, everyone became aware of the absence of Michael Carlisle. Vincent Rhea was also gone, presumably safely escorting the old lawyer to his home. Jack sat slumped in his chair with tears in his eyes as much from the humiliation of the old lawyer's presence at the wake as from the loss of an ex-wife who had not loved him. In a way and in effect, for him she had died long ago; still, his faithfulness remained intact. If nothing else could be said of Jack Llewellyn, he was tenacious in his love for someone that he loved and in his hatred for someone that he hated.

And as much as he loathed the man called Michael Carlisle for his long love affair with his ex-wife and the consequent dissolution their marriage, he also resented him for his romantic involvement with his first love long before the introduction of Julia into their lives. If there were ever two men who were more ill-fated than Llewellyn and Carlisle, their histories are not described in any record.

Father O'Halloran concluded the Rosary in efficient fashion and walked over to Jack, David and Jana. "These are hard times for all of you," he began, "Try to make the best of it by holding on to each other." With that the priest announced the wake's conclusion to the still crowded chapel. And the crowd noisily dispersed. Altogether, it was indeed a rather entertaining evening. Generally, those in attendance had a pretty good time. Tomorrow, the Grove would be abuzz with eye-witness accounts of the tension between Llewellyn and Carlisle.

IN EXITING, THE SMALL CROWD FUNNELED TOWARD THE chapel's double doors to form a human bottleneck. Jana held her father-in-law close to her amid the disorder. As she did, David fell behind and brushed against the scrum's tail end. He found himself forcibly dove-tailed toward the one person in all of Cottage Grove that intimidated him and whose meeting he wanted to avoid – the incomparable Mikaela Rhea. Along with her daughter, she was pressed against David as they reached the chapel doorway. Once in the hallway the crowd dissipated and Mikaela and David were left behind against the wall looking at each other in obvious apprehension. For both of them, it was pretty much the icing on the cake and a natural conclusion to a disastrous evening.

"Mikaela, thank you for coming tonight," he greeted, uncertain as to what else to say, "I cannot tell you how crushed I am about my mother's death and how embarrassed I am about tonight. Her memory deserves better than the bad behavior of Michael Carlisle and my dad."

"Yes, David, it is all so tragic and so unnecessary," she

volunteered, "Whatever demon she possessed I know that there were people who loved her that would have gladly helped in any way."

There was little more that could be said constructively and so the silence became an awkward recess in the brief conversation.

"By the way, this is my daughter, Lauren," Mikaela continued, "Lauren, this is Mr. David Llewellyn, an old friend of mine."

"Hello, Mr. Llewellyn," Lauren said dutifully and with only mild interest.

"Hello, Lauren. It is very nice to meet you."

They looked at each other briefly without comment because there was more to say without words than with them. Over the years their paths had crossed every now and then without incident. She was a few years older and they naturally went their different ways. For both their marriages this absence of interaction probably circumvented calamity. But… and this was the thing that they could not put a handle on… there was something either missing in their friendship or something extraordinary. In either case, they didn't know the something that was unknown and unidentifiable.

And so their relationship was long-distanced, sporadic and superficial. Even as much as they may have wanted it to be different, they could not make it so. The love for their own spouses and that missing thread of connection prevented them from becoming intimate. Though slightly uncomfortable, deep inside both Mikaela and David there resided a sense of relief and maintained order because their relationship would always be incomplete. Sometimes things are better left unsaid, sometimes a lack of resolution is better than a revolution.

At the end of the long corridor of the funeral home appeared Jana still holding her emotionally spent father-in-law. "David, are you coming?" she called with a hint of desperation in her voice.

"Right now, Jana," he answered.

"Good night Mikaela," and he looked at Lauren. "Good night, Lauren.

Thank you both for coming to my mother's wake. It really was very kind of you."

He walked briskly to the corridor's end and helped Jana with his father through the exit door and out into the night. Mikaela and Lauren watched the Llewelyns until they were out of sight. After a brief silence the question was asked, "Mom, why do Mr. Carlisle and Mr. Llewellyn look mean at each other in the chapel?"

"Sometimes, Lauren, adults misbehave as children do. It seems that no matter how old we become, we are still not sure how to behave."

"But that's not the real answer, is it Mom?"

"No," sighed Mikaela, "The real answer is that they both loved Mrs. Llewellyn and they have always competed for her affection. And, in doing so, they have learned to dislike each other very much."

"It seems to me that Mr. Carlisle won because didn't Mrs. Llewellyn like him better in the end?" reasoned Lauren.

"Oh, no, child, no one won. Everyone lost in some way. It is a sad story altogether."

"Still, I like Mr. Carlisle very much. He is always so nice to our family," Lauren countered, "Don't you think so?"

"Yes, he is very nice to us."

"But I like David, too," the girl declared. "Do you think that I could call him Uncle David the next time we meet?"

Lauren inquired. "He seems so nice, just like a family member."

Mikaela looked down at her daughter in wonder. "I'm sure he would like that very much, dear. I am glad that you like him so." With that the two of them walked slowly down the otherwise empty hallway hand-in-hand and left the building to its quiet resident.

ON THE FOLLOWING MORNING THE SKY WAS BLUE, THEN gray, then blue again, as the sun played hide-and-seek for most of the morning behind scattered clouds. At ten o'clock and without the benefit of Holy Mass, Father Timothy O'Halloran gave a blessing over the casket at the only Catholic cemetery in Cottage Grove.

"Eternal rest grant unto her, O Lord, and let perpetual light shine upon her. May she rest in peace."

Present at the burial were only Jack Llewellyn and David and Jana. The projectionist had insisted on a very private burial. The projectionist's thought was to let people come to the wake as they wished, but let the actual burial be brief, without much ceremony, and only for the immediate family. From a safe distance and silhouetted against the rolling cemetery skyline stood Michael Carlisle. Not wanting an encore awkwardness with his fiercest enemy, the old lawyer kept his distance out of respect for the decent civility of a quiet burial.

Michael Carlisle thought about Julia and how she died and wondered why she did what she did. Maybe that would never be known and that was most troubling. But as time passed his musing gave way to the origin of his battles with the projectionist. It was not for the love of Julia as many in

Cottage Grove had surmised. Rather, it was another woman from another time over whom war was first waged. Because, as the fates would have it, she was also the first love of Jack Llewellyn.

With the burial rite concluded Father O'Halloran used both his hands to clasp the hand of Jack and offered kind words of sympathy. He did the same for David. The three family members turned away from the grave and walked with the priest back to the gravel road that was adjacent to the cemetery. Car engines started and slowly the hearse led the other automobile off of the grassy grounds and out onto the streets of the Grove.

The lawyer still stood there and watched the Llewellyns prepare to leave with the priest. He placed his hands in the pockets of his suit pants and leaned just slightly and casually as if he was supported against thin air. He thought to himself with a sense of victory, "Yeah, Llewellyn, you got to bury her, but I took the woman away from you." He smiled with some satisfaction, "Come to think of it, that was the second time I took a woman away from you."

Then, his faint smile went away because he reminded himself that he lost his lover and that a new one seemed unlikely in the near future. He took his hands out of his pockets and walked briskly out of the graveyard. After all, there was work to be done at the office and, right now and in the foreseeable future, that was going to be foremost on his mind.

As the lawyer reached his automobile that was parked on an adjoining road, he realized that Jack Llewellyn was standing next to the driver's side. Apparently, the retired professor had stayed behind, after all, to have a word with his ex-wife's lover.

"What do you want, Llewellyn?" Carlisle asked with some wrinkle in his voice.

"I want to deliver a message to you," was the reply. "It comes straight from my heart." With that, the projectionist rammed his fist onto the left cheek of the lawyer and the feeling of knuckles on cheekbone made a slight crunching sound that rocked Carlisle and vibrated the hand of Llewellyn. The attorney's body lifted in the air and dropped to the ground with weighted force. Pain buckled the hand and wrist of the projectionist and a red soreness formed on it instantly.

Carlisle laid there motionless for a time as Llewellyn stared down at him admiring his handiwork. "Did I get your attention, Michael? I hope the message from my heart was conveyed to you well enough." The projectionist rubbed and held his right hand with his left and calmly walked away. He stopped briefly and turned back at the man still laying on the ground, "If you want to make something of it, just let me know. I'll be available."

Eventually, Carlisle staggered to his feet and stood wobbling in the morning sun next to his Mercedes. He climbed into his car and sat for a while as if trying to return to sobriety. His face was covered with redness and was beginning to swell. And as the numbness was receding, the pain was increasing. He used his hands to press and play with his cheek and jaw. Thankfully, other than the immediate discomfort, there really didn't seem to anything broken or left ajar.

Finally, as he turned the ignition key and started the engine, he said aloud to himself, "Okay, Jack, you win round one, but I get the next round very soon, very soon. My turn is next on the agenda."

Chapter 6

A WAY OF KNOWING

With his mother properly buried and after a brief late lunch with his father at the café, David and Jana traveled back to Wauwatosa to resume their life together. Because it was only about a hundred miles, they returned home in the early evening just in time for the rush-hour traffic.

In truth, David intended to drive back to Cottage Grove the next day to conduct some very personal business without the company of his wife. He could handle his contracting business with the use of his cell phone and laptop computer. After all, he paid good money for the employment of good people.

As they approached the Milwaukee suburb and began the ordeal of stop-and-go traffic, David turned to Jana, "I will have to go back to the Grove tomorrow. There are some loose ends concerning my mother that need my attention."

"Really, can't it wait for a while, David?" suggested Jana. "It has been difficult these past couple days. You look pretty well roughed-up."

"No, Jana, I don't want to wait," he pressed, "It may take me a couple of days, but I want to talk to the police and Michael Carlisle."

"Michael Carlisle!" gasped Jana, "I understand you may want the police to fill in some blanks about your mother's death, but why on earth do you need to see Michael Carlisle?"

"Jana, he was my mother's… lawyer," he countered. 'He may be able to shed some light on her frame of mind during the last few weeks."

FOLLOWING A RESTLESS NIGHT, THE MORNING SUN ROSE above a fluorescent red horizon and across the eastern sky. David and Jana awoke in each other's arms and stared at one another's morning smile. After a while they unraveled from the bedding and placed bare feet on the soft rug that lead them to the hardwood floor of the bedroom.

A quick shower for David became a prelude to a ham and egg breakfast sandwich prepared by Jana. She would return to her interior decorator job and volunteer work the next day while her husband traveled back to Cottage Grove for the two interviews that he felt he had to conduct. It was a quiet breakfast as David was seemingly deep in thought about the next couple of days. Jana left him to his thoughts as he ate, understanding that the untimely death of his mother naturally yielded hard days for him.

"Thank you for breakfast, Jana," he began. "I will be back tomorrow night sometime." She looked at him and said nothing. "I'll stop by one of our construction sites on the way out of town. I'll call you tonight from the hotel."

"Drive carefully, darling," she said. "I love you."

They kissed good-bye because they had already missed each other and there was nothing else left to say. They both hated to leave one another and it was like that every day of their marriage.

Only the Grass Suffers

HEADING WEST ON INTERSTATE 94 FOR THE SECOND TIME in two days, David set the Explorer's cruise control at the speed limit and settled in the travel lane while traffic passed him on the left intermittently. He was in transit and his thoughts carried him to a previous time when his mother had come to his home for a brief Easter visit.

JULIA LLEWELLYN WAS STILL BEAUTIFUL AND ELEGANT AS *a slim auburn brunette. Her delicate hands were adorned with golden rings and her earrings shimmered behind her shoulder length hair. She rarely wore slacks and most often was seen in public wearing stylish dresses or colorful blouses and solid skirts. Because she was already tall enough, she avoided high-heels and stayed with flats for fashion and comfort. She looked ten years younger than other women who were ten years younger.*

She was educated and intelligent and was very much her own master. She was a creature of possessions and occasions, but not of enduring commitments and responsibilities. She excelled eminently in social graces but failed miserably in personal relationships. Those who knew her were enchanted by her, even though they were cognizant of her frailties. Her dearest friends thought of her as having much personality but little character. In the end, it was thought that one could very well love Julia Llewellyn, but one could never really trust her.

Of course, her son was acutely aware of her strengths and weaknesses. Through the years they had weathered a stormy relationship. Loving each other as mother and child while scraping against one another from time to time over contentions great and small. They never confided in each other because they were never close. Still, they loved as mother and son even with some reservation or, more likely, caution.

Jana had gone to bed early. Company had always exhausted her both in the preparation of house cleaning and meal planning. She considered having company a strenuous endeavor. Being company was easier, but still one had to be "on point" at all times.

Julia and her son sat in the living room and had just finished watching a 1940s film-noir movie. She loved the genre because of their stories and well-developed characters. David tolerated the old black and white format with the absence of any special effects because his mother was their guest. Otherwise, he would have just as soon poked his eyes out.

After a while, David retrieved a bottle of wine that his mother preferred. Unlike her son who always found any wine disappointing and far less refreshing than a good cold beer, she loved white wine because of its taste and how she looked while drinking it. She felt so sophisticated and liked the way it made her feel – a little dizzy, but still under control.

And so they drank, Julia her wine and David his beer. And they drank some more until they both relaxed and felt somewhat invincible. It was a different kind of mother and child reunion, so to speak. In the course of the first bottle of wine, she expressed her admiration for Jana and her career and her volunteer work, as well as the casual elegance of their home. Her wish to be called grandma by potential, if not inevitable, offspring was far less pronounced. The conversation moved on as a second bottle was offered and duly accepted.

Midway through that bottle Julia sat there with a tipping wine glass in hand and glazed expression across her face. Her son had never seen her like that before and he decidedly did not like either the circumstance or resulting effect.

"You know, David, I really did love Jack," she began with just a slight slurring of speech. "He was always very good to me. Getting a divorce – I mean dissolving our marriage – wasn't all bad though." She hesitated, then resumed, "He was a good father to you, wasn't he?"

"Of course, Mom," he replied, "But we were never alike, you know, not even when I was a little boy. We just never clicked that well." David momentarily stopped and thought to himself, "But I sure did respect him." He wanted to say it out loud but he was approaching intoxication now. Still not quite there, yet. He would stop with this last beer because he was with his mother.

"Well, you know, that is the way I planned it. I wanted you to have the better father, David," she babbled. "So, I just went ahead and planned it that way."

Again, she sat there just staring ahead into a nothingness that her white wine provided. Her only son sat in front of her dumbfounded in silence.

"What do you mean, Mom? What are you saying?" he slowly asked.

There was quiet in the room. Conversation and glances froze. Silence was both deafening and meaningful.

"I don't mean anything, David. I've just had a little too much to drink tonight. Please forgive me. I think I'll turn in. Good night." She got up with difficulty and managed to walk awkwardly toward the guest bedroom.

"Mom, is Dad not my father?"

Julia stopped and leaned against an easy chair and turned slowly to face both her son and her new future. "I am sorry, dear. I never wanted you to know and, least of all, to find out like this. I am so sorry."

She left it at that and without further explanation struggled to her bedroom and closed the door. There was neither movement nor sound from her during the remainder of the night.

David sat in the living room stunned and crushed. Yet, a part of him also finally understood how his father and he could have been so different through the years. Now, all the disparity in their likes and dislikes, vocations and avocations, interests and hobbies, as well as characteristics and temperament, could now be explained. For literally decades, there had always been a pain between the ears of David Llewellyn as he tried to understand his father and to be a good son. There were always mixed results. Now he knew why. What she was telling him was eminently believable and believing it almost gave him a more orderly world.

But as his mother retired to her bedroom and intoxicated slumber, the obvious question that remained unasked and unanswered was "Well then, who IS my father?"

BY MID-MORNING DAVID HAD ARRIVED IN COTTAGE Grove. A couple of blocks off of the main square a side street turned into a curving paved road that led to the city jail and police station. It was an attractive facility given its purpose and age. Inside, the police chief was waiting for the young man who had requested the meeting just a couple of days earlier.

"Good morning, Chief," David began.

"Hello, David," was the response inside the chief's cluttered office. "Please have a seat. Would you like some coffee?"

"No, thank you."

Off his desk the chief picked up a folder and plopped it down in front of David. "Here is the autopsy report, son. You can read it, but you can't take it with you."

"I don't need to see it, Chief," replied David. "I know how my mother died."

"Well, then, let's get to it, shall we?" The veteran policeman pulled out a pouch of Red Man and stuck a wad between his tongue and cheek. "Can you tell me anything about your mother's mental state during the last couple of weeks that might have made her want to kill herself?"

"Frankly, no, Chief. I was hoping that you could shed some light on the cause of my mother's death."

"I did not know your mother well, son. Only by sight and reputation."

The words came out too fast for the chief to stop their flight and all the damage was done and there was no correction to be had.

To his credit, David did not respond to the remark. His mother's legacy was what it was. She had been well liked in Cottage Grove, but not particularly well respected. Her son had known this for a long time. Her lengthy and public affair with the lawyer Carlisle and the consequent divorce cemented any opinions that anyone had of her. There was no point in either reinventing the past or trying to polish her tarnished image.

"I am sorry, David. That came out all wrong. I just meant I knew who she was by sight and that she was Jack's ex-wife and your mother."

"Forget it, Chief," was the curt reply.

"We were hoping that you would have some insight as to her state of mind during the past couple of weeks. You know, we found some anti-depressants in her medicine cabinet."

David sat quietly for a moment and seemed lost in thought. And then he spoke slowly, "Well, everyone we know has felt some kind of personal pain at one time or another. Sometimes, every once in a great while, it's just too hard for us to forgive ourselves, even if others have already done so. Maybe that was the case with my mother, I don't know. But the last time we saw each other was on Easter Sunday and everything was fine at that time, as far as I know."

The policeman wanted to ask why it was so long ago since he had seen his mother. But instead he accepted the vague explanation and decided to let it go. Obviously, there was a family problem and it didn't make any difference really. There was no foul play other than the nature of suicide itself.

"No one seems to know why she killed herself. Certainly, your dad has no idea. He hadn't seen her in several weeks. We have talked to her lawyer, Mr. Carlisle, and he also is unable to shed any light on what happened. You were pretty much our last hope. I am sorry."

"I am sorry, too, Chief. Thank you for your time." And David ended the conversation there. He rose from his chair, nodded to the policeman and went quietly on his way and out the front door.

JULIA MET HER SON IN THE HALLWAY ON HER WAY TO THE *bathroom the following morning. She avoided eye contact as long as she could, but as she stepped into the bathroom she heard her son say,* "We need to talk right now, Mom."

"I'll be out in just a moment, David."

They returned to the living room in their bathrobes. Jana still slept the sleep of the innocent and David wanted this conversation now and he wanted only between his mother and himself. Without the benefit of coffee or tea or toast, the son began the conversation.

"Okay, Mom, who is my natural father?" The question was blunt and very much to the point and it was volleyed without sympathy. It had been a sleepless night for David and there was neither warmth nor patience in his voice even to a mother that he had loved all of his life.

"Your biological father is Michael Carlisle, David," she revealed in a hushed voice. "But I kept the secret all of your life so that you would have a better father in Jack.

"You see, Michael would never have acknowledged your existence, even if the entire community of Cottage Grove knew about it. So, why punish you for my transgression."

"How kind of you, Mom, to think of someone other than yourself," he answered with sharp sarcasm.

"I did what I thought was best under the circumstances, David. Was I really that wrong in my assessment of either man? Michael Carlisle was interested in only two things – being a district court judge and the color of my panties."

David was uncertain what shocked him most about his mother's rejoinder – her blunt honesty or the sexual reference. But he could only sit there in amazement at both the revealed circumstances and the candid conversation on an Easter Sunday morning between mother and son.

"David, what I did was out of love for you and it was in your best interest. You know that," she entreated, but without effect. Her son only looked at her in cold condemnation.

"You have lied to me all of my life, made of fool out of both my dad AND my father – all in our best interest? Really?" he exploded.

Her face was flushed with remorse and regret and complete forlornness. A late-night intoxication had illuminated an entire lifetime of misbehavior encapsulated in a singular promiscuity. She had purloined the heritage and identity of her own son for her own convenience and that of her illicit lover. And they both knew it.

Now, there was only her shame and his outrage that was left between them.

"Mom, I want you to collect all of your things and get out of my house." And, then, finally, "I never want to see you again." He got up from his favorite easy chair, walked out of the room, and never saw his mother again.

Julia Llewellyn gathered her things and left quietly before Jana stirred from her sleep. When she awoke, she no longer had a mother-in-law. Her husband sat pale-faced at the kitchen table staring into his cup of coffee.

EVEN THOUGH IT HAD BEEN A NUMBER OF WEEKS SINCE his mother admitted that Michael Carlisle was his natural father, David had not attempted to contact the old lawyer. It took that long for him to digest his new lineage and reconsider his relationship with the other man who had raised him. He did not know Carlisle well, he only knew of him. There was neither indication nor recognition of their clandestine consanguinity at his mother's wake. Moreover, as shocking as the situation was to David, it would be equally appalling to Jack whenever he learned of the prolonged deception. In any case, he had decided that the wake was not the right time to confront his biological father or approach his childhood dad with such a revelation.

It was the intention of David Llewellyn to confront Carlisle with his new knowledge and demand some kind of satisfaction, although he did not know what kind of satisfaction there was to be had.

The young Llewelyn pulled at the heavy glass double doors of Carlisle & Rhea during late morning. Lunch time was approaching but he didn't care. He was not hungry and he didn't care about the appetite of Michael Carlisle. He stood patiently in front of the matronly legal secretary for longer than he thought proper; however, she did seem awfully busy.

"Good morning, sir," Cosie said matter-of-factly as she shuffled file folders onto a pile before her. "May I help you?"

"My name is David Llewellyn and I would like to see Michael Carlisle."

Even though she knew the answer, she asked, "Do you have an appointment, Mr. Llewellyn?"

"Of course not," he replied. "Tell him the son of Julia Llewellyn would like to see him. She was a… client… of his. It is personal."

Cosie picked up the telephone receiver and pushed the speed dial number of Carlisle. After a brief moment, she said, "A Mr. David Llewellyn is here to see you. He says that he is the son of Julia Llewellyn and that he is requesting a personal conversation with you, Mr. Carlisle." And then, "Yes, sir."

She looked up at the young man and said, "Mr. Carlisle will see you in just a few minutes. Please be seated."

David complied and surrendered to the memory of his last conversation with his mother. Did the lawyer know that he was his father? If he did, what an outrageous circumstance the conversation would present and what did it say about Carlisle after all of these years? If he didn't, could David really approach him with such an announcement? What would be his reaction? In either case, he was beginning to doubt that this was the right time and place for such a confrontation?

The intercom feature of the secretary's telephone rang and she casually placed the receiver to her ear. Another brief moment, and then, "Yes sir, right away." She returned the receiver back onto its cradle and motioned at David. "He will see you now, Mr. Llewellyn. Please follow me."

Down the corridor David followed Cosie to the law office of Michael Carlisle. The legal secretary left and returned to her desk and a modest brown bag lunch amid stacks of documents for review and disposition.

The old lawyer stood behind his large desk of red cherry and motioned David to have a seat. Llewellyn sat.

"Well, this is a pleasant surprise, David. It is very nice to see you again. What can I do for you?"

The young man was stayed still for a moment so that he could better observe the man in front of him. He finally began, "Mr. Carlisle, it is my understanding that you are handling my mother's estate. Is there anything that I should know as we proceed with the legal administration of that estate?"

The lawyer relaxed back in his chair and began filling his pipe with his special blend of tobacco. "No, everything is in order. You will receive a copy of her will and the original will be kept in this office." He sighed, and then, "Of course, you are the only beneficiary, David." He concluded, "There really aren't any complications to worry about. There is the condominium, a quarter of a million in mutual funds, and a few thousand dollars in cash."

"Were there any personal papers or property that I will be receiving?"

"Personal property? Only what is in her condo and her Lexus," was the reply. "If there are personal papers or keepsakes, those you will have to discover for yourself as your father and you go through her things."

The lawyer paused for a moment and then added, "I would have thought that Julia… I mean your mother… would have left something for your dad, but apparently not."

David studied Carlisle for a moment, perhaps even longer than he should have, sizing up his words, tone of voice, and facial expression. He came to no real conclusion other than a continued ambivalence as to whether the lawyer felt he was talking to a deceased client's son who happened to be a once-upon-a-time lover or his own biological son who he had ignored since birth. It was apparent that either the old lawyer was one seriously cold bastard or he didn't recognize that his only son was sitting before him in a leather chair in his elegant office.

At last, he decided that the latter was the case. And the more he thought about it, the more obvious it became that Michael Carlisle did not know who David really was. In a moment's decision, the young Llewellyn concluded the conversation with affected politeness and the absence of inquiry. It was not the right time for such a profoundly emotional disturbance. His introduction as the lawyer's son could come another day.

VILLAGE SQUARE CONDOMINIUMS WERE LOCATED OFF OF Interstate 94 just outside the city limits of Cottage Grove. They were stylish up-scale condos and apartments for retirees with some financial wherewithal and athletic inclinations. Historically, Julia Llewellyn enjoyed both because of both her intelligence and beauty. She continued to earn the wealth-giving of Michael Carlisle and the ego-satisfying attention of Jack Llewellyn for most of her adult life in one fashion or another.

But, now, things were going to be different. Because of an unfortunate slip of the tongue, her only son had effectively disowned her and complete scandal and shame would soon be visiting her. She had made a train wreck of her life. She betrayed her husband, brought embarrassment to a respected legal mind, and shattered the legacy of the one person she loved most – her son. The final blow came with the apparent early symptoms of a cancer.

For eight weeks she waited for the hammer to fall. But all was quiet. Finally, she had enough. She grew weary of waiting and her health further declined. She saw her doctor for the depression and the disease, but the medicines helped neither condition. And there was no cure for self-absorption and betrayal.

Then, one early summer evening when the sight of daffodils and fireflies and the smell of freshly cut grass filled the front lawn of her residential property, she decided it was time. There was no rush, no rashness, no panic, no emotion. In business-like form, she ran the hot water for a relaxing bath. She climbed in the tub, bathed with luxurious soaps and scents, and rose again with towel in hand to dry the softness of her body.

As she placed her arms in her bath robe, she removed the cloth belt of her robe. With the robe open exposing her naked body she walked over to her bedroom closet and placed a chair just below the 1-1/4" steel tube that supported the hangers of her wardrobe. She placed her closet clothes on the bed and returned to the chair. She stood on its seat and attached the belt to a hook that rested high near the ceiling of the closet. The other end of the cloth belt was knotted around her neck.

She stood still for a moment and felt a tear run down her left cheek. Then she kicked the chair away and was welcomed into the kingdom of God.

Only the Grass Suffers

Toward the evening, David checked into his hotel room off the interstate highway. Because his father's flat was small and the two of them barely got along, anyway, he stayed at hotel rooms when he came home to Cottage Grove.

Back at the hotel, David entered the lobby and headed for the elevator. He paused long enough to notice a Coke machine in an ante room adjacent to the two elevator doors. He pumped in a handful of coins and received his canned soft drink. Taking the elevator to the second floor, he took a quick swig of the Coke to relieve the dryness in his mouth.

In his room, he sat down the soda on the dresser and stripped to his black boxer briefs and laid on the bed. After a while, he took his cell phone and called home to Jana. The telephone lined whirled its buzz a couple of times before there was an answer.

Chapter 7

TRUTH & CONSEQUENCES

David decided to stay in Cottage Grove one more day and head home as the weekend approached. In every sense, he felt that he deserved to set the record straight with both his biological father and his dad who raised him. It seemed to him that everyone should know what is true and let the chips fall where they may.

He decided to lunch with his father at a place called Schweiss' Ford near the confluence of Sweetwater and Outagamie Creeks. It was a place where automobiles traveling the gravel road could cross Sweetwater without risk. A concrete slab connected the two banks of the creek and water flowed through large steel tubes below the surface of the bridge. So, the creek's current remained intact and the locals could pass in safety. There, in the shade of several pin oaks, they positioned themselves on a couple of dead tree stumps and enjoyed sandwiches and coffee.

"You were a good son to your mother, David. She loved you very much," the projectionist began after their appetites were appeased. "She was so very proud of you and would have done anything for you."

"Yeah, Dad, she thought quite highly of us both," David said calmly, "But, you know, there was some treachery in her, too."

"Why David, what brought this on?"

"Oh, come on, Dad," he exploded. "She had a lengthy affair with Michael Carlisle that crushed your heart and destroyed our family."

"It destroyed our marriage – yes, David – but not our family."

"More than you know, Dad," he continued with hesitation but also with resolve to get on with it. "Last Easter Mom and I had a knock-down and drag-out fight that pretty much ended our relationship." Jack Llewellyn sat there stunned with what was obviously a tortured narration by his son.

"What are you saying, David? What are you talking about?"

"The night before Easter Sunday, Mom drank a little too much wine," he started. "Does that sound familiar? She let it slip that she was always thinking of my best interest. So much so…" he paused for effect so that the other shoe would fall with the appropriate impact, "she even chose the better father for me." He let the words settle into the mind of his father. "Do you understand what I am saying, Dad? You are not my biological father. That is how she destroyed our family."

David looked at Jack expecting a grimace of devastation, but it did not arrive. What he saw on his father's face was an expression of mild sadness and somewhat labored patience. The silence was broken by Jack collecting the debris from their lunch and placing everything in a plastic trash bag that he pulled out of his pants pocket.

"Yes, I know, David," was his only response. It was said matter-of-factly and without further comment.

Jack gathered his things and got up to go, but David stopped him. "Wait a moment!" he cried, "Are you kidding me? You mean you knew about this?" His shock and outrage were complete, but the man who raised him was calm to the point of being almost reassuring.

"Well, yes." said Jack. "Maybe we should sit down again and let me explain." With that, they sat and David did not know whether to laugh or curse, so he did neither and, like his father, he gave in to patience.

"First, your mother was right from the beginning. Michael Carlisle would have made a bad father. But there is no use in dwelling on that," was the initial salvo. "The more important issue for me was that your mother betrayed me with their affair, but I still loved her. So, I decided to steal what I thought was the best part of your mother… and that was you, David.

"When we learned that she was pregnant with Carlisle's child, we decided that our marriage could not survive, but that our family, so to speak, just might," he continued. My only sadness is that your newly found genealogy and the circumstances under which it was discovered will trouble you for the rest of your life." He continued, "But don't misunderstand me, I don't regret our relationship or even the pretense under which it existed.

"David, nothing has really changed, you know. Your mother still loved you and the man who raised you still loves you. And I know you still love them. Knowing your biological father changes nothing. As they say, it is an inconvenient truth, but it has little meaning unless you give it that."

By this time, David was slumped forward and focusing on a time and event that he could not fully appreciate. Still, his effort continued. "So, for all of my life, you and Mom have lied to me about who I am."

"No, David," his father countered, "We never lied about who you are, we just didn't tell you who provided the sperm, that's all." You are my son and if your mother had blemishes, well… so do we all. But no matter what, she and I did what was in your best interest. Hell, even Carlisle would agree if he knew any of this."

"I think that is a fairly casual attitude to take about the origin of your son."

"Maybe, but from my angle I got the best part of your mother and you got a father who actually loves you. Go see what you can get from Michael Carlisle. It should really be an eye-opener." And, finally, "Hell, he would have sold you in a heartbeat for a few extra years on his district court bench."

David now understood that his biological father was woefully ignorant of the personal machinations of his parents in decades past. "I would have thought that you would have said something to my biological father so that he could have taken *some* responsibility."

There was no hesitation in Jack's voice, "He would have caused trouble and would have fought me every step of the way in raising you. And he would have done so not because he cared about you but because we have always been enemies. Even before we met your mother."

"That is a pretty mean-spirited assertion, Dad, especially when you are denying the parental rights of the real father."

"He had no parental rights and still doesn't and he is not your father, David. You are looking at your father."

"Tell me, Dad, what if I confront him with this information? What will happen to us all, then?"

Jack paused for just a moment and then, "It doesn't much matter one way or the other, David. I really don't see what difference it will make, other than making you both uncomfortable.

"Really, nothing will change. He isn't going to tuck you in bed at night or coach you in a Little League baseball game or attend open house at your school or teach you to drive a truck or paint a room or cut the grass or advise you on dating or send you to college or help pay for your wedding or worry about you or even love you.

"The truth is your mother and I lied to you. If you feel that you got a raw deal and got the short end of the stick, then you are very much mistaken. Even with all of our faults, we have always loved you, David, and we have a lifetime of memories to prove it."

With that the projectionist got up to leave again. "Right now, you are very upset and rightly so. We may have lied to you, but we didn't cheat you. Give it some time. Give it some thought.

"Take me back to town, David. I'm tired."

AGAINST HIS BETTER JUDGMENT, DAVID DECIDED TO return to the law offices of Carlisle and Rhea. Somehow, he was convinced that he deserved some satisfaction from the old lawyer and it was his intention to get it.

Once again in the front office before Cosie, David stood erect and made his request to see Michael Carlisle.

"I am sorry, Mr. Llewellyn, but Mr. Carlisle is not in his office right now. Would you care to speak to Mr. Rhea?"

"No thank you," he began and then abruptly changed his mind. "On second thought I will see Mr. Rhea." It seemed to David that if he could not again access his natural father, perhaps he could learn something about him through his law partner. In any case, it was worth a try since he was already there.

"Mr. Rhea, David Llewellyn would like a few minutes with you," she telephoned. "Very well, thank you, sir.

"Mr. Llewellyn, you may go in. Please follow me."

As David entered the neatly organized and stylish law office of Vincent Rhea. he glanced at the right side of his desk and saw framed photograph of a beautiful wife and beaming young girl at her side.

He clasped the hand of the young lawyer in greeting and remarked, "You have a beautiful family, Mr. Rhea." David did not mention that over the years Mrs. Rhea and he have been flirting and that underlying fondness still existed. And because that fondness has always been undefined and distracting, they had gone their separate ways and something in both of them encouraged that emotional and physical distance.

"Thank you, Mr. Llewellyn, but let's be on a first-name basis. We can call our fathers mister when we see them, but you and I will be Vincent and David, okay?"

"That's fine, Vincent. Thank you."

"So, what can I do for you this afternoon, David?"

"Well, I met Mr. Carlisle earlier to discuss my mother's estate. He was very kind. It seemed necessary to me to stop back and thank him for both his good work and consideration."

"I will relay the message, David, when he returns to the office later today."

"He is an interesting man, Vincent. And, we both know that he was very close to my mother for many years. But I never did know him because of the strain he placed on our family and, then eventually, I married and moved away."

Feeling slightly uncomfortable with the conversation's direction, Vincent smoothed the awkwardness as much as he could. "Michael has been extraordinarily generous and kind to both Mikaela and me over the years. We cannot say enough good things about him.

"He gave me a partnership with this firm and he has been like a father to Mikaela. He adores our daughter Lauren, of course," Vincent summarized.

"I am sure that everyone loves your wife and daughter, Vincent," countered David. "Mikaela is beautiful and bright and Lauren is a special effect unto herself."

With the conversation settling into a more comfortable tone, Vincent relaxed and became forthcoming. "If you're staying in town tonight, why don't you and your wife come by for dinner tonight? I know that Mikaela would like to finally meet Jana. It just didn't seem like the right time to visit with you at your mother's wake. Also, we are having Michael over so you could see him again."

It was one of those times when one's thoughts raced through the mind at a hundred miles an hour. Images and words flashed across the forehead of David Llewellyn as he envisioned seeing Mikaela again and conducting a pointed conversation with his would-be father.

"Well, Jana did not come back to the Grove with me today, but I will accept the invitation, Vincent. Thank you."

"Excellent, shall we say come by about six o'clock for cocktails and we will eat at seven? Here is our home address." He handed David a small piece of note paper with an address that was already known.

With that, Llewellyn got up, shook the young lawyer's hand and turned to leave. "You know, David, Mikaela and you have known each other for a lot of years. You probably have some good stories to tell."

"Not really. I have always been very fond of your wife, but we never really spent any time together. She had different friends than I did growing up. But I always thought she was very attractive and very bright." He concluded, "You have a beautiful family, Vincent. All three of you are lucky to have each other."

That was the moment that Vincent Rhea decided that he liked David Llewellyn, but he was still not certain that he could ever trust him.

THAT FRIDAY EVENING, THE SUV SLOWLY MOVED ACROSS town to an older neighborhood until David reached Scuppernong Drive, the street on which the Rheas lived. It was in the more picturesque part of Cottage Grove. Scarlet maple trees lined both sides of the street and engulfed the street with a leafy canopy that gave a sheltered feeling to any driver or pedestrian as they made their way through the neighborhood. It was considered the most beautiful of streets in town, although not the wealthiest. The mixing of old Victorian and Cape Cod homes along with the maple trees and pin oaks gave Scuppernong an inviting setting on a cold winter's night or during an autumnal evening or on a warm summer's day.

Finally, David applied his brakes and pulled over to the curb with the engine still running. He rolled down his window and looked out across the street at the old Victorian with its prominent veranda. The incandescent glow of light fought through the cotton sheers of the picture window yielding an effect of warmth and comfort.

He could see a crinoline and lace cloth laid neatly across the dining room table and some kind of floral setting as a centerpiece. Sparkling glasses and shining utensils laid properly next to their companion settings. It was early in the evening and the Rheas were moments away from accepting guests for a summer's night supper. Llewellyn stared across the way in lonely silence and with mixed emotions and wondered how this young family was faring that evening. Were Mikaela and Vincent content in their marriage? Why was the old lawyer so involved in their personal lives? A business partnership was one thing, being nearly a family member was quite another.

Already parked on the other side of the street was the black Mercedes-Benz of Michael Carlisle. Good, he thought. If the Rheas are so close to the former judge, then maybe they can encourage a conversation and an understanding. David wanted both.

Confronting his biological father at this time and in this way may be a mistake, but he was out of patience with people who were given credit for being something they were not. If the old lawyer got his mother pregnant and he was the result, then he wanted the record set straight. All the rules applied to his father as much as to anyone else.

Reaching the veranda of the house, he gently pushed the doorbell button to announce his arrival. A little girl of ten opened the heavy front door and welcomed the handsome man she saw at the funeral.

"Hello, Mr. Llewellyn. Please come in," she directed.

"Thank you, Lauren. It is very nice to see you again," was the cordial reply and came with an appreciative grin.

Mikaela met him in the foyer with an engaging smile and welcoming hand. He took it and gently moved it up and down briefly. "Come into the front room and make yourself comfortable, David."

"Thank you, Mikaela. You look beautiful tonight."

As he entered the front room Carlisle and Vincent ended an animated conversation and turned their attention to David Llewellyn.

"David, how nice to see you, again," began Carlisle. "Would you like a drink?"

"Yes, that would be fine," and then turning, "Hello, Vincent." They shook hands. "Thank you again for the invitation."

"My pleasure, please have a seat," the younger lawyer gestured.

In a moment, Carlisle handed David a rum-and-tonic and the evening began with the entrance of Mikaela and Lauren into the room. It was pleasant conversation and charming personalities kept their guest entertained with the latest news in Cottage Grove.

Later, dinner was served and a roast was consumed with eagerness and sincerity. Unfortunately, the evening did not end with dessert.

Lauren was full and a little bored with the Cottage Grove news report, so she asked to be excused and, thankfully, Mikaela did not object. With the absence of innocence now in effect and the aid of alcohol once again showing its usefulness, Llewellyn felt the time was at hand for truth and consequence. If the Rheas were like family to the old lawyer, then they may as well be part of the conversation.

Still at the dining room table, Carlisle poured more red wine into David's glass. "Vincent said that you stopped by my office today for a second time to thank me, David. That was very good of you."

"Yes, sir. I wanted to thank you for the way you handled my mother's affair – I mean my mother's legal affairs – over the years." But his words obviously lacked sincerity. "Probably you knew my mother longer than I have been alive, don't you think?"

"Probably so, David," answered Carlisle, but he did not know where the young man was going with the line of thought.

"I should think that you have known her at least nine months before I was born," suggested David. The quiet in the room that followed was more than a consequent silence, it was a pregnant pause. Carlisle sat without emotion, Vincent and Mikaela looked at the old lawyer anticipating a response. But none was forthcoming.

Until, "Why, yes, I suppose so. We knew each other for a very long time, David. And you know that we loved each other. That is no secret. It is old news."

"Yes, that is old news," David repeated, "but what isn't old news is that a few months ago my mother admitted that you are my real father, not Jack Llewellyn."

The shock of revelation absorbed all conscious thought in the dining room and a surreal atmosphere permeated all four inhabitants of Earth. Nothing else and no one else existed for a brief undeniable moment in time. Then, the silence was broken by a loud and belligerent denial.

"That is preposterous, David," shouted Carlisle. "Was your mother dead drunk when she claimed that?"

"No, but her lips were loose with wine," admitted David. "Tell me, what should I call you? Father? Dad? Michael? Mr. Carlisle?" Mikaela and Vincent rose from the table and left for the kitchen clearing as many dishes as they could take with them.

Both men still sat facing each other at the table with the older one pouring himself another glass of wine. "It is a lie and I will not listen to this nonsense anymore. I think you should leave immediately. And take your imagination and wishful thinking with you," fumed the old lawyer.

Now, young Llewellyn realized that this conversation had become a disaster and he was damaged badly. Whatever satisfaction or clarity he thought was going to be achieved had become ephemeral and was now irretrievable. Any hope of a relationship was doomed by the time the words of his announcement were fully formed.

"All right, then," he said as he stood and stepped away from the table. "Perhaps you should have a conversation with my real father. Both my mother and dad were right. They did me a great favor in keeping me away from you." With that, David turned away and left quickly and quietly. Mikaela and Vincent stood in the kitchen listening to the words of the two men and heard the front door close with loud conviction. Then, they heard it close a second time with the same authority.

As David approached his car, he turned back to look at the house on Scuppernong Drive. He observed the black Mercedes pulling away from the curb directly across the street. David looked at the vacated spot left by the black sedan and climbed into his own car. Before placing his car in gear, he observed the Rheas through curtain sheers at their dining room table in animated conversation. After a few minutes, Mikaela kissed her husband and began to clear the table.

THE TIRES OF THE BLACK MERCEDES SCREECHED AND screamed with every sharp turn from Scuppernong Drive to the stately residence of Michael Carlisle. The old lawyer was angry and hurt and deceived and humiliated. In his heart he knew that David had told the truth. He knew it instantly, as soon as he heard the words, *"Perhaps you should* have a conversation with my real father. Both my mother and dad were right. They did me a great favor in keeping me away from you."

It did not make any difference that Jack and Julia were right in their assessment of the better man for fatherhood. Something had been deprived of him. That is, someone that he had a right to have in his life was kept hidden through secrecy and deception. He had been played for a fool and that was the worst of it.

IN TRUTH, DAVID'S VISIT TO COTTAGE GROVE SET UPON him a reminiscence that was unshakable. Jana was his life's love for the last decade and beyond, but Mikaela was still a vivid memory of attraction. For the last few years his love and joy toward his wife was uncompromised. Still, in a blanketed corner of his heart there was the remarkable Mikaela. He wanted to see her again, but only briefly and from a distance.

After the predictable disaster on Scuppernong Drive in front of Mikaela, David readied for the trip back to Wauwatosa. He paused long enough to notice a Coke machine outside a gasoline station adjacent to the interstate highway. As he turned onto the station tarmac a summer rain began its soft shower. He pumped in a handful of coins and received his canned soft drink.

Back in his vehicle, he sat down the soda in the console between the front seats and engaged REVERSE gear, then DRIVE, and then just sat there thinking. The raindrops hardened and turned into a summer storm that required the windshield wipers to clap with a labored purpose. After a while, he took his cell phone and called home to Jana. The telephone lined whirled its buzz a couple of times before there was an answer.

The conversation was brief and sincere. He would be home in a couple of hours and they were both the happier for it.

"Good-night, Jana. I love you, too."

That was enough for David. Now, it was time to go home.

He pushed the END button on his cell phone and laid it on the passenger seat. After a protracted moment, he placed his foot on the gas pedal and drove out into the darkness and loneliness of nighttime highway travel.

Chapter 8

A TOUR OF DUTIES

The Coppaway Shoe Company of Cottage Grove, was housed in one of the oldest buildings in the state. It was a three-story red brick structure built in the early 1900s that was home to one of the handful of shoe manufacturing companies left in America. Its founder, Gordon Coppaway was a self-made man who also happened to be from one of the Indian tribal nations of Wisconsin. He was from the Bad River Band of Lake Superior Chippewa, but he had long ago discontinued any real involvement in tribal affairs. His passion was the shoe manufacturing company that he built from the ground up and that bore his name.

Two strong-willed men met at eight o'clock sharp on an early Saturday morning in order to survey the shoe factory and assess the plant's strengths and weaknesses. It was their intention to also test the other's heart and commensurate resolve in their continued war of wills. For Gordon Coppaway it was either secure concessions and avoid a strike or lose the business that he spent a lifetime building, a business that had become an extension of his own being. For Dirk McGuire it was either realize the union's reasonable demands or strike until all hell broke loose while jeopardizing the livelihood of 300 men and women who worked in the shoe factory.

Together with no other employees, they surveyed over 200 manufacturing operations during the course of the day. In the Cutting & Clicking Department, they watched the recently purchased computer-monitored cutting machines that increased speed and limited manual labor. Similarly, new computers and equipment dotted the entire plant at key locations, all designed to increase production of goods while reducing man-hours.

Coppaway and McGuire walked through Closing & Machining, Lasting & Making, Finishing, Inspection, Warehousing, and Shipping. In total, all seven departments had been modernized by the inclusion of new computers and elegantly sophisticated machinery that used less energy to make leather goods faster and with less hands-on involvement. These installations had been going on incrementally since the beginning of the calendar year. Every employee understood that their work day was easier because of the additions and that they were the beneficiaries of a more relaxed work schedule. There was less work to do and they had more time in which to do the work. Unfortunately, the owner of the company was also aware of these facts.

By the end of the day, Coppaway had gained negotiating leverage by virtue of the new equipment that was already in place and operational. McGuire was compelled to acknowledge the improvements. "Yes, Mr. Coppaway, the new machinery will go a long way toward increased production," he admitted. "And that will free up manpower for other places to keep the logistics chain at high performance." He concluded, "Now, you have the machinery *and* the manpower to be at the top of the shoe industry."

It was a nice sales pitch, Coppaway thought to himself. But in his own mind he declined the offer of continued high-volume labor when it didn't seem necessary to his company or his bottom line.

"Well, McGuire," he replied, "I really don't see it that way. But if I can increase production and sales and profit without *raising* my labor burden, then I might think about not laying-off anybody. But we're not there yet, are we?"

As they strolled back through the aisles and toward the front offices, machines and equipment throttled down and quieted as they passed by. Another day of production was ending and the men and women of Union Local 555 were closing up shop as the five o'clock horn blared briefly across the airspaces of the old brick structure.

The old Native American led the Irish union steward into his large cluttered office that boasted plenty of windows because it was located at the front corner of the building. Dan Joda arrived at about the same time and sat down in the chair next to McGuire and across the desk from Coppaway.

"Well, what do you think, McGuire?" began the Indian with a matter-of-fact tone of voice. "You can see for yourself that when your contract with the company ends, there will have to be some changes." He sat back in his chair and studied the reaction of the union employee.

"Dirk, you have to be reasonable," Joda offered. "We are a struggling business and we need your help in our making a go of this shoe factory. As plant manager, I want to work with Mr. Coppaway and you to make our company strong for future years. We owe it our community and to ourselves."

McGuire looked at Joda and heard the words, but he also listened to the voice and watched the face and hands. He liked the words, but he could see that the plant manager was only trying to soften his labor union.

"Aye, Danny, I only want what's best for the company, too. As it is, though, the company is all of the people that come to work here every day. So, on that point, you and I agree. Let's all move together in the same direction."

"I'll tell you what we're going to do, McGuire," replied Coppaway. "We're going to set up a meeting with both our legal counsels and settle all differences once and for all, okay?"

HAROLD CHATHAM WALKED ACROSS THE PRISTINE SLICK concrete floor of his cereal plant as the first shift had already geared up for their day's work. The ovens were vibrating noisily and exhausting pure heat while running at full production. The Chatham Cereal Company was an attractive manufacturer for a lot of the name brands of cereal boxes that sat on the kitchen tables across America. Although CCC did not sell their own brands of cereal, the company did manufacture twelve different brand names for three different national companies of breakfast foods.

A short, portly, and balding man in his sixties, Chatham seemed to be a man of unending energy and positive attitude. He was married to the idea of making cereal and was passionate about his company and the people who worked for him. Like all of his employees who worked in plant operations, he wore a white hard hat, safety glasses, ear plugs, hair net and steel-toed shoes. Adherence to FDA requirements and safety were always foremost on his mind at CCC.

Climbing the stairs up and onto the mezzanine of his two-story plant to survey the cereal ovens, Chatham was surprised to be met by his secretary. She approached him with a green slip of note paper and shouted through the noise of the ovens below, "There is a Mr. Coppaway in your office, Mr. Chatham, and he insists on seeing you right away."

"Tell him that I will be just a moment." The cereal president knew of Gordon Coppaway and once met him at a Chamber of Commerce meeting before they both got too busy to attend the community activities with any regularity. Eventually, they both decided to send company representatives to the Chamber meetings in order to keep an ear to the social and political machinery of Cottage Grove.

After a while, Harold Chatham walked into his office and greeted Gordon Coppaway with an enthusiastic handshake. But the cereal king was busy and there were many miles to go before he slept, so he got to the point. "Gordon, how nice to see you again," he remarked. "What can I do for you this morning?"

"I'll get right to it, Harold," the Indian began. "And I want this conversation to be strictly confidential."

"Okay, it's confidential."

"A long time ago you expressed interest in purchasing my company as part of a business expansion of your cereal plant. Right now, I may be in a position of interest in selling my shoe company or at least the building and its contents for the right price."

Chatham removed his hard hat and safety glasses and placed them on his desk before him. Leaning back in his chair he looked at Coppaway with some hint of reflection.

"Well, that is an interesting change in circumstances, Gordon. Why now would you want to sell a business that you have built with your own hands your entire adult life?"

"I have grown weary of the fight, Harold. It's pretty much that simple."

"It is my understanding you have purchased a lot of new equipment just this year for the shoe factory. You're going to lose money on that investment if you sell, you know."

"I don't care and, really, the investment wasn't as great as I have led people to believe, especially the union and its lawyers."

"What about all of the employees that work for you, Gordon? They would lose their jobs."

"Oh, yeah, those are the loyal employees who are thinking about striking and destroying my business. Do you mean those employees?" Coppaway shifted his position in his chair because the conversation was beginning to become more problematic.

"I understand that some people may lose their jobs, Harold. But some will be able to work for you. After all, you would need additional manpower it you expand."

"Yes, Gordon, but it would take a couple of years for the expansion to be realized."

For a moment there was quiet in the office of Harold Chatham. Neither businessman moved, but rather, they only sat and thought. Coppaway looked at the wall-mounted photograph of an aerial view of the cereal plant while Chatham pretended to scribble a note to himself on a small yellow notepad.

And then the conversation was continued by Chatham.

"As a matter of fact, Gordon, I am still very much committed to our company's growth and I would still like to buy your business. Or, that is to say, I am still interested in buying your building and the surrounding property." And then he added, "I would even be willing to purchase all of your equipment and machinery, new and old. I could write all of that off toward capital loss and depreciation when we file our corporate taxes."

Harold Chatham tore off the previous daydreaming scribble that he penned before and on a clean four by six notepaper wrote down a dollar amount, tore that sheet off the small pad a pushed it across his desk in the direction of Gordon Coppaway.

The Indian leaned forward and collected the scrap of paper and lifted it before his eyes. He looked across the desk of his contemporary and smiled without comment. It was the golden parachute that would make Coppaway a winner even if he lost his business to a Local 555 strike. Now the leverage was his to be used against that devil Dirk McGuire.

Chapter 9

FATHER, BUT NOT DAD

With both dinner guests storming out the front door in the early evening the night before, Mikaela and Vincent were left with a Saturday night unto themselves and much to talk about. They were still preoccupied about paternal claim of David Llewellyn. They cleared the dining room table, tagged-team the kitchen clean-up, and finally sat down in the family room troubled by the fireworks that they had witnessed.

When the young mortician's assistant and future concert pianist decided it was time to brush her teeth and begin preparations for bed, her parents decided it was time to place the last evening in perspective.

"Vincent, either David Llewellyn has lost his mind or Michael is his biological father and Cottage Grove is going to be turned upside down," Mikaela declared.

"We do live in an upside-down world, Mikaela," Vincent said quietly as he thought about how this news might affect his mentor. "I do believe David. This is not something that one lies about carelessly," he continued. "Still, knowing Michael, he will want some proof as to what David claims. Michael is going to go through some rough waters in the next few days."

"Yes, that's true. But I wonder how David is handling things," she thought aloud. "And what about Jack Llewellyn? If he has known all of these years about David's real father, how could he have raised the only son of his worst enemy? Answer me that."

"Maybe it was done out of spite," Vincent speculated. "Maybe, denying that enemy his only son was sweet revenge after Michael's affair for as many years."

"No. I don't think that is the way Jack operates," replied Mikaela. "I am more inclined to think that if he lost Julia, he would accept the consolation prize of her son."

"Maybe. After all, if David is the biological son of Michael, Jack kept the secret for three and a half decades." And, then after pausing, "Come to think of it, so did Julia Llewellyn." It was clear that Vincent turned his thoughts to Julia, now. "You know, she was a strange animal. Beautiful, smart, but also she was a train wreck."

"Vincent, stop it. Like each of us, I am sure she did her best."

"Yes, but she pretty well crossed up the lives of some people around her," he countered. "Especially her husband and lover. She was the type of person who didn't end up in a car crash, but she caused other people to get into car crashes."

"Right now I am more worried about Michael. What a crushing announcement it is to know that you have a grown son and that he grew up in the same town all of these years," said Mikaela.

She got up and walked to the window and reflected, "Michael has treated us so well, Vincent. He has been instrumental in your law career and has been even more involved in our family life." Then she turned to face her husband, "He is more than your law partner, he is family. And not just because he is Aunt Helen's brother."

"I know that, Mikaela. Sometimes, I just think he gets a little too close to Lauren and you."

"Vincent, how unkind of you," was the sad retort.

"I'm sorry, but tonight sheds a different light on Michael," he explained. "He denied the existence of a son, but we all know that David was telling the truth. I believe his mother and I believe him."

It was getting late now and they were both tired after a trying weekend. David Llewellyn had exploded the relaxation with stunning news the night before, Michael had stormed out the front door without his usual civility, and Vincent had begun questioning the role of their benefactor in their family. Finally, she still did not know what to make of her relationship with David. There was some feature either missing or additional in their knowing each other. After all of the years of their friendship, she still could not name what it was.

AROUND LUNCH TIME THE FOLLOWING MONDAY JACK Llewellyn pushed through the screen door of the Devil's Elbow Tavern. The smells of burgers and beer partnered with the warm summer temperature to caress those passersby who were hungry or thirsty.

The saloon was becoming a little crowded and a little noisy. It was the place to be in the heart of Cottage Grove. Cash McDermott and Shadow worked the patrons with steady and efficient determination. People waited for service because the burgers were tasty, the beer was cold, and the conversation was lively. Every now and then, there was a scraping skid and crash of chairs that prefaced a brief skirmish in which tempers flared but no one got hurt. There was pushing and shoving and yelling. After all, it was a saloon.

Llewellyn found his table near the door of the men's toilet at the back of the tavern. A few more steps down a short hallway there was an exit door that led to a small parking lot adjacent to the alley. This was where Cash hoped to fashion a beer garden in the near future when capital was available. He began preliminary plans three years ago, but the funds had yet to arrive.

After a long wait, Shadow finally served the burger and beer to Llewellyn. Generally, he enjoyed eating alone because there was no social obligation to fulfill toward conversation and he could chew and swallow at his own pace. It was a small thing, but he had long ago enjoyed the small things about being alone.

And then, from out of the back exit and across the darkness of the companion hallway, there appeared rays of light offered by the mid-day sun. And before the exit door could close again the shadow of a man climbed up a wall and gave way to darkness as the door collapsed tight against the jambs.

Jack heard a voice and felt a strong hand upon his left shoulder. "Hello, Jack. I see you're eating alone. Mind if I join you?" It was the voice and hand of Michael Carlisle.

"Get lost, Carlisle. I would like to maintain my appetite," Jack grumbled. And he took a swig from his beer glass without looking in the direction of the lawyer.

"I want to talk to you, Llewellyn," he began, "There are some things that we need to discuss at my office about Julia's estate." The lawyer sat down at the small table opposite of Jack.

"Someone is playing a practical joke on you, Carlisle," Jack said coolly. "Somewhere along the line somebody gave you the impression that I give a rat's ass what you want." The projectionist grabbed a paper napkin and wiped his mouth and glared at the enemy.

What amazed Llewellyn the most was how quickly Carlisle could move for an old overweight lawyer. Out of the corner of his eye, he saw the black object flash from the side to the front, and then came the collision. He felt the lawyer's blackjack land across his forehead and propel him backward. Both his chair and his body crashed loudly onto the hardwood floor simultaneously as his feet kicked the small table and his beer and burger exploded into the air with proportioned violence.

"Just so you know, Llewellyn, this message is from really deep in my heart. Was I eloquent enough for you?" He looked down at the projectionist and smiled with calm retribution. "This is just my official reply to your message that you offered me at the cemetery, Jack."

Llewellyn laid there for a while in brutal agony with his hands covering his head. Beer and meat and condiments covered his clothing until Cash McDermott arrived to help him back onto his chair.

"That's enough, Carlisle, now get the hell out of here," shouted the bartender as he held the projectionist tightly in his chair to forestall the probability of a counter-attack. Shadow set right the table and began cleaning up the mess on the floor. After a moment, both adversaries seemed to regain their composure, but Llewellyn was very much worse for the wear.

"It is in your best interest to talk to me, Jack," the lawyer persisted, "and it is in the best interest of David, as well.

There are some questions that need to be answered before any estate distributions can be made."

Still feeling dazed by numbness emanating within his head, Jack moaned, "What kind of questions?" He was too incapacitated to be angry at the moment. That would come later when he was fully recovered from the head trauma.

"Come by my office later this afternoon at your convenience," was the only response. Carlisle shoved forward his chair and it clashed against the still upright table. As he stood there staring down at Llewellyn, he opened his wallet and threw a ten-spot down onto the table.

And then the old lawyer delivered a remark that the projectionist did not understand, "Here, Jack, lunch is on me. It is the least I can give you in return for all that you've done for me."

Llewellyn finally looked at Carlisle for the first time as the lawyer exited down the short hallway and through the back door. Once again, the sunlight washed across the hall floor and walls for just a moment and then the door closed again.

"Jack, I saw everything," said McDermott, "Do you want me to call the police?"

"No, Cash, no police. This is between Carlisle and me. Let's keep it that way."

"Well, okay, if you say so. But you better have that head of yours examined, if you know what I mean," suggested the bartender.

"I'll be okay. Thanks, Cash."

Jack was pretty much finished with his lunch, such as it was, and so he simply paid his bill as his forehead throbbed and showed the reddened tattoo of an unrecognizable shape. Shadow enjoyed the ten-dollar tip that was left under the small porcelain white plate that once held the grilled burger. He forgot to mention the generous windfall to Cash McDermott.

ORDINARILY LLEWELLYN WOULD HAVE WAITED ABOUT three days to comply with the request of Julia's estate attorney. But, in light of their physical altercation earlier in the day, he was more than anxious to continue the conversation, such as it was. Still, he wasn't totally angry. In some strange way he acknowledged to himself a slight respect for the way Carlisle showed some spit after decades of acrimony. That, at least, he could understand. Anyway, the aura that lingered in his head was fast dissipating, so the retired professor was regaining his strength. Moreover, Carlisle said it would be in the best interest of David to discuss the estate. For now and after two short rounds, they were even and he could live with that for a while.

By the time Jack walked up to the front door, he had decided not to aggravate the situation unnecessarily until the time came when it better suited him. Then, he would certainly aggravate the situation unnecessarily. In any case, around three o'clock in the afternoon he entered the law offices of Carlisle & Rhea and asked Cosie if he could see Michael Carlisle.

Seeing the red lump across the forehead of the projectionist, Cosie felt compelled to inquire, "What happen to you?"

"A canister of film fell from a high shelf and smacked me in the head as I was trying to reach for it."

"Do you have an appointment, Mr. Llewellyn?" she asked, even though she always knew what clients had appointments.

"No, Cosie, but he is expecting me," he disclosed, even though he knew that she knew.

After the usual office ritual of intra-office communications, Jack was allowed to show himself into the office of the former district judge, now turned premier lawyer in Cottage Grove.

They did not shake hands; they did not acknowledge each other. Llewellyn promptly sat in one of the stylish, but small, leather chairs and faced Carlisle who sat in his large leather chair behind his imposing desk that suggested power and knowledge.

"Thank you for coming," the lawyer mumbled and looked straight at the projectionist. "Llewellyn, I have only one question for you concerning Julia." He inspected his empty pipe and then reached for his tobacco pouch and began filling the pipe and tamping the tobacco gently.

Llewellyn sat there stoically amused at the visual cliché that sat before him making every attempt to appear scholarly and sophisticated. "And what is that, you two-bit shyster?"

The attorney looked up from his pipe and smiled as he enjoyed the obvious discomfort of his nemesis. Just then, the attorney attacked, "Last Friday night, your son announced to me that Julia had told him earlier in the year that *I* was his father and *not* you!" he burst out. "What do you say to that?"

Sitting back in his chair and into a more relaxed position, Llewellyn returned the smile and said, "Well, I don't know what David expected to gain from telling you that, but it is true," he answered. "But, more to the point, you are only the sperm donor. I am David's father." The projectionist stood-up and leaned forward with both hands on the large desk. He whispered in a hoarse voice for effect,

"And that is the way it will always be, Carlisle. Because you cannot retrieve the years of his growing-up and change the formation of his manhood. Thank God." And lastly, "You may have stolen Julia from me, you low-rent shyster, but I got the best of her and I got him for a lifetime."

Carlisle pushed back his leather chair and stood behind his desk, "I should have been told. I had a right to a son!"

"Take it up with Julia, you insolent ass. I owe you nothing. David is my son and you cannot undo three and a half decades of a father-son relationship, even if you wanted to – which you don't, of course. You just want to kick and scream because you lost and I won."

As both men were standing now, Carlisle still behind his desk and Llewellyn between the large desk and his own chair, they grimaced red-faced and postured themselves for physical combat. Suddenly, the desk telephone rang with seeming authority and obvious interruption.

Carlisle maintained his glare as did Llewellyn. The lawyer handled the telephone receiver and placed it at his left ear. "Hello." There was silence in the room but not on the other end of the telephone wire. "Very well, Helen, I will take care of things. Stop by tomorrow and we will discuss what should happen. Good-bye."

He placed the receiver back onto the telephone base and with his composure returned sat down again and requested his adversary to do the same. "Please sit down, Jack. Let's be civilized about this."

Once again taking his chair, Llewellyn's tension dissipated and the two men faced each other seated and adopted a mutual non-threatening posture.

"It is true that I don't like to lose. It is also true that you made a better father than I would have if given the chance," the attorney conceded. "I know my faults, Llewellyn. You are not needed to point them out to me.

"But I tell you this. From this day forward I will be a better father to him, man to man, than what you have been since your divorce." And with all the conviction that he could muster, "That I swear to you and to him!"

"Knock yourself out trying, Carlisle. But you cannot change the stripes on a tiger. After a few weeks, you'll run out of gasoline and grow weary of the effort," was the retort.

After a lengthy pause, Llewellyn finally asked sarcastically, "Is that all of the estate related questions that you want to ask?"

"Yes, that about does it for now."

The projectionist got up and without looking at his late ex-wife's estate attorney began to walk out of the room. But he stopped and turned. "Was that your sister Helen on the telephone?" inquired Jack casually. "It has been a long time since I have talked to her."

"Yes, that was my sister Helen."

"For what it's worth, Carlisle, I always thought she did an unbelievable job raising Mikaela by herself. She is a credit to your family."

It was the first time in forty years that a thin veneer of civility presented itself between the two men and it lasted only for a few seconds and then it was gone.

The lawyer did not respond to the compliment. He only watched Jack as he turned and walked through the doorway, down the corridor, and eventually into the sunlight of Cottage Grove.

As usual, Tuesday followed Monday during that midsummer week. For Michael Carlisle that was pretty much the only normalcy he found during the course of those summertime days. Promptly at nine o'clock Helen Quesnell walked through the door of Carlisle & Rhea to confer with her brother.

She was a few years older than her brother and in recent years had become somewhat elderly in her speech and dress and mannerisms. Long ago she had come to terms with being aged because of her frailty and inclination toward ailments and aches. But Michael and Helen did dearly love one another because they grew up liking each other. And actually liking each other made all the difference in all the good that they accomplished and, also, in all the bad that they accomplished – depending on your point of view, of course.

She was active at St. Matthew's Catholic Church and a former officer in the Ladies Sodality, as well as an expert in cooking chicken and dumplings for the annual parish festival. She was a soprano in the church choir for many years and was a steward of Wednesday night bingo. Her quilting talent was renowned throughout the county. Unlike her brother she was not feared; but she was well respected. Most importantly, she single-handedly raised Mikaela Rhea from infant to womanhood. In spite of her quiet and gentle demeanor, even Michael Carlisle paid attention to her. If there ever was a need for a textbook example of the proverb "still waters run deep," Helen would do quite nicely.

Cosie dialed Michael's extension to announce that his sister was here to see him. In a moment later, Mrs. Quesnell walked into her brother's office and kissed him warmly on the cheek. "Hello, Michael, how are you feeling these days?"

"I'm okay, Helen. These are hard days for anyone who knew Julia. But I'm getting by."

"I'm sorry for your loss, Mike. I know that you loved her very much," consoled Helen.

"Thank you. Now what is the problem with the St. Matthew's Parish Festival later this summer?"

"Yesterday, I attended Mass and instead of a homily Father O'Halloran talked about the festival at the end of summer. Apparently, the Vincentian priests have agreed to accompany a small group of Daughters of Charity sisters from the Cincinnati province."

"Are you kidding me?" gasped Carlisle with open mouth. "Why in God's name do the Vincentians want nuns from Cincinnati coming to our small town, small time, festival?"

"Young Father O'Halloran is from Cincinnati and he thinks it would be a treat to have his former teachers see how well he is doing," she explained. "The Archbishop of Cincinnati will bring with him an entourage of Vincentian priests and Daughter of Charity sisters to our festival."

Carlisle sat mesmerized by the thought of clergy and religious women from Cincinnati coming to Cottage Grove. "Where does O'Halloran get such clout as to compel the archbishop and a religious entourage to come to the Grove? And why from Cincinnati, for godsake?"

"Well, Mike, when Father Tim was ordained a few years ago his family donated ten million dollars to the Archdiocese of Cincinnati," Helen deadpanned.

"Ah, I see." There was no other response beyond silence and introspection.

Then she added, "Of course, it doesn't hurt that the archbishop is a long-time dear friend of the O'Halloran family and that Father Tim is the godson of the archbishop. I think Cottage Grove is only the first step for Father O'Halloran, you see," continued Helen. "I suspect the archdiocese has great plans for his future."

"But why should the archdiocese in Cincinnati send him to a small town in Wisconsin for his initial parish work?" questioned the brother.

"According to the president of the Ladies Sodality, they didn't. The Vincentians did," she explained. "Apparently, the archdiocese and the Vincentians don't quite see eye-to-eye on the future of Father Tim.

"What complicates the whole situation is the fact that Father Tim is not a diocesan priest. He is a religious priest," explained the sister.

"Huh, what do you mean, Helen?"

"Well, because he is a religious priest and not a diocesan priest, the Vincentians get to direct his assignments, not any diocese," she continued. "According to my information, the archbishop in Ohio is trying to get the original ordination mission of Father Tim changed to diocesan so that he can control his whereabouts. It is church politics at its finest, Mike."

"Whatever," sighed the attorney. "Do we know what nuns will be coming to the festival?"

"Here is the list of priests. And here is the list of the sisters," she offered. Carlisle ignored the list of priests and grabbed the list of sisters from the hand of Helen.

"She is on the list, Helen," he sighed quietly and with distress.

"Yes, I know."

The attorney thought for a moment and his sister watched him think. "We have to contact her, Helen, and encourage her not to come to the festival. She is the head of the convent in Blue Ash, Ohio, and should have some say as to when and where she travels."

"She has taken a vow of obedience, Mike. If the archbishop instructs her to be part of that entourage, how can she say no?"

"She will have to make up some excuse. Do you want to talk to her or should I?" asked Michael.

"She does not know me; I am only a name to her. If you cannot persuade her to stay in Ohio, then it may be the beginning of the end for both of us," Helen replied. "Although, frankly, she may have much to lose, as well."

"What do you mean?"

"She has spent almost her entire adult life in the service of God. Do you really think she would want to give up that mission for a past that can never be reclaimed?" she reasoned. "She is the Reverend Mother of her convent. What good would come from revealing a secret past? It would only hurt everyone involved."

"You're right, Helen, she is an intelligent woman. Why should she now jeopardize all that has been accomplished? All that was done was done in the best interest of all parties involved."

At that moment both brother and sister felt slightly better about the situation because elementary logic and rationalization were soothing balms. But neither was a guarantee that the woman's arrival would be averted and the worrisome possibility of catastrophe remained. Michael Carlisle had no intention to forfeit whatever social standing his sister and he commanded in Cottage Grove.

But the fact still remained that one name on the list of sisters needed to be excluded from the late summer festival at St. Matthew's. This was to be accomplished at all costs. With that, Carlisle decided on preliminary travel plans to Blue Ash.

Only the Grass Suffers

He stared down at the list of sisters again as if by doing so he could erase the name of Larae Savignac.

Chapter 10

BLUE ASH, OHIO

Michael Carlisle sat there for the longest time... watching, waiting. He watched people come and go in the restaurant. He watched them talk and laugh and carve their steak and eat their Italian bread and drink their cabernet sauvignon. Eventually, the old man became tired and restless with his rum and tonic from a tall glass even though he was sitting in a high-class joint. After a while, he changed over to a domestic lager beer that was served in a long-neck bottle.

The place was called Ristorante Martinelli and it was located in the upscale village area of Blue Ash, Ohio. This is where he knew to sit and wait and, eventually, Larae Savignac would show up with friends to dine. Carlisle had received a telephone call from his sister explaining that Larae's routine included dining out on an occasional Friday night. Apparently, it was "ladies' night out" in her circle of Blue Ash friends.

Helen Quesnell had provided the cursory information requested by the old man for his use while in Ohio. That information included her address, telephone number and a brief letter that described her favorite restaurant in Blue Ash. It was Martinelli's where she was often seen with friends on Friday evenings.

That was all that Carlisle knew at this point, except that there was a thin manila envelope that laid atop his hotel dresser contained a little more information about Larae. But, because he was so rushed to arrive at Martinelli's early, he left the envelope unopened. He would see to it tomorrow. Tonight was for an initial observation only. No real contact was planned by the old man – just observing a woman of once-upon-a-time.

It was an elegant restaurant, filled daily with professionals from Cincinnati and the surrounding environs. The clattering of plates and the clinking of glass mixed with discordant conversations. The conflict of sounds created a human cacophony much like the Devil's Elbow on a Saturday night. The only difference was that these people were dressed less comfortably and paying more for their leisure than the patrons of the tavern.

Carlisle sat in the corner of the main dining area. It was a discreet location that he had requested upon entering the restaurant. He wanted to observe, but not be observed. That was important – he was not to be seen under any circumstances. After all, he was not altogether psychologically prepared for an actual meeting. He just wanted to watch and observe and, maybe, even decide on what he wanted to happen.

The steak and potatoes arrived and he ate slowly, thoughtfully. He noticed a small group of nuns being escorted by the maitre d' to their table. Two bus boys pushed two tables together gently, arranged the chairs properly for the guests, and then left quietly. The older man gingerly laid a menu in front of each nun, made some kind remarks and left them to themselves.

Among the arriving sisters there was no Larae Savignac.

The old lawyer was crushed. His heart was beating fast and he almost willed the presence of the familiar face of long ago. But she was not there - only unfamiliar women of God who were of no interest to him. So, again, he waited and only watched with casual interest.

Later, Carlisle enjoyed a couple more beers and continued to monitor the restaurant without a single remarkable incident occurring. But he watched the young and the old enjoy their friends and family and he envied every single one of them. Because what they were doing, he could not do – that was part of the purchase price of being Michael Carlisle, former district judge and current successful attorney-at-law.

On a summer evening a long time ago, while sitting in lawn chairs and enjoying brats and beer in the back yard, Helen asked him why he had not considered marrying. Carlisle looked at her at length and said, "Helen, I am a man who has loved another man's wife so much and for so long. How is it that you think I could ever look at or live with another woman with the same passion and conviction that I have in loving Julia?"

Helen looked down at her plate of food and felt flushed with sadness and understanding. She never again asked her brother that same question. Even then, there was reaffirmed an abiding love and respect and compassion for her brother.

And so Carlisle could never open his heart again for any woman, except maybe Larae. His enemy's wife had been his life's love, but Larae was his first love. Unfortunately, that was also true of Jack Llewellyn. Through the years he had lost touch with her naturally. She was most attractive decades ago and he assumed there was a graceful aging.

Finally, Carlisle was growing impatient. Picking up his napkin from his lap, he pushed back his chair so that he could go use the men's room. As he was shoving the chair back toward the table, he glanced across the dining patrons to the middle of the room – and there she was. He saw her face, beaming in light conversation with her friends. He had missed her coming into the restaurant because she had blended in with the blue of the other nuns' religious habits.

The lawyer fumbled with his chair for a moment longer and briskly walked to the men's room as discreetly as possible. Inside the lavatory, he was alone momentarily. He walked up to the urinal and unzipped his trousers to conduct his business. While the warm stream of urine flowed, his face flushed with warmth in the surreal recognition of Larae. The nature of the discovery further dumbfounded Carlisle. It was upsetting enough to recognize one's first love after three and a half decades. Although he had always known of her vocation, to actually see her in the dark blue religious habit of a nun was still difficult to accept.

He took care of his basic hygiene and stopped briefly to look at himself in the mirror… an old man not worth very much anymore. Gee, he didn't write the great American novel or save the whales or cure cancer. He looked closer. No, he didn't do those things, he thought to himself. But, along the way, he knew that he had practiced law, served on the bench with distinction and monitored the raising of Helen's Mikaela so that she grew up strong and straight. In his heart, he also knew that he had been a good provider for his heirs and was a good and decent citizen.

He decided not to leave just yet. He had traveled too far and at great expense and inconvenience. Carlisle wanted to see what he came to see – even if his first love had been transformed into a nun. The attorney thought, "My dear God, you really do have a curious sense of humor!"

Now, back at his table, Carlisle sat in his chair with his elbow on the table and hand slightly covering his chin and right cheek. Occasionally, he drank from his glass pretending to care about his drink, but really just sitting there watching Savignac the nun. A thought occurred to Llewellyn, "Now, if I want Larae, how do I compete with God?" But he really didn't want Larae, he just wanted to re-introduce himself to her and ask that she not travel to Cottage Grove later in the summer. It was such a simple request.

She was still beautiful, of course. The old man expected that. And, although the years showed on her as much as anyone else, she remained stylish and engaging, even in a nun's habit and even from a distance and for the brief time that he observed her.

After a while, Carlisle became more comfortable in his present state. It did not seem that his presence would be discovered and so he sat back in his chair in a casual manner. He folded his hands, hands that had held pen to paper or gavel to bench for over three decades and now displayed an impulsive clumsiness with glass and bottle above the linen table cloth.

She talked with her sisters and laughed and ate delicately and seemed to genuinely enjoy being out and about with good friends. She sipped her red wine sparingly and mostly played with her food with only an occasional morsel being consumed. Her habit flattered her in some way that Carlisle could not describe. The crisp, starched white collar against the navy blue skirt and companion head-dress gave a measured innocence to her. Above all else, she seemed so… happy.

Carlisle just sat and watched. He sat back, legs crossed, elbow on the table and fist to chin and observed for himself a woman of God enjoying the company of her friends in a gala setting. He was visually eaves-dropping on an unsuspecting vision of yesteryear. He barely knew what he was doing – it was a somewhat surreal experience for him. In a way, he felt it was slightly unseemly in that he was invading her private world without her consent.

And, then, the evening was over. The nuns negotiated the contents of one check for proper disbursement. Eventually, they agreed that the division of expense was correct and each contributed their cash onto the pile of money at the table's center. In concert, they got up to leave and Larae looked casually in the direction of Michael Carlisle.

A flush washed across his face and he turned toward the wall in hopeful avoidance of recognition. If there was recognition, there was no acknowledgment on her part. By the time he turned toward the nun's table again, they were gone and on their way back to the convent.

Again, and because it was a long trip back to the hotel, the old man went to the restroom. At least there, he found physical relief, the comfort of privacy and time for reflection. At the porcelain urinal, he thought about what he had come to see at Martinelli's. He decided it was more than for what he bargained.

Michael had had enough for one night in a foreign town hundreds of miles from the familiarity of Cottage Grove. He zipped up, washed his hands and left the men's room. Once again in the main dining area, he weaved through the elegant dining tables with his head down and looking away from the nuns' table even though they were no longer there. After, paying for his beers and leaving a most generous tip – he did not wait for change – Carlisle left as quickly as reasonable. He wanted to get back to the hotel and open the thin manila envelope that Helen had given him.

The warm summer night afforded a light breeze that cooled the man's face and but gave him a singular sense of loneliness. He watched the hustling movement of village traffic on a pleasant Friday night. The warm and inviting lights from every building glowed to remind him that he was not at home – and he wished he were home, back in his upscale condominium where he belonged.

All he wanted to do now, all he really could do now, was to take a taxi back to his hotel room and try to get some sleep, if he could sleep. Because tomorrow was a new day and maybe he would not feel quite so flustered after seeing Larae. It had been nearly half a lifetime since he had even seen her and he did not know how he really felt… excited, fearful, embarrassed, disappointed, intimidated, fascinated, enchanted – maybe all of those things. He needed time to reflect and decide.

However, instead, he took an easier path to ease his anxiety – straight to a local bistro called O'Reilly's Bar & Grill. There he purchased a bottle of high-grade scotch – nothing but the best to celebrate a reunion of sorts – and proceeded to get plastered until the early morning's daybreak.

THE OLD MAN LAID FACE DOWN ON THE GRITTY CONCRETE. His right hand clutched the empty fifth bottle of once-upon-a-time scotch. As he laid motionless two cockroaches played tag across his back. The alley with the exception of this kingly sight was empty and dark.

Up against two trash cans the man sat up and bellowed a guttural moan, then fell back to the pavement once again in reassuring sleep. But it didn't last long. A short dream later he awoke to a stream of yellow warm urine in his face. For just a split-moment he welcomed the embracing shower, then the horror of what was happening gripped his head and he sprang to his feet punching and shoving.

"What the hell are you doing, you dumb sonavabitch!"

But the second drunk could not answer. By this time, he laid folded up on the ground unconscious. It was simply a way of one friend waking another for the promise of a new day.

Wiping his face with his shirt tails the scotch drinker picked up his hat and gathered together his composure. A quick glance at his Bulova nudged him forward to hurry along. It was a new day, just before the dawn, and all of his movements would be terribly painful on this day.

EVENTUALLY, CARLISLE MADE IT BACK TO HIS HOTEL room. After an incredibly long shower that washed away dirt and grime and shame, he crawled between the sheets of his bed and slept for several hours. By noon he awoke with a splitting headache which he dulled with three Bayer aspirins in a throated gurgle and gulp.

Carlisle sat on his bed in his black boxer briefs for a long time and absorbed the hangover as best he could. He looked over at the dresser in thoughtful hesitation. A manila envelope laid atop his dresser still crisp in its newness and still unopened by its owner.

He got up and walked across the room and picked up the manila package and walked back to the bed. Gingerly opening the envelope, he poured out the contents onto the bed sheet and fanned the paperwork so he could see at once his treasure.

He looked through the credit reports and municipal documents which told him virtually nothing of what he wanted to know about Larae. She had no legal history in the courts and her credit was excellent. Although she had a handful of addresses, the paperwork showed that she had moved to Blue Ash, Ohio, many years ago and her address remained the same – 2900 Fairy Chasm Lane. There were no photographs.

On a separate report, there was a short listing of possible relatives – a female named Helen Quesnell of Cottage Grove, Wisconsin, and Mikaela Savignac with the same original address as Larae. It was a rural route address from Gills Rock, Wisconsin. There were no other names listed.

"Mikaela," the old man softly spoke out loud to himself. "Mikaela," he slowly repeated. "Her name is now Rhea and her husband's name is Vincent," he said to himself. "And my granddaughter is Lauren." There was a pain between his ears, now. But he let it go.

He dressed casually with a crisp white shirt and gray dress pants and polished black shoes. He slowly prepared with measured ceremony and care. He looked as good as he was going to look. One last glance in the mirror and he was out the door to find a once-upon-a-time love who now happened to belong to God by virtue of her being a nun.

The taxi lumbered through the Blue Ash village and headed north on Fairy Chasm Lane. It was a scenic asphalted road sandwiched by scarlet maples on both sides of the thoroughfare. It curved left and right for nearly a mile before bridging a deep gorge which cradled a vibrant stream. The roadside sign read "Kazareen Pass." Beyond the bridge, the convent could be seen from a great distance.

An ornate sign with blue letters and white background was framed by a black wrought-iron border against an equally black wrought iron fence nearly six feet in height. The sign read "St. Rose of Lima Convent" and was freshly painted or cleaned. As distance prevailed on either side of the large gated entrance, the rigid iron fence gave way to a less imposing chain-link fence. In the background was the convent, itself. An imposing edifice largely made of white-gray limestone which gave it a somewhat foreboding atmosphere.

Because it was not a long drive through the Cincinnati suburb, maybe a couple of miles, the lawyer decided to forego a return trip by taxi cab and enjoy the wooded scenery and rolling hills by foot. He had become somewhat portly in recent times and he needed the physical motion.

Carlisle paid his cab fare at the iron-grated entrance gate. He wanted the time that it took to walk the lane to compose himself and prepare his introduction to Larae. He observed the expansiveness and peacefulness of the grounds that laid before the convent proper. Out-buildings consisted of a four-car garage, equipment shed and a small cottage, perhaps for a groundskeeper. Most striking was the incredibly large and well-kept lawn that surrounded the convent. The entire campus was enclosed by a chain-linked fence and the massive grounds were kept impeccably landscaped and neatly mowed. This pristine care provided a delicate sense of decorum in a pastoral environment.

Finally, after his lengthy walk and at the front door, Carlisle stood at rest and hesitated. "Is this what he really wanted to do?" he asked himself. His self-retort came immediately, "Yes, what do I really have to lose?" He pushed the doorbell button twice and knocked for good measure, then took one step back in anticipation.

In a moment, the large wooden door opened slowly and an elderly nun in an apron and with a pleasant expression looked inquiringly at Carlisle. "Good afternoon, sir, may I help you?" she asked.

"Good afternoon, Sister, my name is Michael Carlisle and I would like to see Larae Savignac," he offered.

"The elderly housekeeping nun replied, "I see. Please wait here one moment." She closed the door quietly and Carlisle was left standing before the large closed door in continued anticipation.

And then he thought to himself, "I cannot do this. This isn't right." Fear swelled up between his ears and was absorbed by his own blood. In only a moment panic rushed through his heart and crushed whatever was left of his desire to see Larae.

Losing his composure, the old man curtly turned away from the stone convent's threshold and walked briskly back toward the front gate of the grounds. After three and a half decades, he simply could not bring himself to confront his first love in life. She had to remain in his mind a constant idea whose physical existence would not be verified. He wanted her to be considered only as a memory across time and geography.

It would be impossible to hail a taxicab from Fairy Chasm Lane. Only traffic dealing with the convent used the road and there really wasn't all that much of that on any given day. Service trucks and supply vehicles used it the most. Occasionally, automobiles from the archdiocese would bring visitors, but that was only on certain occasions and for specific purposes.

Though not a cloistered convent, there wasn't much activity to be observed on Fairy Chasm. It would take the rest of daylight to get back to Blue Ash, now. But the old man didn't care. He needed the time to think, anyway.

Emblazoned in his mind was the face of Larae and how happy she seemed and how utterly engaged in her friendships she seemed to be. Yes, to be sure, she looked considerably older. Why shouldn't she? After all, she was older and so was Carlisle. But, even with age, she still looked beautiful and charming and captivating.

Michael slowed his walking pace as he approached the wrought-iron entrance gate at the end of the drive. On the other side of the gate was Fairy Chasm Lane. He stopped to look back at St. Rose of Lima Convent and formed a frown of disappointment in himself. "I have come all this way from Cottage Grove, only to get stinking drunk and end up embarrassing myself in front of some old nun."

From a distance Carlisle heard the sound of a lawn mower start and idle down to a hum. He looked across the grounds and saw a boy riding a mower at the far edge of the acreage and along the chain-linked fence line. "There has to be more of an effort than this," he thought to himself. He sighed heavily and tightened his face with what passed for determination at that moment in time and began walking back up the lane to the convent.

Again, standing before the great wooden door of St. Rose of Lima, he knocked yet again and waited for a response. He thought to himself that seeing Larae was going to be a mistake – that renewing the relationship had become very much against his better judgment – but he had come this far – he gave in to the notion that he may just as well see it through. He had to make the effort.

Once again, the massive door creaked upon opening and slowly it traversed inward presenting the elderly nun wearing the apron. "Oh, it's you again, now what?" Her tone was cross because the interruption was repeated and she had lost her patience with the strange man.

"I'm sorry, Sister, to bother you again. May I see Larae Savignac, after all?"

"Well, you may see *Sister* Larae, I suppose. Please come in and wait here... and wait this time, will you?"

"Yes, Sister," Carlisle responded with his best-behavior voice that he had not used since grade school. Like St. Rose of Lima, his grade school was operated by the Daughters of Charity. He remembered them being stern, but fair, educators.

The housekeeper closed the door rather roughly behind him and he stood in the large foyer and waited patiently. It was an ornate foyer made of strong and imposing woodwork, painted plaster walls and a wood floor with a large, colorful, throw rug that had a Mexican flavor to it. In anticipation of seeing Larae, Carlisle began to feel somewhat faint. He wanted to sit down, but there was no chair in the foyer and he did not want to be presumptuous enough to enter an adjacent room. So, he continued to stand there, albeit with neither physical nor emotional resolve. He was beginning to panic and he was literally afraid to meet Larae.

In one of the far rooms and from the back of the convent he heard a door open and close and the footfalls of hard-heeled shoes grew louder as someone approached. He heard soft voices being exchanged on the other side of a door that had a frosted glass as part of the top half – like that of an old elementary school classroom door. From inside this ante room, he saw two blue ethereal images converge and then separate. Llewellyn stood frozen in anticipation of his past coming to greet him.

Slowly, the door opened toward the foyer and out came Larae Savignac.

Chapter 11

THE PLEASURE OF HER COMPANY

"Ah, Mike, how nice to see you." She extended her hand in salutation and offered a harmless smile. Her habit was navy blue with white trim and she was as impeccably dressed as a sister could be.

"Hello, Larae, I am glad to see you, again," he replied. "I hope that you are doing well. Do you have a moment to talk?"

"Well, it's very nice to see you, Mike," she repeated, "What do you want to talk about?" she asked curtly. She stood there waiting for an answer to a question that was unanswerable from a man who traveled nearly five hundred miles and over three decades. Llewellyn was not prepared to stand in the foyer of a convent and defend his presence to a woman that he had not seen in all of that time. He expected to see the first love of his life, not this strange, but vaguely familiar, woman he knew once upon a time – but, of course, not now.

"I just thought it would wonderful to see you again and spend just a little time with you, if you could," he stumbled.

"Well, I'm sorry, Mike. I have so much to do today. I really can't spend any time with you. Perhaps, some other time… but it really was nice to see you again."

She smiled a second time.

After the necessary pregnant pause, she walked toward the front door and opened it. "The next time you are in Blue Ash, please call, I'm sure I will be able to see you then." Carlisle stared at her in disbelief at his quick dismissal. But, being a gentleman, he complied with what was her obvious wish – for him to go away quietly and without incident.

"I am sorry that you are not able to see me, Larae. Please take care of yourself." He looked at her intently, searching for some vague acknowledgment. But there seemed to be only a hint of his being a temporary nuisance for her of which she was about to dispatch.

"I will," she replied with a good measure of conviction.

From the corner of his eye, Michael believed he saw her give a bland smile. He walked across the threshold and the door closed gently behind him. He heard the door lock slide and click into place. If the night before at Martinelli's was surreal, this day's meeting had turned nightmarish.

He felt flushed and weak and a little faint as if his blood was warmer than it should have been. After a moment, he could not breathe normally and he became physically ill. He sat down on the stoop to compose himself and surveyed the front lawn of the convent for fear of embarrassment at his condition. And, then, Carlisle experienced an aura that accompanied a profound migraine headache. Feeling sick to his stomach and not being able to see through a darkened and blurry vision, the lawyer laid down on his side in utter defeat, both physical and emotional.

"No one should see me like this," he thought to himself, intuitively. So he crawled off the convent's entryway and toward the back side of the bushes for concealment. There he laid for several hours without discovery.

The day had turned to early evening and the coolness of dusk gently wakened Carlisle from his unconsciousness. Eventually, and slowly, he sat up and stared into the bushes that had protected him from the embarrassment of his condition. Dirt covered the left side of his face and was held intact by the coming of his beard's stubble. It occurred to him that he was going to have trouble returning to his hotel room any time soon. For one thing, he did not think that he could stand up, much less walk with any usual coordination.

So, he sat there with tears forming in his eyes from his physical duress and emotional confusion. He felt gladness that the pain had subsided, at least for that, but he was disoriented and the curtness in Larae's tone of voice lingered. It was as if she had been cross with him. He marveled at how efficiently she had dispatched him out through the front door.

"Well, I guess I had better begin my trip back to Blue Ash," he mumbled aloud to himself. With that, he braced himself and, then, ratcheted his body upward against the exterior wall of the convent until he stood leaning against it. A few breaths later, Carlisle staggered momentarily and then began the long night's journey back to his hotel room.

By whatever time he got back to the hotel, it had been a walk to remember. Dusk had turned to night and Fairy Chasm Lane morphed from an enchanted thoroughfare to a foreboding roadway shrouded by forest and darkness. The damp night was a cold companion to Carlisle, but it cleared his mind and encouraged his body to move with increased locomotion to stay warm.

He had thought long and hard about Larae and Julia… the former his first love, the latter his life's love. The miles gave him an opportunity to measure what he knew of Julia against what he could only surmise about Larae. Simply, there had been too many years to remember all that much about the now "daughter of charity." Once, when they were young, he had loved her. But that was a lifetime ago. She was a total stranger to him, now. The day's interview with the nun was both disappointing and disturbing, but in no way surprising. He rolled the dice and lost. And that was all there was to it.

Thankfully, the moon was full on the night of his walk back to Blue Ash. So, he had no real trouble seeing the edge of the road as he walked on its left side back to the village. With the migraine's aura now dissipated, his vision was better and his collapse behind the bushes of the convent and resultant sleep served to restore some strength in him for the long walk back to the hotel.

The cool evening air soothed him as he walked the stretch of Fairy Chasm. For the moment the cadence of his step lulled him to a comfortable rhythm of locomotion and he began to remember a winter's night nearly a lifetime ago…

> …It was a bitterly cold wintry evening. He held her close as they walked toward the front entry way of the dormitory. They stopped, still in the shadows away from the golden light of the lobby. In the blue of night, he closed both of his hands around the collar of her gray woolen car coat and pulled her to himself. He kissed her longingly, lovingly, and with a deepness of sublime affection. He opened her coat by unbuttoning the front and separated the two halves of the scarlet scarf and gray lapels. He slid his hands into the inside of her coat and wrapped his arms around the

warmth of her waist. He held her closer and smelled her scent as his cheek caressed her forehead.

She discreetly pulled away and they looked at each other for just a split moment. "I have to go in now, before they lock the doors," she said quietly.

"I will call you when I get home. I'm glad we had this time together," the young lawyer answered. They walked to the glass door that led to the dorm lobby and he opened it for her. At that late hour, he was not allowed to enter. "Good night, Larae, I will call you later." She smiled and walked through the doorway and, then, across the lobby and to the elevator. He watched her through the exterior glass wall that separated the winter from the dormitory until the elevator door closed...

The night stayed cool, so the old man did not sweat as much as he otherwise would have while walking back to Blue Ash. Yellow moonlight glimmered off the scarlet maple leaves and left a burnt-orange shine on the asphalt. In a distant field he noticed movements of some sort. Then, he could see by the silhouettes the movements were cows grazing on the moon-drenched pasture.

Again, the cadence of his steps kept a brisk rhythm for reverie and the mind of Carlisle flashed another memory before he could stop its appearance.

... The young lawyer came out of the shower, his water-beaded body was clean and he smelled of the bar soap that he had used. He wrapped the powder blue cotton towel around his waist and walked quietly toward the bedroom door. He pushed it gently open

and she was standing there almost naked. Wearing only her lavender panties, she stood there waiting for him, inviting him. At first, he looked at her face and her long dark brunette hair that shined even in the darkness, and then his eyes fell to her breasts and stomach. Before this night, he had never seen perfection. He came close to her, caressing her arms, then pressing his frame against her body. They kissed deeply and then slowly fell onto the bed...

It surprised the old man that the walk was not laborious, but rather, somewhat pleasant. The coolness of the summer night and the glow of the moon kept him comfortable. That was good because he was no longer in top bodily condition. He had frequented the Devil's Elbow too many times over the years and had drunk too many beers to maintain a physical endurance.

"Are you ready to go, Larae?" the attorney asked as he entered her apartment. "I thought that we could go to a park, if you like."

"Sit down, Mike," she said and he complied. After a pause longer than what he would have expected, "I think our relationship has gone as far as it can go. I don't think we should date anymore," the young woman announced.

It took a moment for the words to register, then a flush came over the man and there was no breath in him. She looked intently at him and he could not return the eye contact. There was nothing that he could say. He could not beg, nor plead, nor defend himself from whatever pain the revelation of unrequited love implied. He did not see it coming, it never occurred to him that she would not grow to love him.

After that, he could not remember anything else about that afternoon.

The sojourner's feet began to ache terribly as he approached the outskirts the Blue Ash proper. By then, he was sweating and aching and felt the grime of asphalt dust on him. Moreover, his spirit was lethargic and his soul darker than the night through which he walked.

Back at the hotel, he slept much and ate little during the following twenty-four hours. He was physically weary and too emotionally drained to do much else. He needed to recuperate from the emotional trauma that had been named Sister Larae and the companion migraine seizure at the convent's entry.

Two days later, Michael Carlisle left the hotel and had breakfast at a local diner. He sat in his booth and looked out the window at passers-by with a natural lack of interest. He stirred his coffee and looked at his aged hands that he invariably wrapped around a porcelain cup of coffee and waited for the arrival of another western omelet.

It was Monday and Blue Ash was alive and well. Adults hurried to work and their children were casually making their way to playground and parks. Summer vacation had arrived in weeks past and was held in fullness. The night before the old man had decided to make a final attempt, but no other. This would be the last of it, no matter what the outcome.

He paid his bill and offered a generous tip to an attractive waitress. She reminded him of Wish McGuire back in Cottage Grove. She, too, was blonde and appeared exceedingly attractive in her pink uniform. After leaving quietly, Carlisle hailed another taxi and instructed his chauffeur with directions that were not necessary to him.

The sky had turned gray even though the morning was not old. Eventually, later in the day, it would rain, he thought to himself. Now, Fairy Chasm Lane had regained its initial charm. While the early leaves no longer glistened because of the sun's absence, the vibrant red and orange colors from the maples still persisted for that is the way of Nature.

This time Carlisle did not dismiss his transportation. With the taxi meter running and the driver in a slumber mode, the lawyer knocked on the heavy door for the third time. Again, the familiar housekeeping nun opened the door and gave a slight look of recognition, but not approval. She gave a look of anticipation and questioning.

"May I help you, sir?" she offered politely.

"I would like to see Sister Larae Savignac, please," was the response.

"Just one moment, please." And she closed the door and left the familiar stranger on the doorstep to wait one more time.

It was a long time before the door opened again. The old man had grown impatient and a little angry at the reception and impoliteness of it all. Still, he remained calm and altogether determined. Finally, Larae slowly opened the grand door and looked without smile at her old acquaintance.

"Mike, you're back. I am surprised," she deadpanned. "What is it that you want?"

"Larae, I would like to have a conversation with you," he said with as much determination as he could put in his voice. "I have come hundreds of miles to see you – admittedly without invitation or warning. Still, I have come at great expense and inconvenience. And, if you have an ounce of Christian charity in you, you will see me."

It was an incredible announcement when you think about it. Here was a relative stranger demanding a conversation without any prior appointment. In the process, he was challenging her by questioning her Christianity if she did not comply. It was a bold move on his part.

"Well, Mike, if you insist, I suppose I can spare a few minutes," she acquiesced without much enthusiasm.

She turned her back to him and walked across the foyer to the anteroom which adjoined the grand foyer. Carlisle followed pensively with some embarrassment, but also with a measured determination to engage his first love in spite of both her unreceptive attitude and intimidating religious habit.

The anteroom was clearly meant as a welcoming place to receive visitors. There were two large easy chairs at each end of an enormous and colorful oriental rug and two long leather sofas, each covered with a pastel blanket, facing opposite at the other two sides. Completing the arrangement was a handsome maple coffee table surrounded by the furniture at the center of the room.

The room was large and was lit by sunlight flooding from the oversized windows from two different sides. The dark and heavy window drapes were always open, so an opulent lighting chandelier that hovered over the coffee table was needed only at night.

Sister Larae sat down in one of the easy chairs and motioned Carlisle to be seated on one of the leather sofas. He did not ignore the gesture and sat at the end of the sofa to be close to Larae. She did not smile.

"Larae, I will not keep you long," he began cautiously. "It has been a very long time since we have seen each other and I thought it best if I would come in person to talk to you."

"Mike, it has been over thirty years... I am a sister, now... What is the point?" she stopped and let the information sink into the mind of her visitor. "Why even see each other now after all of these years?" she continued, "Frankly, why come to St. Rose of Lima? What kind of reception did you imagine you would receive?" Besides the obvious aggravation in her tone, there was a suggestion of injury, as well, perhaps because he was invading her present life and he belonged better as a distant and vague memory.

The old man looked at her blankly as if not certain what he could say that would change her obvious annoyance. Then, he himself became defensive and somewhat put-upon, "Even if you are a nun, you can still be civil to an old friend," he argued.

"I am not a nun, Mike, I am a sister. There is a difference," she countered. "Obviously, we are not going to become romantic."

"We were once upon a time," he said with a hint of amusement because he understood that it would place her off-guard. It did. He reached for her right hand and gently held it between the two of his.

"That was a lifetime ago, Mike," was her rejoinder. "Moreover, all of that will stay in the past," she said with conviction. She moved her hand just slightly as it was becoming warm sandwiched between his two. Surprisingly to Carlisle, she allowed it to remain.

He gave movement to his own hands to better feel her flesh and bone and pulse and to emphasize what he was saying. "Larae, I know that it has been a very long time, but I had to come to Blue Ash," he began. "It is my understanding that the archdiocese is requesting that you come to Cottage Grove later this summer for our St. Matthew's Parish Festival."

The woman stared at him for a while and slowly stiffened, and then remarked, "I am aware of that, Mike." She paused just briefly, then, "But that's not going to happen. I have officially petitioned the archbishop and requested that I be excluded from the list. I could not survive a visit to Cottage Grove, Mike, and you know it."

Carlisle was in a trance-like state in hearing not only her words but also the profoundly sad tone in her voice. But he rebounded quickly because there was relief in knowing that his mission was going to be successful. It was now only his ego that needed soothing.

"You may not have loved me those many years ago, Larae. But, surely, you cared for me to some extent," he challenged. "We were intimate once. You cannot deny that."

"No, Mike, I cannot deny that. But that was decades ago. I don't know you anymore."

"That's right, Larae," he confirmed, "You made certain of that by giving me my walking papers." He was becoming angry, "You had had a lifetime supply of Michael Carlisle, didn't you?" He continued, "How does a person become intimate with another human being and then, a few weeks later, tell them that they never want to see them again? That they do not want to know them any longer? I don't understand that Larae? What does God say to you about that?"

Now, it was Savignac's turn to be angry. "God tells me that I have a free will, Mike. And that just because you may have loved me does not mean that I was required to love you back!" She had to catch her breath and now whispered hoarsely, "Furthermore, my dear Michael, we both gave up an incredibly precious gift from God to save your career on the bench and maintain my mental health. Neither one of us really had a choice. The sanctity of your judicial career and my inability to be a good mother trumped the formation of a family. And I did not need to stay with the man who also was my accomplice."

Now, they both were angry and the harshness of their words intensified the silence that had subsequently followed.

Then, the old man sighed the sigh of a lifetime. He offered, "I have come here uninvited without your consent and I have invaded your privacy. I apologize. But for everyone's sake, I had to be assured that you would stay away. Your coming to Cottage Grove would be disastrous for a lot of people, Larae."

At once, Larae's shoulders dropped, almost imperceptibly, as she sensed the annoyance of his visit concluding. "Perhaps, he would go away soon," she thought to herself. She said nothing, but only kept staring at him, waiting for him to get up and leave her company.

"It is true that I did love you, once. But that was a long time ago," he started again. "Now, I no longer know you. And, really, Larae, that is the worst thing that we have done to each other – to disallow our presence in each other's life. But, in our case, we had no choice. As brutally painful as our decision was, Larae, how wrong were we?

"Still, Mike, there is that pesky notion that we declined a gift from God because we put ourselves first. If things worked out for the best for everyone, it was pure dumb luck."

"Yes, there is that, Larae. Fortunately for me, I found my life's love in someone else. Unfortunately for me, she died an untimely death. In a way, so did I, although in a less dramatic and corporeal fashion.

"And you found God or at least a way to serve Him. Do you think He can forgive us, Larae?"

"Of course. He did long ago. That's not the problem, Mike." And with a sadness that exceeded the expectations of Carlisle, "Can we forgive ourselves by convincing ourselves that we did the right thing?"

They looked at each other for a while because there really was not much else to say. The lawyer got up from his chair. The sister did the same. Michael Carlisle stepped toward her and planted a gentle kiss on her left cheek. She neither moved nor responded, but stood there stoically. He took one last look at her and turned toward the door that led to the grand foyer.

"How is she, Mike. Is she happy?"

He turned to face her and smiled. "Eminently so, Larae," he said simply. "Our plan has been a great success."

The sister stood there and faintly smiled in return, "I'm glad."

Chapter 12

IN THE CONFERENCE ROOM

Like so many other shoe manufacturers in the country, his company was at a crossroad. For it to survive, Gordon Coppaway needed to find a way to offset the poverty-level low wages of foreign competition, especially that of China. He found less expensive leather and plastic and rubber from distributors and he invested in state-of-the-art machinery for each department in order to facilitate production and lower the cost per skid of shoe, but it was still not enough to intelligently compete with imports. The only savings left to be had would have to come from labor.

The conference room at the shoe factory was small and cluttered. An unused coffee urn sat on a scarred and warped credenza. The room was little used except for visiting salesmen offering their products and services to the factory's general manager.

A secretary entered the empty room with a box of coffee mugs that had imprinted on them the name and company logo of Coppaway Shoe. She placed the mugs about the table and positioned them to correspond with the location of each chair. She then lifted from the box embossed nameplates for those people that would be in attendance at the meeting.

At 10:00, Dirk McGuire and Tony Fedoryshyn walked in the room and began unloading their paperwork onto the conference table. Shortly thereafter, Gordon Coppaway and Dan Joda entered and slapped their leather binders on the flat surface of the table and sat on the opposite side of the table without acknowledging their adversaries. Lastly, Michael Carlisle walked in with briefcase in one hand and his smart phone up against his ear in conversation. He quickly ended his telephone call as Coppaway glared at him in disapproval. Finally, the secretary sat at the corner of the table with a tape recorder in front of her and a stenographer's pad readied for use.

"Well, let's begin, shall we?" offered Coppaway. "I see that Local 555 is now being represented by counsel, Dirk. Would you please introduce your legal representatives for the record?"

"Yes, of course, Mr. Coppaway. This is Mr. Anthony Fedoryshyn of Fedoryshyn and Davis. Their office is located in Crown Point, Indiana, and their firm is now the legal representative of Local 555."

"Very well, Dirk," answered Coppaway. "Let the record show that Mr. Michael Carlisle of Carlisle & Rhea is present as attorney for the Coppaway Shoe Company. Also, present is Mr. Dan Joda, our plant manager, who has met with Dirk McGuire on previous occasions to establish some groundwork regarding possible union demands and concessions."

The tape recorder was already spinning silently as the secretary transcribed in furious shorthand.

"Let me begin, gentlemen," the old Indian began. "Perhaps we can save some time. It is my understanding Mr. Joda and McGuire have met previously on several occasions to discuss 555's complaints and requests. Of course, these meetings were informal, unofficial and preliminary in all ways.

"As you know, we are in an extremely competitive market. Dan, here, has saved the company a great deal of money by purchasing leather goods, rubber, and plastic at reduced wholesale costs. Also, he has brought in some new equipment and electronics to streamline various steps in our machining processes. But it is still not enough savings to beat the foreign companies in most price points."

"We are not taking a cut in our wages, Mr. Coppaway," interrupted McGuire with an explosive voice. "We want better working conditions and real safety regulations that are actually followed by the company. We want a better healthcare plan that reduces premiums and is something other than catastrophic insurance. We want to be paid for overtime that goes beyond the forty-hour work week." And then he concluded, "And yes, Mr. Coppaway, we want higher wages so that we can have decent lives in exchange for the hard work that we do every single day."

"Let me finish, McGuire," Coppaway fumed in return and then spoke in a calming voice, "So, here is what my company will submit to Boot & Shoe Union Local 555… We will agree to all of your demands, including higher wages for a single concession from you."

Dirk McGuire and Tony Fedoryshyn exchanged glances in subdued surprise and then looked over at Michael Carlisle for verification of the good news. The old lawyer sat there without expression. They both noticed Dan Joda staring across the table at them, apparently waiting for their next reaction as the other shoe was about to drop.

"What is the single concession?" asked Fedoryshyn with a blank tone of voice. He was a veteran of labor negotiations and was not quickly moved in altogether terms.

"Coppaway Shoe will need to reduce the number of employees working at the factory," he deadpanned, and then added, "By one-third."

The old Irishman nearly fell out of his chair as his lawyer sat next to him holding down his arm so that no pencil or tablet would be transformed into a projectile launched from one end of the table to the other.

"Are you dead drunk, Coppaway!" shouted McGuire.

"Mind your manners, Dirk," countered Joda. "You happen to be talking to the president of the company."

"Shut-up, Joda. This meeting is for adults only," was the Irishman's rejoinder. And then Dirk turned his attention to Coppaway and Carlisle. "Listen here, there ain't no way you can slice the manpower of the factory by one-third. It's not possible." He argued looking straight at the owner, "Look, you got seven different departments working at over 200 separate operations by the time a pair of shoes leaves this plant. And you want to cut the manpower by one-third? Are you serious?"

"That's right, McGuire," explained Joda with exaggerated patience, "Each department will show a reduction in available labor. But production will remain the same because of more sophisticated equipment and better use of time and space.

"Here is the rundown. Each department will have forty workers, including supervisors: Cutting & Clicking, Closing & Machining, Lasting & Making, Finishing & Inspection, and Warehousing & Shipment. Finishing is being combined with the Inspection and Warehousing is being combined with Shipment. So now we have just five departments."

"I don't care what new equipment you bring into this building or what computers you've bought to run things, you can make boots and shoes only so fast," countered Fedoryshyn. "There has to be a limit otherwise quality and safety become vague concepts of the past."

The first salvo had been discharged and received in what was apparently going to be a bitter time in the history of The Coppaway Shoe Company. Propriety, politeness, decorum – all left the negotiating table in a heartbeat. "Mister" would be no longer used in address. It was clear that Gordon Coppaway had brandished his sword and Dirk McGuire would soon answer with equal measure.

"You're talking about one hundred families without employment, Michael," suggested Fedoryshyn with a sigh of resignation. "Is there no alternate solution?"

"Yes, Tony," replied Carlisle. "Three hundred workers can take a significant pay cut with longer hours and very little healthcare benefits." The old lawyer continued, "And, by the way, the employees' union will have to agree to pay for any cafeteria or restroom improvements during the next five years. That would definitely have to be in the new contract"

At the table, the players sat looking at each other for a moment, both sides perplexed at the other's attitude in seeming not to recognize the reality and consequent implications of the confrontation. The possible closing of the factory, or the possible undertaking of a strike, or the possible laying-off of a hundred union workers at Coppaway.

"Well, I think we're done here," Fedoryshyn replied with calm as he gathered up his papers and notebooks and stuffed them in his attache case.

The three company men remained seated and watched their two adversaries push their chairs toward and then below the surface of the conference table.

Dirk McGuire turned just slightly toward Gordon Coppaway and whispered even though he meant for all to hear. "Listen here, lad. The next time we meet you had better come up with some better ideas than what you did today or there sure as hell will be a strike. We'll close this plant if we have to. You can place your gambling soul on it, Indian."

Coppaway smiled wryly and said quietly even though he meant for all to hear. "Listen here, Irish. If you pull off a strike on me, I will sell my building and property to that cereal plant across town and you can go make corn flakes for the rest of your life."

Chapter 13

MISSIONS ACCOMPLISHED

On Tuesday morning Michael Carlisle arrived at General Mitchell International Airport in Milwaukee. His flight from Cincinnati had been pleasant enough and he had his early morning coffee while in transit. He grabbed the shuttle bus to the outlying long-term parking lot, climbed into his car and headed west for nearly a hundred miles back to Cottage Grove.

The former district court judge and current attorney-at-law was feeling good about his mission to Blue Ash. He had accomplished what he wanted – an unqualified assurance from Larae that she would not be coming to Cottage Grove later in the summer. Her absence would continue his good standing in the community and would preclude unnecessary upheaval for people that he loved in the way that he was able to love.

It was late morning when he turned his car into the short concrete driveway of his sister. She lived alone in a small Cape Cod house on a quiet side street. Although the house was not in disrepair, it needed updating inside and new siding on the outside. It was a pale-yellow house with brown shutters and a crumbling walkway that led to the front stoop.

There was not much of a backyard for the neighborhood houses were like postage stamps – very small and close together. So, she made up for the lack of a yard by planting bouquets of marigolds before and below the two front windows that bookend the covered front stoop. The bold colors of fluorescent orange and vibrant yellow were punctuated by ones of rust-color. Geraniums provided bas-relief in both flower gardens with colors pink and fuchsia and red and white. Complementing these arrangements were small peony bushes of white and pink on one side of the walkway and purple lilacs on the other.

Already home from weekday Mass, Helen Quesnell was preparing a modest lunch for herself when her doorbell rang. She wiped her hands using the dish rag and walked to her front foyer. After peering out the front door's window, she opened her house to her brother.

"Hello, Mike. Come in," she invited.

The lawyer smiled and said, "Thanks, Helen."

He wiped his feet on the foyer rug because he knew that he should and then closed the door behind him.

"I am making a tuna casserole. Do you want to stay for lunch?"

"Okay, thank you, I will," was the warm reply. "I have some good news. Larae has assured me that she will not be coming to the parish festival." Carlisle watched his sister accept the news because it was important to her, as well.

Helen stood somewhat stoically in front of her brother and then said, "That's good, Mike. She is still thinking of what is best for everyone." After a faint smile, she led Carlisle into the kitchen and allowed him to help complete preparations for lunch.

As they both sat at the kitchen table Helen served the casserole to her brother and then to herself. They sat and ate quietly for just a few minutes before she began her inquiry. "How did she look, Mike? What did she say to you?"

"She looked fine, Helen," he began. "A lot older, of course, but still beautiful in a wholesome way." He continued, "And she still seems to be a force and not one to accept a song and dance routine. He thought awhile and then, "I mean it seems like she would know how to take care of herself if she were cornered in a bad situation."

"I don't understand, Mike. What do you mean she could take care of herself?" She sipped from her coffee cup.

"I think she is just as determined to keep things the way they are as much as we are, Helen. After all, she is the mother of her convent. Anyway, she seemed very comfortable or at least content, but there did seem to be an underlying sadness about her."

"Mike, that is true about you and me, as well. No matter how well things have turned out, there will always be an underlying sadness about our lives. That's just the way it is."

She served herself a small portion of the casserole because her appetite was waning as the conversation continued. She looked at her brother as she placed the fork and food in her mouth.

"Sometimes I think love is too expensive," she admitted. "It seems like we pay a too great a price to love people and have people love us. Maybe, you and I think alike in that way, Mike."

He looked at her with a slightly surprised expression and then set his own fork on his plate. He sat motionless for a moment to consider. His elbows rested on the table and his hands were cupped in front of his face as if to hide what he was thinking. After the moment had passed, he picked up his fork and continued eating.

Michael finished his portion of the casserole and gulped down the last of the coffee. He stood and kissed his older sister good-bye and thanked her for lunch. She watched through the front picture window and saw him drive away. She loved him. He had given her a gift of love and life, but in tandem that gift brought along doubt and fear and guilt. For Helen Quesnell the exchange rate for a family was a constant and dull awareness of calculated odds that Larae Savignac would remain true to her religious calling. After her brother's successful mission to Ohio, Helen still had both her daughter and the natural dividend whose name was Lauren.

CARLISLE LAID IN BED LONGER THAN USUAL ON WEDNESday. The trip to Ohio had taken its toll on the lawyer. He was just plain tired and somewhat mentally worn down. At about ten o'clock the sun's light and warmth flooded his bedroom so much so that he was compelled to rise and shower. He would telephone Cosie to state the obvious – he would be late for work.

With hard steel slicing whiskers and scraping lather he decided to talk to Vincent about David's outburst at the Rhea residence. He wanted to set the record straight without misunderstanding or ambiguity. Vincent would come to the old lawyer's point of view. Carlisle dressed, grabbed an old but valued briefcase, and drove into town.

Both Vincent and Cosie were waiting for him as he entered the office.

"Good morning, Vincent, Cosie," he greeted as he came

in from the back door of the offices. They replied in kind and both colleagues were all business with Cosie reminding him of an appointment with Dan Joda at the shoe factory and Vincent handing him legal briefs that were prepared for him in his absence.

With greetings concluded and updates given, Carlisle asked Vincent to step into his office for a brief meeting. There was neither smile nor indication of congeniality. Vincent followed his partner down the corridor with a feeling of a student headed for the principal's office. After Rhea entered Carlisle' office the senior partner closed the door gently behind him showing a marked intent for privacy.

"Please have a seat, Vincent, this won't take long."

Unbuttoning his suit, the junior partner sat before the large desk of Carlisle. "What's on your mind, Michael?" he asked.

The old lawyer sat his briefcase on the floor beside his chair and sat relaxed behind his desk. "Vincent, first I want to apologize for making a scene at your house a while back. Obviously, I was very upset with what David Llewellyn said and embarrassed at the way the conversation was handled."

"Is it true, Michael? Is David your son?"

"According to both Jack and David Llewellyn, it's true," Carlisle answered. "But I don't know… I suppose I can take their word for it. In a way, it really doesn't matter anymore. I mean what difference does it make now?

"Look at it this way, Vincent," he continued. "David is a full-grown adult now. What does he need from me that he doesn't already have? What am I going to do for him that Jack Llewellyn hasn't already done or is doing?"

It was a persuasive argument, of course. Neat, concise, clean, logical, and altogether wrong in the mind of Vincent

Rhea. "But Michael you can still have a son. Belatedly, yes. But you can have a lot of years and a new life with David. Everyone needs a family," the partner argued.

"Well, I have Mikaela and Lauren and you, you know."

"Yes, Michael, we are *like* family to you, but we are not *blood* relatives. My God, man, he is your son. How can you not pursue that relationship?" implored Rhea. "You are a part of our family, Michael, by virtue of friendship and circumstance, but he is your family by virtue of consanguinity and the result of your love for Julia."

The old lawyer was feeling pressure from within his own soul at hearing the words of his partner. But the nature of a man has many features and what constituted the greatest part of Michael Carlisle would not permit his paternal instinct the final word. His drive for self-realization and his own viewpoint of his personal world would not allow for the belated entry of a son who he did not know even existed until recently.

Additionally, Carlisle reasoned that since David resided nearly a hundred miles away from the gossip of the Grove, there was little likelihood that the townspeople would ever discover that he had a son. In any case, the news of the discovery would not make much difference to Cottage Grove because Carlisle was no longer on the district bench. The attorney felt assured that David would always be known as the son of Jack Llewellyn.

"Let me explain some things about me to you, Vincent. I am a man who can love only so many people. I can't help it. That is just the way I am constructed. I can count on one hand all the people in the world that I have ever loved other than my parents. Helen, Julia, Mikaela, Lauren, and someone you don't know and is none of your business.

"And I do not forget anything and I cannot forgive anyone. That's also the way I am and I can't help that either. For over thirty years David has been the son of Jack Llewellyn and I cannot forget that and I cannot forgive my son for that. Of course, it's not fair. But, really, that's quite beside the point.

"Your family is enough for me, Vincent. My devotion to all three of you is complete and exhaustive. Along with Helen, there is no room for anyone else. Certainly, not at this late date in my life."

"But Michael…"

"What should I do now, Vincent?" Carlisle violently interrupted. "Drive a hundred miles each day to his house, push his lovely wife aside, and tuck him in at night? Will he want my advice on dating his wife, Jana? Don't you see the problem? It is too late to be a father to him.

"Enough of this, Vincent," he protested. "This is all that I wanted to talk to you about now. I wanted you to know how I felt and hopefully you can understand my feelings in this matter. The subject is now closed."

"Well, I don't understand. How does a man give up a son?"

"He doesn't," Carlisle exploded, "but David Llewellyn will never be my son. Jack Llewellyn will see to that. What remedy do I have? The old bastard has a three and a half decade jump on me. What am I supposed to do? Erase time?"

By the end of their heated exchange both men realized that neither was seated any longer. Both had somehow rose to their feet and were standing facing each other on either side of the desk. Vincent offered an emotional retreat from the argument by slumping his shoulders and taking a step back because the elder had the moral authority to control his own fate whether he was right or wrong. After all, it was Michael's decision to make.

"Okay, Michael, have it your own way," conceded Vincent. "It is your life to live as you see fit. I just want to see you as happy as you can be.

"Mikaela and I think the world of you and so does Lauren. If you want your world to stay the way it is, then we have to accommodate you. It's just that even if you do it your way, you're still going to lose."

"Maybe I even know that," the elder admitted. "But, for me, this is the way it has to be. By now, there is too much Jack Llewellyn in David. It would just be bad chemistry between David and me, Vincent. That much I know."

Then Vincent offered a nod to Carlisle as if to say "So it is written, so it shall be done." But in his heart the young lawyer knew that his decision about his natural son shortchanged his employer and probably David Llewellyn, as well.

JANA LLEWELLYN WAS JUST ARRIVING HOME FROM THE grocery store. She opened the back door of her SUV and grabbed one of the paper bags and her leather purse and made her way to the front door of their home. It was a small bungalow style house that exuded character and charm and offered comfort and warmth on a cold winter's night. Its casual elegance provided comfort and coziness in every room whether first or second floor. In the summers, the floor plan included varied rooms whose windows created cross breezes which made air conditioning unnecessary.

She returned to her SUV for the remaining grocery bags when David pulled into the driveway, home from work at one of his company's construction sites. Their life together was a happy one. They loved each other and considered everything else only details. No children yet, but it was neither for a lack of effort nor for a lack of enjoyment in the effort. But they also knew that time was running out.

He helped her with the remaining paper bags and into the house they went with Jana talking about her day and David smiling the entire time. With the groceries put away in the proper places, the perky brunette began the task of preparing a modest dinner while her husband went through the mail as was his regular routine. Interrupting their conversation the doorbell rang once, then twice. David laid down the mail and answered the door. It was Michael Carlisle.

"David, I apologize for disturbing you at home like this, but I think we need to have a conversation," Carlisle greeted. "May I come in?"

"Sure… come in," said David hesitantly. "We were just now making dinner. Would you like to join us?"

"No, thank you. I won't be here that long."

The old lawyer looked around the living room and gave a discreet approval with a slight smile and then sat down without invitation. Jana entered the room cautiously because she did not know whether she should be part of the conversation or not. David was talking to his biological father for the first time as his father. She decided to stay in the room unless there was an objection raised by father or son.

"I guess I still don't know what to call you," confessed David. "I'll go along with whatever you like."

"Don't call me anything, David. That's why I am here this evening," he began. "So you understand." The lawyer cleared his throat and looked at Jana and then back at David. "I don't think it wise for us to alter our relationship just because you recently discovered a secret from your late mother." He looked down at his hands as they were rubbing against his knees in embarrassment. Jana observed in dull awareness the old man's self-consciousness. She could not believe what she was hearing.

"In other words, I don't feel like there is any point in beginning a relationship between us at this stage of our lives. You already have a father who I can only assume is of some use to you. In any case, I don't believe that I could wrestle out of you enough 'Jack' to do you any good. I am sorry to be so blunt, David. You seem like a nice young man, but that's just the way it is."

If young Llewellyn felt stress over the years on construction sites where tradesmen curse and spit at one another on a daily basis, where bravado and brawn and bullshit conquered decorum and civility, that stress paled in comparison to the sledge-hammer remarks of his biological father in his own the living room. For a flash moment, David wondered what kind of man was Michael Carlisle and how much did he naturally inherit from the son-of-a-bitch.

It is hard to say how long Jana and David sat there so stunned at the words of Michael Carlisle. But there came a point in time when even the lawyer thought somebody should say something.

"Well, I hope eventually you will come to understand my point of view, David," he pressed. "Really, nothing has changed. You are still a Llewellyn and you may as well play out the hand that you have been dealt. That is true of all of us, don't you see."

"I don't know what kind of man you are, Mr. Carlisle," Jana began, "but it seems to me that you are throwing away a perfectly good son just because he is used and not brand new."

"Stop, Jana," David said bitterly. "It's no use. You can see it in his face that he has nothing to give, even to his own son who he has just met."

"Believe me, this way is the best way for everyone concerned," Carlisle argued. "Given time, you will come around to my way of thinking. I'm thinking of everyone's best interest, of course."

"Well, as long as it is in the name of expediency," Jana said with as much quiet contempt as she could muster.

Carlisle looked at her, then at David. Finally, the conversation was over and the lawyer stood and said, "I'm sorry. I had better go. Good luck to both of you." With that he walked straight to the front foyer without looking back. The door opened and closed and he was gone.

Jana went back into the kitchen and continued making dinner, but she did by setting pots and pans onto the electric range top with vigor and slamming pantry doors with a vengeance. In an attempt to save kitchen cookware and cabinetry, David hurried into the room and placed his hands on her shoulders to steady and soothe his wife.

She stopped what she was doing as he did so and observed, "You know, your dad and Carlisle must really hate each other." She continued, "I can imagine them at each other's throat as they throw themselves off a cliff, punching and kicking and gouging each other all the way to impact." It was an image in their minds that they both held for a long moment.

"It's okay, Jana. The ass-hole is right about one thing. I still have my dad and nothing has changed, really."

She stopped what she was doing and braced herself against the stove front and turned around to face her husband. 'I know, dear, but it is all such a shocking way to begin and end your relationship with your real father."

"No. My real father is back in Cottage Grove threading film through a 35- millimeter film projector right now. The man you saw tonight only furnished and installed sperm," he concluded. She smiled at him because she loved him and because she knew that she would acquiesce to his attitude by evening's end.

ON INTERSTATE 94 NOW, THE BLACK MERCEDES OF Michael Carlisle hummed with a silver slick cruising motion that defied the feel of concrete beneath spinning rubber tires. Once again, his mission was accomplished. This time his efforts and consequent success were more altruistic. He had spared the good son the bad father.

In his heart, he knew that David was truly Jack's son, not because of blood but because of time on task and three and a half decades of father and son interaction. The fates were unkind to the lawyer, but there was no compelling reason to defy what mutual love existed between the Llewellyns. It would be spitting in the wind. And that was something Michael Carlisle never did.

In his musings across the miles, the would-be father thought about his enduring war against Jack Llewellyn. First, there was Larae, then Julia, now David – except that now he was forfeiting David because Llewellyn had had him as his son during the formative years and beyond. In other words, now the return on investment would not be appreciable and he felt his efforts would be wasted in a lost cause.

For a brief moment it occurred to the lawyer that David and Mikaela were half-siblings. But that relationship would have to remain secret because he had no intention of revealing it to either. The delicate judgment by the Grove's general public would be unforgiving. For that matter, he concluded, there was no reason to interrupt the lives of either offspring with an embarrassing biological complication. Again, he believed it was in the best interest of all parties that such a relationship should not be made public.

For the second time in a week the old man felt good about what he had accomplished. Larae would stay at St. Rose of Lima Convent and not attend St. Matthew's Parish Festival and David would keep the only father that he has ever known. In both circumstances he knew in his soul that all involved would be better served by the absence of Larae and himself, respectively. And he admitted to himself that both outcomes benefited him greatly and would allow him to continue his life without encumbrance. His world order was maintained and that was pretty much the signature concern of Michael Carlisle.

Chapter 14

A PREGNANCY IS ANNOUNCED

In the days following the unexpected visit of Michael Carlisle, David became quiet and reflective to a point of lethargy. Jana left him alone to sort out for himself where his place was in his personal world. She had confidence in him that he would work through the shock of rejection and with his internal resilience regain his self-worth. There was much pride and strength in David Llewellyn. His wife was certain of that much.

Eventually, she was proven right. Her husband rebounded because he reminded himself and fully acknowledged that his real father – the one who loved him almost in spite of his biological origin – still was part of his life and would always be there for him. Just for a few days, David forgot that he already had a father; now he realized that he did not need a new one. It was a fictional crisis and he let it die a natural death.

In the Llewellyn household it was in the division of labor that Jana always planned and prepared the meals and David always washed the dishes and cleaned the kitchen afterward. All other inside duties belonged to her. David was responsible for the exterior of the house and yard work except for flowers.

So it was when David was just completing his kitchen

patrol duties when Jana entered from the living room to offer her announcement. "David, I want you to know that we are going to have a baby."

She stood there waiting for his response as he lifted the dish towel from his shoulder and turned toward her with an expression of sublime delight and amazement. In just a flash, he threw aside the towel and embraced his wife, at first with a loving compaction. Then, realizing what they were celebrating, he relaxed his affectionate hold as to not cause her any possible discomfort. They gazed at each other longingly and with a renewed and elevated love because they had created a new human being and would be introduced to that living soul in just a few months.

Finally, after a lengthy embrace, David found his words to speak, "Jana, I cannot tell you how happy I am. I love you so much. Please sit down and rest for a while." He practically pushed her down onto a kitchen chair in spite of her efforts to remain standing.

"David, I am perfectly fine. You don't have to treat me like a china doll. I am not going to break," she assured him.

"When did you find out? How did it happen?"

"Last night I took a pregnancy test and then I saw my doctor this morning. And you know perfectly well how it happened."

Her husband blushed briefly and then came to his senses. "Well, this is incredible news. When can we start telling people?" he asked.

"Let's wait a few weeks. Otherwise, it will seem to people that I will have been pregnant for a year instead of the normal nine months."

"Okay, Jana. We'll wait."

During the subsequent weeks of Jana's pregnancy, David

watched and waited. He watched her every subtle movement as one who is on call and ready to remedy the slightest discomfort shown on her face. Moreover, he remodeled the third bedroom in their bungalow and transformed it into a nursery. Further finish work would begin and colors selected when the sex of the baby was known.

Through the warm summer David hurried home from work to see to his wife. Although he allowed her to continue with the making of dinners, he insisted on doing the laundry in the basement and all house cleaning chores other than dusting. Under no circumstances could she stand on anything higher than a throw rug. Without fail he escorted her to the grocery store so that she never lifted the bags and bottles that they purchased. More so than at any other time in their marriage he gave deference to Jana. For her part, she did not object to the arrangement. At all events, he continued to watch and wait with forced patience.

AFTER SEVERAL WEEKS' DURATION, THE SECRET OF JANA'S pregnancy could no longer be kept. As with all such announcements, the young couple were eager to exchange their privacy for celebration. Jana's side of the family was told first because that was what she wanted and David congenially agreed because he liked them, too. So, a brief excursion to Algonquin, Illinois, was planned and executed. Of course, her parents were delighted as this would be the first grandchild in their immediate family.

A few days later Jack Llewellyn received the good news while licking the side of a vanilla ice cream cone at Suzy DeSoto's Custard Drive-In. Jana decided it was time to satisfy her craving for frozen custard and David happily agreed to share in the summer delight. So, when they came to the Grove to deliver the good news to Jack, it seemed like a good idea to announce it while enjoying the best frozen custard and ice cream east of the Mississippi River. Everyone knew that it was the best frozen custard and ice cream because there was a sign at the parking lot entrance that said so.

The drive-in was located at the edge of town. There were no parking spaces per se. One just drove across a gravel lot and pulled up to the small rectangular building with a lighted overhang and parked one's car. There was no curb service of any kind. You just walked up to a sliding glass window on either side of the building's front and placed your order, got your frozen custard or ice cream, and went back to your car. However, for the more sociable there were three sets of white wooden picnic tables and plastic chairs if you wanted to eat and talk under the long linear canopy that stretched away from the front of Suzy DeSoto's.

It was an uncomplicated business with an abbreviated menu that did a splendid business during the summer months. Two teachers, a husband-and-wife tandem, from the local high school owned and managed the place during their summer vacations.

At one of the tables the three Llewellyns were deep in their conversation involving the next generation and all the possibilities, challenges and joy that were certain to follow. For the first time in as long as they could remember the frozen sweetness at the drive-in took a distant second place to a topic of discussion.

"You know, David," Jack began, "I remember when your mother was pregnant with you. We would lie in bed at night and sometimes before we fell asleep she would feel you moving about. I suppose you were trying to get comfortable because your mother was lying down.

"Anyway, I would place my hand gently on her stomach and feel you moving, and when she would raise her pajama top to exposing her stomach we could see small bumps of skin rise and fall to show us that what we were witnessing was something more than indigestion. It was the new life of a brand-new human being. It was an awesome moment and we were very much intimidated by it all."

Jana brushed back her long hair and set it against her shoulder. She looked at her father-in-law intently and said, "How did the movement feel to her?"

"I don't know, Jana," the retired professor replied. "It must have been a strange sensation, though. Not ticklish, not painful, but some movement inside and independent of her, a life that was uniquely human that was slowly developing.

"Oftentimes, I wonder how civilized people can end human life like that. For those people convenience of not raising a child must trump the life a of human being. In any case, they choose to ignore what they learned in their high school biology class."

David and Jana listened quietly and momentarily forgot their custard dishes as they wondered if they would feel and see the same thing in the coming months. They knew the answer was yes, of course, and it gave them something else to look forward to and to think about.

Eventually, Jack's ice cream was history and the younger Llewellyns finished their frozen custard by scraping their spoons across the inside of their dishes. Just then a late model SUV drove up and stopped near them. It was Mikaela and Lauren Rhea.

"Hello, everyone," greeted Mikaela. Lauren only smiled.

David stood up and waved for the Rheas to join them. "Mikaela, we are so glad to see you." And then he looked at Lauren. "Hiya, Lauren." Again, she only smiled, but did manage a wave of the hand.

"Lauren, take my wallet and order each of us an ice cream cone," instructed her mother and the daughter eagerly complied.

In short order, Tom Pfefferkorn drove into the graveled lot to join what was becoming a small gathering of old acquaintances. "Tom, David and Jana have just told me that they are expecting their first child," Jack beamed. "I'm going to be grandfather!"

"Jackson, that is great news," the editor answered. "In fact, I'll put a brief announcement in the paper's next issue. People in town will want to read about it."

Lauren was just coming back with the two ice cream cones for Mikaela and herself. She handed one of the cones and the wallet to her mother.

"I'll tell you what. Everyone stay right where you are and I'll get a picture," said Pfefferkorn as he reached for his smart phone from his trouser pocket. "Okay, let's get everyone in this photo for the newspaper."

He shuffled together the three Llewellyns and the two Rheas and had them pose for as much drama and interest as he could muster for the photograph. After all, Tom Pfefferkorn knew that people who bought his hometown newspaper liked pictures of locals and seeing the names of their neighbors in the articles. He could imagine it – local retired professor announces the birth of his first grandchild while friends gather to celebrate at Suzy DeSoto's. Who knows, maybe he could get the two teachers to buy some advertising along the way using the family friendly photo opportunity.

"Hey, Tom, when can I get some copies of that for everyone," asked Jack, who was glad to return to some normalcy after the death of Julia. He had been somewhat uncertain that he could find happiness again. It had been a pretty tough life for him for so long. He could not remember the last time he felt this kind of happiness.

"Tell you what, Jack. You stop by the office tomorrow and I will make a copy for each of you and I'll e-mail you the electronic version," offered Pfefferkorn.

With that the gathering concentrated on their ice cream cones and custard dishes all the way to completion. There were smiles and hugs and Mikaela planted a kiss on the cheek of David that made him blush. The watchful eyes of Jana noticed and she would make an inquiry while they were on their way home in the privacy of their SUV. The kiss did not bother her, but the blush did. And while there was no known history between the two, she knew that they were both extraordinary people who happened to admire one another.

WITH THE BIG NEWS DELIVERED AND THE ICE CREAM consumed, they were finally homeward bound. The oldies FM station played the Motown sounds of the Four Tops as background music to the conversation between David and Jana. They talked about the baby and when she would begin showing in earnest her condition and what plans they should make for the extra bedroom that was now envisioned to become the nursery.

Then suddenly, Jana reached over and turned off the radio and looked over at her husband. "Tell me, dear, did you enjoy the kiss from Mikaela?"

"Ah, come on, Jana. It was a kiss on the cheek!" he admonished his wife. "She was just congratulating us, for goodness' sakes."

"Then why did your face turn beet red, David?" was the retort from the young emotional woman with child who was glaring at him. Now, tears were forming because she had worked herself into the kind of emotional state that men could not understand. "You are not going to leave me, are you?" she sobbed.

Suddenly, she was out of control and her husband was frantic to have her regain both her composure and common sense.

"Jana, you know that I love you and the baby and there is no one else," he pleaded. "Mikaela is a friend to both of us and has been for more years than we can remember." And, finally, he said with conviction and persuasion, "But, honestly, she and I have never dated although we did grow up together. No matter what, you are my life, even more so now that we are going to be a family."

With that Jana eased back into her seat and patted her eyes with a Kleenex. Eventually, she smiled and even laughed under her breath more because of the affirmation than the relief. He told something that she already knew, but still wanted to hear. Women are like that sometimes.

THE *JOURNAL SCENE* WAS PUBLISHED TWICE WEEKLY IN Cottage Grove and was distributed through the mail and available at certain locations throughout the county. In the following Thursday issue, the Suzy DeSoto celebration photo was placed on page four. The cut-line below the picture identified those in attendance and an accompanying four-inch article explained the circumstances, thus officially announcing the Llewellyn pregnancy.

Jack Llewellyn spent the latter part of that Thursday accepting congratulations from virtually everyone that recognized him and subscribed to the *Journal Scene*. The projectionist was pleased that the buttons stayed fastened on his shirt and he could still feel the ground below him as he walked about the town. He was proud and happy and felt somewhat invincible, much like his son nearly a hundred miles away.

As evening drew near, the town square grew quiet and parking spaces became freely available in front of those stores that closed early. Jack Llewellyn was making his way back to his flat after an unnecessary haircut that gave him an extra opportunity to share his good news with old cronies at the barbershop.

Turning a corner toward home he was abruptly accosted by Michael Carlisle. With the *Journal Scene* folded under one of his arms and carrying a briefcase in the other, the lawyer bellowed, "Look, Llewellyn, you can have David because you already have David," he growled. "But the grandchild is *mine!*"

It was obvious to Llewellyn that Carlisle was drunk. He looked harried and disheveled as he blurted out his challenge. It occurred to him to shove the old lawyer to the sidewalk because there was no one about, but he resisted the urge and with exaggeration walked around him – pretending to ignore him, but obviously not doing so.

"Llewellyn, do you hear me!" Carlisle was shouted as loud as he could.

"You are drunk again. What is it with you and alcohol?"

The projectionist continued to stare at the drunk and finally said so softly that the words were engraved onto the mind of the attorney. "Carlisle, you have no son and you will have no grandchild."

In his inebriation, the lawyer stumbled aggressively toward Llewellyn. But the sober man quickly grabbed him by the lapels of his suit and supported him standing with a hateful glare, face to face. Jack hesitated for a moment and then released him without harm.

But the lawyer would have none of it, at least the effect would not be reflected on his face for his enemy to see. And so with false bravado he protested, "That is not for you to say, Llewellyn. You will see. I will wrench that baby from you and you will sit in your second-story flat and you will curse the day that you ever danced with me." Carlisle would have bellowed more, but he was drunk. Still, he knew enough to realize that the encounter should conclude. So, he gave a military salute to Llewellyn, even though neither had been in the armed services, and went on his way pretending to be neither physically nor emotionally unbalanced.

As far as Jack was concerned, he had shown strength in the face of Carlisle's weaker hand. David was still a Llewellyn and his child would also be a Llewellyn. Perhaps, the baby would be born without the Llewellyn DNA, but it would come into and exit this world very much a Llewellyn, nevertheless.

The off-duty projectionist continued on his way home somewhat flushed because of the personal skirmish with his only enemy on earth. And while he knew that this day belonged to him, Jack also understood that their personal war was not over… and that it would never be over.

As Michael Carlisle walked into his office the following Friday morning, a copy of Thursday's paper laid on the small coffee table in the foyer of the office. He grabbed it for a quick inspection and flipped the pages casually until he reached the fourth page and saw again the photograph of Mikaela and Lauren sitting with the Llewellyns under the canopy of the ice cream drive-in. But what continued to mesmerize him most was the article below the picture that highlighted the future arrival of David and Jana's baby. To his chagrin, the story had not changed from the reading of it the day before. And because of that, his reaction had also not changed.

"Look at this, Cosie," exclaimed Carlisle to his legal secretary who he oftentimes ignored when coming through the front door. "David Llewellyn is going to be a father."

"That's nice," replied Cosie without looking up because there was too much work to be done before the weekend.

The old lawyer folded the newspaper and placed it under his arm and walked back through the corridor to his office and closed the door behind him.

While the news of the upcoming arrival of Jack Llewellyn's grandchild was interesting and made for pleasant conversation for the general public, the identity of the true biological grandfather remained shrouded. Only a handful of people knew the story and it was unlikely that those who did know would have any reason to approach the subject.

Still, while Michael Carlisle had decided to forgo a claim on his biological son, the grandchild was a different matter. After all, Jack Llewellyn had no more history with the grandchild that was yet unborn than him. And while he may never see a relationship with David because his father-son bond with the old professor was strong, that was not the case with the grandchild, girl or boy.

So, Carlisle sat in his big leather chair behind his imposing desk and gently rocked and thought and thought some more – mostly about how he enjoyed being like a grandfather to Mikaela's daughter and how he would enjoy another little child to whom he could bring gifts. Admittedly, it was the softer side of the lawyer and he considered it a benign weakness. But he should have known it was really his Achilles' heel.

After lunch Vincent Rhea was back from court and was anxious to see Michael about the page four photo and story. As he hurriedly entered the front office, he asked Cosie if Carlisle was in his office.

"He is," she said, again without looking up because there was still a lot of work to be done before she left for the weekend.

The young lawyer walked briskly back to Carlisle's office and knocked on the door as he entered without waiting for a response.

"Michael, have you seen the paper?" he asked.

"Yes, Vincent, I have seen it."

"Comment?" was the natural inquiry that Rhea was compelled to make.

"I don't believe it will be necessary for me to comment on every life event of the Llewellyns from now on, will it Vincent?" was the old man's retort. "If that's the case, I will begin working from home.

"But, for the record, I really don't have any comment at all. I congratulate David and Jana. Now, if you don't mind, there is work to be done. I have to prepare for an important meeting with Dan Joda at the shoe factory. The union is being stubborn and is threatening a strike if we don't settle soon."

It was a relief to Vincent that Michael was taking such a casual attitude about the pregnancy. Upon seeing yesterday's newspaper, he was almost certain that Carlisle would become overly agitated and unpredictable with the prospect of continued descendants that would continue his lineage. Perhaps Michael was different, though. After all, he was a singular individual with a focused purpose only on his professional career.

He watched the elder lawyer scribble notes in preparation of his upcoming meeting at the shoe factory. After feeling ignored long enough and satisfied that Michael was indifferent toward what would be a grandchild, Vincent left the office and continued his work at his desk and in the firm's library for the remainder of the day.

With Vincent gone, Carlisle laid down his pen and rubbed his eyes and then his cheeks and then his head as he leaned forward over the paperwork on his desk. Then, as he held his head in his hands and elbows on the desk, he muttered to himself, "Okay, Jack, you got David. You won that battle; but I'm going to get the grandchild." He paused, and then with face flushed with determination, "But I'm going to get the grandchild!"

Chapter 15

DECISION & DISCOVERY

As with his now deceased ex-lover, Michael Carlisle also lived in the Village Square Condominiums adjacent to the interstate highway service road. When Julia Llewellyn lived on the same campus there was an obvious convenience built into their relationship. Sometimes he would stay the night at her place, sometimes she would spend the weekend at his. For a long time they enjoyed each other and their freedom simultaneously. It was a splendid match all around.

But now the lawyer was alone and troubled by the memories of both Julia and Larae Savignac. He had loved them both and had lost them both in one fashion and another. And, because it was an upside-down world, this was also true of his lifetime enemy. The recent death of Julia and the even more recent journey to Larae reminded him of his blemished past and an uncertain future in claiming an unborn grandchild who he did not publicly acknowledge as his own.

Carlisle set about the cleaning of his residence because it had been so long since that chore was completed. Moreover, it was good therapy for the man and he knew it. Just returning from Blue Ash, he started the laundry of worn clothes, made himself lunch and set out a trash bag filled with accumulated junk mail and useless travel paperwork that he intended to discard.

Because he had been out of town for the last few days, the attorney decided to go into the office over the weekend. He would be able to work more efficiently without interruption. No phone calls, no Cosie, no Vincent, no clients. So, with chores eventually completed and his condo in reasonably good shape, he showered and climbed into bed and, sleeping restless in his dreams, waited for the weekend to begin with the morning sunrise.

MONDAY WAS TRASH PICK-UP DAY AT VILLAGE SQUARE Condominiums. A large green and white rear loader garbage truck entered the parking lot from the interstate service road and noisily lumbered across the way toward the rear of the buildings. Shubel Terhune was behind the wheel making his scheduled rounds that consisted of various routes detailed by the Public Works Department.

Although the cab, itself, was virgin white, the rest of the garbage truck was Forest green. The rear lift bucket, compactor, compress box, and hydraulic tank were all shimmering green in the morning sunlight. It was said and generally accepted that his truck was the showcase of the fleet because he cleaned it at the end of the day every day without fail.

Shubel wheeled his way to the trash bin area and backed into position for the loading of trash and garbage and whatever the condo owners had left for him to take. As he did his work with gloved hands, baseball cap on head and dirty tee shirt already absorbing the smell of garbage, the early morning summer breeze still cooled him. In another hour the sun in the higher sky would begin to beat on him and the heat of the garbage truck and its hydraulics would begin to wear on him.

With the trash bins selected, maneuvered, lifted, poured, and set back into place, the same breeze blew and scattered light cardboard and paper alongside the curb and Terhune made an effort to gather by hand the misbehaving scraps and toss them into the rear lift bucket. But as he picked up one small pile, he noticed that it included an e-mail hotel reservation from Blue Ash, Ohio, for Michael Carlisle, a United boarding pass to Cincinnati and a map of Blue Ash, as well.

One last crumpled scrap of paper rolled across his shoes and he quickly reached down for it before it got away. Instinctively he opened it and read its brief contents.

Dear Mike,

Good luck in Blue Ash. I know that Larae will be reasonable. She once loved you and still wants what is best for your daughter. It may be just as well not to mention the granddaughter. It would make things even more difficult for her. We don't want her to dwell on what might have been any more than what she has done already over the years.

Love,
Helen

"I don't know who Larae is but it looks like Mr. Carlisle went to Ohio recently," he mumbled to himself. "Man, I don't get to go anywhere like that." Then, for just a brief moment

Terhune paused to reflect how it must be to be able to get on an airplane and travel to another part of the country. "Someday, I think I would like that very much. Maybe, I could take Wish someplace out of state."

Then, the reverie was over and Shubel went back to his work because there was work to be done and he was taking care of his business. Nobody was going to do it for him.

THE SUMMER NIGHTS IN COTTAGE GROVE HAD BECOME warmer and no longer provided the refreshment of the early summer. Still, the warmth was a fair bargain in juxtaposition to the hot, steamy nights in the lower climates of the Midwest.

Shubel Terhune sat in his fire-engine red Chevrolet pickup outside Danbury Café waiting for Wish McGuire to appear after a long day of work. He knew that she would be tired because she had worked the afternoon and evening shifts, but he had to talk to her eventually. The radio station announced the time of 9:00 and he waited patiently while listening to the news beneath the metal-halide lamps that flooded the parking lot. His truck shimmered and shined whistle-clean for the admiration of Wish McGuire. Shubel had worked the better part of the evening in getting the old Chevy in mint glistening condition.

More than that, he scrubbed and scoured his hands and face and spent much of the early evening in the shower washing away the trash and garbage smells that lingered in unforgiving fashion. He washed his hair twice and applied a conditioner. Afterward, he tied his long black hair in a single ponytail behind his neck. It was his opinion that he cleaned up quite nicely.

Suddenly, the warped screened back door opened with authority and Wish McGuire came dancing out past the trash bins and into the parking lot. With a sense of purpose and a determined step, Skyler unlatched his door and made his way to intercept the blonde beauty.

From a fair distance, he hailed, "Wish!... Wish!" He waived to her as he kept approaching. The girl looked his way and stopped, not really knowing what to expect. Finally, he was upon her. She could smell the Aqua Velva aftershave lotion just a short time before his arrival and she could tell that he was dressed with new shirt and trousers. This was a different boy than what she had seen on a regular basis at breakfast.

"Shubel, hello, what are you doing here?" she asked with quick surprise.

Although the boy beamed with nervous enthusiasm, his response was noticeably measured and suspiciously practiced. "Hi, Wish," he began. "I just thought I would stop and see if you needed a ride home."

There was a long pause – perhaps longer than either of them wanted. Shubel began looking at the shoes of Wish McGuire and then the asphalt which supported those shoes. For her part, the blonde beauty stared in awkward surprise at the face of the boy who blocked her path to retreat. She could see that Shubel Terhune was not going to break the silence. It was apparent to the waitress that he was overcome by the moment, that his courage had ebbed and that he made his best effort in his initial approach. Skyler was toast. She let him down as gently as possible.

"That was nice of you, Shubel. But my car is just across the way, so I'm pretty well on my way home. But, thanks anyway."

The blonde smiled weakly as Shubel looked toward the street past the far side of the restaurant. He only nodded in agreement to her response. Then, Wish just quietly walked away and toward her pale blue Mustang. It was a classic 1992 convertible that had been given to her as a high school graduation present from her father. He had labored over two years to restore it to pristine beauty.

Not until she had driven around the corner and out of sight did Shubel regain his composure.

A little embarrassed and a little disheartened, he knew that it would be a while before he would recover from the encounter. For him, Wish McGuire was everything good that life could offer him. Somehow, he had to find a way to get her attention and turn her glance toward him. It would be a problem that he would work on during the course of his work every day until a solution came to mind.

He pulled out his wallet to assess what cash he had on hand, got in his pick-up and drove away. Two minutes later he stopped at a convenience store for a six-pack of beer before heading home. On his way out the door he ran into Jack Llewellyn who had just pumped gasoline into his old pick-up truck.

"Shubel, how's it going, son. I see you got your truck looking sharp tonight," Llewellyn started. "I hope everything's going okay for you these days."

"Mr. Llewellyn, hello," Shubel said. "Everything is going okay, sure." The front door of the convenient store closed behind the young would-be lover as he shifted his carton of beer from his left arm to his right arm.

"How is work going for you?" the projectionist asked.

"Oh, fine. Sometimes it gets a little wearisome driving a garbage truck. I mean, it ain't real romantic, you know," Shubel explained with some seriousness. "But every now and then I'll come across something interesting that people throw away and tells me something about their life."

Llewellyn grinned because he liked Shubel and because he could see a little wisdom inch out of him from time to time for someone so young and rough around the edges.

"Take for example, today," continued Terhune with a relaxed self-interest. "I was picking up trash at those Village Square Condos and I saw on the ground some scraps of paper. There was a plane ticket to Blue Ash, Ohio, and a hotel reservation and a map."

Llewellyn waited for him to continue, but he just stopped as he apparently was thinking about what he had found. So, the old man decided that a prompt was necessary. "Well, who did all of that belong to, Shubel?" asked Jack.

"Why, it belonged to Mr. Carlisle," he answered. "Heck, I didn't even know he was out of town lately."

"Well, I guess he comes and goes," speculated Llewellyn. "I suppose he has to be *somewhere*."

"Yeah, and I found a note to him from someone named Helen. She wrote good luck talking to somebody about his daughter," Shubel responded. "Does he have a daughter, Mr. Llewellyn?"

A crinkled forehead and squinted eyes became the countenance of the older man whose mind was engaged in a problem-solving sequence. But nothing made sense. "No, Shubel," he mumbled slowly almost to himself, "he may have a son, but he doesn't have a daughter that I am aware of." Llewellyn paused and then asked, "Do you still have the letter, Shubel? I'm just curious."

"Oh no, sir. I wadded it up and threw it in with the rest of the trash. We ain't supposed to keep anything that's in the collection."

With the conversation dying a natural death, the old man decided it was time to pay for his gasoline and it was time for Shubel to do whatever it was that he did on weekday summer evenings. They exchanged farewells as congenial acquaintances who lived in different worlds but in the same small Wisconsin town.

Eight hours later, Jack Llewellyn was just coming out of his early morning shower and making ready for his day. His immediate focus was scrambled eggs and fried ham in the same skillet over an electric range burner. The coffee was hot and ready and strong.

Standing over the stove, he cracked a couple of brown eggs and poured just a little milk over them as the butter sizzled in the skillet. His hands reached the counter, gently folded a handful of ham slivers, and slipped them into the same frying pan. A comforting crackling noise accompanied the aroma of daybreak breakfast. The sound of hot toast popping up from the shiny toaster on the counter completed the meal preparation.

Sitting at his kitchen table the projectionist ate slowly and with satisfaction. As he did, he looked over to a picture of Julia and his heart was troubled once again. But there was no choice but to continue on with whatever his life was going to be. He still had David regardless of what Carlisle may initially envision. David would always be his son no matter what the DNA claimed.

It occurred to him that if his life's love was gone forever maybe he could reunite with someone else in whom a closeness once existed. Perhaps it was foolish, but he had very little to lose, in any case. He decided to give it some thought. There was no rush and it gave his mind something of a diversion from his loss of Julia. After all, if he was problem-solving one issue of the heart, it gave him relief from the ache of another.

In his lifetime, Jack Llewellyn had loved only one other woman. He had met her while in college and before Julia's arrival into his life. She had no equal in beauty and intelligence and he still loved the memory of her. As with his wife, he fought Carlisle for her affection, as well. Neither man won her heart because there was no evidence that one existed. But that dissuaded neither the promising new lawyer nor the doctoral candidate in those early days. Both were young and perhaps a little naïve. Eventually, both suitors were given their walking papers. For Jack's part, he surmised that her gentle, but insistent, dismissal was the language of politeness and that she used it to discard a worn-out relationship.

Even so, there was a time when the young coed was the wind and earth and life itself. He had loved her, then, and still did now, but in a different way. Now, he loved her more as an ideal than as a real person of flesh and bone. Whatever missing pieces his memory could not provide, he filled in with imagination. That is the way with an old love that is nearly, but not quite, forgotten.

Was it possible to love two women from different times at the same time? For Jack, it was an unequivocal yes. And for years he had the physical existence of two vastly different women as proof positive of such ambivalence. Although he dearly loved Julia, there remained his conflicting longing for someone else, even now after all of the years.

In any case, he did not know where she was or if she had married or what kind of life she had lived or if she had changed. He only remembered the college co-ed and that he loved her a lifetime ago. It never occurred to him that she might have died. Until recently, death was not a reality of which he gave much thought.

After firing-up his desk-top computer he waited patiently for the Windows logo to appear and assemble itself before him. He clicked onto a new tab away from his homepage and typed her name when the browser prompt became evident.

No dice. Nothing. His luck ran out before he even began. He got a list of ten different sites with French wording and images of unrelated and peculiar interests. But nothing that came close to what was of interest. He tried Facebook and was left with similar results. No soap. Nothing.

Then, it occurred to him that the university might be able to locate her. But he wanted to wait a day before calling the Registrar's Office in Madison because he wanted to be sure of his plan. A long-time friend still worked there and might be willing and able to help him find an alumna. It would have to wait because Llewellyn wanted a day to think, to evaluate what it would take to renew the relationship, to calculate the odds of success, and to assess the risks that were inherently involved.

In the meantime, Llewellyn washed the breakfast dishes and exchanged his pajamas and robe for a collared shirt and khaki trousers. He exited his second story flat, climbed into his old Ford pickup and headed for the quiet running water of Schweiss' Ford. Of all places, there he could think and organize his thoughts about what he was about to undertake. It was more than a trip down memory lane, it was a chance to recapture a friendship when he needed one most.

Only the Grass Suffers

He stayed there on the boulders that separated the Sweetwater and the Outagamie creeks and watched the waters collide in quiet inevitability. The currents would have their way even when they became one and traveled farther down-stream in a blended consonance.

After a while, Llewellyn rose to his feet and gingerly traversed the boulders to the shoreline. Again, he climbed into his truck and drove slowly away. This time he drove over to the Catholic cemetery where the freshly mounded grave of Julia was covered by decaying flower arrangements.

He stood there for a lengthy time thinking about her. With a sense of finality, he whispered to himself Macbeth's soliloquy of Lady Macbeth's death. After another moment, he silently mouthed a prayer of his own making and his eyes burned with salty tears. Still, his life had to continue on. Really, what other choice was there?

"Good-bye, Julia," he said quietly. And then in utter understatement and while staring blankly at the dirt mound before him, "It was nice knowing you." And then he realized that there was nothing left to say, no other prayer to recite, and no other passage to quote. He turned to feel the warm summer sun on his face and placed his heart on an imaginary shelf for future reference and maybe even some use.

ON WEDNESDAY JACK LLEWELLYN HELD HIS TELEPHONE in his hand and tapped the number of the Registrar's office in Madison. His ear accepted the whirl of ringing as the invisible transmission lines did their magic and connected him to another disembodied human voice for an early morning call. Summer session was in full operation and the university was very much in business.

He had said his farewell to Julia and had given himself a day to think things over and he decided that there was little to lose and much to gain. So, he began his journey is earnest.

"Registrar's Office. How may I help you?" offered the young female on the other end of the line.

"Hello, good morning," began Llewellyn. "May I speak to Dr. Eric Faircloth please. This is Dr. John Llewellyn calling."

"Just one moment, Dr. Llewellyn. Please hold the line," she returned.

Llewellyn held his telephone to his ear and thought how strange it was to refer to himself as "doctor" after so long a time in retirement from academia. Still, he had collected many friends during his lengthy career as an English professor and film historian. He had managed to avoid campus politics and had published just enough to maintain a respectable tenure. His textbook entitled *Film and Novel: A Comparative Analysis of Two Art Forms* was still used in both novel and film courses.

"Jack, it is good to hear from you," exclaimed Faircloth as he came on the line. "How have you been, my friend?"

"I am fine, Eric. It is also good to hear your voice," Llewellyn countered. "I know you are busy with the summer session so I'll be brief. Would you do me a favor and locate an alumna for me?"

"Sure, Jack, I can do that for you; but you can't ever tell where you got the information," cautioned Faircloth.

"Yes, I understand, Eric. You have my word on that. I would like the current address of a young woman who attended the university around the time that we did. So, you may have to go back in your records quite a ways to find her," explained Llewellyn.

"It doesn't make any difference, Jack. All of our records are in the computer database. Give me a day's time to get back to you. What is the name?"

"Larae Savignac."

DURING THE LATE AFTERNOON ON WEDNESDAY JACK received an e-mail message from Eric Faircloth. He had checked his inbox just before he was about to leave for the January-Wabash Theater. As he anticipated, his old friend did the work in journeyman fashion and provided the information in a timely manner. His message was brief and on target:

> *Jack, here is the address that we show for Larae Savignac. We have been sending her alumni literature at this address for a few years and we have received transcript requests from her on a couple of occasions, so the address is probably still current. We do not show a telephone number or e-mail address associated with her name.*
>
> *2900 Fairy Chasm Lane*
> *Blue Ash, Ohio*
>
> *Good luck with your search.*
>
> *Your friend,*
> *Eric*

That was good enough for Jack as he decided that a road trip would be in order. If one is to start a new life with an old love, he had to get there first. Of course, coming unannounced was problematic. But he was retired and his part-time work at the theater was mostly a fill-in position with both flexible hours and flexible days. Besides Santosh Pulvermacher was not only his boss, he was also a friend. Sandy would work around his absence for a few days.

Then he stopped himself as blood rushed and circulated from heart to brain and back again. *Blue Ash*, where had he heard that name before? Of course… he heard it from Shubel Terhune in front of the convenience store earlier in the week. It was the recent destination of Michael Carlisle. What business did *he* have there?

Selecting a new tab on the internet, Llewellyn type on his keyboard "BLUE ASH, OHIO." He saw that it was a suburb of Cincinnati.

After a day of pain between his ears the old projectionist came to some disturbing conclusions. Carlisle had gone to see Larae. What other business could there have been for him in Ohio? But, why? Was it for the same reason that he was contemplating? If so, the old bastard had a head-start on him and that was something that he could not allow. This time, he would wrestle away their contested first-love. He may have lost Julia, but he could still regain Larae.

Llewellyn waited until the following Monday to leave Cottage Grove for the Cincinnati area. After all, the weekend was profitable to the January-Wabash in terms of both ticket revenue and concessions and it was important that all went smoothly. The younger employees would be under less stress mid-week as opposed to the weekend, so Jack stayed through Sunday night. Even though he was only part-time his time was valuable to the movie theater.

Because he hated airports and the human compaction inside metallic tubes soaring 35,000 feet above the earth, Jack drove to Blue Ash in a rented Ford sedan. There really was no way that his old Ford Ranger pickup could make the trip and he did not own a car. In any case, driving up to the doorstep of Larae Savignac in an ancient gravel road-worn truck was not the image that he wanted to convey.

It was a long day's journey, yes, but other than going through perilous Chicago, it was an easy drive. Civilization existed north and south of the Illinois metroplex. Therefore, once through Chicagoland, he could enjoy the sunny flatlands of Indiana all the way to the green hilltops that welcomed him at the Ohio border. And then into metropolitan Cincinnati that contained the beautiful suburb called Blue Ash.

At the end of the day and across all of the miles Jack Llewellyn was tired and sore and cranky. He needed to relax for just a short while and then get some sleep. He arrived in Blue Ash and checked into his hotel and did just that. It was Monday night and the cool summer evenings of Cottage Grove gave way to the hot and humid nights of southwestern Ohio.

By now, he was having second thoughts about arriving at the doorstep of an old lover that he had not seen for decades – and unannounced, no less. Was she married with children? Divorced? He was just now beginning to worry about the reception that he might receive. He thought to himself belatedly, "No matter how old we get, we still don't know how to behave." He began to regret his impulsiveness and the long-distance journey on which he had embarked. Already, he wanted to go home.

After arriving at his hotel in Blue Ash, he unloaded his gear, checked-in, and relaxed in his room for a while before going for a long walk out into the warm and humid Cincinnati suburb. He stopped in a local pub across the street from the hotel and enjoyed a couple of beers before heading back to his room. There, he studied the map that showed him the road called Fairy Chasm Lane.

The next day brought sunshine and heat by mid-morning and Llewellyn was not used to the humidity of the river town. He brought out his GPS and tapped in 2900 Fairy Chasm Lane. In seconds, he was on his way out of the parking lot with one hand holding the steering wheel and the other wrapped around an insulated cup of coffee.

On the outskirts of Blue Ash, he found the narrow road of asphalt that had shown the way for his long-time nemesis earlier in the summer. As the sedan approached the address shown on the GPS screen Llewellyn became more and more perplexed. This was no residential area.

He steered his sedan across a narrow bridge that announced Kazareen Pass and continued on until he saw that the road brought him to the entrance of a great property. In fact, before him there appeared a massive stone residence accompanied by smaller buildings set on an expansive piece of wooded landscape.

The address on the iron gate matched the address that Eric Faircloth had given him. He stopped the car at the property entrance and looked blankly at the sign that read, "St. Rose of Lima Convent." Llewellyn did not understand. Did Larae work here? Did she live here? He had hoped that his old friend Faircloth did not make a clerical error and give him the wrong address. He had driven such a long distance and he had trusted his former colleague.

Llewellyn drove through the entrance and up toward the gray stone building until reaching a small parking area meant for visitors. He got out of the car and walked slowly to the front door while surveying both the building and grounds with no idea of what to expect from the residents inside. But he steeled himself in his desire to find Larae after making such a great effort, so he approached the large door and placed his hand on the door bell button and waited.

Momentarily, the large door slowly opened and gave way to the sight of an elderly nun dressed in blue habit and white trim. She wore a white apron and held a soiled rag in her hand. It was clear that Llewellyn had interrupted her morning chores.

"Good morning, sister," he greeted with a measured politeness. "I am sorry to disturb you. My name is Jack Llewellyn. I was wondering if Larae Savignac lives here. If so, I would very much like to see her, if that's possible."

The old Daughter looked at him cautiously and decided that he seemed harmless enough, so she said, "Wait here." And she abruptly closed the door in his face. And so the weary traveler stood uncomfortably on the front stoop of the convent and waited without the benefit of hospitality. He waited nearly twenty minutes for a sign of welcome or acknowledgement or even life. But on this morning, there was none of that. He almost considered to pound on the door out of frustration when he heard the sound of the door being unlatched and watched it slowly creak open for a second time.

There, before him, the opened door revealed the body of another Daughter of Charity with the face of Larae Savignac.

Chapter 16

STRIKE ONE

On early Monday morning, the Business Manager and Union Steward of the Boot & Shoe Workers Union Local 555 announced over the public address system at the Cottage Grove factory that an organized work stoppage was to officially begin at 10:00 a. m. The company office manager burst into the communications office and grabbed the microphone away from Dirk McGuire and turned off the P. A. system control console. The Irishman gathered his lambskin briefcase, walked through the doorway left open by the flummoxed office manager and with a measured cadence walked out the front door and onto the parking lot that was adjacent to the old brick building.

At exactly ten o'clock in the morning, every piece of equipment, every machine, every computer, every motor, and every tooling device throughout the three-story plant was de-energized and sat quietly dormant. Every motorized rolling door, fan, and light fixture was turned off. Every forklift and truck was abandoned. Every union employee left his or her station, gathered personal belongings and walked out onto parking lot in visual solidarity and loyal obedience to Dirk McGuire. Three hundred strong with a mission to break an Indian from the North Woods of Wisconsin.

Tony Fedoryshyn stood next to Dirk McGuire inside the bed of a metallic blue pick-up truck. With bull-horn in hand the lawyer slowly shouted, "Ladies and Gentlemen, please collect a picket sign from the red van across the street and walk on the public sidewalk only.

"You must move your vehicle off of the company parking lot and onto the street," he continued. "Remember, this parking lot is private property and right now you are trespassing because of the work stoppage. You must stay on the public sidewalk carrying your sign. Thank you."

The union membership complied gaily with intentional good humor. It was a pleasant summer day with plenty of sunshine and the exciting notion that they were not having to work that day gave them a sense of play. The realization that they could not provide for their families would come later.

With an entire parking lot emptied, because Local 555 members were no longer employees, and picket signs in hand, a raucous band of strikers began its long day's protest at the front walkway of the Coppaway Shoe Company. A second set of revelers closed off the back entrance to the warehouse and loading docks so that no materials could come in the plant and no products could leave. These measures precluded attempts by any scab laborer to apply for a job and any union contractor or supplier to deliver any materials for manufacturing.

For the next few days, only management employees were allowed to pass the picket lines. Dan Joda was escorted by two uniformed policemen as verbal attacks were littered at him with every step he took; however, the office manager and her staff were allowed entrance without incident or harassment. With tangled logic the union members looked at the secretaries as merely innocent bystanders performing office functions necessary for the shoe factory to exist until the strike eventually ended.

ONCE AGAIN SHUBEL TERHUNE SAT IN HIS FIRE-ENGINE red Chevrolet pickup outside Danbury Café waiting for Wish McGuire to appear after a long day of work. He had showered and shaved and paid for a haircut in which even Dirk McGuire would have given his approval. Shubel was fortified with the determination of Terhune generations to solicit the attention and eventual affection of Wish McGuire.

The young waitress eventually exited the café a little after nine o'clock with a tired expression washed across her face. Her golden hair seemed a little matted as a result of a long day of smoke and grease that permeated from the back kitchen. Grease stains dotted her crinkled blue uniform. She looked more than ready for a well-deserved hot bath and a cold drink.

"Hello, Wish – I mean Kathryn," he said with just a little bravado and an engaging grin as he stood erect next to his truck. "I've come to take you home."

This time Wish needed a ride home. A friend had dropped her off at the café because her car was being serviced at a gasoline station across town. She was about to call her friend when she noticed the red pick-up outside of the restaurant.

"Okay, Shubel, you can take me home. Thank you."

He opened the door of his truck and helped her in and gently closed the door behind her. Walking around to his door he noticed that she was watching. He stepped lively and climbed in to start the engine. He smiled as he turned the ignition key to the right.

They drove for a while without words and then he asked about her and if she liked her job. She told him it was fine but she would take some classes at the junior college in September. Some day she would own a flower shop and have plenty of money.

They arrived at her home and he turned off the engine and turned toward her as he sat behind the steering wheel.

"Thank you very much for the ride," she said demurely. "I know I must look bad. I probably smell like grease and food."

"Well, let me see," was the reply and Terhune scooted quickly over to her side of the cab and placed his body against her and smelled her neck. "No, you smell sweet to me, Wish. I'm sorry. I have to get used to calling you Kathryn."

"It's okay, Shubel. You can call me "Wish." My dad wouldn't mind it if someone special in my life called me that.

He held himself there against her with bold abandonment and she at first was taken aback. But she did not stir, she let him stay as long as he wanted. She simply forgot that she was tired and hot and dirty. He turned her chin so that they were face to face and then he kissed her and they melted into each other for a long time.

THE PICKETERS MARCHED AND MARCHED SOME MORE IN front of the three-story brick edifice and at the rear of the building. Refreshment vendors arrived after a couple of days and did a brisk business in offering bottled water, sandwiches, and mandarin orange ice cream push-ups. In the beginning, it was a festive atmosphere because there was hope and optimism about a strong employment future with generous wages, clean and safe working conditions, handsome medical benefits, and a 401K for their children's sake. The union was strong and resilient and failure was not an option.

TIME PASSED FROM DAY TO DAY AS SHUBEL AND WISH saw each other on a regular basis. She asked varied friends for a ride to work knowing that Terhune would be taking her home in a shiny red pick-up truck. Their relationship developed during that August and suddenly the summer nights were more pleasant than in any time during their young lives.

Wish was never taken directly home after work. Before arriving at her front door at midnight, she had been at the January-Wabash or at Suzy DeSoto's or at Schweiss' Ford or at the city park or at Shubel's apartment. It was clear to the both of them that they had become "involved." It was equally clear to Dirk McGuire that his daughter had fallen in love with Shubel Terhune.

This was not particularly bad news to McGuire. Kathryn was of legal age with a good head on her shoulders. To him, Terhune was a hard-working fellow, reasonably intelligent, who came from a modest background. The Terhunes were strictly blue-collar down-to-earth people and Shubel would likely end his career as a Public Works Director for the city. As much as anything else, Shubel's shorter haircut and the absence of a ponytail endeared him to the old Irishman. In short, Dirk was beginning to warm up to the idea of Shubel Terhune.

On weekends the three of them sat at the kitchen table over coffee and doughnuts that Wish had purchased at the delicatessen out on Highway 61 near the interstate exit. Dirk didn't much care for the pastry; Shubel's sweet tooth was satisfied until morning's end.

"The strike is going well enough, I suppose," said McGuire. "But there is no movement with the Indian and Dan Joda is of no use to either side."

"These things take time, Dad," consoled Wish. "You've been through this kind of thing before."

The Irishman looked up from his coffee cup and at Shubel. "You belong to a union, don't you?"

"Yes, sir," Shubel said. "I belong to the public employees' union."

"Good boy," McGuire replied and he softly pounded his fist on the table and rattled the coffee cups. "That means you won't collect any trash because you would have to cross our picket lines."

"No, sir, I wouldn't cross the picket lines," Shubel said with sincerity, "unless, of course, my boss said I had to."

Wish stared at the love of her young life with bewilderment. Her father's face flushed red and he spoke slowly. "No, Shubel. You don't understand. You can never cross our picket lines. It would be extremely dangerous for you to even say that you might." The Irishman grabbed the forearm of Terhune and squeezed brutally while he spoke his words.

Chapter 17

BLUE ASH REDUX

She had aged gracefully, so she was still beautiful. She still possessed an air of obvious intelligence and her demeanor suggested respect and deference that was both expected and deserved. All of this Jack Llewellyn clearly saw instantly in Larae Savignac. And, in quicksilver realization, he saw that whatever influence he had once held over her decades ago was long gone and forgotten.

"Jack, what are you doing here?" she exclaimed with more concern than enthusiasm. The old friend from long ago ignored the question and made a mental note of the emotion.

"Rae," he started and stopped with a quiet affection. "I cannot believe it's you. I am so very glad to see you again," he said slowly. "I had no idea that you were a sister," he mouthed with a good measure of incredulity. "Please forgive me. It just never occurred to me that you would have joined an order," he continued to stammer. "I mean you never expressed the interest."

After the required lengthy awkwardness, Savignac broke the spell of her old acquaintance. "Jack, first of all, it was a rather long time ago since we knew each other," she explained. "In those days I probably didn't have much interest. But people can change, you know."

"I have been with the Daughters of Charity for over thirty years and I am the Mother of St. Rose of Lima Convent" she expressed with a good deal of pride.

"Yes, Rae. People can change."

Why don't you come inside and compose yourself," she invited. "You really do look a little pale."

With that, Sister Larae opened the door wider and led Llewellyn into the large foyer and through another set of doors and eventually into the anteroom where she had sat with Michael Carlisle just a couple of weeks earlier.

Llewellyn was shaken by the discovery that his long-ago love had optioned for a different kind of life. For a moment he regretted his impetuousness in making the journey to Blue Ash. But he acquiesced to the spirit of the occasion and decided to make the best of it. If he could no longer envision a renewed love affair with Larae Savignac, perhaps he could cultivate a long-distance friendship.

"Rae, I've come to see you because I have been thinking about you lately," he began. "Frankly, you have always been in the back of my mind since our college days.

"Sometimes life gets in the way of two people and they lose touch. Careers and families consume each of us," he offered. "But I have never forgotten you and I was hoping that you would still think well of me."

"Of course I do, Jack, but it has been so long and our lives have gone in such different directions," Larae interrupted. "It was my understanding that you married. Does she know that you have been trying to find me?"

"We were divorced several years ago, Larae," he countered. "I lost her a long time ago to someone else." The old projectionist looked down at his hands as they rubbed and scraped against each other. "I believe you know Michael Carlisle."

Savignac relaxed back into her chair and gave an understanding sigh. She remembered with clarity the consummate enmity of the two men who loved her in the yesteryears of her youth.

"Do you mean to say that Michael Carlisle came between your wife and you and broke up your marriage?" was the obvious question.

"Yes, Larae," he answered. "But that was a long time ago. Like you, we all had to get on with our lives the best way that we could. The point is I could never forget you."

For his selective convenience and not to cheapen the purpose of his coming to Ohio in the eyes of Larae, Llewellyn chose not to disclose the recent death of Julia. For him, this was not an opportunity to rebound from tragedy; rather, it was a getting on with life such as life would allow. In any case, the situation had changed dramatically and now it was a matter of playing out the hand that was dealt him. Immediately, he realized that God had other plans for the "other woman" in his life.

"No one wants to go through life alone and you were the only other woman that I ever loved. So, I thought I would take a shot. You know, find you and see how you are and see if you wanted to spend some time together.

"At this point and seeing the way things are, I just thought I might as well be honest. This looks like a fairly hopeless situation with you being a sister and being the Mother of the convent and all."

The projectionist refused to look at his once-upon-a-time lover. Instead, he memorized the pattern of the area rug to avoid eye contact with the good sister. For her part, Larae just sat there motionless with an open mouth until he finished. Her eyes were slightly glazed because of the faint memory of a long-ago love that had been forgotten and was now undefinable. That memory arrived quickly and quietly and she felt its warmth. But the memory was ephemeral as was its inherent will to survive. It was all gone and could not be recaptured. Just for a brief moment it was there, and then it was gone forever. Both sadness and relief visited the heart of Sister Larae Savignac.

"Jack Llewellyn, that is very sweet of you to think of me in that way. You flatter me with how you remember me and the effort that you made in coming to our convent."

She got up from her chair and said, "Let's take a walk, Jack. The garden is beautiful at this time of year."

Jack stood in front of Larae with a weak smile and without comment. She led him through a door in the far corner of the anteroom and into what was obviously a library where a small group of young novices were sitting at long wooden tables that were lacquered and polished all the way to shimmer. They walked by quietly and no novice looked up from her studies as they passed. Finally, they exited the library at the opposite end of the room and found themselves in the lush green flower garden of St. Rose of Lima.

They took a stone path that weaved its serpentine way through lush green ferns and shrubs. A myriad of flowers boasted fluorescent oranges and yellows and pinks and blues along the way on both sides of the walkway. At the end of the path, small trees encircled and shaded an aged fountain that drove bubbled water into a small basin. From there the water circulated and swirled and recycled itself.

"This is my favorite spot on the grounds," Larae said smiling and then turned toward Llewellyn. "It gives me privacy and peace and I can even think out loud if I want to." There was still that girlish charm that the old man remembered and he like seeing that it was still there.

"I have my own spot back home, too," he contributed. "It is at a place where two creeks come together. When they become one, they make a comforting rushing sound because together they are stronger and faster than when they run alone.

"What is that called? When the whole is greater than the sum of its parts?" He paused to think and then, "Oh, yes, it is called synergy." Then, he looked straight into the eyes of the woman before him. "It is like when two people come together, Larae. They become greater than the two separate individuals that they were before."

This time Larae avoided the eye contact. She turned and walked carefully away into a narrower and unpaved path away from the water fountain. Llewellyn followed closely behind her. Presently, they came to a clearing from the bushes and brambles and the green rolling landscape of the grounds appeared before them. In the distant the main building was still visible, but the out-buildings and maintenance sheds were cloaked by the small trees that stood at the garden perimeter as sentries to the vibrant flowers and lush bushes.

Nearby, there was placed a stone bench that allowed one to survey the landscape while in the solace of reflection. The couple sat down together and remained quiet for a short while before Llewellyn spoke.

"Tell me, Larae, when was the last time you saw Michael Carlisle."

For her part, Savignac had to think and decide quickly how to answer the question without having Jack pursue the conversation further. But, other than an outright deception, there really was no way to circumvent the impending subject of the lawyer's recent visit.

"Why Jack, why do you ask that question?" was the lame reply.

"Because I know that he has been to Blue Ash recently. And why else would he come here unless it would be to see you," he said matter-of-factly.

The sister realized there was no hope in avoiding the conversation, so she acquiesced to the inevitable. "Yes, he came to see me a couple of weeks ago," she admitted. "Like you, he came to see an old friend and, like you, that's all there is to it." She went on, "I assume it's just a coincidence that you both came within a few days."

"I am curious as to why he wanted to see you just now," Llewellyn wondered aloud.

Larae looked hard at her companion and without smiling said, "I really don't know, Jack. If it bothers you that much, maybe you should ask him." Her tone of voice was now without softness and there seemed to be some impatience forming with her words.

And then she thought it would be safe ground to bring up the approaching parish festival in Cottage Grove. "He said that you will be having a parish festival later in the summer. That sounds like a lot of fun for your community."

"Yes, it's the biggest community event of the year for our town. As a matter of fact, it is my understanding that your archbishop will be attending as a way of recognizing our parish priest," he explained. "You may not know it, but our pastor came from the Cincinnati area. Perhaps you know him… Father Timothy O'Halloran."

"Yes, Jack, I know him. He is a young priest with a very bright future in the Church. Apparently, he is well liked by everyone who knows him. Most importantly, the archbishop is a close friend of his family here in the area."

The projectionist decided to change the subject. He reached into his right back pocket for his wallet and unfolded it slowly to remove a photograph.

"Look here, Larae. Here is a picture of my son and daughter-in-law. We were getting some ice cream and they announced that they are going to have a baby."

The sister took the photograph and looked at it out of politeness. "That is wonderful news, you are going to be a grandfather." She looked at the picture a second time, placed her index finger on the pair and asked, "Who is this woman and little girl in the photo?"

"That is Mikaela Rhea and her daughter Lauren," he replied. "They are dear friends of mine. Unfortunately, her husband is a law partner to Michael Carlisle."

Savignac looked at the photograph again; then, she stared at it at great length. After a while it seemed to Jack that she had become mesmerized by it. "Rae, what's wrong? Now, you're the one looking pale."

Tears swelled in her eyes and gravity pulled the wetness down both cheeks until she covered her face with both hands. Still, she tightly gripped the photograph. The old man shifted closer to her on the stone bench and gently placed his arms around her in utter puzzlement.

"Rae, what is it? What has affected you so?"

For a moment she was without words. Then, she regained her composure and braced herself away from Llewellyn. "I'm okay, Jack. I'm sorry. It's just that I am so happy for you."

If Jack Llewellyn did not buy into the reply, he did not let on. He had not come to Blue Ash to give grief to someone that he cared about long ago and even now. Although his mission had become a failure at the moment he met her at the front door because of what she had become, he still loved her and wished her no harm. But there was something very much awry with both her reaction to the photograph and the lameness of her explanation.

"I am sorry, Jack, for the drama. I haven't been feeling very well of late," she said as she stood. It seemed to Llewellyn that she was unsteady on her feet and that she had not yet decided if she was going to faint. Then, she corrected herself to an upright stance and took his arm. She wanted to return to the convent with slow and measured steps.

"Let's go back, Jack. I'm feeling a little weak and a glass of water would be very nice."

Llewellyn held her as they walked back along the narrow and unpaved path toward the water fountain. Midway back the summer thick foliage shielded them in any direction from campus buildings and walkways. Their privacy assured, Larae stopped to rest and Jack turned her to face him. He wrapped his arms around her and lowered his head and kissed her on her mouth and felt her body move only slightly and only for the briefest of moments. Then, he released his mouth from hers and he looked into her eyes for the reaction.

She looked up at him, not angry as well she could have been. She was a Daughter of Charity and deserved a reverent and respectful distance even from those who in any way loved her. Rather, she was satisfied, almost pleased, in spite of herself. She allowed it because she did love him once, long ago, in a faraway place, when they were quite young and full of themselves.

"Why did you do that, Jack?" she asked with the blush of confusion, but without alarm.

His hands remained pressed against her arms just below the shoulders and he looked into her eyes with a gentle sincerity, "Rae, I just wanted to do that one more time, maybe for old times' sake. Maybe because I know that I will never be able to do it again. For the last several days I haven't thought much about anything else. That, in itself, was probably a mistake."

She considered his answer for a moment and accepted both the gesture and the explanation without complaint. "Okay, now you've had your kiss. But what's the point because that's all that there is," she said. "Whatever we had, it was a lifetime ago and we are so very different now. Not just me, Jack, but you, too. Let's remember the past – always; but let's not relive it."

With that, the projectionist had given them both their last chance and, of course, there was no real chance to be had. They both remembered how it was to love one another, but they also knew that that love was in the past where it belonged. Now, the only important thing was that they still liked each other and would go their separate ways as long-distance friends. If he was earlier compelled to intimacy to satisfy a memory, he now was obligated to respect her religious station.

They walked past the water fountain with her holding onto his arm for both support and friendship. They entered the library where the novices had been before but were now gone. They walked across the room and through the door to the anteroom where they had first sat.

She motioned him to sit again. He did so.

"Jack, do you think I could keep this picture. It would mean a great deal to me if I could."

He was surprised and he did not understand, nevertheless Jack agreed that she could keep the photograph. He had copies. "Of course," he hesitated, "if you like."

"Please don't ask me to explain. It would take a lifetime to do so. Let me just say that it will keep you in my thoughts and prayers every day of my life. That would be okay, wouldn't it, Jack?"

"Yes, Rae, that would be very fine."

What Llewellyn understood was that it was not his image in the photograph that moved her. Although she may still have some feelings of affection for his memory and their time together, he didn't really believe that she still loved him. So, he knew there had to be someone else in the picture that was of profound interest to her. Now was not the right time to give the question the effort it deserved. He knew that his time of departure was fast approaching. He would have to think about it during his return trip home.

They sat for a while longer facing each other. He extended his hand and she accepted it. For a long time she allowed him to hold her hand and no words were spoken by either one. It was as if they enjoyed each other's company for one last time and then they needed to say good-bye again.

"You should go now, Jack. Thank you for coming. I loved seeing you again. Thank you for thinking so well of me for all of these years. Please pray for me."

Although Llewellyn did not want to leave, he knew that he had to leave. Larae Savignac belonged to a greater life mission than to provide companionship for him. Moreover, there had been too much of their lives spent apart. Their life together never existed so there could not be anything to show for the sharing of it. It was neither good nor bad. It was just two young lives intersecting and then taking diverging roads.

"Good-bye, Rae. I will always love you."

They both exited the anteroom and walked through the great foyer to the front door where a young novice in blue garb and white apron was on her knees scrubbing the tile floor.

Llewellyn turned to Savignac one last time and said with the young novice not watching but surely listening, "Good-bye Sister Larae. Thank you for seeing me and showing me around your beautiful campus. It was very much appreciated."

"Good-bye, Mr. Llewellyn. Please have a safe journey home."

With that, Larae opened the large front door for Jack and he walked through the opening to begin his way back home and back to his life. After closing the door on her past, Savignac walked over to an adjacent window and moved the curtain slightly to watch the car drive away with no apparent haste.

Once again the Mother of the Convent, Larae briskly walked across the foyer to a set of stairs that led to the second floor living quarters of the sisters. She entered her modest bedroom and walked over to her chest of drawers, pulled out the photograph from her religious habit's pocket, and placed it into a small wooden box within the drawer.

She looked down at the photograph for another moment as if to memorize the faces. Larae knew the name of her daughter and now she knew her face, as well. For the first time in her life, she realized that there was also a granddaughter. "Be happy my dears. May God take care of you because I cannot. That is not who I am."

With the keepsake safely hidden among her private possessions, she closed the small box, slowly pushed in the drawer, and went downstairs to continue her motherly duties. It was a life that defined not only her womanhood, but also her very existence.

ON WEDNESDAY, HE WAS HOMEWARD BOUND AND BACK on the shimmering flatness of blanched concrete that crossed Indiana. Llewellyn began to think about the photograph that Larae wanted so sincerely to keep. What had moved her so? Whose face did she want as keepsake? It was time to problem solve.

He tried to think logically.

David would be of no interest to her because she did not know him and his mother was Julia. Jana was from a solid family in Algonquin, Illinois, so Larae would have no history with her. Although she may have wanted his photograph as a keepsake of her previous life, her demeanor toward him did not suggest a passionate interest. She accepted his visit warmly, but there was no inference that she wanted him to remain in her life. Who was left?

Mikaela and Lauren... Mikaela.

Now, he reasoned further. First, Michael Carlisle had come to Blue Ash just a short time earlier. Why? Second, Shubel Terhune had said that he found a letter that mentioned a *daughter*, not a son. The letter was supposedly written by someone named Helen. That could have been Carlisle's sister, Helen Quesnell. And, third, Larae became so emotional when he showed her the photograph and named those in the picture. What conclusion would explain all three elements?

The retired professor was now skimming over the interstate highway system as fast as practical to push through the approaching vast wasteland of courtesy and civility known as Chicagoland. Eventually, the Ford sedan made its escape across the Illinois-Wisconsin border as his thoughts returned to Larae Savignac.

Llewellyn accepted the idea as soon as it arrived. It came with neither introduction nor fanfare. The concept fell into place with a quiet ease. It was a simple solution and an elementary conclusion to the intricate problem that resided within the Blue Ash convent. Mikaela Rhea was the daughter of Larae Savignac. And with the addition of the Rheas' daughter, the family of Michael Carlisle continued to grow retroactively.

While racing north to Milwaukee and then west to Cottage Grove, Llewellyn wrestled with what to do with what he knew to be true about Carlisle. He would enjoy the devastating public shame that would be brought upon the lawyer, but that same scandal would affect people that he cherished. The sordid disclosure could take on a life of its own and its aftermath would be uncontrollable. Additionally, David's true biological origin would surely be revealed, as well.

Still, the *threat* of disclosure might serve Llewellyn's purpose just as well as the actual deed. After all, effecting mental suffering onto his old enemy would give him some satisfaction. But, at all costs, there must be no danger to the well-being of either David or Mikaela. David was his son in all ways other than DNA and he had always been most fond of Mikaela. He had no intention of hurting either one of them.

It was approaching evening as he gently tapped his brakes in exiting the interstate highway. The western sky was red with the setting sun's fluorescent brilliance. As he turned south and into the city limits of Cottage Grove, he removed his sunglasses and slowed to the first stop light. The town was quiet and he was very tired after a long day's drive across the Midwest.

By the time he arrived home it was too late to return the rental car. He could do that the following morning. After that he would call Helen Quesnell, Carlisle's sister, and ask to have a pleasant conversation with her over a cup of coffee at the Danbury Café.

Chapter 18

QUID PRO QUO

In a few short weeks the St. Matthew's Parish Festival would consume Cottage Grove and the surrounding region. Committees had been formed long ago and now preparations were being made for the most celebrated weekend of the year. Part of that preparation was the one hundred patchwork quilts that were sewn by the Ladies Sodality. These quilts were either to be auctioned off during the course of the weekend or to be given as prizes to winners at the bingo games.

As a long-time member of the group, Helen Quesnell was a veteran quilter with a fine reputation for color selection and pattern arrangement. She was almost out the door for yet another early morning quilting session in the basement of the rectory when her telephone rang from her living room.

She walked from her front door back to the end table and picked up the receiver, "Hello," she said. On the other end of the line Jack Llewellyn spoke pleasantly and asked if she would have a cup of coffee with him later that morning to talk about her brother and a mutual friend who lives in Blue Ash, Ohio.

The old woman bristled at hearing the voice on the other end of the line because it was the voice of her brother's mortal enemy and there was no good that could ever come from talking to him.

"I am not available this morning, Mr. Llewellyn. I have a previous engagement," she said. "Really, we have nothing to talk about." There was a coldness in her voice and she felt the tenseness of her body as she held the telephone to her ear.

"Mrs. Quesnell, we have a great deal to talk about," countered Llewellyn. "I've just returned from St. Rose of Lima Convent, so I am not looking for answers to any questions. I already have the answers. What I want from you are reasons not to expose your brother for the low-life train wreck that he really is. I think our town deserves to know what kind of man is practicing law on the town square."

The face of the woman had turned ashen with the comments of Llewellyn. Her brain churned furiously and decided with dispatch to acquiesce to the meeting. It did not seem there was much choice in the matter. "Very well, Mr. Llewellyn. I will meet you at Danbury's at ten o'clock." With that, she set the receiver down and walked out her front door. She decided to attend the quilting session as usual. But she would do so with a preoccupation of Jack Llewellyn and a gathering fear for her family.

IN A CORNER BOOTH AT THE DANBURY CAFÉ, JACK SAT slurping his coffee as he waited for Helen. She was slightly late because the Ladies Sodality meetings were always eminently social gatherings and it was all she could do to leave the quilting session earlier than usual.

As she entered the restaurant, Llewellyn raised his hand to gain her attention and she saw him immediately. He exited the booth as she approached and sat down again after she was settled.

"Thank you for coming, Mrs. Quesnell," he began.

There was no response from the woman. She gave him only an icy glare. "You don't need to thank me," she replied. "I did not come because of an invitation. I am here as a response to a threat."

Llewellyn was stopped from continuing as the waitress brought pad and pencil to take the woman's order. "Nothing for me," Quesnell offered and Wish McGuire filled Jack's cup and then almost went away, but didn't. Instead, she sat the coffee pot down on the table and looked straight at the sitting man and hoped for a straight answer.

"Mr. Llewellyn, you know Shubel Terhune, don't you," she asked demurely.

"Yes, Wish, I know Shubel fairly well."

"Well, what do you think of him. I mean, do you like him very much?"

Llewellyn paused momentarily for effect more so than to actually consider the question. "Yes, Wish. I think Shubel is a very fine young man. He works very hard and he is talented when it comes to cars and trucks. He would be welcomed at my dinner table anytime."

"That's what I thought," the blonde said and then pensively walked away. He watched the young waitress walk toward another table that served as a hub for other patrons and admired the form fitting uniform that she wore because he was not dead yet.

He turned to his company with some effort; there was business to conduct still in spite of the intriguing scenery of Wish. "As you know, I have an enduring contempt for your brother." Llewellyn gave thought to what he was saying, "We have been at odds ever since we've been adults. We have fought over two women and, to some extent, even a son. Next, it will be a grandchild."

"Yes, I know," she said. "And now you intend to ruin him by revealing a secret so long kept that it would hardly do you any good." She hesitated so she could swallow. "But here is what it would do, Mr. Llewellyn," she continued as she leaned forward in the booth and lowered her voice just a little. "It would devastate Mikaela and her daughter and turn that family upside down. And it would destroy my relationship with Mikaela, as well. I've raised her from baby to woman, would that be fair to me? And for what? So you could even some kind of score with my brother?

"If he won the heart of Larae Savignac and Julia and you lost both times, perhaps the fault doesn't lie in him but in you," she argued. "I'm not saying he is a better man than you, only that he is a different kind of man. I should think that you both ought to respect each other for your differences, let it go at that, and get on with life.

"You both went to see Larae, but you both went for very different reasons. I don't know what your reason was, but Mike went to make sure that Mikaela's life would remain intact because Larae may be asked to come to the parish festival this summer. He didn't want that to happen. He was trying to protect Mikaela. What were you trying to do?"

She was a force greater than her brother. Jack did not know this before about Helen Quesnell, but he certainly knew it now. He had unceremoniously decided that he liked her very much, in spite of her rough handling of him. Perhaps he even deserved it.

She continued on before the old man could get in a word. "Let me explain something to you, Mr. Llewellyn," she started. "There is an old African saying, 'When two bulls fight, only the grass suffers.' That's what is going on with you and my brother. Everybody involved is going to suffer for the rest of their lives because two old fools are too self-absorbed and too hateful to care about the people they *claim* to love."

He sat there and just looked at her and he could tell she was someone that had seen things and had done things and had gone places and had read books in the course of her life. Jack was beginning to realize that there was more to her than the matronly aunt persona that she projected in the Grove. Her opinions were worthy of his attention and he at once realized that she was right and that he was far out-of-line in his implied threat. But he was also a man of some experience, himself, and he knew that the exercise of leverage was a good practice against a bad man.

"Okay, Mrs. Quesnell, I see your point. Your reasoning is persuasive. Just the same, I want something from you," Jack countered.

"What is that?" she inquired.

"It is this… You go to your brother and you tell him about our conversation. After the harsh insulting language subsides, give him this *quid pro quo* offer from me. His secret family in Cottage Grove and his affair with a Larae will be kept undiscovered if he gives up any claim to or involvement with the unborn child of David and Jana Llewellyn. David remains my son and the grandchild will be *my* grandchild.

"Mrs. Quesnell, I'm not trying to damage the people you love or you. I just want to keep what I always have had – my son. And, now, also my grandchild. Tell your brother to leave me alone and I will leave him alone."

She was silent for a moment and she gave the idea some thought. Her brother might accept such a notion if it were presented as if it were a contract of sorts. He would be forfeiting a son that he would never be able to mentor and an unborn grandchild that came from that same son in exchange for preserving his secret family and law partner.

To Helen Quesnell, this seemed to be a reasonable compromise and she hoped that her brother would see the light. "Very well, I will talk to Mike. Someday, I hope you and Mike can end this personal war of yours." Finally, she cautioned, "Maybe there won't be any casualties today, but the longer this war goes on, the better the chance that people are going to get hurt."

MICHAEL CARLISLE SPENT THE DAY AT THE COPPAWAY Shoe Company with its owner, Gordon Coppaway, and Dan Joda reviewing a legal strategy that would out-maneuver the Boot & Shoe Workers Union Local 555. As he was packing his old briefcase with preliminary notes that outlined tactics that would carry out the plan, his cell phone rang with the name of "Helen" being illuminated.

"Helen, how are you? What's going on?"

"Mike, can you stop by the house on your way home. I had a conversation with Jack Llewellyn this morning and I think we should talk."

Thirty minutes later, the lawyer pulled into her driveway, slammed the car door, and pounded briskly on the front door of his sister's house. Within moments Helen came to the door and Carlisle pushed through the entryway with determined force. "What the hell did that ass want with you, Helen?" he exclaimed.

"Mike, settle down and sit down and let me tell you what happened," she implored. And with that she offered a medical advisory, "If you have a cardiac arrest, I will not be able to help you very much."

Slightly amused by his sister's plea for calm, the brother threw his body into the easy chair in the front room of the house while the sister sat straight on a recently reupholstered chair opposite of him.

"Jack Llewellyn has no right to talk to you, especially if the conversation is about me. You don't need to be in the middle of our quarrels, Helen."

"I agree, but here I am, anyway, Mike," she said with some sadness. "He knows about Larae. I don't know how. He has just come back from Blue Ash and he saw her at the convent."

The words took a while to filter through the hard hollow rock that protected the mind of Michael Carlisle, but they did eventually get there with full impact. He reclined back into the easy chair with a reverse slump of the body and stared at his sister. For a long while the house was silent except for the sound coming from the refrigerator in the kitchen as its compressor kicked on to circulate the refrigerant through the copper coils.

After a while, the anger came, but it came this time without words of venom. The lawyer just sat there and seethed. And after a longer while still, Carlisle relaxed because there was no recourse for him. He decided there was nothing for him to do. His worst enemy knew an inescapably damaging truth about him and there would be no mercy shown.

"Well, other than finding out a few details as to how and why all of this transpired, I see no remedy to the situation. Jack Llewellyn has me by the throat. Did he spend the morning gloating? What did he want from you?"

"I am the messenger, Mike. Here is the message: He wants to strike a bargain with you," she replied. "He will keep secret what he knows about Larae and you on the following condition. You not only give up any claim to David, but you must also give up any involvement with the unborn grandchild.

"It's sort of a 'bird in the hand is worth two in the bush' kind of situation, I suppose," she concluded. "You get to keep Mikaela as your secret daughter, but you have to give up your grandfatherly claim to David's child."

Carlisle listened patiently to his sister and realized that the offer was both legitimate and equitable. As always, maintaining the status quo was the great imperative for him. His sister's tone of voice suggested to him that she found the exchange terms acceptable – she even threw in a proverb to make the agreement more palatable.

The brother sat there for a moment without expression and digested what his sister had explained. But it was not a lasting respite. "You know, Sis, the condition seems reasonable and practical and expedient," he concluded with some deliberation. And then he exploded, "However, Jack Llewellyn can go pound sand!"

"Mike!" shouted Helen as she held up both hands to calm her brother. "Please take it easy and let's talk about this."

"I'm not going to be beaten and abused by someone like him, no way, Helen. He's not going to hold anything over my head and get away with it. That grandchild is going to be mine, even if all hell has to break lose for me to make it happen."

"But, Mike, you already have Lauren. She loves you as much as you love her," she argued. "Why jeopardize that?"

"Nothing is going to be jeopardized and there will be no

compromise," he countered. "Llewellyn thinks he has me up against a wall, but I am going to bust down that wall and charge back at him."

Then the lawyer sat forward on the edge of the easy chair and focused on the face of his sister. "Now, listen to me, Helen. This is important. I am not going to agree to the terms. At a matter of fact, I am going to talk to Mikaela and tell her everything."

"Oh, no, Mike, you can't do that. It will destroy everything that we have accomplished. It will destroy what family that we have, both for you and me. You can't be serious."

"Helen, it's the only way to save our family. Let the truth come out. Mikaela doesn't have to tell anyone else about her real mother or where she came from." He thought for a moment, "Of course, she may want to tell Vincent, but that can't be helped and it may be just as well. But the important thing is that they don't have to tell anyone else."

And as an oral post script to his announcement, Carlisle suggested, "Maybe, then, Mikaela and I can have a real father-daughter relationship, out in the open as it should be… and Lauren will know that I am her grandfather."

"What about public opinion, Mike. What about the Ladies Sodality?"

"Nothing is going to change in that way, Helen. Mikaela and Vincent don't have to breathe a word about any of this to anyone."

"What about Jack Llewellyn?" she worried aloud.

"Llewellyn won't push it, "he said. "Remember, he doesn't want anyone to know who David's real father is. And, you know, good ole Jack doesn't like to play too rough in the sand box." And then, "You know, I think he's bluffing, anyway."

"Perhaps, but if all of this becomes public and blows up in our faces… the fact that you have two adult children out of wedlock by two different women and I've been an accomplice to one of the lies… Can you imagine our life in Cottage Grove afterward?" She continued, "You will no longer have a law practice, but you will have an estranged family because they will be humiliated." And, finally, "I will be blackballed by the Ladies Sodality."

"And I'll tell you something else, Mike. I will never forgive you if Mikaela harbors any resentment toward me. I have loved her all of her life. I raised her from when she was a baby. I am her mother, not some religious woman 500 miles away who gave away her baby some thirty years ago."

"I know that and I promise to keep things right. Trust me, Helen."

For now, they sat without further conversation, both thinking about how things could work out, how things might work out. Mike was confident; Helen was frightened. This was how it had always been with the two of them since childhood. Except this time the stakes were as high as they could get.

IN THE EARLY FRIDAY EVENING MRS. QUESNELL BYPASSED the ticket booth at the January-Wasbash Theater and walked into the grand lobby. The teenaged attendant let her pass because of her fast-paced walk and forced frown telegraphed that she was at the theater to conduct business and not to see any movie. The young man had learned early on that when adults were apparently on a mission, it was a good idea to give them a wide berth.

She went through the lobby and made a left turn toward the stairs. With the step cadence of a good soldier delivering a message, she climbed to the second floor and stepped into the projection room with the bravado of her brother.

"Mr. Llewellyn, good evening" she announced herself to the startled projectionist who was concentrating on his preparations for the Friday night shows.

"Mrs. Quesnell, what can I do for you?" He looked a little taken aback because he really did not know what to expect from her.

"Just to let you know, my brother declines your compromise offer regarding your knowledge of the Blue Ash resident," she declared in business-like fashion. "It his intention to pursue his role as grandfather to David's child," she continued without emotion, "and he demands that you allow him that relationship since he is allowing you to remain the father figure to David."

She had practiced delivering the message most of the afternoon to make sure that she would get it right. Her brother had decided that she should not mention his intention to talk to Mikaela about Larae Savignac because Llewellyn did not deserve to know any more information than necessary.

The projectionist was amazed by both the method of delivery and the message, itself. He did not expect Helen Quesnell to be so challenging in her tone. Nor did he expect her to appear in the projection room at the movie house. Regardless, Carlisle had called his bluff – and only a bluff it had been, especially in the wake of his conversation with Helen. He had developed an immediate respect for Carlisle's sister and this conversation did not change his opinion. But, again, there was no need to expose his intentions. Rather, he was more inclined to play out his hand until the game was over.

"Very well, Mrs. Quesnell, if that is the way your brother wants it," he countered maintaining his composure in the wake of her words. He continued his preparations with the opening of 35 mm film cans and placing the reels in order on the work table. "But you may want to remind him that we live in a small community and that his profession relies on the confidence and trust of his clients. Bad public opinion can shake confidence and trust."

The old woman's face paled. She was not use to such conflict in her life. Her brother may have been, but she was not. "Good day, Mr. Llewellyn," she said. Without further comment she left the upstairs of the movie house and walked briskly through the unpopulated lobby where the teenaged boy attendant still kept his distance.

With her role as messenger for both Llewellyn and her brother completed, Quesnell was left with her own thoughts. The truth was that Mike did love Mikaela's mother, but she always looked past him to someone else– or rather in her case, to something else – which held more fulfillment. Larae was both strikingly beautiful and intelligent and had possessed the strength and wherewithal to give her own life a focused, but different, direction in spite of giving birth to a daughter. With profound understatement, Helen thought to herself that she could never understand that kind of women.

Then, her thoughts turned to the young woman that she raised and loved so completely, "My God, Mikaela, what will you think of me and our life together?" It was foremost on her mind and there was no one to turn to for either advice or comfort. "I will just have to wait and see what happens when Mike talks to her," she said to herself. "God help us all if she ever finds her natural mother."

Again, she reminded herself to be a good soldier and trust that Mike knew what he was doing. She even rationalized her position and came to a certain logical conclusion, "No matter what," she assured herself, "Mikaela and I love each other and you cannot throw away all of the years that we meant so much to each other… After all, I *am* her mother."

Later, in the stillness of her kitchen and sitting at the table with a cup of green tea in front of her and the FM radio station playing a soft rock tune, Helen laid down her head on her wrists atop the table and wept uncontrollably.

Chapter 19

INTERVIEW AT JACOBUS

He sat in his black Mercedes on the far side of Scuppernong Drive with the window rolled down. Looking across the street and through the picture window's lace curtain sheers, he could make out no movement, only hazed colors that washed the walls and silhouetted the furniture. Mikaela lived in a beautiful house on a beautiful street in a beautiful town and had a beautiful daughter. It was perfect. Except, of course, it really wasn't, nothing ever is, you know. In a couple days' time, her world was going to be turned upside down.

Carlisle continued to stare across the street for just a little while longer. But he couldn't take it anymore, so he placed the car in gear and drove away quietly without looking again. He decided to see his daughter as soon as possible. It was about time he faced her completely

A couple of days went by before Michael Carlisle decided to talk to Mikaela about her mother. He wanted to formulate in his mind what he should say and how he should go about saying it. It would be more challenging than any closing argument that he ever made to a jury.

He knew there would be family upheaval, maybe even legal implications, that would affect him profoundly. It could get ugly in a heartbeat unless his approach and demeanor suggested kindness and love and deference to both Mikaela and Larae.

It was time to tell the tale and take proactive measures before his life could be turned upside down by something that Jack Llewellyn would say or do before the lawyer had a chance to clarify. His was a defense condition five on a scale of one to five. "I have got to talk to you, Mikaela," he thought to himself. "Before all else, I have to see you to explain." As much as anything else, Carlisle determined that there would have to be an explanation, perhaps even followed by some kind of compensation to pay for an acceptance of how things transpired.

THAT EARLY SATURDAY EVENING IN HIS STUDY, MICHAEL Carlisle sat relaxed in his leather chair, reclining against with hands cupped behind his head. It was early evening and he thought he would take a chance. He sat there and thought through the various scenarios. What if this, what if that? Finally, he decided that he would roll the dice. After all, he could always hang up the receiver if the call went south.

He dialed the telephone number that was branded in his mind. He always remembered it using the prefix. Originally, that is the way she gave it to him and he was very much old school, anyway. He heard the ringing over the transmission lines of A. T. & T. and then a diminutive voice.

"Hello, this is the Rhea residence," the voice announced while offering inquiry.

Carlisle knew that it was Mikaela's daughter. He spoke gently, almost lovingly. "Hello, may I speak to your mother?"

"Who is calling, please?" was the response.

Of course, the lawyer knew that she knew his voice, but he played along with the charade because it was fun for both of them.

"Mr. Carlisle. I work with your father... is she there?" he asked.

"If you work with my dad, why do you want to talk to my mother?" came the rejoinder.

"Well, I also know your mother, young lady," he replied with great amusement. "Would you please tell her that Mr. Carlisle is on the line and would very much like to speak to her?" he countered with a slight tone of endearment in his voice.

For a long time, there was silence. "I will get her for you," the little girl decided and said so. Then he heard the little girl set down the telephone receiver to go get her mom. It was apparent the kid was screening her mother's call.

Carlisle was altogether amused with the little girl. After just a few moments on the telephone, he was reminded that she was very much like her mother. She was both beautiful and business-like. Sadly, his conversations with her over the years were usually of brief duration.

What did Michael Carlisle, attorney-at-law, have in common with a little girl?

The old man waited for Mikaela to pick up the telephone's receiver.

Finally, a voice with the crisp clarity of crystal came on the line in salutation, "Hello, this is Mikaela. Is that you, Michael?"

"Mikaela, good evening my dear. I am sorry to bother you, but I would like to meet you somewhere tomorrow afternoon if it is possible. I have something to discuss with you."

"Well, of course, Michael, but I don't understand. Why

would you want to see me and not Vincent?" she asked. "Should I bring Vincent with me? He isn't here right now, but he should be home soon. He's been playing golf today."

"No, just you, Mikaela, only you," he answered. "Let's meet somewhere private, I want to have a confidential conversation with you without any distractions." He paused, "It is a very private matter that concerns you and I would rather you did not discuss this with anyone, even Vincent."

"I see," she hesitated, "But I don't keep any secrets from Vincent."

"After we talk, Mikaela, then you can decide if that remains so," the old man responded. "In any case, keep an open mind and trust me until tomorrow, please."

"Okay, Michael," she said slowly, "Where and when would you like to meet tomorrow?"

"Let's meet at the gazebo in Jacobus Park at one o'clock sharp."

"And you don't want me to say anything to Vincent?" she pressed.

"Not just right now, Mikaela. Please do this as a personal favor to me, just until after we talk, okay?"

"Okay, Michael," she replied after hesitating, "but only until after we talk."

They both hung up their telephones simultaneously and both were silent in their thoughts. Mikaela could not surmise what her husband's boss could possibly want with her. Carlisle puzzled as to how he would explain a generation of deceit to a woman that he profoundly loved… and feared.

The young woman stood pensively for just a moment and then turned away from the table on which the telephone sat. Her thoughts of the appointment were interrupted by the inquisitive posture of her daughter.

Behind Mikaela stood Lauren in quiet curiosity.

"Lauren, you startled me," she remarked, "I didn't hear you standing there."

"What don't you want to tell Daddy?" she inquired pointedly, "What does Mr. Carlisle want you to do?"

"Only to meet him, dear. Maybe he is planning a surprise for your father," she continued, "I will find out tomorrow. But, please, Lauren, don't say anything to your father just yet. Let's see what the surprise is, okay?"

The little girl looked at her mother suspiciously for a moment, but acquiesced to the request. "Okay, Mom, if you say so, but it seems strange to me that we should keep a secret from Daddy, unless, of course, it really is a neat surprise."

"I'm sure it will be, Lauren. Now, go take a bath and put on your jammies. Your father will be home soon and we will know how his golf game went by the kind of mood he is in."

Lauren Rhea complied with her mother's wishes. The hot bath felt good and she was tempted to lounge in the steaming bath water. Instead, she washed herself to the point of squeaky clean and hopped out of the tub. As she dried herself with a perfectly white towel from the bathroom closet, she heard her father's voice coming from the hallway.

Apparently, he played well this Saturday and was in good humor. His animated voice and her mother's laughter assured her of both a pleasant evening and an early retirement to bed. That is the way it always was on Saturday nights in early summer in Cottage Grove. It was a pretty good deal for all three of them. A few years ago, they had become the perfect family. Of course, that wasn't really true, but they did very well for themselves just the same.

In her tenth year of life, Lauren was having a pretty good year. She was respected by her classmates because of her important job. Her parents were popular in the community and sat in the front row in church. Most importantly, piano lessons were in her immediate future. It was to be a summer of music and an autumn of piano performances.

As much as anything else, though, she sensed that there was some undiscovered treasure on the horizon… that her world was going to change ever so dramatically and she would discover some great secret about her mother. Mr. Carlisle gave her that impression in the urgency of his voice and the way her mother reacted to his request for a *secret meeting*. It was all so very exciting.

Their dinner was a light repast of leftovers. But it didn't matter to any of them. Vincent was satisfied with his game of golf, Mikaela was somewhat quiet but receptive to the conversation, and Lauren was preoccupied with the possibilities of her mother's impending secret meeting with Mr. Carlisle. Their conversation was lively, but not particularly interesting.

That night the Mortician's Assistant slept quietly in her bed next to the open window. The metal screen allowed the smell of the summer to filter through and caress her soft cheeks and tickle her button nose. Her blankets sheltered her warm against the blue coolness of the dark. She slept in perfect harmony with the universe which only a small child of the Most-High God can do on any given night.

THE FOLLOWING MORNING WAS SUNDAY AND THAT meant Mass at St. Matthew's. The early summer sun was bright with its yellow glow. But the air was still cool because it was early in the season. Wisconsin winters are long and harsh, but the summers are sunny, cool and altogether inviting.

Lauren did not mind going to church services because she was pretty much in love with Father Timothy O'Halloran, the Vincentian pastor at St. Matthew's Parish. He was relatively young and articulate and possessed a vibrant attitude that was both engaging and infectious. It did not hurt that he was blonde and eminently handsome.

Generally, his Masses were fast and his homilies were filled with humor and timely lessons. The parishioners liked and respected him and Lauren Rhea was captivated by and enamored with his charisma. She would have applied to become an "altar girl," but the Rhea family attended church only intermittently despite the involvement of both mother and daughter at St. Boniface Grade School. Because of their irregular attendance on Sundays, it was not meant to be that Lauren should serve at the altar of God."

That being the case, Mikaela did allow Lauren to help in the annual parish picnic every summer. It was a good community activity, if nothing else. In years past, Lauren helped out at the "Fish Pond." There, behind a blue wall with painted waves and assorted fish, she would attach toys to fishing lines offered by little children. It was a popular money maker for the Picnic and it was a lot of fun. She worked Sunday afternoons from noon 'til three.

On this particular Sunday, though, Lauren did not pay very much attention to the eloquence of Father O'Halloran. Rather, she spent forty-five minutes speculating about her mother's secret meeting with Michael Carlisle later in the day. It occurred to her that there was not much use in guessing. So, she decided to stealthily follow her own mother to the rendezvous point if it was within walking distance; otherwise, she would have to exercise patience and accept the results of that meeting as her mother was inclined to offer.

After Sunday service was complete the congregation began filing toward the exits. Out the front of church the Rheas proceeded, greeting acquaintances as did everyone else. In the vestibule they approached the welcoming presence of Father O'Halloran.

"Good morning, Rheas. God bless all of you," he exclaimed. Vincent offered his hand in friendship and so did Mikaela. Lauren was mesmerized and flushed with embarrassment. The youthful blonde priest offered both a smile and his strong hand to the little girl. She smiled weakly and managed to look furtively into the ocean-blue eyes of Father Tim.

Lauren was glad that she wore her colorful summer blue skirt. Presently, it was her favorite. Her auburn hair gave an attractive contrast to the crisp white linen blouse that was partially covered by the delicately starched navy frock. It was not her immediate intention to impress the good pastor, but it couldn't hurt for future reference.

AFTER LUNCH THE RHEAS WENT THEIR SEPARATE WAYS. Vincent began his annual rite of summer in cleaning the garage. Every mechanical tool and motorized machine for the proper care of yard and exterior building was evacuated from the winter hibernation of the garage. Moreover, every hand tool, paint can, storage bin, and garden implement were set aside and outside of the outbuilding in which Mikaela was discouraged to enter, save for the occasional soil trowel which was required for the planting of flowers.

Only the Grass Suffers

Mikaela gave explicit instructions to Lauren about her Sunday chores, which included dishes, personal laundry and a walking tour to the neighborhood drugstore to pick up some household supplies. With instructions recorded on paper and her mother gathering the car keys for departure, it became obvious that the daughter would not be able to spy on her mother's secret meeting, after all.

She told her husband that she was off to run some errands in which groceries and lingerie would figure prominently in the afternoon acquisitions. Although he provided sincere encouragement in both of his wife's purchases, he declined to assist in either. It was for him only to claim beneficiary of both.

By 12:45 and with her family properly occupied, Mikaela was in her car approaching the main entrance to Jacobus Park. From a distance, she could see the gazebo that sat as the hub to the city park. Already in the parking lot was the familiar black Mercedes that she had seen parked across the street from her house on more than one occasion.

Three minutes later, she parked her car next to the black sedan. Michael Carlisle motioned to her to join him in his car. She opened and closed her door, locked it and walked around to the passenger side of Carlisle's car. She heard the door lock click open and she pulled the car's handle and slipped onto the front seat next to the old man.

"Good afternoon, Mikaela," he began, "thank you for coming."

He was dressed as casually as she had ever seen him – rough-looking and faded blue jeans and a beige denim shirt with the long sleeves rolled up.

"Hello, Michael," she replied curtly. "What's on your mind?"

"You, my dear, you," he offered. "You have been on my mind for as long as you have been alive," he began. "Now, I have something to tell you. So, please pay attention. This will be difficult for the both of us…"

There was an awkward pause and the lawyer's hand rubbed against and around the steering wheel as he looked forward into the park. He narrowed his focus toward the gazebo. "Let's get out of this car and sit inside the gazebo," he suggested. "It is a beautiful afternoon and we can enjoy the fresh air while we talk."

They exited the car and Carlisle offered his arm to Mikaela. Walking to the gazebo there were no words spoken and Mikaela began to feel uncomfortable with the strange silence of her husband's employer. Finally, they reached the bench within the gazebo and Carlisle brushed off the debris atop its concrete surface.

"Michael, what in the world is going on with you?" Mikaela asked with a good measure of wonderment. "I have never seen you like this. Is there something wrong at the office with Vincent?"

"No, Mikaela. Vincent is a terrific young man and a very good lawyer," he assured her. "I am very glad to have him as a partner." He stopped and it seemed to the young woman that he had gathered some inner resolve to deliver to her what was foremost on his mind.

"What is it, then?"

The old lawyer took and cupped her hands into his and both felt the warmth from each other. The gesture was a comforting one but it also signaled to her some storm had arrived.

"Mikaela, you don't know very much about your parents or the circumstances of your birth," he began. "I want to shed some light on all of that for you and explain some things… so you will understand the way things were and why things happened the way they did."

Instantly, she was mesmerized by the conversation's topic and stared in frozen stillness at Carlisle as he continued on with his narrative.

"You were born in Gills Rock and given up for adoption by a very good woman whose life was meant for something other than motherhood." He stopped briefly to look at Mikaela and then continued. "She gave you up because she loved you and knew that it would be far better for you to be raised by your Aunt Helen.

"You should know that I arranged for the adoption because your mother and I were very much involved at that time and I wanted to help her as much as possible."

"What do you mean you were very much involved?" she asked with some anticipation.

"I mean we were lovers for a brief time."

"What are you saying, Michael?" she urged.

"I am saying, Mikaela, that your Aunt Helen really is your aunt… I am saying, Mikaela, that I am your father."

Without hesitation, she pulled back her hands and placed them hard upon her lap. She became speechless and her fixed expression was one of shock. There was no reply because she was unable to decide on the truth or implications of his words.

In the shade of the gazebo at the center of Jacobus Park, Mikaela Rhea could not think of a proper response. She did not know if she should hug her new found father or strike with the tongue lashing of an Irish sailor. The announcement created an emotional maelstrom.

Eventually, she calmed herself out of self-preservation as much as anything else. "Then, who is my mother?"

Carlisle stood and walked over to the edge of the gazebo platform with his back to his daughter.

"Her name is Larae Savignac. She lives in another state far away."

Mikaela sat quietly again, this time digesting the concept that Michael Carlisle was her father. Thinking about the words he said and what the revelation would imply. Relationships had to change. He was her father. He was the grandfather of Lauren. He was the father-in-law of Vincent.

"Do you mean to tell me that all of my life you knew you were my father but said nothing? You never wanted people to know that I was your daughter? That you had a family in Cottage Grove? For God's sake, Michael, why not?"

He turned to face her as she sat on the bench alone, still looking so beautiful, yet now so vulnerable.

"This is where you have to understand where I was in life, Mikaela," he offered. "I wanted more than a career as a lawyer, I wanted to be a judge in those early years. Your mother and I were only lovers, not married," he explained. "The scandal would have ruined my career on the bench before it even got started."

"So, you gave me away because of a job?" she asked pointedly.

Carlisle had no response in him because she asked and answered her own question at once. His silence was confirmation.

He sat down again next to her and gave explanation. "Mikaela, sometimes there are people in this world who can give only so much. That doesn't make them bad, it just makes them incomplete. Maybe, you should even feel sorry for them. I guess I'm one of those people walking around who have only so much love to give.

Only the Grass Suffers

"You have a right to be angry with me. I know that. But, look at it this way, I have helped you and Lauren and Vincent and Helen over the years. I have not been without some redeeming value to you.

"And I am telling you now, it was out of love that your mother and I gave you away because, frankly, neither of us were prepared to take care of a baby."

"You mean unwilling," she argued.

"Mikaela, parenthood was not an option for either one of us. We're not monsters, we just weren't made for it."

She stopped the conversation for a while to think about the argument that the lawyer was advancing, that neither of her natural parents were equipped for parenthood. She let the words roll around and bounce about in her mind until they settled in like snowflakes falling onto and laying within blades of grass.

Finally, she said, "Baloney."

"What, what do you mean?"

"Baloney, Michael. Either you are lying through your teeth and you are not my father or you gave me away for a job. Or maybe you thought parenthood would be too inconvenient for you; it would take too much effort. Was that it? People don't give up their child because they don't think they would make a good parent."

"People do it all the time, Mikaela," he protested. "Maybe someone is too poor or too young or too infirmed. If people do not have the wherewithal to take care of themselves, and they abhor abortion, then adoption is the best answer, maybe the only answer. Why do you think adoptions exist in the first place?"

Carlisle moved back from Mikaela just a little as a defense measure.

"Look, you have to believe me. I have watched over you ever since Helen adopted you and I have done everything financially to make your life better. Of course, I have loved you. Maybe, not in the way that you would want, maybe not in the way most people do, I can't help that. But I have loved you in the way that I am constructed to love… from a distance and in a measured fashion. I didn't do everything for you, Mikaela, but I did everything that I was able to do."

They paused in their conversation to emotionally rest because they were two people in search of a middle ground. In the wake of all the years that they had known one another and because of those years, neither one wanted to sacrifice the other now. It was as if the young woman checked herself for internal damage and explored what harm had come to her soul.

It came to her that she had survived quite well with the love of her Aunt Helen and the financial support that she imagined was given by the old lawyer. While it was true she had had no normal family, she did have a healthy, loving family life. Perhaps, she thought, she could reconcile the difference between what could have been in a perfect world and what she walked away with in her imperfect beginning.

Finally, she sighed and with a tone of resignation said, "Perhaps, there are times in which we must accept what other people can give us, even if it isn't enough," she said looking at him. "And maybe we can only give back what they allow us to give.

"In a way, Michael, you are right. I do feel sorry for you. You gave up having a daughter and a granddaughter all of these years because you are lacking something inside your soul. I pity you."

From no one else on the face of the earth would Carlisle have taken that comment, except from the person he loved the most. For him it was a crushing moment. For the first time in his adult life, tears formed in his eyes and he wept. His daughter watched him for a while and then began to leave the gazebo platform.

But before she left, she stood above the seated lawyer and asked, "Michael, I have two questions for you... Does Aunt Helen know all about Larae Savignac?"

"Yes, she does."

"What did you mean when you said her life was meant for something other than motherhood?"

Chapter 20

STRIKE TWO

As the dog days of August progressed and no movement in negotiations was discerned, the strikers became less enthusiastic about the monotony of their marching, and so the picket signs were not held as high as they once were. Still, they persisted in their new line of work, that of striking, and became fierce in their loyalty toward one another and their contempt for the old Indian. They would follow the Irishman all the way to hell because they knew that he would get them back again and back to their work safely and with higher wages. Except that some of Local 555 really did not think that way.

After a few days of pounding pavement beneath the summer sun there began quiet rumblings of unrest on the line in the whispers of small group meetings. Every now and then clusters of would-be workers gathered up against the exterior eastern wall and in the shade of the old brick building, lit up cigarettes, and held clandestine impromptu discussions about what they should be doing instead of striking.

It became apparent that fewer workers gathered at morning to collect their pickets and walk the lines. A rumor circulated that a handful of men from shipping applied to the cereal plant and were hired immediately. Other former employees were never seen or heard from again in Cottage Grove. It was said that they moved to Madison to seek employment there.

And so the strike force was diminished in numbers and in volume. Only a handful of picketers walked the front entrance and not enough men and women attended the lines to prevent anyone from the loading docks at the rear of the building. Each passing day introduced fewer strikers at the doors of the shoe factory. Dirk McGuire began to worry, but his hatred for the old Indian was a soothing salve that assuaged his fear of failure.

Day after day Gordon Coppaway noted the diminishing attendance on the picket lines and in his parking lots. For him it was now a race between the strikers acquiescing to his terms and the losing of once loyal customers on a one-by-one basis. It seemed that by the time the strike would end, he would no longer have any customers left. Still, in the back of his mind he held the trump card that was the generosity of Harold Chatham. Beyond that, he had lived too long and too hard to lose to a man that he called "an ignorant mick" in private conversations and on a daily basis.

Harry Glick sat with his back against the cool building bricks and reclined on the warm asphalt of the parking lot and assessed their station. "Ya know, I don't think we got as many people walking the lines as we started out with."

"It looks like it to me, too," agreed Riley Turnbull, who only recently was made foreman of the Cutting & Clicking Department. "I know damn well that some of us ain't showin' up for the work we got to do here on the line." He took another drag on his cigarillo as he leaned against the shaded brick and mortar.

Glick crushed his cigarette butt against the brick and rubbed the back of his neck before grabbing his picket sign for another marching session. He was the foreman of the Closing & Machining Department and a long-time friend of Turnbull. Together, they made life a lot easier for Dan Joda because they were men who knew their trade.

"I heard a group of scabs were applying for work in the Lasting & Making Department," Glick offered. "But I ain't seen anybody come into the plant other than the front-office people."

"Ah, that's just rumor crap, Harry," countered Turnbull. "You hear stuff like that all the time during a strike. That kind of junk is put out for the public consumption to make workin' stiffs like me and you start worryin' and gettin' yellow."

Turnbull threw down the cigarillo and smashed the stub with his foot. Glick handed him a picket sign and they left the cool shade of the eastern wall. "Let's get on with it, Harry. We got a job to do. I sure hope Dirk knows what he's doin'."

"I know one thing, Riley," he whispered leaning closer to the ear of his long-time friend, "if things don't start happening soon, then maybe I'm goin' make somethin' happin' myself."

"What do you mean, Harry?"

"I mean a little blood might make the Indian bend a little."

Turnbull stopped and looked at Glick with alarm but said nothing. The two men slowly walked toward the line that was adjacent to the loading docks. With about a hundred of other brothers of the Boot & Shoe Workers Union, they marched in a long and narrow oval that suggested a continued solidarity, even if it was not entirely so. In truth, there was a waning sense of optimism within the troops. The brotherhood was beginning to blink.

THEY SAT DOWN AGAIN. THIS TIME IT WAS AT A NEUTRAL site so that neither side would command a home court advantage. They decided that neither written nor audio transcriptions would be conducted. This meeting would not be for the record; rather, it was a meeting of the minds, an exchange of attitudes and perspectives. It was a coming together of two divergent forces – management and labor – headed by two strong-willed egos to save a struggling company and three hundred jobs. It was a meeting that was held at farthest picnic table at Suzy DeSoto's Custard Drive-In.

Because of the location of the meeting, the conversation would be limited to point blank efficiency without long-winded rhetoric or obnoxious hyperbole. Rather, the attendees were compelled to say what they had to say with dispatch and a minimum of emotional codswallop. And they had to say it with controlled and muffled restraint because on a warm August afternoon Suzy Desoto's place always had customers coming and going. It was the worst place for such a meeting and it was the best place for such a meeting.

Gordon Coppaway and Michael Carlisle sat on one side of the picnic table while Dirk McGuire and Tony Fedoryshyn sat on the other. All four of them enjoyed their sundaes with quiet satisfaction and with boyish enthusiasm.

Eventually, they had to get down to business with Coppaway reclaiming that he needed to cut the plant's labor forces by one third in order to survive. McGuire wrote on his white napkin the demands of the union which included greater wages, benefits, and working conditions. It was the familiar refrain that they both advanced before and would not yield to the other. Carlisle and Fedoryshyn looked at each other with continued resignation as if they both were cavalrymen headed for the Little Big Horn.

As they reached another silent impasse, a little blonde-headed boy with a dirty face and a baseball in his hand ran past them. He was followed by a smaller red-headed boy with freckles who carried a bat and glove.

The little blonde boy shouted as he looked over his shoulder, "We're not going to play if you don't let me bat first."

The red-headed boy panted his reply with hurried steps not far behind, "No way, it's my bat, I get to bat first!"

"Then, we ain't playing, Red."

They went on their way and after them came eight other boys of similar age and height with frantic faces because there was only one ball and only one bat available for their use that day.

The little boys left the custard stand with a swirling cloud of dust trailing them. From the nearby baseball field they came and did not stop for refreshment at Suzy DeSoto's. For them negotiations were being held while in transit and there would be no peace until a stout solid wooden stick of ash greeted a sphere of cork, yarns, and cowhide. The blonde boy with the baseball and the red-headed boy with freckles did not seem burdened by the eight other boys wailing close behind.

It was a brief commotion that was ignored by the four adults with stomach for neither more frozen custard nor reasonable compromise. And although the disruption was ended at the custard stand, so was the meeting. The

Only the Grass Suffers

four men gathered up their plastic cups and spoons and napkins and disposed of their trash along with any hope of reconciliation.

Chapter 21

BREAKFAST ON SCUPPERNONG

The afternoon stayed warm and sunny. Lauren remembered seeing a cloud earlier in the morning, but an uninterrupted azure blue washed across the sky for the day's remainder. With the assigned laundry in progress and dishes washed and dried, her final duty was a trip to the drugstore to purchase household supplies for her mother. Her father had given her a twenty-dollar bill toward the payment for those items. She was debating with herself if she should return the change or accept the windfall profit that was bound to materialize. Ultimately, she decided not to bother her father as he would still be preoccupied with cleaning the garage. She was pleased with her consideration for her father.

On the way back from the local mercantile and with supplies in hand and the cash windfall in the back pocket of her jeans, the ten-year old walked casually and without much purpose. It was a pleasant break not to have to hurry as was her custom in her daily delivery of death cards around the Grove.

She wondered how her mother's meeting with Mr. Carlisle went. Hopefully, her mother would share the results of that meeting and together they would conspire to safeguard a terrible secret from unknown adversaries. No other children on Scuppernong Drive would be allowed to know what dark secret was held by her mother and her. She would have to devise an elaborate ritual to execute in order to ensure that the secret was safe. Something akin to "crossing my heart and hoping to die" ritual would probably suffice. After all, Lauren felt that her mother was generally trustworthy.

It was late afternoon by the time Mikaela arrived home. She looked tired and red-eyed and very much distracted. She walked quickly into her bedroom without saying hello to her daughter but only offered a weak smile. The ten-year-old stood outside of the bedroom with her ear pressed against the door to listen but heard nothing. After a while, Lauren sensed trouble and decided to leave her mother alone until she seemed herself again. Her curiosity did not extend so far as to test her mother's apparent upset condition on a Sunday afternoon.

By the time Vincent had finished his work in the garage and banged the back door upon entering the house, Mikaela had regained her sense of well-being. To Lauren, she seemed almost back to normal except for the tired expression that still washed across her face. Vincent did not see it because he was not looking for it.

"Hello, babycakes. How was the shopping?" he asked with a casual gladness in seeing her home.

"I didn't get very much accomplished," she replied. "I didn't see anything that I really liked, so I just came home."

Lauren watched her mother, but did not say anything. Secrets could be shared the next day when her father was at work.

They sat down in the dining room and ate sandwiches made of cold-cuts and potato salad made with mustard and mayonnaise. It was an easy and satisfying summer dinner after a busy weekend for all three of them. What conversation there was came mostly from Vincent as he recounted his afternoon in the garage. The light work of cleaning seemed to provide welcomed therapy for the young lawyer after a week of law books, legal briefs, and the occasional human drama of clients. And while the husband did not comment on his wife's pensive state, he did unexpectedly clear the dinner table and wash the dishes with Lauren's assistance.

Mikaela went to bed early that night while Vincent stayed up and read. The little girl laid in her bed and looked out at the moon and stars and wondered what magical secret her mother would share with her the following day. Lauren listened to the quiet until the sound of her father's footsteps through the hallway ebbed, then disappeared.

Mikaela was asleep when her husband came into the bedroom, so there was no conversation to be had – except she wasn't really asleep, there was only a pretense. Vincent was sound asleep after a short while and she laid there with eyes wide open thinking about her father and the woman who raised her and a Daughter of Charity living in Ohio who happened to be her natural mother. Sitting on the park bench inside the Jacobus gazebo, Carlisle had narrated the entire story eventually and reluctantly including the current life of Larae Savignac. She really didn't know whether to laugh or cry. And she didn't know if she should tell anyone what she had learned or just let it go… just let it go… just let it go. After a while, she slept restlessly.

Only the Grass Suffers

THE ALARM CLOCK STRONG-ARMED THE RHEAS TO CONsciousness at six o'clock the next morning. It was unrelenting and forced Vincent to shake away the slumber in deference to a new summer day. It was Monday and there was a formidable agenda of clients to advise before he would be able to sleep again. Mikaela was nowhere to be found until he heard the clanking noises of colliding pots and the subdued sounds of cabinet doors closing from the kitchen. The familiar early morning banging and clatter suggested breakfast was being prepared and would be ready by the time he showered, shaved, and dressed himself. He entered the open doorway to his daughter's bedroom because she was not yet stirring from her nighttime slumber.

"Lauren, Lauren" he said quietly as he gently jiggled and joggled her to wakefulness and reintroduced her to the morning sunshine that cascaded silently through the venetian blinds. "It's six o'clock, my child. Time to get up."

The young father tugged on the string and raised the venetian blinds with vigor and the morning sun flooded the room with light and warmth. The scraping sound of the blinds rising up and the new daylight encouraged the young girl to climb out of bed and her bare feet hit the rug with a familiar soft thump.

She rubbed the sleep from her eyes and headed for the bathroom before her father could assume ownership of the toilet and shower. After a moment, she descended down the staircase and into the kitchen in order to greet her mother and perhaps solicit some information regarding the previous day's meeting with Mr. Carlisle.

"Good morning, Mom," she greeted with both smile and a watchful glance.

"Well, hello, Lauren," was the reply. "How did you sleep, dear?" she asked while preparing omelets over the cooktop for her family.

"Fine." Then, hesitating for only a moment, "What did Mr. Carlisle want yesterday?"

Mikaela could sense the determination in her daughter to know what secret may exist in the wake of her meeting with Michael Carlisle. She realized that Lauren would never let it go. But it didn't matter because Mikaela, herself, would never let it go either. Secrets and lies were never part of the Rhea family culture and full disclosure was always expected regardless of what consequences the situation implied.

"Let's wait until your father comes down to breakfast, Lauren," she said and saying so increased the drama for the little girl. The daughter realized that this was going to be big.

"Okay, Mom," she agreed and sat at the kitchen table with both legs swinging forward and backward in excited anticipation.

By six-thirty Vincent came down the stairs dressed in business casual and with briefcase in hand. He set down the luggage at the entryway to the kitchen and walked over to kiss Mikaela good morning and then his daughter, as well. "Good morning, ladies. It looks like everyone is present and accounted for" was his usual morning greeting.

Mikaela placed the omelets in front of her husband and daughter and sat down next to them. Vincent applied the pepper and ate hungrily as Lauren played with her fork and watched her mother watch her father. After some time, Vincent realized that his wife was not having breakfast but was staring at him with a look of concern.

"What is it, Mikaela?" he asked, "Is something on your mind?" Lauren sat down her fork on the untouched plate and waited for the payoff that was surely to come. But it didn't. Because, at that moment, the doorbell gave announcement that someone was on the front veranda for an unexpected early morning visit.

Without hesitation and with a little relief Mikaela quickly left the kitchen to answer the door. Her daughter also got up from the table and stood in the front room waiting to see who was calling at such an early hour. The mother opened the door and there stood Aunt Helen in her best church-going clothes and obviously requesting entrance.

"Aunt Helen, well, come in." Mikaela said with hesitation. "What are you doing here so early in the morning?"

The old woman entered into the foyer and sat her purse on the small table that stood near the front door.

"I wanted to talk to you as soon as possible, Mikaela," Helen began. "I know that you talked to your father yesterday. He called me last night; he was very upset. Mostly, he was angry with himself in the way he handled things. I didn't want an hour of daylight to pass without seeing you." And, finally, "We need to talk."

"Come into the kitchen, Aunt Helen," Mikaela said, "Vincent and Lauren don't know anything yet. I suppose we should tell them together."

With that, Helen looked past her adopted daughter and toward her adopted granddaughter. "Lauren, good morning, sweet child. Do you have any breakfast for me?"

"Nana!" she cried and ran to her grandmother for a huge hug of mutual affection. "What are you doing here?"

"I've come for breakfast and conversation," Helen said, smiling and looking down at her. "Let's go talk to your father."

They all went to the kitchen and surrounded Vincent as he swallowed his last piece of toast. The four of them sat at the table as Mikaela poured hot coffee for both Helen and Vincent. Lauren was five years away from enjoying a cup, so she settled for hot chocolate even though the summer mornings had become warm.

"Aunt Helen, this is a pleasant surprise," Vincent said with a genuine smile because he liked his wife's mother. "What on earth is going on this morning?"

"Vincent... Mikaela and I have something to tell you that you should know," Aunt Helen began. "Your wife learned of this only yesterday afternoon when she met Michael at Jacobus Park."

Of course, he was stunned that his wife had met with his partner. He had no idea, but it did partially explain her quiet disposition yesterday evening.

"You see, dear, Michael is my father," Mikaela explained. "My natural mother is living in another state. She gave me up for adoption when I was born. And Aunt Helen adopted me and became my real mother."

That Mikaela felt that she was still her real mother made Helen's heart soar with an even greater love and pride than she had known through the years. It was obvious that she had raised her daughter better than she imagined.

Vincent sat at the kitchen table mesmerized by what his wife and mother-in-law were saying to him. Just now, he realized that his senior law partner was also his father-in-law and that Mikaela also had a half-brother in David Llewellyn. Everything seemed to hit him at once. He looked at his wife to see what was shown on her face. It was apparent to him that she was getting used to the idea.

What neither Mikaela nor Helen did share with Vincent and the ten-year old was that the birth mother just happened to be the Reverend Mother in a convent of sisters. Neither Vincent nor his daughter had the presence of mind to ask the woman's name.

Lauren sat there without saying anything, but with her mouth just slightly open. Although her father sat frozen and keenly interested in the conversation, there seemed to be more agitation than excitement in his reaction. In her bewilderment as to whether her parents were glad or sad, she wondered what it all was going to mean for her. What was going to change? Was Nana no longer her grandmother or was she going to have two grandmothers? When would she meet this new grandmother that she had never known?

With the conversation paused and no one seemed to have much more to say, Helen spoke hesitantly, "Of course, this situation is upsetting for all of us, especially for you, Mikaela," she continued, "and I know that Michael didn't ask this of you, but I will." The old woman stopped and with obvious discomfort said, "Nobody in Cottage Grove needs to be any wiser about this situation. We can all continue on as we have always done. This is a family matter and our family has changed only in that now you have gained a father that you did not know you had.

"Mikaela, I know that Michael has explained everything to you. There is nothing else to tell. Can you live with things the way they are, dear? Can we continue on as we have always done – just loving each other and being a family?"

Mikaela looked across the table at Helen and thought for a moment. "I honestly don't know. Right now, I don't know what to think. I know that I'm going to need some time to sort out things."

"Of course you will. Take all the time you need. Call me when you want to talk some more," Helen replied with a compassionate tone of voice. "But remember this... You have always been loved by Michael as much as he can love, and you know that I have loved you since you were a baby and I love your family now. How could you do better than that?"

"Tell me, Aunt Helen, why did you adopt me in the first place? It was always a financial struggle for us over the years."

The old woman took her daughter's hand into her own and looked squarely into her eyes, "Mikaela, because I had a love to give, even if your birth mother did not. That is a sadness for her and a joy for me. Not everyone can give love so freely and not everyone is meant to be a parent."

The three of them sat silently for a while and every now and then a bite of egg disappeared or a muffled crunch of toast was heard or a sip of coffee was slurped discreetly. No one spoke, but each of them tried to measure what it all meant to their lives and to their relationships.

"You know, the strange thing is..." Mikaela started and stopped reflectively, "is that I don't know if everything has changed or nothing has changed."

Again, neither Helen nor Vincent said anything because neither really knew what to say. All Helen could do was to be there for Mikaela to answer the questions that would naturally come. All Vincent could do was to be there to escort her through the navigation of those answers. Lauren was beginning to sense that she was a participating audience and she would probably not be harmed very much. Like her newly acquired grandfather, her priority was maintaining an orderly universe.

Finally, Vincent ended his morning breakfast. "Aunt Helen, Mikaela and I have a lot to talk over, but right now I have to go to work." He folded his napkin, pushed back his chair, and stood to kiss each of the three females good-bye. Grabbing his briefcase, he turned and looked back at Mikaela. She was pouring a cup of coffee for Aunt Helen as they settled in for more time together. Lauren continued to watch the faces of the two women at the table as if to learn her fate in the family drama. It didn't seem like anyone had eaten very much of a very good breakfast.

BY THE TIME VINCENT ARRIVED AT THE OFFICE, COSIE was immersed in typing and organizing and telephoning. Carlisle was entrenched in a discreet conversation with Gordon Coppaway and Dan Joda regarding the on-going strike at the shoe factory. It was a closed-door meeting in which their attention was turned more toward strategy than negotiation. Talks with the union local had floundered and civil unrest seemed like a natural conclusion.

Eventually, Coppaway and Joda left with stern facial expressions and determined steps. Carlisle whispered some clerical instructions to Cosie and approached the entryway to Vincent's office.

"Do you have a moment, Counselor," the old man asked.

"Sure, Michael, please come in," was the quick response.

Before Carlisle could seat himself, Vincent said matter-of-factly, "Your sister came over to our house earlier this morning and, apparently, I have a father-in-law, after all." He set aside some large manila folders to the left side of his desk and sat back to wait for his partner's response.

"Yes, you do. How is Mikaela this morning?"

"She is fine. I don't think she slept well last night, but she seemed better this morning, at least she was a little more relaxed," Rhea replied. "Aunt Helen suggested that we may as well keep the revelation in the family and not share it with the town."

"That was good of her to suggest that."

"But why, Michael? Why hide anything at all? You are no longer on the bench and you are not running for another election anytime soon, so what's the concern?"

"The concern, Vincent, is that I have had two children out of wedlock over the years. How much dirty laundry do you think I can have viewed before I am run out of town?"

The young lawyer sighed with a measure of agreement because he knew that sometimes it was harder to live in a small town where everyone knew your business than in a metropolitan area where anonymity could offer privacy. "Mikaela and I have a lot of talking to do, Michael. Of course, because we are partners, your reputation affects my ability to make a good living for my family," he reasoned. "You've put me between a rock and a hard place. As I said, we have a lot of talking to do in the next few days."

Carlisle could tell that he made an impression on his junior partner, so he let the subject of confidentiality slide by. He didn't want to oversell the concept of keeping the family secret just that. The old lawyer was mildly surprised that Vincent had not remarked about Mikaela's mother being a nun. But then he supposed the fact that Larae was religious made little difference in the long run.

"Now that we are family," Carlisle began, "you may as well know that your family will enjoy a handsome inheritance some day in the distant future." He stopped just momentarily with a glazed expression across his face that suggested some aching reverie. "David will get nothing, though. He is a product of John Llewellyn. This is a great sadness for me." Then, in an instant his face was aglow, "But I have Mikaela and Lauren and you, now. And you know that you have me."

"Yes, Michael, but you don't want anyone in Cottage Grove to know that you have us and that we have you and that we are a family. What kind of family is that?" challenged Vincent.

"We've been through this already," he answered. With his fist pounding the desk of his partner, the old lawyer got up and exited the room without further comment. Even with the acknowledgment of a second secret paternity and the addition of a son-in-law in his law practice, the primary focus in the life of Michael Carlisle was maintaining the status quo.

THAT NIGHT THERE WAS VERY LITTLE CONVERSATION AT the Rhea residence. Mikaela was adjusting to the idea that her father was Michael Carlisle. She worked steadfastly on rationalizing how and why he conspired with Aunt Helen to secure her welfare in the wake of her abandonment by the natural mother. She could not comprehend what kind of woman could not be a mother but could give her life in service to God. She began to feel a desperation to meet and to understand such a woman, especially if it were her own natural mother.

Vincent considered what the old lawyer had said as he connected the reputation of the law firm to the financial stability of the Rhea family. What Michael had said was true – for the Grove to learn of two secret paternities would devastate the firm's credibility by highlighting the old lawyer's robust history.

Lauren pretended to read while really assessing the potential in having two Nanas offering their affection. She was guaranteed the love of one, perhaps she could have the love of two by summer's end. The idea brought excitement to her small-town world without regard to the unforeseen and inherent complications that it would present to her parents.

Once again moonlight washed over Scuppernong Drive with the scarlet maple trees drawing shadows and night shade across the face of the Victorian house. The summer was continuing on and now the nights were warm, but never humid. The little girl slept deeply as now the window air conditioner purred and cycled chilled air across the room and onto her quilt and sheet.

Mikaela and Vincent laid in their bed holding each other and looking at the ceiling fan and listening to the soothing hum of their floor fan. "Did Aunt Helen tell you the name of your mother?" he spoke gently.

"Larae Savignac," was her reply. She hoped that he would ask nothing more.

"Where does she live?"

"Someplace in Ohio, she said," replied Mikaela.

"Do you know anything else about her?"

Mikaela thought for a moment and realized that the conversation should end because there really was no reason for it to continue. Of course, she was naturally curious about her birth mother, but she accepted the adoption long ago and knew that there was little to gain in reaching out to someone who had abandoned her decades earlier. Apparently, the woman found more fulfillment in a religious life than loving a daughter for a lifetime. What would be the point of it all now after so many years? So, she gave the only answer that might suggest the subject's conclusion.

"No."

And then, something that she had not considered happened – something that she wished he had not said…

"I'll see what I can find out about her for you," the husband offered.

"I wish you wouldn't," was the quick reply.

She rolled out of his arms and onto her side looking at the distant wall through the bedroom's darkness. He sensed that she was serious in her reaction.

"But why not, Mikaela? Don't you want to know about her? Wouldn't you want to meet her someday?"

"No, Vincent. I don't want to know about her or meet her, either." She gave up the right to know me when she gave me away. What could she say to me now that would make anything better? What could I say to her? Thank you for throwing me away?"

It took no effort for her husband to sense the pain that she felt. The loss, the rejection, the abandonment, the discarding of a human being. He would acquiesce to her wishes, of course. He rested for a while as he laid on his back thinking about the day's events.

And with that he fell asleep, but she did not.

Chapter 22

LARAE SAVIGNAC

The golden Lexus sedan shimmered through suburban Cincinnati and across the Blue Ash geography. It slowed only as it approached the narrow bridge that spanned Kazareen Pass. With the iron gate opened, the automobile traveled up the driveway and stopped abruptly in the visitors' parking area of St. Rose of Lima Convent.

The priest got out of the car and walked briskly to the convent's front door. Before knocking he took the time to clean his eye-glasses with a soft cloth that he removed from his coat pocket. He was a young archdiocesan bureaucrat who happened to be the personal secretary to Robert M. Czajka, Archbishop of Cincinnati. For the archdiocese, he was the no-nonsense make-it-happen clergyman who made things happen regardless of ambient obstacles. He was a handsome, brilliant, and tenacious problem-solver. All of these things made him the invaluable right-hand man of the archbishop.

After several moments, he returned his glasses to his face as his knock was answered by a young novice with bucket and mop in hand. "Good morning, Father, may I help you?"

"I am here to see Sister Larae Savignac. My name is Monsignor Daniel Carmody. I am with the archdiocese."

"Please come in, Monsignor. I will get the Reverend Mother for you."

The young novice sat down her bucket and mop and walked across the foyer and into the anteroom. After a short while the novice returned and led the priest to the library which was without use at that time. He sat at one of the long mahogany tables and waited patiently for Savignac.

She entered in the same way that the priest had come just a short time earlier. He stood and introduced himself, "Good morning, Reverend Mother. My name is Monsignor Daniel Carmody. I am with the archdiocese."

"Good morning, Monsignor. Welcome to St. Rose of Lima," was her reply.

They both sat on the same side of the table directly facing each other.

"Archbishop Czajka has instructed me to speak with you about an earlier request that you declined," he began. "As you know, the small town of Cottage Grove in Wisconsin is presently the home of Father Timothy O'Halloran."

"Yes, I am aware of that, Monsignor. I remember Father O'Halloran when he was a seminarian here in Cincinnati."

"Then, you also probably know that Father O'Halloran's family and Father O'Halloran, himself, is a very close friend to the archbishop," reasoned the priest.

"Yes, I am aware of that, as well."

"His Excellency has drawn up a list of invitees to the small town's parish festival and you are on that list, Reverend Mother. To show his support and approval of Father O'Halloran, he is asking for one hundred per cent participation by those on that list," the monsignor deadpanned.

Savignac's reaction was delayed briefly, but it was delivered with concreted resolve. "But I have already explained in my letter to Archbishop Czajka that my duties here at the convent prevent me from traveling to Wisconsin." She continued, "Unfortunately, the archbishop will have to be disappointed. I'm sure he is able to understand my responsibilities at St. Rose take priority over a one hundred percent showing in a small Wisconsin town."

"Sister Larae, I can assure you that the archbishop has no intention of being disappointed. You are being instructed to attend the St. Matthew's Parish Festival in September in celebration of Father O'Halloran and out of respect for Archbishop Czajka."

"Monsignor Carmody, I appreciate the facts that Father O'Halloran is from the Cincinnati area and that his family is close to the archbishop, but I have duties to perform at St. Rose and, furthermore, the archdiocese has no authority over the mission of the Daughters of Charity. Only our Mideast Province in Cleveland has that privilege."

"That is true, Sister. However, the archbishop has many favors available to him and people are eager to be at his disposal."

The priest shifted his body position slightly in order to lean forward and speak in a hushed, but strong, tone of voice, "My dear Reverend Mother, you *will* attend the parish festival in Cottage Grove during the first weekend in September. If not, you will no longer have any duties as Reverend Mother to perform here in Blue Ash. This statement is both sincere and incontrovertible and comes straight from His Excellency."

The archbishop's envoy had delivered the message with force and clarity so that there could be no misunderstanding by the recipient. Savignac leaned back in her chair absorbing the intended will of Archbishop

Czajka. The good monsignor delivered the blow with the subtlety of a sledge-hammer and there was no escaping the inevitable. She was compelled to go to Cottage Grove in September. It was as if God in His Heaven had meant it to be so. She complied with the obedience of a loyal Daughter of Charity.

"Very well, Monsignor," she sighed with lowered shoulders. "Please inform Archbishop Czajka that I will make travel plans to Wisconsin in September. May I take a companion from the convent with me?"

Monsignor Carmody smiled and said with gentle deference, "Of course, Sister. You may recall that His Grace has also placed on the list a Sister Elyse from your convent for that very purpose. She may accompany you."

The priest got up from his chair in readiness to leave Savignac when something occurred to him. "You know, Sister, it seems to me that in your file I saw that you are from Cottage Grove. Is this not so?"

"Yes, Monsignor, I am from Cottage Grove."

"Well, then, this should be a homecoming for you. Why would you not want to attend the festival in any case?" was the obvious question.

"Because my life is here at the convent; my motherhood here at St. Rose is all-consuming."

"Do you not have family in Wisconsin?"

"No, Monsignor, I have no family there."

Carmody accepted the answer at face value and continued to conduct his business. "By the way, since the archbishop has sent out the invitations by way of the published list of requested attendees, you should know that all expenses will be paid by the archdiocese."

"Thank you, Monsignor. Is there anything else?"

"No, that is all, Sister. I shall be leaving now. I will inform Archbishop Czajka of your accepting his invitation. He will be very pleased."

With that, the personal secretary to the archbishop took the hand of Savignac into his and said his good-bye. He left without escort to the foyer and through the front doorway. Larae listened to the quiet engine hum dissipate as the Lexus rolled down the driveway and back onto Fairy Chasm Lane on its way back to Cincinnati.

Savignac walked toward the rear of the convent and into the chapel where she signaled a novice for her attention. "Please ask Sister Elyse to come to my private quarters right away." The novice bowed toward the chapel altar and left without comment.

In her room, Larae gently opened her bureau drawer to reveal the photograph that she received from Jack Llewellyn. She took it in her hand and placed it before her eyes as if to give inspection to its contents. "So, my dear Mikaela, it almost seems like God wants me to meet you and your daughter," she mused to herself. "I suppose there can be no other way in this matter. But know this, my daughter, our meeting will test the mettle of who we both have chosen to become." And, then in a postscript moaning, "It frightens me so."

A knock on the door interrupted her thoughts and Larae hurriedly returned the photograph to the bureau drawer and closed it. "Please come in," she invited. Into the room walked Sister Elyse as instructed. She was youthful and capable; moreover, she wore the inviting smile of an admirer of Sister Larae. By all accounts, her demeanor suggested a pronounced kinship toward mother.

"Did you want to see me, Reverend Mother?"

"Yes, Elyse. I want you to make travel plans for the two of us. We will be traveling to Cottage Grove, Wisconsin, on the first Friday of September and return home the following Monday."

"Will we fly or drive, Mother?"

"We should fly, Sister. That way we won't be so exhausted by the time we get there. It will be an exhausting weekend enough."

THE REVEREND MOTHER WALKED TO HER WINDOW AND looked out at the vibrant green lawn of St. Rose of Lima. She loved her life and her home and her work at the convent. She was taken aback at the heavy handedness of the archbishop and the stern delivery of his secretary. But she realized that this was a personal to Czajka and that he took her response personally. Nobody insulted the archbishop without consequence, especially if it meant offending a family friend like young Tim O'Halloran. It was not known if it was the archbishop, himself, that meted out such punishment or Monsignor Carmody who would not allow His Eminence to be disappointed. In any case, Czajka was not to be harmed. Gathering even greater mystique to his persona, it was said that this was the year he was to become a Cardinal in the Church.

Although it was not a foregone conclusion that she would meet her daughter at the parish festival in Cottage Grove, the smart money would be on God's curious sense of humor that would insist they collide into one another somewhere on the festival grounds. Larae could feel life's gear wheels slowly spinning and accelerating to compel a mother and daughter reunion. Whether the reunion brought joy or catastrophe was quite beside the point.

She continued to stare out across the lush emerald lawn and allowed herself the same reverie that she owned for over three decades.

The young woman sat quietly in the waiting room among other women who were showing their pregnancies with what seemed to be a good measure of pride and understandable self-importance. After all, they were carrying new human life within them; right now, there existence had become "two for the price of one."

But Savignac was sitting there in the waiting room only to verify what she had strongly suspected – that she was with child in an untimely manner. So, she waited some more and pretended to read a magazine. But it was only something to hold in her hands and flip the pages every now and then. She was more interested in watching the other women and wondering what their stories were.

By and by, a heavy-set older nurse opened the interior door that lead into a hallway and clearly spoke the name of "Larae Savignac."

Larae looked up from her magazine that she was not reading and slowly stood to gather her purse and jacket. "Here I am," she said.

"Dr. Ligouri will see you now," the uniformed nurse announced.

She was led into a vacant room without instructions other than to sit and wait. Because she had been at the OB/GYN office for a previous examination, there was no need to undress for the subsequent consultation. Still, she climbed up on the exam table in case there was need of further evaluation on the part of the doctor. Eventually, Dr. Mary Ligouri gently knocked on the door and entered the room with chart in hand and stethoscope wrapped around her neck that complemented her pristine white doctor's smock, bluish blouse, and stylish black skirt.

"Good morning, Larae. I am Dr. Ligouri. How are you today?"

"Fine, Doctor. It's very nice to meet you," the young girl nervously replied.

The obstetrician looked down at her chart and then smiled at Larae. "It looks like you are going to have a baby, Larae. Congratulations."

Savignac swallowed hard and accepted the anticipated news with grace and aplomb. It was only a confirmation of something that she already knew to be true.

"Thank you, Doctor. I pretty much thought as much."

"Of course, you are not very far along. I want you to come back in about three or four weeks and we will do a checkup on the baby's progress. Okay?"

"Yes, Doctor. That will be fine. I'll make an appointment before I leave."

"Right now, Larae, everything looks fine and normal. The baby will do very well and so will you."

The young woman made the next appointment at the front desk before she left and walked out of the medical office building and along the street. She was deep in thought in where she was in her life and what plans she should make for her baby that was on the way, a baby that she could not keep. In her heart, her life was meant for something else. Not motherhood and marriage.

In recent times she had made love to two very different young men. They had both loved her and she had loved them both, as well, or at least as much as she was capable of loving. But it was the physical expression of those loves that now burdened her and would always burden her child in the years to come. That was her great sorrow, but her course was set and she would not change that course.

Of the two young men, she knew which was the father. But what was most important to Savignac was the kind of life her baby would live and so she had to make preparations for that life in clear and certain terms. And so she planned as she walked in the sunshine along the busy street and back to her apartment that was located just a few blocks away from the university campus.

SHE CROSSED THE ROOM AND LAID ON HER BED BECAUSE she was emotionally tired. She placed herself down softly with effort so she would not wrinkle her navy blue habit. She knew that she would have to rejoin the convent activities soon so she wanted to still look presentable. Staring at the ceiling, she angled both arms and placed her hands between her head and pillow and recalled a time and place of which she had not given thought for a time longer than she could remember.

In truth, that time was a watershed moment in which the future of her child was set into motion. The decision that she made and the plans that Michael orchestrated gave redirection to the life that was within her body. And now it seemed that God wanted to extract from her interest and add that payment onto the price that she had already paid throughout her religious life.

Over the transmission lines of American Telephone and Telegraph the voice of Larae Savignac suggested a sense of urgency to Michael Carlisle. He knew her well and understood that she was not a frivolous person whose few requests should be ignored.

Only the Grass Suffers

"I don't know when I can get there, Larae," he cautioned. "I have clients to see and a campaign for the bench to deal with."

"Michael, it is important that I see you as soon as possible. Can you come tonight?"

The young lawyer hesitated but knew that he could actually make the trip to her apartment. So, with some degree of reluctance, he agreed to be at her apartment by 8:00 p.m.

"Thank you, Michael," she said and rang off hurriedly.

He ran late because his campaign meeting ran late. A young lawyer who was running for the district court bench against a long-time incumbent has a lot of work to do and he needed all the help that he could get. He assured his supporters that he knew how to return a favor someday down the line.

A half-hour passed the agreed time, Savignac opened her apartment door and allowed Carlisle through the entryway. She welcomed him and they both sat in the living room facing one another. He waited for her to begin.

"Thanks for coming, Michael," she started. "I know you must be very busy with your practice and campaign… But there is something that you should know."

"What is that, Larae. What's going on?"

The natural hesitation of the young woman that followed set a readiness in Carlisle for the delivery of bad news. He was becoming used to the sensation of anticipating bad news. This feeling was the result of dealing with unscrupulous clients.

"Michael, you need to know that I am going to have a baby."

Although braced for impact, the news bulletin hit him hard and his personal mechanics of self-preservation was engaged instantly. At once, the wheels in the mind of Michael Carlisle began spinning and spinning even faster than ever before. There was much to consider. The success of a relatively new law practice, his campaign for the district bench, and the still forming reputation that he enjoyed in Cottage Grove. With all of that now in question, he coolly kept his composure and offered a facial expression of concern for the situation and, to a lesser degree, for the young woman who sat before him.

"I see," he muttered. "Well, I'm sure that you have given this situation a great deal of thought. What is it that you think we should do about it?" He continued, "You know, just a few weeks ago you handed me my walking papers, Larae. What should I do now, take you back?"

"No, Michael, in that regard nothing has changed," she countered. "I will tell you now that I will have this baby, but I will not keep this baby. You should know that for some time now I have decided to join a religious order. The Daughters of Charity. It is my intention to have the baby adopted and then devote my life to God." She looked down at her lap and said quietly, "It must sound crazy to you, but I am not meant to be a mother." And then she looked up at Carlisle, "I am meant to be a servant of God."

Carlisle sat there dumbfounded for the first time in his life. The silence between them and the exchange of eye contact was more than the lawyer could withstand. "Larae, you have never indicated to me any religious fervor. When did this come about?"

"It has been inside of me ever since I can remember," she explained. "But I have other desires, as well. I may have a calling from God, Michael, but I am also human in all other ways... as you know."

He digested the comments of Larae for a moment. He considered her point of view, but frankly did not understand it. But, no matter. He was off the hook in terms of marrying her and accepting the responsibility of fatherhood. His law practice seemed safe and his campaign seemed safe. Those were the important issues in his life right now. If he had actually loved her, it would have been a one-two punch for the ages. As it was, her announcements of pregnancy and religious calling were academic conundrums that challenged both his influence and problem-solving skills. Immediately, he felt equal to the challenge of setting things in order for both Larae and himself.

Still, there were present details to be considered. Michael Carlisle trusted people, but he insisted on cutting the cards. Having control of any given situation that could potentially threaten him was of paramount importance.

"Then I will help you, Larae," he offered. "I will set up the adoption paperwork, pay for all expenses, and contact an excellent OB/GYN."

"I have a doctor already."

"Yes, but all of this must be done discreetly because you intend to enter religious life, Larae. The Daughters of Charity will not look approvingly at you if you have had pre-marital sex and gave away your baby. Discretion and distance are your allies, now. That is why you will need to relocate to Gills Rock in Door County. There, I know people in both the medical profession and in Social Services. Until you leave this apartment, I will hire a full-time nurse to assist you with your affairs."

"Why do you need to be so involved with all of this Michael? You don't need to take charge of every detail."

"I want to have full knowledge of the situation because the baby is mine, too. I will see to its placement in a good home and will help the child financially until it becomes an adult. The closer I am to the people and surroundings of the child, the better I can control how it is raised. We both will want that."

"But Gills Rock is far away from Cottage Grove," she complained.

"But, Larae, the baby will only be born in Gills Rock for the purpose of privacy. After all of the adoption paperwork is completed, the baby will move to the Grove so that I can monitor all events."

"You can make such things happen like that, Michael?" she questioned.

"Yes, and much more, Larae. You can trust me. I want to be part of the baby's life, but only at a distance and only anonymously. You can go on with your religious devotion to God and I can go back to the practice of law and the baby will have a comfortable life. It is in the best interest of everyone, you know.

"One last thing, Larae, and this is most important... You cannot see the baby. To do so would invite a change of heart. Seeing the baby could alter the trajectory of your life. If you are compelled to be a religious woman, then you must not hold the baby in your arms. Do you understand?"

"Yes, Michael, I understand what you are saying. I just don't like it very much."

WALKING OVER TO HER BUREAU, SISTER LARAE OPENED the drawer and removed the picture of her relatives. Slowly, she turned and walked to her bed and sat down. Staring at the images she thought back to decades long ago. With a practiced determination of remaining stoic, she wondered how the young woman had fared in her lifetime. Savignac thought she looked happy and healthy in the photograph. But perhaps it was best not to think about such things in spite of those thoughts reviving in her mind from time to time. This forfeiture, then, was the price of her religious life and her singular devotion to God.

And she studied the man in the picture who had meant so much to her so long ago, yet he could never have had a place in her life. Not then, not now. She traced her fingers along the borders of the paper and again was lost in thought of a lifetime ago.

The telephone rang and rang. Eventually, the young woman had to answer. The duty must be performed so that she could go on to the next step. "Hello," she answered.

"Rae, it's Jack," he began. "I've just finished up with grading papers. I'm free the rest of the day. Can I come over?" *As always, there was enthusiasm in his voice. He loved his job at the university and he loved Larae. Life was not easy for him, but he loved it anyway.*

"Okay, Jack, come over. I'll make some coffee for us."

Thirty minutes later the young assistant professor entered the apartment with a bounce in his step, but Larae avoided the offered kiss and asked him to sit down. Immediately, he saw through the doorway that there was another young woman in the kitchen pouring coffee into a cup. She went into the kitchen and returned with his coffee and she sat intentionally across the room from him.

"Who's your friend?" he inquired.

"She just that, a friend," she answered. "You don't know her. She's sharing the apartment with me and she's going to be a traveling companion for me."

"Where are you going?"

"I'm going away for a few months; and then, I'm going away to another part of the country."

"Rae, what's going on?" he asked hesitantly and with animation. "No kiss hello and a lot of distance between us?

And now you're telling me that you're leaving permanently. What's this all about?"

"Jack, I will make this quick and clear," she spoke with exaggerated emphasis and a little too loudly, "I don't want to see you anymore."

"Are you serious?" he exclaimed. "What are you talking about?"

"I've allowed you to come over so I could tell you face to face. But now... I want you to leave now... please."

"But why?" he implored. "Why are you doing this?"

It was a fair question, but it would go unanswered. Her only response was that she wanted to go a different direction in her life and that she no longer loved him. Further, it was her hope that he would respect her wishes and go away quietly.

The young man sat there not understanding and yet not able to ask any more questions because he had not yet received answers to those he had already asked. Apparently, there was no more conversation to be had from the young woman that he loved. He was being dismissed out of hand and without ceremony or even explanation.

He sat down his coffee cup on the adjacent table and just sat there for a brief time. Finally, he decided that there was nothing left to do but to walk away. He stood to leave. "May I have one more kiss in saying good-bye?"

"No."

He looked at her in utter bewilderment. But he could see that there was nothing to be done and nothing more to be said. As he opened the apartment door and looked back into the kitchen, he still wondered about the other young woman. It occurred to him that she was a confidant and that she allowed for their privacy as Larae sent him on his way without any real explanation. It was obvious that she had given advice as to how he should be shown the proverbial door. But he did not ask about her again. He only looked at Larae before him and said, "Please take care of yourself."

"I will," she replied flatly.

THE KNOCK ON THE DOOR BROUGHT SAVIGNAC BACK from her daydream to her personal quarters. She returned the photograph back to the safety of the small box that rested in the chest of drawers.

Looking toward the door, she said, "Yes, what is it?"

Sister Elyse stood on the other side of the door and spoke through it dutifully. "Reverend Mother, the novices are ready for today's instructions. They are assembled in the library."

"Thank you, Elyse. I will be right down."

Chapter 23

STRIKE THREE

On Wednesday, Gordon Coppaway drove his car through the picket line at the rear of the factory. The strikers let him pass without interference or even comment. After all of the acrimony between management and labor, the old Indian was still respected and still somewhat feared. He parked his car in the now spacious parking lot and walked slowly to the rear man-door next to the loading docks. As he opened the metal door that led into the warehouse area, he turned to look at the strikers. He loved that he hated them; he hated that he loved them. The heavy metal door slammed shut behind him as he entered and vanished from sight.

Sometime in late morning, a Cottage Grove garbage truck gave a turn signal as it approached the rear entrance to the shoe factory. The picket line held its place and waived the truck driver to stop at the parking lot entrance.

"You can't cross the picket line, Shubel," commanded Dirk McGuire as he stood on the truck's footstep and against the driver side door. Looking eye to eye at Terhune, he said, "You're a union public employee. You have to respect our strike!"

Shubel looked at the strained face of Wish's father and then looked at the humanity in front of the entryway to the parking lot.

"But all I want to do is collect the trash, Mr. McGuire," he replied with a hint of panic in his voice. It was a Terhune trait that given a job to do, the job would get done no matter what. Besides, his supervisor would have his head on a platter if he did not complete his rounds. "Don't ya think I should do that at least one more time?" he pleaded.

"Shubel, you get this truck out of here. You're not coming through our picket line," warned McGuire.

For the young driver it had become an immediate conflict between his affection for Wish as shown in his respect for her father and his profound sense of duty that all Terhunes historically felt toward their jobs. The fact that he belonged to a public employees' union was a slightly less compelling argument.

Terhune toggled his glances between the crowd of strikers in front of the imposing garbage truck and the face of Wish's father framed by the open cab window at his immediate left shoulder.

Before words could exit the mouth of the young man, a police squad car pulled up alongside the truck and behind the cruiser was the Audi that transported the shoe factory's general manager. The Chief of Police, two uniformed patrolmen, and Dan Joda all climbed out of their vehicles and surrounded Dirk McGuire as he stepped down from the side of the garbage truck.

The plant manager spoke first, "McGuire, this is to inform you that the strike is over. You need to send everybody home right now."

Dirk looked at him as if he spoke in a foreign tongue. "What are you talking about, Joda?" he fumed. "We've been at this for just a few days and we have a helluva long way to go!"

"Not anymore, Irish," Joda countered. "Mr. Coppaway will be selling the building and property to the cereal plant just like he promised at our meeting on Monday. This morning he reached an oral agreement with the cereal people and signed an 'Intent to Purchase/Sell Agreement.' Oh, and by the way, this is the shortest strike in the history of shoes." Coppaway's lieutenant offered a deadpanned expression so that the nearby strikers could witness his contempt for Dirk McGuire.

"You're a liar!" shouted McGuire. "What about all the new machinery and computers that Coppaway bought? He's too smart to throw away an investment like that."

"That's right, Dirk, he is," he answered. "Fortunately, there is a very nice aftermarket for that kind of specialized equipment. The cereal people are very happy to pay him close enough to the market value and turn around and sell it all for a modest profit as part of the agreement." And, then with a viciousness that he had not shown before, Joda added, "He told you that if you walked out, he would sell the business."

Then, McGuire looked at him, "What about you, Joda? What are you getting out of all of this? You're out of a job, too."

"It's called a golden parachute, McGuire. My retirement starts tomorrow."

With this new information being processed by Terhune, he placed his garbage truck in first gear and slowly pulled away from the impromptu meeting at the back entrance of the property. As he did so, he heard the menacing sound of a gun's loud report, felt the instantaneous crackled explosion of the truck's windshield, and then realized a sharp unforgiving pain deep in his chest.

For a moment he applied the brakes but then slumped over onto the floorboard of the cab. The truck rolled aimlessly toward the brick building and abruptly collided with the exterior wall. A mass of men rushed to open the driver's side door and retrieved a bloodied and unconscious occupant. It was then that chaos ensued in the parking lot.

"Shubel! Shubel!" screamed McGuire as he pushed aside the men who had converged on the young driver. "Somebody call 911!"

He lowered Terhune to the ground with the help of a couple of strikers and laid him gently on the asphalt of the parking lot. Someone ran through the gathering and stuffed a canvas bag of soft rubber underneath his head. But he laid there unconscious and with his chest bleeding.

Near the street the police chief was directing his men to seal off the parking lot and the doors at the factory building's perimeter. A uniformed officer was calling for an ambulance and additional back-up manpower. Apparently, the county's sheriff's department was on the way, as well.

Within minutes the EMTs arrived and administered what medical procedures they could before loading Terhune into the ambulance. The harsh and discordant sound of the siren cleared the way through the chaos. Out of the parking lot and into the street with red and blinding flashes atop the EMT van, Shubel Terhune was on his way to the hospital's ER entrance.

With the strike's lone casualty off site, tempers flared and accusations were thrown in every direction. In a rushed altercation, Dan Joda was pushed back into his car by the police chief and driven away from the fray. By then, the police increased their numbers and shoved back and eventually dispersed factory workers who were just now beginning to become belligerent in their desire to protest.

McGuire jumped onto the back end of a pick-up truck's bed with the tail gate up and against his shins. With his megaphone in hand he turned on the switch, "Listen up, everyone. May I have your attention, please." The crowd quieted down some and the Irishman made the best of the situation.

"Local 555, listen up," he began. "It looks like the strike is over because there ain't no more shoe factory. Coppaway sold the place – lock, stock, and barrel – to the cereal people." The announcement was followed by a collective gasp then groan then silence then emptiness. The once brightly fluorescent and robustly shiny balloon was now feeble and fallow.

He turned off the megaphone briefly to catch his breath and his thoughts. Then he switched it on again. "We should all go home now," he continued. "Each of us has to make his or her own way now. I will talk to Coppaway one more time – maybe I can do some good with some kind of compromise. Maybe it's not too late, yet. We'll see. But you'd better plan on looking for another job, people."

He placed the megaphone down in the truck bed and climbed down onto the asphalt pavement. The men and women of Local 555 stood as a group and watched him walk away. It was obvious that there was no more argument and no more reason to stay if there was no more company at which to work. In a few days they would all learn to hate Dirk McGuire as much as they hated Gordon Coppaway.

Toward the end of the day and under a dusk sky, a handful of strikers and now former shoe factory employees collected pickets and signs that still cluttered the sidewalk in front of the old three-story brick building that once housed their livelihoods. Even with the abysmal failure of their short-lived strike, the former employees maintained a sense of propriety and order. It was their mess, after all, and they always cleaned up their own messes.

Alone and inside the shoe factory offices, Gordon Coppaway sat at his desk and shuffled and then stuffed the Intent to Purchase/Sell Agreement into his attache case. The factory was quiet with machinery and ancillary equipment sitting dormant. All the lights were turned off in the offices except for the banker's lamp atop of the Indian's desk. The darkness and the quiet gave the entire building an eerie atmosphere of abandonment and waste.

The office door opened slowly and Dirk McGuire entered with neither announcement nor ceremony. Coppaway thought to himself, "He came to talk. Okay. let's talk."

"Have a seat, McGuire," he offered. "What can I do for you?"

The union leader sat himself as a weary warrior might have done in the wake of an arduous campaign. "Listen, Coppaway. We've got to come to some kind of agreement or this whole situation is going to blow up in our faces."

"But, McGuire, you still don't get it. It already has." He explained with some slowness so that the idea would be absorbed by his nemesis. "Look, I don't work for my health. Either I'm going to make some good profit running a shoe factory or I'm going to sell the whole damn thing and make a one-time big-time load of money.

"As it turns out, you decided for me when you decided to strike. Now go explain that to your out-of-work buddies who will probably want to lynch you whenever they realize that the both of us have screwed them."

"So, you admit wanting to screw the people who have worked for you for all these years?"

"Not at all. It's just that that's the way it worked out," countered Coppaway. "I'm not going to let a Mick like you get the better of me and you're not going to let an Injun get the better of you. We just naturally hate each other, McGuire… Do you know anything about making cereal?"

"You sorry bastard. You're willing to sell-out 300 families because you're a hateful, bigoted, selfish man with some kind of grudge against anyone who stands up to you."

"Not any more than you, McGuire. In your arrogance, you thought you had enough leverage behind you to make me dance. You used those 300 families to try and squeeze me for some things that I just couldn't afford to give you. And, by the way, do you think those 300 employees ever cared about me or even the company as a whole? I doubt it."

The Irishman kept quiet for a while so that he could collect himself. At this point, there was little more to lose and just about anything to gain.

"Look, Coppaway, let's put aside our personal dislike for each other and see if we can save your company and our three hundred jobs." And then McGuire made his final offer, "What if we compromise and just keep all wages and benefits the same." He leaned forward to complete his pitch, "We can go back to work tomorrow morning making American shoes and boots and you can make the same kind of money that you always have. I know I can talk to the membership and persuade them to go along. What do you say? Can we make that happen?"

"You look, McGuire, I've already made a sweet deal with Harold Chatham at the cereal plant. Hell, even Dan Joda gets rich off of this strike." The Indian sat back in his chair with his arms folded and smiled at his former employee. "Welcome to the wonderful world of corn flakes, Dirk, or any other job you can get. Except, of course, you ain't goin' to be so popular in Cottage Grove anymore."

The conversation concluded with as much mutual hatred as can be endured without spontaneous violence occurring. McGuire got up from his chair and glared at his enemy and the facial expression was returned in kind. Surprisingly, the Irishman walked out of the office without further comment and without physical confrontation or destruction of personal property. Actually, it was a credit to both men regardless as to how short-lived the circumstance.

Chapter 24

THE DEVIL'S ELBOW

The dog days of summer had come and gone and the evenings were noticeably cooler. The leaves were still green, but one could feel that Nature was readjusting her thinking and was contemplating autumnal color schemes. The feel and smell of cooler air circled the town and the citizens were beginning to wear light jackets and an occasional sweater. Summers were gorgeous in Cottage Grove, but they were also short-lived. The first weekend in September was only two days away and that signaled the annual rite of festival.

From the Archdiocese of Cincinnati and at the request of family friend Robert M. Czajka, ten clergymen and ten religious sisters made their way to the small town in Wisconsin to acknowledge the good work and modest achievements of Father Timothy O'Halloran. The archbishop had chosen ten Vincentian priests and ten women from the Daughters of Charity. All twenty had graciously accepted the invitation and all expenses were being paid by the archdiocese.

It was a travel day for the religious contingent from Ohio and from different parts of the archdiocese they made and executed separate itineraries in getting to Cottage Grove. There, in a small Wisconsin town that had nothing to do with either Cincinnati or their important religious vocations, they were going to assemble out of obedience to their spiritual leader. Robert Czajka wanted his godson and protégé to feel the professional encouragement of former instructors and acquaintances from his past. Tim O'Halloran was a solid young priest and he would go far in the Church.

Of the ten Daughters, two were from St. Rose of Lima Convent in Blue Ash. Together they deplaned at General Mitchell International Airport in Milwaukee and walked slowly up the concourse toward the main terminal. Each sister lugged their small carry-on satchel over their shoulder as they made their way down to the lower level baggage claim and carousel number two.

"Here are our bags, Mother," Sister Elyse said as she lunged for the suitcase of her mentor and then her own.

They walked across the sheltered driveway and into the rental car area and Elyse placed the convent's credit card and her driver's license on the counter. Thirty minutes later they were headed west on Interstate 94 toward Cottage Grove.

THE CHARTER JET GLIDED SOFTLY AND LANDED SMOOTHLY on the VIP runway just beyond the western shores of Lake Michigan. Then, tires skidded and screeched and smoked for a short distance down the runway and the twin-engine jet slowed to a moderate speed as it turned and approached the tarmac. Aboard were the pilot, Archbishop Czajka, and his personal secretary, Monsignor Carmody. There were no other passengers; the archbishop believed in traveling light.

Monsignor Carmody procured a rental car as the archbishop waited in a VIP room adjacent to Concourse A. After some time, a porter collected the baggage with a luggage cart in tow, and eventually followed both clergymen to the parked automobile and loaded their gear into the trunk.

Ordinarily, Czajka would arrive in a chauffeur-driven limousine to any and all destinations; however, he was traveling to small-town USA and the less ostentation, the better. Also, his discretion in this way would facilitate a better control of his activities before and after his attendance at the festival. Sometimes, it was easier to be the archbishop when there was less ceremony and fanfare. Although he enjoyed his work and his celebrity status, he preferred the position not be a 24/7 proposition of "pomp and circumstance" in spite of his pledge to Rome.

"Dan, how long will it take to get to Cottage Grove?" asked the archbishop.

"It will be a couple of hours by the time we get there, Your Grace," he responded. "But I have booked rooms in nearby Madison because there will be less notice of your coming and going."

"Yes, that sounds good. Thank you."

"Also, you will enjoy an upscale hotel there, as well. Frankly, there is no suitable hotel for you in Cottage Grove."

Czajka did not react to the last statement. He grew up in a large family that was relatively poor and "upscale" surroundings impressed him less than anyone knew. If he ever had to sleep in a cardboard box, he would make himself comfortable by adapting to the accommodations. There was no self-importance to archbishop. After all the years, his humility still was his finest quality.

WITH ELYSE DRIVING, THE TWO DAUGHTERS WERE

approaching the interstate highway exit to Cottage Grove.

"Keep driving, Elyse," said Larae. "I want to drive to the UW-Madison campus for just a bit."

The young sister kept the gas pedal pressed as the Grove's exit ramp materialized and then vanished from view.

"It's just as well, Mother. Our hotel reservations are in Madison. We can't have you staying at a motel off the interstate."

They drove through downtown and eventually into the university campus. They noted the football stadium and a handful of dormitories and archaic buildings where her scholarship blossomed decades ago. Finally, they reached an area of town called College Hills where she rented her apartment for the latter half of her undergraduate career.

"Stop here, Elyse," she said as she pointed, and they pulled over to the curb of a side street. Larae sat and looked at the surroundings that were no longer familiar, only the intersection, itself, remained the same. Her apartment was no longer there. It had been replaced by a gasoline station and a generic mini-market. She still-stared at the location as if the newer buildings would evaporate and her old stomping grounds would magically reappear. After a while, she sighed and tears bubbled in her eyes and ran down her cheeks. All of which gave instant alarm to Sister Elyse, who was not used to seeing the always-in-control façade of Mother Larae.

"Mother, are you okay?" she asked as she placed her hand on the shoulder of her traveling partner.

"Yes, Elyse, I am fine," she answered. "It's just that I have so many vivid memories about this street. I'm afraid my apartment house is gone now. Like so many things, it has become only a memory, too.

"Why don't we drive to Cottage Grove, now. It will be daylight for quite some time yet. Maybe we can get a quick look at the town after we check-in at the hotel."

"Okay, Mother, its only fourteen miles away, so it won't take us long to get there."

Sister Elyse checked her mirrors and made the requisite U-turn onto the main thoroughfare and they were on their way to the hotel located on the edge of the city.

In their hotel room, they changed from their religious habits to lay clothes because of comfort and casualness. It was their intention to relax as everyday citizens in Small-town, USA, and to assume an affinity with a simpler life. Casually, they drove to the Grove with the intention of dinner and a quick glance at St. Matthew's Church and the festival grounds. However, instead, they would soon find themselves on a collision course with an incredibly memorable evening that included a drunken bar fight and a little jail time for the participants.

AFTER A BRIEF BUT NECESSARY NAP AND SUBSEQUENT shower, the archbishop was ready for the evening drive to Cottage Grove. Both men changed into clean clerical clothing as the journey from Cincinnati left their original attire crumpled and crinkled. Czajka wore his usual bishop wear of black cassock with red piping, red buttons, and a large red satin sash around his waist that offered a tail to his knees. Carmody wore the more understated black suit and shirt with fuchsia piping running vertical down his chest.

The monsignor led the way out of their hotel in downtown Madison and brought around the car to the front entrance beneath the porte-cochere.

"Let's see what this small town of my godson looks like, Daniel."

The monsignor placed the automobile in drive and they traveled east to the Grove.

Thirty minutes later the two clergymen were circling the square for a place to park and they finally pulled up to an empty space in front of The Devil's Elbow Tavern. Carmody turned off the engine and the two men sat looking ahead at their surroundings as if deciding how they should now proceed.

"Well, Daniel, why don't we get something to eat and drink in that tavern?" remarked the archbishop. "It looks quiet enough, not too many people around, so maybe we won't be bothered."

"Very well, Your Excellency," was the response. "I'm up for some refreshment."

"Turn here on Scuppernong Drive, Elyse," she said. Looking down at the piece of paper, Larae read the address that she had acquired earlier in the week while still in Ohio. "Here is it, pull to the curb."

The younger sister complied and the automobile sat silently under a large maple tree. Larae looked out of her window and at the old Victorian house. There was no sign of stirring, but she still stared for the longest time until her partner became restless. Elyse did not understand what attraction the house held for the Reverend Mother. For the second time within the last hour the young sister was asked to turn here or there and then stop to look at a location that signified something from the past of Sister Larae Savignac.

"Is there some history here, Mother," Elyse asked. "Is there someone you know who lives in that house?"

"No, Sister, no one that I know," was the cryptic reply. "We can go now. I've seen what I wanted to see."

Eventually and accidentally, they found the square without the help of a map. They walked around for a short time and then found the front door of The Devil's Elbow. Looking at each other the two women chortled with a sense of adventure, if not mischief.

"Okay, Elyse, we are going to see what the inside of a tavern looks like. What the heck, here we go!"

The two women opened the warped wooden door and walked into the sweet and sour smell of drink and grease. The place was empty and they walked gingerly passed obstacles of tables and chairs and sat against the far wall facing each other at the back of the tavern. Already they realized that they were not so brave, after all. Now their concern was to maintain a furtive and temporary patronage only, then leave as quietly as they had arrived. Fortunately, there were no other customers at that time of day.

The forever unkempt Shadow greeted them agreeably and they ordered hamburgers and colas and he left them alone.

THEY GOT OUT OF THE RENTAL CAR AND CARMODY pumped in four quarters into the parking meter. Looking about the square they noted an absence of activity. It was early evening, that time between the close of business and the beginning of night life, such as it is in a small town. On the square, the only nightlife belonged to the tavern and the movie theater. It was a little too early for either establishment to be at its vibrant best.

And they entered cautiously as the creaky wooden screened door announced their arrival to a not-quite empty saloon. Behind the bar Shadow watched them as they selected a table and sat against the far wall toward the front window.

Shadow approached their table with some reverence as he recognized immediately the clerical clothing of important priests. He looked into the kind eyes of Czajka and swallowed hard because he felt he was in the presence of God's personal friend.

"Good evening, Your Holiness," he began. "May I get you anything?"

"Yes, thank you, my son. Would you have some iced tea on hand?" was the reply from the archbishop.

"Yes, sir, we sure do. I'll get it for you right away." Shadow looked at Carmody with pencil and pad at the ready. "And you, Your Worship?"

"I'll have a Budweiser, thank you," ordered the monsignor who happened to be grinning because of the salutations.

Behind the bar and in the kitchen, Shadow worked tirelessly and as efficiently as he could. Cash McDermott was due back from an errand soon, so help was on the way. He slapped together two hamburgers with pickles and onions on the side and delivered them on a tray to the two women in the back corner of the tavern. He went back to the bar to collect the colas and delivered the glasses of dark soda and paper straw with dispatch.

Then hurriedly he popped open a long-neck bottle of Budweiser and began preparing the iced tea. He hesitated for a moment to think and he reached into a side drawer at the end of the bar and pulled out a booklet entitled, "The BarKeeper's Book."

Shadow paged quickly through the manual until his search reached its conclusion – Long Island Iced Tea. He went to work with a furious intensity because His Holiness was waiting and the Budweiser was getting warm. Vodka, rum, gin, tequila, and everything else on the list was poured into the mixture and shaken. Both the beer and the tall glass of iced tea was delivered without incident with all the pride and professionalism that Shadow could invoke.

"Here you go, Your Majesty." He sat down the tall glass of iced tea in front of the archbishop. And then, "Here you go, Your Honor." And the empty frosty mug and long-neck bottle of beer sat tall before the monsignor. He stood grinning from ear to ear with accomplishment, bowed, and then walked back to the safety zone that was behind the long mahogany bar.

Robert Czajka slugged down the iced tea with gusto and with a raised voice exclaimed, "Holy Toledo!"

"What is it, Your Grace?" broke in Carmody as he cleared away the beer suds from his mouth.

"This tea is extremely good, Daniel, but I don't think it is tea." Czajka took another swallow and rolled the liquid around within his mouth and seemed delighted with the results. "It has a unique bite to it. I don't think that young man gave me the right order, but I'm going to enjoy it just the same."

The archbishop had his secretary order another round for both of them. Shadow was preparing the "iced tea" mixture as Cash McDermott returned from his errand. The owner walked behind the bar to survey the room and its inhabitants. He acknowledged the clergyman at the front of the saloon and noticed the two women sitting at a table near the back hallway. The ladies were in deep conversation using hushed tones and appeared to be utilizing the darkest part of the room for privacy.

"What is the matter, Mother? You don't seem yourself," asked Elyse.

She leaned forward so that her head was just above her plate and whispered, "Don't look now, but Archbishop Czajka and Monsignor Carmody are having a few drinks at the other end of the tavern."

Instinctively, the younger sister ignored the instruction to "not look now" and turned and looked over her shoulder and, sure enough, she saw sitting there the two clergymen gulping down their drinks in large swallows and with noticeable satisfaction.

"Oh my goodness, Mother!" she hoarsely whispered in reply. "What should we do? Should we say hello?"

"Not at this point, Elyse. I think we'd better stay back here and keep being unnoticed." She reasoned, "Otherwise, the archbishop might feel embarrassed." And with a little more concern, "I've already had to deal with Monsignor Carmody. Who knows how he would react. He is extremely protective of the archbishop"

So the two Daughters of Charity turned their attention back to their burgers and colas and waited patiently for "the coast to be clear" so that they could make their escape.

About an hour later the Archbishop of Cincinnati had downed his fourth Long Island Iced Tea that Cash McDermott had personally prepared for "His Highness." The other guy who they subsequently called "His Lordship" finished off a six-pack of long necks and no longer cared how many drinks his traveling partner consumed. It was the end of a long travel day and both were exhausted. Shadow realized this upon noticing the two of them were slumped over their table in an unconscious state.

Unfortunately, the two ladies in the back of the room did not notice this new development, so they did not get up to pay their bill at the bar and make their way out of the saloon while the going was good.

Suddenly, the front door of the tavern opened with undo force as Gordon Coppaway entered abruptly and climbed onto the first barstool in his path.

"I need a drink," he bellowed to McDermott and the bartender looked over at him with slight aggravation.

"Okay, fella. Keep your shirt on. What will you have?"

"Jack Daniels, straight up. Make it a double."

McDermott poured the drink and the old Indian chugged it down in a heartbeat. "Give me another," he demanded.

Cash answered the demand with an efficient response. Coppaway drank for a second time as the front door crashed open again. This time it was the imposing manhood of Dirk McGuire silhouetted against the evening daylight coming through the open door.

He stopped for a moment to study the room. From the corner of his eye he saw the two men in black slumped across their table. No threat there he thought. He walked up to the bar and stood next to Coppaway. Without looking at his enemy, he ordered, "Jameson Irish Whiskey."

McDermott looked at him and got the bottle and poured the shot. The union man drank and slammed down the glass on the bar and looked into the face of Coppaway. Both men wore the face of leathered redness and glared with hatred at the sight of one another.

"Do you understand that you are ruining the lives of three hundred families because of your outrageous greed?"

roared the Irishman. "People's livelihoods are at stake and you threw that out the window today!" He took a breath and continued the lashing, "People have to eat, pay their mortgage, raise their families! You have a responsibility to keep that plant in operation, Coppaway."

The old Chippewa Indian looked at the Irishman square in the eyes with equal contempt, "Not if I can't make any money, I don't.

"What do you think I'm running here in town, a charity? This is business and if I can't pay lower wages with less benefits, then I am out of business. That's just the way it is, McGuire." And then, "But you and your lawyer turned down my last offer, so we all go home with nothing. I got no more factory and you got no more jobs. The factory closes at the end of next month."

"You dirty, stinkin'..." cried the Irishman and grabbed the Indian by the throat and threw him across the room. Coppaway landed atop the table of the archbishop and glass splayed across the floor with the table collapsing along with the two clergymen. All three men laid there momentarily but the old Indian got to his feet quickly and assumed a defensive position with a chair held in front of him.

Cash reached across the bar and grabbed the arms of McGuire from behind, but his hands could not maintain their purchase. The tradesman lunged forward recklessly and Coppaway swung the chair and it crashed against the head of McGuire, sending him pell-mell across the room and onto the floor in front of the two sisters.

Coppaway wrangled with his old body among the splinters of tables and chairs. Pieces of glass and splashes of alcohol surrounded the clergymen as they laid on the floor. In his quicksilver motion to stand beyond that fray and hurl his knife, he miscalculated the exact position of his target, not seeing the young woman who abruptly began to kneel at his adversary's side.

The glint of the Indian's long-blade knife lasted only a split-second before reaching the end of its flight. As Sister Elyse knelt above the vacant expression of McGuire the cold steel entered just below her right shoulder and took her to the floor. She collapsed like a rag-doll and fell on top of the Irishman with a four-inch blade firmly imbedded.

Larae bent over to aid her protégé and shouted to Shadow, "Call 911 now!"

Cash jumped over the bar to see what help he could give to the young woman and Shadow made the telephone call as he was ordered by the older one.

The ambulance and police arrived at about the same time. Because the evening crowd had not yet arrived, the number of onlookers was less than what there would have been otherwise. The EMTs attended to Elyse efficiently and she was out of the tavern and into the ambulance within just a few minutes. The siren blared the entire way across town to the hospital. Larae followed behind closely in the rental car. Before exiting the saloon behind the gurney that carried Elyse, she exchanged glances with Monsignor Carmody but with neither expression nor acknowledgment.

The two adversaries sat at different tables with both heads lowered and hands clasped in handcuffs behind their backs. One uniformed officer stood sentry over and between them, while the other officer stood over the two clergymen as they sat on stools in front of the mahogany bar. Their heads were also lowered above the flat surface of the bar and each priest supported his head with both hands.

Only the Grass Suffers

Cash McDermott had locked the front door upon the order of the police chief, so townspeople that formed in front of the tavern could not enter. However, nothing prevented the gathering crowd from shielding their eyes and peering through the large glass front windows. Tom Pffefferkorn was there with camera and notepad in hand for any information that he could extract for his reading public.

IT WAS EARLY EVENING BEFORE ALL THE STATEMENTS had been taken and recorded by the police. The archbishop and his personal secretary were allowed to leave the tavern by way of the back door in order to avoid public embarrassment. Daniel Carmody removed his black suit coat and shirt and white collar. With only his white tee-shirt and black trousers on, he went around the front of The Devil's Elbow and collected the rental car for his boss. He pulled the vehicle around to the back alley of the tavern and Czajka climbed into the back seat and fell recumbent as the car drove away. In less than forty-five minutes they were back in their hotel room, both physically and emotionally overwhelmed.

Gordon Coppaway and Dirk McGuire spent the night in jail in side-by-side cells and screamed at each other until dawn.

THE NEXT MORNING WAS THURSDAY, THE DAY BEFORE ST. Matthew's Parish Festival was to begin its three-day celebration. Archbishop Czajka was due at the rectory that morning for a breakfast meeting with Father O'Halloran. After a day of visiting on Thursday and a little rest on Friday, their plan was to walk the festival grounds on Saturday night and say Mass on Sunday at St. Matthew's. Then, the Ohio clergy and religious women would travel back home on Sunday afternoon.

Monsignor Carmody called late morning on Thursday to apologize for the missed breakfast and offer the archbishop's best wishes to Father Tim. They agreed that the archbishop could rest all day Thursday and reschedule their time together on Friday.

"Please give the archbishop my very best regards, Monsignor," said Father O'Halloran.

"I will, Tim. We will see you tomorrow morning, eight o'clock sharp."

TONY FEDORYSHYN SHOWED UP AT THE POLICE STATION early on Thursday and bailed-out his long-time friend and client. "Well, Dirk, what a mess!" he sighed with exasperation.

"I didn't hurt that girl; Coppaway did, Tony," McGuire countered.

"No, but you started the physical confrontation that ended up with the girl being stabbed," his lawyer argued. "That makes you equally culpable. And, by the way, that girl happens to be a nun. A Sister Elyse."

The Irishman was stunned to hear both that he was equally to blame and that the young girl was a nun. At that moment he was very glad to know Tony Fedoryshyn. He needed a good lawyer.

MICHAEL CARLISLE SPOKE TO THE CHIEF OF POLICE IN

hushed tones outside of the police station that early Thursday morning. With his right hand on the chief's left shoulder, he leaned in and offered in explanation the delicate nature of his client's position. Moreover, the old lawyer led the chief to infer that it was indeed possible to reverse the decision to close the shoe factory if his client received some extraordinary consideration "in this unfortunate situation." At least, that was the inference that the chief believed.

"You see, Chief, if there are no fingerprints on the knife, there is no way anyone can prove who threw the blade," Carlisle suggested.

"Well, it wasn't the damn archbishop, Michael," exploded the police chief. "What are you suggesting? That I wipe off the fingerprints from the knife?"

"Of course not, Chief. But if there were multiple prints on the knife handle to the point where none were identifiable... Well, then, there would be a much lesser case against my client."

"The fight between Coppaway and McGuire still caused the nun to get stabbed," complained the policeman.

"Yes, but it puts both men on equal ground and makes for a lesser offense and lesser punishment." Then Carlisle tossed up the only ace that he had in his possession. "I know that Gordon Coppaway would be very grateful to Cottage Grove and he may even reconsider the fate of three hundred employees that might still hold jobs."

The police chief stood silent for a moment and watched the slow traffic as it passed in front of the police station. He thought about the stakes and the risk-benefit factors involved and said, "I'll think about it Michael. That's all I can promise right now."

"Of course, Chief. That's all I can ask at this point."

An hour later, Michael Carlisle escorted Gordon Coppaway out of the police station and they drove away with both of them talking to each other in animated fashion.

SISTER ELYSE HAD GONE THROUGH THE EMERGENCY room the night before and surgery was performed on her right upper chest and shoulder. The knife was gingerly removed and all had gone well in repairing muscle and nerve tissues. She rested comfortably in her room and Larae never left her side the entire night and into the morning hours.

During late morning she became aware of her surroundings and smiled at her mentor. "Good morning, Mother. How are you doing?"

"My goodness, Elyse, how are *you* doing?" came the reply.

"My right side aches something fierce, Mother. I don't dare move my body one way or the other. But I'm okay."

"Get some rest, Elyse. I'm going back to the hotel to change my clothes and then I'll return this afternoon."

"Okay, Mother. Thank you." But her voice trailed off and she fell back to unconsciousness.

Savignac looked down at her as she slept because of the painkillers. She loved Elyse like a little sister or, at least, how she imagined one would love a little sister. She kissed the sleeping patient on the forehead and walked out of the patient room.

Now out of the room and away from the hospital's hustle, she was immediately approached and pushed sideways into a small corridor alcove by Daniel Carmody. His face was darkened with a serious expression and his signature resolve of purpose.

"Monsignor Carmody, what are you doing?" Larae demanded, although in a hushed voice. He had startled her and she did not like the stern façade he once again wore in her presence.

"Sister Larae, the archbishop is extremely embarrassed about last night. I think you will agree that it would be best if you went back to Blue Ash today." Carmody argued, "If His Grace sees you at the festival, he will be reminded of a very ugly evening. I will see to the needs of Sister Elyse, of course."

"Monsignor, first of all, I don't agree that it would be best if I went home today." She continued, "Furthermore, I am not leaving Sister Elyse under any circumstances, even if the archbishop is uncomfortable." And then, "Third, take your hand from my arm or I will scream from the top of my lungs – do it now!"

Immediately, the monsignor released his grasp from Savignac and stepped back to a more relaxed stance. "Larae, you have go or His Grace will be beside himself with shame."

"Monsignor, he should be ashamed. It will be good for his soul." The statement was given and received with glares of approaching fury by both combatants. Then, they both regained their composure and acquiesced to a mutual silent civility.

With that Savignac turned her back on the monsignor and down the second floor corridor she walked in measured steps and he could only look after her. She pushed the elevator's down button. She waited, the door opened, she entered and subsequently exited. Out the hospital's front doors she felt the late summer sun on her face. Her dear friend laid in the hospital bed with a knife wound encountered in a bar fight that included a drunken archbishop on the first night they had been in Cottage Grove. None of this was expected to happen. She had not even gotten to the hard part yet – that which she considered inevitable – coming face to face and being introduced to her personal sacrifice, to Mikaela Rhea, her daughter.

Chapter 25

PARISH FESTIVAL

I t was festival time.
The annual rite of summer had arrived for St. Matthew's Parish and Cottage Grove was alighted with a pronounced excitement. It was the singular money maker for the parish and secured financial stability in operating costs for the subsequent twelve months. The Catholics hosted the three-day event but the Presbyterians and Methodists were just as eager to enjoy the year's biggest celebration of beer and brats and rides and games and bingo and large quantities of the finest home-cooked meals in the state. The Baptists were less excited about the fanfare and the Lutherans were purely jealous but attended in sporadic small groups nevertheless.

The annual celebration was held in a farm field just outside the city limits and consisted of an imposing dining hall cluttered with long linen-covered tables and wooden benches, a small once-upon-a-time dance hall that also included offices, storage rooms and areas of display that housed hand-crafted quilts, paintings, artwork and crafts for purchase. Scattered throughout the festival grounds were a variety of canopied booths from which food and souvenirs were sold and carnival-style games were played.

Of course, Bingo was the main-stay of the festival for thousands in attendance. This was the one event game that elderly women bettered their husbands as they played multiple cards and did so with a determined vengeance. These games were conducted beneath a large open-air grandstand filled with tables and benches to accommodate both determination and greed. Stylishly sewn quilts of vibrant colors and patterns were to be won by those who were both focused on their game cards and plain lucky.

There was a permanent cylindrical structure that housed a long-standing carousel of wooden horses that were ornately painted. The electrical and mechanical equipment that powered the old carousel was kept always in good repair by the Terhune family for generations and had been used for as long as anyone could remember. In those days, Shubel ran maintenance checks and scheduled practice runs once a month throughout each spring and summer leading up to the festival.

But Shubel would not attend to the carousel this year during the festival because Shubel could not attend to the carousel, or to anything else for that matter. The gunshot wound to his chest pretty well concluded any enjoyment of summer's end and much of his fall. So, the Terhune clan tipped their collective hats to the Fates and simply inserted a cousin as a replacement. As a family the Terhunes were religious in their dedication to the carousel. After all, it was the centerpiece of the festival and they would not relinquish their responsibility.

The imposing steam engine train that encircled the grounds and the fluorescent-colored miniature cars tethered to long tubular arms that ran in a circle were equally popular to the children through the years. And, while those children squealed with fear and delight at all kinds of locomotion, the old timers were kept refreshed sitting in the cool shade under the oaks and maples that served as a mammoth beer garden.

Deep-fried chicken and dumplings and kettle-cooked beef and slaw and potato salad invited an entire community for lunch and dinner. They came and feasted in all-you-can-eat fashion at the sit-down meals in the dining hall for the entire weekend. It was said that twelve good men fried chicken in deep vats of lard for two days and another twelve good men carried the largesse in greasy coolers from the back-kitchen frying room to the dining hall.

Dumplings were made in the kitchen proper along with coleslaw, potato salad and various pies. While the older women completed this work, the younger girls served the patrons in the dining hall. Out in the grounds, old men served the beer and brats and the high school football team made and sold the homemade vanilla ice cream. And no one left the picnic grounds without eating the famous ice cream.

But the Fish Pond was the domain of Mikaela and Lauren Rhea who managed the booth like the business that it was. With the help of a handful of Girl Scouts, they allowed the smaller children to place their fishing line over the side of a wooden blue booth on which was painted various kinds of fish and different sizes of waves and drop in their line. On the other side of the booth's wall, the Rheas would tie a toy onto the string and give it a tug. When the child pulled back his fishing rod and line, there for the taking was their new toy. All for the price of a dollar.

With the end of the shoe factory strike now a reality Cottage Grove was beginning to worry about its inevitable effect on the St. Matthew's Parish Festival. Not only would three hundred families have less money to spend during the three-day celebration because of the loss of jobs, the general attitude of the community would be far less festive. There was trouble that had to be considered.

Still, the festival was on. The priests and sisters from Cincinnati were nowhere to be seen on that Friday evening. Their appearance was scheduled to commence on Saturday night in the Dining Hall for a celebratory dinner with Father O'Halloran and a few members of the town's political inner circle.

Only one sister was seen on the festival grounds on Friday night and that was Sister Larae Savignac. She was alone. And she was there in response to what she believed was the insistence of God and even, perhaps, to His seemingly curious sense of humor. How else could she explain it?

Three decades ago she relocated nearly four hundred miles away to a new life without connection to her home town or the daughter that she gave up. Now, after all of the years and across all of the miles, the godfather of the local pastor of her home town who just happens to be her archbishop requires her presence at weekend festival where she will surely stand face to face with that daughter. One may call it simply chance, but to Savignac the odds of ever meeting her daughter always constituted a statistical monstrosity. For Mikaela meeting her natural mother was always an impossibility. After all, it was her understanding that her mother had died in childbirth.

So it was that Savignac decided to just get on with the encounter if that is what God wanted. Perhaps there would come about some kind of closure or peace of mind in seeing Mikaela. She was entitled to hope for that, at least.

Her knowledge of her daughter consisted of knowing her name, her place of residence, and that Michael's sister, Helen, had raised her in Cottage Grove. Recently, Carlisle had assured her that Mikaela was happy. The last piece of information came to her by way of the parish bulletin that she read earlier in the day in the narthex of St. Matthew's Church. Inserted within the bulletin was a pamphlet listing the festival duties of each parishioner. She saw the name of Mikaela Rhea below the Friday night Fish Pond heading. All of that totaled what she knew about her daughter. Still, she knew she would recognize her immediately.

She walked for a while across the midway and the ground's dust dulled her parade black shoes and the bottom of her navy blue habit. She drank in the sights of children running and people gathered in small groups drinking and eating and rides twirling and rotating and lights shining and splashing across the festival grounds. She admired the carousel of wooden horses and observed the large crowd of bingo players beneath the open-air building. She glanced at the beer garden and noted the picnic tables that were available for people who just wanted to rest and visit. The festival would be a success, in spite of the strike and discord in the community. Because, after all, the annual "picnic" was too much a part of the life of Cottage Grove.

Eventually, she stood in front of the Fish Pond and watched a young mother and her daughter take tickets from parents and offered fishing poles to their children. She watched for a long time because she knew who she was watching and she just wanted to study them for a time. It never occurred to her that she might be a grandmother. Now she could see that she was, but she still watched from a distance with an emotional restraint.

On a small piece of paper she wrote a note that read: *"Meet me at the far end of the beer garden at 8:00 p. m. tonight. We need to talk. Sr. Larae Savignac"*

The sister handed the note to one of the parents standing in line in front of the Fish Pond and asked that the note be given to Mikaela Rhea. And then Larae turned and walked away and disappeared into the festival crowd.

AT EIGHT O'CLOCK MIKAELA AND LAUREN ARRIVED AT the far end of the beer garden with Vincent catching up to them at the last moment. The three of them walked beneath the amber festoon lighting that was stretched across the tables and benches of the designated area in a less than symmetrical fashion. The garden was crowded and a little noisy with the music of a nearby country band playing some sad song about the broken heart of an owner of a pick-up truck.

Mikaela recognized the out-of-towner immediately as the woman in blue and white garb sat with an expectant expression on her face at the edge of the beer garden. The trio walked slowly toward her and stopped before the table that Savignac occupied.

The three of them stood there at the picnic table and no one spoke at first. Lauren looked up at her mother with a puzzled expression. It was not like her mother to just stand and stare without salutation.

"Hello, Mikaela. Please sit down."

She sat across the picnic table from Larae with Vincent on her left and Lauren on her right.

"This is my husband, Vincent, and our daughter, Lauren." She looked left and right and then said, "This is Sister Larae Savignac from Ohio."

Immediately, Vincent knew who was sitting across from them, Lauren did not yet understand. The introduction was followed by an awkward silence that was quickly broken by the Daughter of Charity.

"You are very beautiful, Mikaela, and you have a beautiful family," Savignac began. "There is so much to say and, yet, there are no words that can adequately explain either what happened over three decades ago or what is in our hearts now."

Mikaela stared trance-like into the eyes of her mother as she braced herself in engaging her for the first time. She looked at her face and then her blue and white religious habit and then watched her fingers as they rubbed the top of her hands as she spoke.

Vincent said nothing but sat observing his wife from the corner of his eye. Lauren sat quietly wishing the interview was over and that she could go on the festival rides. The nun seemed nice but what was the point of this conversation?

"Aunt Helen and my father have explained the way things were when I was born, so we don't need to go into any of that," Mikaela offered. Larae cringed and steeled herself against the reference to Michael Carlisle but said nothing. "But what I want to know is what are you doing here?" was Mikaela's only question.

Savignac explained her presence at the parish festival and why she believed it was God's plan that they finally meet. She did so without exposing their relationship in consideration of Lauren. That would be up to Mikaela to reveal to her daughter if and when she decided to do so. That deference was the least she could give.

"I will be returning to Ohio after the festival. We have had some trouble here in Cottage Grove. A dear friend of mine has been hurt, so I need to accompany her back to the convent as soon as she is able to travel."

Finally, Mikaela had had enough. Vincent could see the emotion beginning to boil over from within his wife. He took hold of her left hand and held in against the table top to steady her.

"You give too much credit to God," she announced. "He doesn't care about you coming to Cottage Grove and making a cursory appearance for my sake or for your sake. You've created a rationale of your own that justifies throwing away the care of a baby and the raising of a daughter."

Now Larae sat blanched-face across the table and began to tremble. Lauren looked at her mother wondering what in the world she was talking about and why she was apparently scolding this nun. But what baby and what daughter?

"Vincent, would you please take Lauren on some of the rides now? It is time for her to go," Mikaela requested.

"Okay... Let's go, Lauren."

The father and daughter dutifully got up and made their polite good-byes to Sister Larae. And they were gone.

"She is beautiful, Mikaela, and Vincent seems like a very nice young man." The mother of the mother smiled a smile that blended joy and sadness at once and Mikaela could clearly see both emotions imprinted on her aging face.

"They are both special. I wish you could have known them."

They sat silent for a little while.

"Vincent knows who I am, doesn't he?"

"Yes."

"Will you tell Lauren who I am, Mikaela?"

"I really don't know. I haven't decided."

"Mikaela," Savignac began and then hesitated. "Don't ever think that I got off scot-free. I've thought about you every day of my life and I have loved you every day of my life. It was a terrible sacrifice that I made long ago so that I could serve God in my own way. Tell me, Mikaela, how wrong was I?"

"There are all kinds of ways to serve God."

"Yes, dear, there are as many ways as there are people trying to make their own way in the world," was Larae's rejoinder.

"Will I see you again?"

"Only if you write and ask to see me."

Mikaela considered the possibility for a moment and then let it go. Perhaps someday she would, she thought, but it didn't seem likely. She could not envision what circumstances would arise that would compel her to make the request.

They sat silent for a little while longer.

"Tell me, are you happy with your life?" Mikaela asked with hesitation.

"Did you make the right decision?"

"Yes, Mikaela, I am as happy as one can be in this world," was the reply. "There was sadness in my decision to give you away, but there is joy in my service to God."

They sat silent for a little while longer, again.

"Well, then, I am glad for you," Mikaela said finally and abruptly stood over her mother with a pained smile. "I have to get back to the Fish Pond stand to help close up for the night."

Larae got up from the table and stepped toward her daughter. Reaching with her right hand, she touched the left forearm of Mikaela who quickly pulled away and then quickly walked away, leaving her mother standing there to watch her as she did so. Mikaela disappeared into the dissonant chorus of the festival crowd. That was the first and last time Larae ever saw her daughter.

ON SATURDAY EVENING, ARCHBISHOP CZAJKA BROUGHT his religious delegation from Ohio to the St. Matthew's Parish Festival. They convened en masse in front of the dining hall entrance along with Father Tim O'Halloran. Also attending the archbishop was a handful of the town's better known citizens that included the mayor, the police chief, Tom Pfefferkorn of the *Journal Scene*, and a few others. Michael Carlisle promised to be there, as well, but had not yet arrived. Of the religious from Ohio only Sister Elyse was absent. She was recuperating nicely, though. Monsignor Carmody wrote a handsome check to St. Matthew's that more than covered the cost of the dinners for the entire group.

From a distance across the midway, Jack Llewellyn observed the congregation of the religious and civic VIPs in front of the window-screened dining hall. He walked slowly toward the gathered group and was surprised to see Larae Savignac standing there among the visitors.

As they gathered and mingled, a red-faced Llewellyn approached Savignac at the periphery of the crowd. "Larae, I had no idea that you were coming to Cottage Grove."

As Jack spoke the words that Monsignor Carmody overheard, the priest turned to look toward the two old friends. Jack stood close to Larae and then offered a sincere embrace that he shouldn't have given. Now, Savignac was red-faced and stepped back just a little to offer a cordially prim handshake for the benefit of the monsignor.

"I had no choice, Jack," she said. "The archbishop gave me no choice."

"But do you understand what an awkward position this may put you in?" he cautioned. "Carlisle will be joining us later in the dining hall."

"Jack, no one is going to know about our past," Savignac whispered with soothing assurance. "Just let it go."

The out-of-towners and designated hosts entered the dining hall and sat at long tables under large ceiling fans that circulated the cool evening air and shooed away flies from the banquet food that was set before them. Llewellyn decided to mix in with the other hosts because he decided that he could not keep a distance from Larae now that she was at the festival. The old man maintained a pleasant cordiality throughout the dinner as Savignac was positioned between Llewellyn and Tom Pfefferkorn. For as much awkwardness as Sister Larae may have felt, she hid the discomfort well and was congenial to both men. Monsignor Carmody sat on the other side of the same table, toward the middle and alongside of the archbishop, but he kept glancing in her direction from time to time because he found it impossible not to watch her. For the monsignor's liking, she was too independent and too outspoken.

Just before dessert was to be served Michael Carlisle entered the dining hall and offered his welcoming hand to the archbishop and waved acknowledgment to the mayor and police chief before finding a place at one of the long tables. It was obvious that he had stopped by a drinking hole before his arrival at the festival grounds. The look of personal dishevelment and liquored breath pretty much gave away his condition. Maybe it was understandable as he did play a background part and felt some vague responsibility for the shoe factory upheaval, the shooting of Shubel Terhune, and the stabbing of Sister Elyse. It was a circumstance of failure during a difficult summer, and he was succumbing to some measure of regret.

He was served a plate dinner by a young waitress and as she moved away the other visitors came into his view. There between his fiercest enemy and the newspaper editor sat the one person who could do serious damage to his world order. His entrance and salutations were keenly witnessed by both Larae and Jack. From the corner of her eye, the Daughter could see the expressions of fear and hatred form across the face of Michael Carlisle. The fire in his eyes and a paled expression signaled warning to the Reverend Mother. But there was nothing that she could do to stop the inevitable explosion that she knew was coming in spite of everything that they both had to lose.

Finally, Carlisle could not contain himself any longer. He stood up and marched over to where Savignac sat. And in front of those around her and within earshot of the archbishop and Carmody, he exploded.

"What are you doing here?" fumed the lawyer in whispered hoarseness as he stood in front of and across the table from Larae. "You promised me that you weren't coming."

"I'm sorry, Michael. But I had no choice," she replied quickly, looking up at Carlisle.

But the answer was not sufficient and the old lawyer attacked out of instinct and left reason behind. "What have you and this bastard been telling Pfefferkorn about me?" he demanded with words that slurred in rhythm, motioning at Llewellyn.

"Nothing, Michael. No one has said anything about you," was her reply.

"No soap, Larae. I know Llewellyn better than that."

"That's your problem, Carlisle," challenged Llewellyn. "You judge other people in terms of yourself. You think the worst in people because you are the worst of people."

By this time, the dining hall was quieted by the apparent rancor so that the entire building had become audience to the verbal skirmish. Archbishop Czajka and the monsignor had gathered close and stood near Sister Larae in some small attempt to settle down the obvious conflict.

But it was too little too late.

The drunken lawyer leaned on the dining table in front of Savignac with both hands placed flat on the surface, quickly glanced at the newspaper editor, and queried without filter, "Did you tell Pfefferorn?"

But she just looked at him in puzzlement. "What are you saying, Michael?"

Again, he demanded an answer, "Did you tell Pfefferorn, I said?"

"Tell him what, Michael?"

The old lawyer swayed unsteadily and with saliva forming at the sides of his mouth sprayed in a guttural exclamation, "Did you tell Pfefferkorn that we had a baby together?" He stood erect now as he was proud of the implied condemnation.

A deafening silence absorbed the dining area and a surreal atmosphere enveloped all those who were within hearing distance. Czajka and Carmody stood open-mouthed behind Savignac. The others looked on with blank expressions awaiting the next shock wave.

In abject horror and humiliation, Larae rose to her feet and screamed back in self-abandoned self-defense at Carlisle, "We never had a baby together, Michael! The baby's father was Jack!"

At this point a gasp and roar ascended across the dining hall and through the screened doors and windows to the outside. Emotionally exhausted in the wake of Elyse's trauma at the tavern, her second confrontation with Carmody, the first-time meeting with her daughter, and now this humiliating attack, Sister Larae promptly fainted and collapsed onto the sawdust covered floor of the hall. A crowd of colleagues hovered over her to assist and, once again, the EMT ambulance was called into service.

Michael Carlisle and Jack Llewellyn stood and stared at the fallen Larae. Both were stunned by Savignac's outburst and were processing the new information as fast as their minds would allow. They both were staggered by the concept of lost and found fatherhood for the second time that summer. Once again, their histories were circling back to intersection, altering their progeny, and affecting the people they loved as well as themselves.

Carlisle and Llewellyn faced each other as two gunfighters might have done on the street of a lonely prairie town. They stood and stared at one another and made mental preparations for yet another skirmish. But they checked their desire to punish one another because of the commotion and clamor of the scrum that surrounded them. There would be a better time for just retribution. Right now the center of the universe was lying unconscious on the floor of the festival dining hall and all hell had broken loose.

Upon regaining consciousness inside one of the emergency room stations, Savagnac's blurred vision focused first on Archbishop Czajka as he leaned over and watched her come back into the world. He was gently holding one of her hands. They smiled at each other.

"Welcome back, Sister Larae," he said quietly and with a gentleness that was most becoming of him.

But then she realized where she was and what had happened and her smile gave way to pallor. "I am so sorry, Your Grace," she lamented and tears watered her eyes and trickled down the sides of her face.

"Don't worry about any of that, Larae," he said with real reassurance. "Everything will be set right after you've recovered." The archbishop stood erect and motioned to his secretary. "Monsignor Carmody has made arrangements that you will stay in the hospital just for tonight, only as a precaution, you understand. We will talk tomorrow, Sister."

Czajka squeezed her hand as if to say good-bye and he left the ER station and closed the curtains behind him. Carmody looked carefully at Savignac for a moment as if he was evaluating her condition and then left. Larae thought to herself that no one ever knew what the monsignor was thinking and that made her very nervous. She rested in her lateral recumbent position for a while and studied the medical equipment that surrounded the ER bed and to which she was tethered. By ten o'clock that night she was wheeled into her own private room where she slept until morning.

BY EARLY SUNDAY MORNING A PREJUDICIAL ACCOUNT OF the personal drama that had occurred in the festival dining hall had become common coin. The archbishop and Father O'Halloran and Carlisle had all gone through phases of shock and embarrassment and anger in the wake of Savignac's announcement. Llewellyn was shocked, but neither embarrassed nor angry. At least not at first. Those feelings came later as he waited for Larae to explain in a singular defense of herself. But, no matter what, he did not understand the events of over three decades past. Why did Larae give up her baby? Why did she convince Carlisle that he was the baby's father? And why was he deprived of the daughter that he should have had?

By mid-morning Jack Llewellyn positioned himself on a bench in front of the hospital and waited for the arrival of Savignac. He had been told that she was to be released momentarily and he decided to wait and approach her privately outside and away from the hospital's sterile ambience.

Eventually, she exited the front doors and walked gingerly down the front steps and onto the walkway.

She looked across the way and saw Llewellyn sitting there and obviously waiting for her. "Ah, it's you."

"Larae, how are you feeling?" Jack inquired with caution.

"I am very fine, Jack. I really didn't need to be here. The archbishop insisted that I stay one night just to be on the safe side."

She walked over and the projectionist stood to greet her and with a hint of bravado gave her a gentle hug with both arms encompassing her. They sat together as old friends and new acquaintances.

"Talk to me, Larae. Tell me everything or as much as you can."

She did. She told him of how Michael Carlisle had helped her place the baby for adoption and how the lawyer knew the right people in Gills Rock as well as Cottage Grove. She told him how her destiny was to serve God as a religious woman and not as a mother or wife. Giving up her daughter was the sacrifice that she was compelled to make whether anyone liked it or not. She knew this to be true in her heart. The choice was not made out of carelessness or coldness, but out of love for God and love for the daughter that she was not meant to raise. She had never seen Mikaela before Saturday; she knew only that she was a young woman that lived in Cottage Grove. She did not know that she was a grandmother, but she had surmised as much after seeing the photograph that she was given at the convent in Blue Ash.

"Larae, why did you let Carlisle believe he was the father?"

"Because of his position and potential financial standing, Jack," she replied. "I thought he would be able to help her better financially throughout her life. I am sorry if that hurts you. I never wanted that. I just wanted what was best for the baby."

"You wanted what was best for the baby," mimicked Llewellyn incredulously. "Really? What about her knowing her father, if not her mother, Larae? Wouldn't have that counted for something? Didn't she have a right to know who her father was? Didn't I have a right to know that I had a daughter?"

Jack rested for a moment to collect his thoughts and resist the urge to pummel her with recrimination.

"You may have thought you had the best interest of the baby at heart," he continued. "But what you did is a textbook example of the proverb that the road to hell is paved with good intentions."

Savignac sat there without reply because she could see the storm forming in the eyes of Llewellyn.

"It is profoundly insulting and hurtful that you prevented Mikaela and me from knowing and loving each other as father and daughter for all of these years." He said it slowly and seethed as he said it.

Then he delivered the final blow.

"I will always love the Rae that I knew decades ago and I will always love our daughter and I will always love our granddaughter." He paused to look deep into her eyes as if to discern those things that made her what she was. "But I never want to see you again.

"I know you will understand, Larae, if I do not forgive you."

The projectionist stood up and looked down on the Daughter. And she looked up at him without either tears or reply, but with slumped shoulders and with the pallid and blank expression of a dirty dishtowel.

"Good-bye, Larae."

There was still no reply. And he walked away from her for the last time.

MICHAEL CARLISLE SAT AT THE KITCHEN TABLE IN HIS sister's house with his head in his hands. Helen sat across from him drinking her green tea methodically taking a sip every few seconds, both wondering how to react in response to Savignac's revelation in the festival dining hall. For over three decades both have been committed to Mikaela, especially Helen who raised her and was mother to her.

In a way, she ultimately supposed, it really didn't matter who the father was. True, if she were Michael's daughter, it would have been a more meaningful adoption because of the inherent consanguinity. In a real sense, if she were Llewellyn's baby, it really would not make any difference that would affect the state of her motherhood. She would have loved and cared for Mikaela just the same.

But for Michael, it did make a difference. Because for over thirty years he monitored Mikaela's life and discreetly guaranteed her well-being as much as practical. Of course, this is what Larae Savignac had in mind all along. So, the sister sat with her brother and wondered how she could console a man who had sort of lost a family and sort of did not.

"Well, Michael," she started. "It's like this. In one way, things have changed, but in another nothing has really changed."

"What's that suppose to mean?"

"Well, what happened to you is the same thing that happened to Jack Llewellyn, isn't it?" She explained, "He lost Julia's son to you, except that he really didn't because he raised David. Now, you've lost Mikaela to Jack, except you really haven't because he will never be as close to her as you are right now. Am I wrong?"

"I guess not, but I wonder just how close I really am to Mikaela," worried Carlisle. "I wonder what Mikaela will think of all of this."

"Mike, I know Mikaela and I know you both have gone through a lot in recent weeks. Try to be patient." She paused and then went on, "Remember, she has just recently found out about her birth mother and now she learns about her birth father. That's a pretty hard row to hoe. But remember this... We have been her family all of her life. That cannot change because people don't throw away family because of a technicality."

The brother looked at his sister and saw the sincerity in her face and heard the certainty in her voice. He felt a small measure of relief and gave a timid smile and shook his head.

"These are maddening times, Helen."

Chapter 26

A SOFT SHOE DANCE

By Monday morning the confluence of the shoe factory's demise and the festival's religious embarrassment had left Cottage Grove in public disarray. On one hand, three hundred families had lost employment as a result of the failed strike and the corporate misdirection of an old Native American. On the other hand, both the visiting archbishop and St. Matthew's pastor had suffered embarrassment because of the ill-advised declaration of an overwrought visiting Daughter of Charity. Not only that, but a respected local attorney as well as a retired university professor had been proportionately humiliated. Finally, and equally regrettable, was the hospitalization of two fairly innocent by-standers, one from a stabbing and one from a gun-shot wound. Cottage Grove had never experienced such a week.

THE TELEPHONE RANG WITH A CRISP CLARITY IN THE office of Harold Chatham. On the other end of the line was Gordon Coppaway. He was agitated and he wanted some assurance from the cereal plant president.

"Harold, I want to postpone the purchase of the shoe factory for a few weeks," he began. "I have some things to work out with the city and then we can go ahead with the sale. Is that satisfactory?"

"Of course, Gordon, take your time. I can wait a short while, but not too long, you know. Is there anything that I can help you with?"

"No, no. I just need to receive some political concessions from the city and then it will be smooth sailing. It won't take very long to get everything I want accomplished."

"Okay, good luck with that. Talk to you then," Chatham replied.

The two men ended the conversation amicably and set their plans in motion. Chatham telephoned his lawyers to begin laying out the terms of the formal and final purchase agreement and ancillary documents required by state law. Coppaway dialed the chief of police to set up a quiet meeting later on in the day to discuss keeping the factory going and what it would cost.

THE POLICE CHIEF SAT ON A PARK BENCH AT JACOBUS Park sucking on a soda straw when the old Indian drove up and parked his vehicle. He got out and walked over and sat down on the bench next to the policeman. With his arms spread out on top of the bench back and one leg crossed over the other, the shoe company president casually surveyed the area and readied himself for a friendly conversation.

"Let's have it, Mr. Coppaway," the chief said still working on the last of his soda tumbler.

"Tell the mayor that the shoe factory stays open if I get the police file on the nun's stabbing. Otherwise, three hundred families got no jobs."

"Understood. Anything else?"

"You make a new file and it shows the stabbing as an accident, Chief. Which, by the way, it really was. I never meant to hurt that nun. Please believe me."

"I do, Mr. Coppaway. But she got hurt just the same." He took one last pull on the plastic straw. "I'll let you know what the mayor says."

The policeman got up and walked away without further comment. The old Indian watched him as he finally drove away.

SHUBEL TERHUNE REMAINED UNCONSCIOUS IN THE HOSpital's intensive care unit long after the slug was removed from his chest. Eventually, though, he did come around after a few days. The first thing he saw after slowly coming back to consciousness was Wish McGuire sitting next to his bed and staring at him.

He tried to move, but he couldn't. He tried to talk, but he couldn't.

"Stay still, Shubel. You've been shot. But now you're going to be okay," she whispered. And tears formed in her eyes. "I love you."

BACK IN THE CORNER OF THE DEVIL'S ELBOW Harry Glick and Riley Turnbull sat at a table and leaned forward over their respective beers. The two burly tradesmen spoke in gruff, short sentences that suggested urgency and secrecy.

"Look, Harry, I'm not goin' to get involved with you shooting that Terhune boy. You had no cause to do that."

"Riley, shut up! I ain't takin' the fall by myself, so you had better keep your mouth shut. You understand me? We're both in it together."

In fact, they were in it together; however, as luck would have it, no one in the striking crowd saw either the gun or the man who shot the handgun. Because all eyes were trained on Dan Joda and Dirk McGuire and the garbage truck, no one saw the aiming and firing of the handgun. As it happened, both Glick and Turnbull were standing at the back of the crowd. The noise of the acrimony and chaos cloaked the shooting sufficiently, so that when people turned to see from where the gun was discharged, it was too late to observe who fired.

And so it was that after a few weeks of sweating it out by the two factory foremen, they began to understand that they were not suspects in the shooting, but rather good union tradesmen who walked the line and did their part during the Local 555 strike.

THE CHIEF OF POLICE HAD CALLED GORDON COPPAWAY and arranged a meeting at Jacobus Park. The chief carried a manila file folder in his hand and gave it to the old Indian who opened it up and studied the contents.

"That's the complete file, Mr. Coppaway," the policeman said. "The new file is already in place at the police station. The file that you are holding contains all the evidence that has been collected or could be collected pertinent to the case." And then he gave his final reassurance, "You have nothing to fear at any time in the future. You have a clean bill of health."

"Thank you, Chief. This is very good of you."

"Just keep the shoe factory going. Will you, Mr. Coppaway?"

"Of course, Chief, of course."

IN THE MCGUIRE KITCHEN TONY FEDORYSHYN SAT across the table from Dirk McGuire. Both men were recovering from the death of the Coppaway Shoe Company and the consequent funeral of Local 555 of the Boot & Shoe Workers Union.

"Dirk, you gave it a helluva run," commiserated Fedoryshyn and then gulped down a slug of his beer, splashing the glass mug's contents as he did.

"Yeah, Tony, we did," agreed the Irishman. "But Coppaway held all the cards and he played his biggest trump card with a joker named Chatham.

"What will you do now, my friend?"

"Well, I guess there's always the cereal plant." And then he thought about it. "But to tell you the truth, I think I'll drive over to Madison and see what kind of work there might be there. Larger cities usually have better opportunities."

"Well, good luck with your search, Dirk," Tony offered. "As for me, I guess I should be getting back to Crown Point. I have a partner who would like me to reintroduce myself to him. Apparently, we have a lot of work that has been left unattended."

"Do you think all of this could have been handled better, Tony?"

The lawyer got up from his chair and finished his beer with one last heave. He placed his mug firmly onto the table. He looked Dirk squarely in the eyes and said, "Well, to tell you the truth, I don't think the mutual hatred between the Indian and you helped very much. Maybe, if that wasn't such a stumbling block, you would have had a better shot at saving the company and all those jobs. But, what the hell, Dirk, it's all water under the bridge now."

With that, the lawyer gathered his things and smiled at Dirk one last time and he went out the door and back to Indiana.

IN THE SECOND WEEK OF SEPTEMBER DAN JODA SHOCKED the entire community by placing a notice in the *Journal Scene* that all shoe factory employees were to report back to work immediately. The strike was over and the Coppaway Shoe Company was back in business with ten percent raises for all employees and full medical benefits offered on a *gratis basis*.

The following day and with the exception of those who had taken jobs elsewhere, every employee had arrived at the starting whistle and horn to begin work. However, the ramping up of work was slow going because the strike had compelled the company to reject purchase orders and turn away customers. Because of that there was little work to be performed in any of the departments. Still, the company's doors opened and 250 employees shuffled throughout each day in a pretense of productivity.

Dirk McGuire did not return to the shoe factory along with his comrades. He had fallen out of grace. In Cottage Grove, he had become *persona not grata*.

Two weeks later Dan Joda shocked the entire community by placing a second notice in the *Journal Scene* announcing the closing of the shoe factory and the immediate demise of the Coppaway Shoe Company. No one other than the mayor and police chief realized the faithless municipal chicanery of an old Indian from the Bad River Band of Lake Superior Chippewa. And they both realized that there was really nothing they could do about it without incriminating themselves.

AUTUMN WAS COMING TO COTTAGE GROVE. A sky of flawless azure and chilled-to-crisp air replenished an optimism into a fast-recovering Shubel Terhune and his companion nurse Kathryn McGuire. They walked slowly on the sidewalk that outlined the hospital's front circular driveway and ran beneath the porte cochere. After a while they found a bench within the Healing Garden that was positioned in front of the driveway and sat among the fading flowers to soak in the sun and rest in each other's arms.

"What are you thinking, Shubel?"

"I guess how nice it is to be getting well and just being here with you," he replied. "The doctor said I can go home tomorrow and maybe go back to work in a couple of weeks." He paused for just a moment. "My boss said that my job will be waiting for me."

"I'm glad."

"How is your dad doing, Wish?"

She looked down at their hands which were still clasped together as they sat side-by-side. "Well, he's been struggling with how the strike failed and how people lost their jobs," she said hesitantly. "He's been drinking quite a lot lately. Right now, his full-time job is trying to get a full-time job.

"But honestly, Shubel, I think he's going to be okay. It's just going to take some time, that's all." And then, "By the way, he always asks about you. I don't think it's just because you got shot. I think he likes the fact that we're dating. He says you got a lot of spit in you."

Terhune smiled at that.

"Let's talk about your college classes and your future flower shop," he said. And they did just that for the rest of the afternoon.

Chapter 27

A FAMILY TRADE AGREEMENT

On the Sunday morning of the parish festival Archbishop Robert M. Czajka co-celebrated Mass with Father Timothy O'Halloran at St. Matthew's Church. Afterward, there was a brief reception in the basement of the church and then the religious delegation from Ohio promptly headed back to Ohio.

Before leaving Cottage Grove with the archbishop, Monsignor Carmody escorted Sister Larae to her rental car located in the parking lot. They were alone.

"Sister, the Archbishop has asked me to convey to you his disappointment and embarrassment at your outburst in the dining hall on Saturday night," he announced. "Also, you have embarrassed Father O'Halloran at the very moment in which he should have been honored by His Eminence and old friends from Ohio in front of his current parishioners."

"I am sorry that His Grace was embarrassed, Monsignor. It was a night in which I was emotionally overwhelmed. You see, I met my daughter for the first time just the evening before we sat down to dinner."

"Yes, well nevertheless, Sister, His Eminence has asked me to inform you that you are no longer to be addressed as Reverend Mother. You may keep your place within the Daughters of Charity in the Greater Cincinnati area; however, you will no longer serve as Mother of St. Rose of Lima Convent."

She looked at him with an expression of devastation and lowered her upper body and folded into a slump across the hood of her car. She placed both her hands over her face and quietly wept.

The priest looked down at her and almost felt sorry for her. "It's nothing personal, Sister. It's just business."

She stopped, removed her hands from her face, and looked up at him. The priest's cold demeanor left her aghast. Both his message and tone achieved their purpose.

"You see, Sister, we always have to be sensitive to the optics these days. The Church doesn't need any more bad press than it already gets.

"One last thing, Sister… Archbishop Czajka understands that you will want to stay with Sister Elyse until she is fully recovered. He appreciates your friendship and loyalty to her. I'm sure the archbishop will be in touch with you when you both get back to Ohio."

The priest nodded slightly to Larae and went on his way without further comment. Savignac watched him walk back to the front of the church and meet with the archbishop. Eventually, they drove away and from a distance she saw Father O'Halloran stare briefly at her and then turn and reenter the church.

The Daughter would go to Elyse later in the day. The younger Daughter was doing well and would be able to travel in a few days. But first, Savignac wanted to see someone else who deserved both an acknowledgment and a conversation.

The rental car pulled up alongside the curb in front of the old Cape Cod house deep within the modest neighborhood. Larae surveyed the front yard and watched the autumn leaves dance across the front lawn as the breeze picked up and toyed with her blue and white habit.

She rang the doorbell and waited without much patience. She knocked on the door and waited again. Eventually, the front door opened and standing in the foyer was Helen Quesnell.

"Hello, Mrs. Quesnell," Larae began. "May I come in?"

Instantly, Helen knew who was standing before her and she flushed with intimidation. Still, she was a veteran of all kinds of circumstances and emotions and she braced herself for yet another trial that life might hand her.

"Please come in, Sister."

They both entered the living room of the house and sat across from one another with considerable awkwardness.

"May I offer you something to drink, Sister?"

"No, thank you, Mrs. Quesnell. I won't take up much of your time."

"Please, call me Helen."

"No, I don't think I should," Larae replied and hesitated to begin, but did anyway. "I have no intention of interfering in your life and I have too much respect and gratitude for you.

"Because I was required to come to the Grove by my archbishop and because it seemed inevitable that my presence become known to your daughter, I thought you were owed some kind of conversation."

"It is not necessary, Sister. I understand."

"Mrs. Quesnell, thank you for adopting Mikaela. You have done a wonderful job with her. She has grown up to be a bright and beautiful young woman. You must be very proud of her."

"Yes, I am. And you can be proud of her, too, Sister."

"I gave her life, but you gave her everything else – love, a home, a family. She is truly your daughter and I am happy for you both. I just wanted you know how much I respect you and how grateful I am for all that you have done for her.

"Now, with that, I want you to know that I will not be returning to Cottage Grove nor will I try to contact Mikaela. She is your daughter. I made that sacrifice decades ago and I have no intention of making the same sacrifice all over again.

"You were meant to be a mother, Mrs. Quesnell. I was meant for something else. I have always known that. We have both served God in our own way and we will continue to do so for all of our lives. Both are worthy endeavors."

"But why lie to my brother about the paternity, Sister?"

Savignac paused and adjusted her posture to explain. "Michael had the greater wherewithal to provide for Mikaela in one way or another. Jack Llewellyn would never have been able to take care of a daughter and pursue an academic career. And, most importantly, Michael had you and I counted on that. I counted on Michael and you to take care of Mikaela. I took care of my daughter the best way I knew how."

Finally, the Daughter got up from her chair and Quesnell followed suit. They looked at each other briefly and Larae embraced her counterpart warmly.

"Thank you for coming, Sister. I am very glad to finally meet you."

"And I am glad to finally meet the mother of my daughter," she said smiling. "I wish you both all the happiness in the world."

"God bless you, Sister."

And Larae Savignac turned and walked out of the life of Helen Quesnell forever.

During the week following the St. Matthew's Parish Festival the law offices of Carlisle and Rhea were pretty much closed. Although Cosie was stationed at her desk all five days, neither law partner was anywhere to be found. With a slurred and stuttering voice, Carlisle left a vague telephone message explaining that he would be out all week. Rhea left his own voice mail message that assured the secretary he would be in mid-week, but he ended up being a no-show, as well.

Sisters Larae and Elyse made their way back to Milwaukee and then on to greater Cincinnati for an uneventful return to St. Rose of Lima Convent. The news of her demotion and the reason for it had arrived the day before the two of them. E-mail correspondence from the Provincial Mother Superior had explained the circumstances and the request of Archbishop Czajka that Sister Larae continue duties as a Daughter but not those of Reverend Mother. Another sister was temporarily assigned the position of Mother until a permanent selection could be made. Sister Elyse was met with sympathy and deference; Sister Larae was met with sympathy and avoidance.

Because she was no longer the Reverend Mother, Larae was asked to remove her personal possessions from her room and transfer her residence to more modest quarters toward the back of the convent. She complied without complaint and was grateful for the new Mother's kindness. Savignac kept to herself in the room for the remainder of the week. She prayed constantly and ate sparingly until she conceded to a vaguely approaching and increasingly bothersome illness.

Jack Llewellyn did not contact Mikaela Rhea right away. He did not know what to say to or how to feel about his new daughter. He knew her well enough and he knew that she had a lovely young daughter and a fine husband, but he did not know her well. Because they were so intertwined with Michael Carlisle, he generally avoided Scuppernong Drive.

Eventually, he could no longer stay away. He wanted to meet his new daughter and new granddaughter for the first time. He wanted the family that Larae had denied him all of their lives.

Llewellyn stood on the veranda of the old Victorian house with his pick-up truck parked on Scuppernong Drive. He had telephoned the day before and asked Mikaela if he could come for a visit. She had nervously agreed to the meeting, but Vincent would be at work and Lauren would be in school. Before he had a chance to knock on the door, it was opened by his daughter and she invited him in.

They sat at the kitchen table and the young woman served iced tea and cupcakes.

"Mikaela, I don't know where to begin," her father began. "How does one introduce himself to his own daughter?"

"You don't have to do that," she replied. "We already know each other." Then she stopped herself and thought quickly. "Of course, I suppose I shouldn't call you Jack anymore. I should call you Dad."

The old projectionist smiled and they talked about everything and nothing for a while.

"I want you to know that I loved your mother those many years ago and that I love both Lauren and you so very much," he said. "I want to be an important part of your life, Mikaela. I want to be your dad and Lauren's grandfather and Vincent's father-in-law."

"We want that, too," she replied. "But you must understand Michael Carlisle has been a part of our family since forever and we cannot turn our backs on him because you now are coming into the family. Somehow, you both will have to accept one another or you will end up with nothing. This is as much true for Michael as it is for you."

She placed her hands around his hands on top of the table and looked into his eyes, "Right now, Michael and you have two families, the same two families. If you continue your war with him, you both will lose your two families and we all will suffer along the way and Michael and you will become the less for it."

There was a pained expression on the face of Llewellyn but he knew that his daughter was right. Things were the way they were. On one hand, Carlisle had seized an irretrievable part of David and now he, himself, was doing the same with a part of Mikaela. It was an extraordinary set of circumstances that twisted in a permanent knot a forced kindred connection between the two men, as well as to their families, both assumed and actual.

He looked back into her eyes with a fearlessness. "I will try, Mikaela."

He repeated with reflection, "I will try. Maybe we can make it work. I promise you I will make an effort."

Then the conversation turned to her mother.

"Will you tell Lauren about her grandmother?" Llewellyn asked.

"Not now, Dad," she said with a tone of sadness. "Maybe someday in the distant future. What good would it do her now? Aunt Helen volunteered to be her grandmother long before she was born. Why muddy the water for Lauren? She is just a little girl." Mikaela thought a little longer. "Maybe someday years from now she can know that her biological grandmother is a Sister, but she doesn't need to know that now."

They talked some more and then some more again. Jack made Mikaela go first and would not let her stop talking about herself until the morning was done. Then he spoke of himself and his life, but gave only an abbreviated version because there was too much to tell and he did not want to overstay his welcome. At the front door and just before he left, the retired professor asked, "Do you think it would be okay for me to take my granddaughter for an ice cream cone sometime?"

"She would love that." And both looked at each other's smile and embraced in saying their good-byes.

FOR WEEKS THE OTHER SISTERS WHO WORKED IN THE convent with Larae Savignac noticed an increasing daily fatigue in her. More often than not, Larae was not able to complete her household chores during the course of a given day. Moreover, she never slept well and was given to wander about the convent during odd hours of the night.

On one particular day, Savignac did not come down to breakfast and a worried Sister Elyse climbed the long stairs to the second-floor bedrooms. She walked down the long hallway and gently knocked on the wood paneled door once, and then twice, before a weak voice from the other side said, "Come in."

Elyse slowly turned the door knob and pushed the door inward and saw her dear friend still in bed with her face flushed and covered with perspiration. She walked over to Larae's bed and was alarmed immediately by the sweat-soaked bedding.

"Oh, my goodness! Sister, what is wrong with you?"

"Elyse, my chest hurts so bad!" she cried. She tried to inhale and exhale, but it took great effort. "I can't breathe!"

In the time of a heartbeat the young Sister reached into her pocket and called 911. Minutes later the ambulance roared and whined on Fairy Chasm Lane through the front gates and into the driveway of St. Rose of Lima. Two paramedics bounded through the front door, flew up the staircase, and raced down the corridor into the private room of Sister Larae. They found her still struggling to draw breath and massaging her own chest to relieve the discomfort there. The two men purposely pushed Elyse out of their way as they attended to the older Sister.

VINCENT RHEA WAS IN HIS OFFICE WORKING ON A BRIEF when his computer ringed a tiny tinned bell to announce another e-mail message had arrived. He opened his in-box and saw the sender was from a St. Rose of Lima address. He opened the message, read it, and printed it immediately.

"Cosie, I am leaving the office and won't return until tomorrow morning," he said as he made his presence brief in the front reception area."

"Okay, Vincent," she replied. "I'll see you tomorrow morning. Have a nice afternoon."

He arrived home and collected the leaf rake that he had left on the front lawn the night before. As he did, the postman, carrying the heavy burden of a full mail satchel, walked up to him in front of the house and delivered the mail personally. They chatted a bit and eventually the government employee went on his way, leaving the young lawyer to assess what he had been handed.

He laid down his rake next to the front door and walked pensively into the house and called for Mikaela to come downstairs. From the upstairs she came down and he handed the e-mailed letter to her. She took the paper from her husband while offering him a puzzled expression.

"You'd better read it, Mikaela," Vincent said with a slightly grim face. "Something has happened."

She unfolded the e-mailed correspondence with deliberation and read aloud it to her husband…

Dear Vincent,

I regret to inform you that Sister Larae Savignac died last night at St. John's Medical Center here in Blue Ash. Of course, it was important to inform you as soon as possible. According to the doctors at St. John's, Sister Larae died of an acute heart attack. We called for an ambulance as soon as we realized that she was ill.

The paramedics did everything that they could, but she was in a very bad way by the time they arrived at the convent. She lived for a few hours after arriving at the hospital and the doctors did their best, but to no avail. The damage to her heart was too great.

When I was in the hospital in Cottage Grove, you asked that I keep you informed if there were any important news about Sister Larae so that you could keep her daughter, Mikaela, aware of her life events. So, I am doing just that.

Also, please know that Sister Larae wished to be buried in the Catholic cemetery in Cottage Grove. As you know, her roots are there and her natural family lives there, as well. I think she wanted Mikaela and her daughter to be able to visit her from time to time. I hope you will honor her wish.

Please e-mail or call me if you would like to make arrangements for the body to be transported to Cottage Grove. Our local funeral home will keep Larae's body until I hear from you.

Just so you know, your Sister Larae was a wonderful Reverend Mother. She was loved, respected, and admired. She was a dear mentor and friend to me. We will all miss her very much.

Yours in the service of God,
Sister Elyse Morgan

Mikaela carried the piece of paper into the living room and sat down on the sofa. Vincent followed her and sat beside her. There really wasn't anything to say, so they just sat for a while.

Finally, Mikaela sighed and without a show of emotion asked her husband, "Why don't you go ahead and make the funeral arrangements with Alan Riedelsheimer? He can contact Sister Elyse at St. Rose of Lima." She stopped briefly and then added, "They should bring the body to Cottage Grove for burial if that was her wish."

"Okay, I will."

"I will inform Jack of mother's passing," returned Mikaela. "And you tell Michael. They both should be told as soon as possible and they will want to know about the funeral arrangements, as well."

"Okay." He kissed his wife and left.

The following day Vincent called Carlisle to detail the funeral arrangements for Larae Savignac. After the conversation, Michael placed his cell phone on his desk and went back to work on a stack of paperwork that would not go away without his grinding attention.

After a moment Cosie called on the office line and the old lawyer responded with a grunt.

"Mr. Carlisle, David Llewellyn is here to see you."

A little aggravated at the interruption, Carlisle agreed to see the young construction manager.

"Hello, David, please come in."

David entered the office for the first time and sat across from his father.

"I wanted to come and see you, sir. This won't take long," he began. "I just wanted you to know that you are going to have a grandson in a few months."

Carlisle leaned forward and was mesmerized by the idea of a grandson. "Well, David, congratulations!" he grinned. This is wonderful news. A grandson!"

"Yes, and we've decided on a name that was suggested by Jack Llewellyn," David continued. "It was a champion idea of his."

The old lawyer grimaced at the mentioning of Llewellyn's involvement and was chagrined to learn that the name was a suggestion of his old enemy.

"Wait a minute, David. There is no way that Jack Llewellyn should be naming my grandson," countered Carlisle.

"Well, the name he came up with is 'Michael Llewellyn.'"

In a rare moment, the old man had nothing to say. He looked at his son and thought about what he had heard. Michael Llewellyn. He thought about it a little more and then some more again. Michael Llewellyn.

"Do you mean that Jack Llewellyn suggested that you name the baby 'Michael?'" he asked with a good measure of disbelief.

"Yes, sir, that is what I'm saying."

Carlisle sat there without movement and joyfully considered his grandson sharing his name. He also was moved by the fact that this was the first time Jack Llewellyn ever gave him any accommodation in all of the years that they have known one another. It literally took away his breath.

In his internal reverie, the lawyer remembered the clashes over Larae and her compromised passion for him and her now discovered and realized love for Jack. He remembered the clashes over Julia and her intermittent passion for him and her faithlessness to Jack. He reminded himself of Mikaela who is his lost daughter and David who is his found son. Most of all, he thought of his grandson, the extremely young Michael Llewellyn, who, apparently, Jack was now willing to share.

"My goodness, this changes everything."

AUTUMN ARRIVED IN COTTAGE GROVE ON A SATURDAY morning and the leaves that were once emerald green had turned to fluorescent orange or scarlet red or dandelion yellow. And they tumbled across the lawns and streets by the chilled western wind and became brittle by their dryness and then soaked soft by intermittent rains.

Lauren Rhea was in a hurry. She had a job to do and was determined to complete the delivery of funeral notices by lunchtime. At 2:00 p. m., she was expected at the home of Mrs. Patty Worms for her piano lesson. Just as with being reliable for Mr. Riedelsheimer, she was committed to the elderly and recently widowed Mrs. Worms who was a gentle taskmaster. The ten-year-old girl had found both an instructor and a dear friend while realizing her love for the piano and the joy of music.

But, first things first. She dutifully and methodically circled the square and dispatched the notice from one business to the next. This time there was no photograph on the four by six card, only the name that read, "Sister Larae Savignac, D. C. with her dates of birth and death. Funeral and burial arrangements were private."

The little girl pulled open the heavy outer door of the saloon and then pushed against the screen door. As always, the sour and sharp smells of beer and whiskey and fried burgers surrounded her as she walked toward the mahogany bar.

"Good morning, Lauren," greeted Cash McDermott, who was cleaning and straightening his watering hole after a night of noise and commotion.

"Good morning, Mr. McDermott," she replied good-naturedly and placed the card stock notice on the bar before the proprietor.

"Who died this time, Lauren?"

"Sister Larae," she answered. "I met her at the parish festival. She was very nice." She hesitated because she wasn't sure as to how her mother felt about the Sister. "It seemed like my mom knew her when we talked to her at the picnic." She stopped again and tried to remember what had occurred. "But it seemed like they were a little upset with each other for some reason. Anyway, I met her just that one time."

"Well, I guess it doesn't matter too much now. It's like Huck Finn said in his book, 'I don't take no stock in dead people.' "

Lauren looked at McDermott with a puzzled expression because she had no idea what he was talking about. But she was in a hurry because piano lessons were waiting, so she went out the door and on her way.

From the back room carrying a case of long-neck Budweisers, Shadow Pleasance came hurrying into the bar area. He sat the beer case on the floor and walked over next to McDermott and looked at the funeral notice.

"Oh, yeah," he began, "That's that nun who died. You know, Cash, she was in here the night that the other nun got stabbed."

"Really, was she one of those nuns? I didn't even know they were nuns. They were wearing regular street clothes."

"Alan Riedelsheimer told me that both Mr. Carlisle and Mr. Llewellyn were making the funeral arrangements," Shadow confided.

"You don't say? You mean they was doing that together?" Cash asked incredulously.

"Uh huh. Alan said that he never saw two men more polite and considerate of each other over funeral arrangements. He said he didn't realize they could be in the same room together without one strangling the other."

Shadow continued with his narration, "Alan said that after a while the two men began trying to outdo each other in niceness and almost got into it because neither one of them wanted to get a favor without giving a favor in return.

Only the Grass Suffers

"They both offered to pay for the funeral. And get this, they both wanted to have a Mass said for the other along with the nun. So, they both did that and then one of them, I forget which, wanted to pay for a High Mass in Latin, and then the other one wanted to pay for a six-pack of novenas in return. Finally, Alan said that they could split the cost of the funeral and any Masses or novenas was up to them at a later date."

McDermott held the card in his hand and stared at it for some time. Finally, he said only, "Well, go figure."

THE FUNERAL AND BURIAL OF LARAE SAVIGNAC WAS VERY private. The Rheas, Carlisle and Quesnell, and Llewellyn attended. Tim O'Halloran said a prayer at the Catholic gravesite, but there was an impatience in his manner as if he thought a prayer just wasn't enough celebration of a religious woman's life. Alan Riedelsheimer employed four good men to carry the casket to and from the hearse and then they left as soon as they had completed their task.

After the service Mikaela invited the others for lunch on Scuppernong Drive. They all accepted and arrived at about the same time. Michael and Helen came together and Jack pulled up in his old Ford Ranger pick-up. Helen went on inside the house and left Michael and Jack standing out on the veranda.

"Say, Jack," Carlisle placed his hand on the arm of Llewellyn and stopped the projectionist as he was about to enter the front door. Slowly and with a good measure of effort, "I want to thank you for suggesting that we name my grandson 'Michael.'"

Llewellyn instantly remembered the promise that he

made to Mikaela, that he would try to get along with Carlisle. Somehow he knew this was the watershed moment from which his daughter would begin collection of that promise. He did make the effort and the first installment payment was made. "Why not, Mike. He is your grandson, after all," he answered and then added, "I will always think of him as mine, as well." He looked at Carlisle for his reaction.

The old lawyer nodded his head and offered in return, "Well, I just thought it was very good of you. It was very much appreciated."

"Look, Mike, we're never going to be friends in this life. There is too much water under the bridge by now," Jack explained. "But maybe we can coexist because we both have two beautiful families. We are the patriarchs of those two families. And they just happen to be the same two families. Not too many people can say that."

"Yes," Carlisle admitted. "It is obvious that we are inextricably intertwined and will be for the rest of our lives."

"But here's the thing," Llewellyn continued. "There is no one else on earth who can appreciate what we both have been through except for you and me, loving in our own way the same two women and, really, being betrayed by one or the other, as well. So, it just makes sense that only you and I can understand what price we've paid and how much those families mean to us."

"You mean maybe we can help each other?"

"Yeah, Mike. Maybe we can help each other be a part of the two families that we love. The one that we each always had and the other one that we each just recently inherited. If we can concede and compromise, then maybe we can have both families."

Only the Grass Suffers

And then Llewellyn looked Carlisle straight in the eyes and seemingly into his soul, "Or we can battle on without goodwill and our families will suffer for the lack of it and we will be left to ourselves."

The projectionist smiled slightly, "Your sister Helen once advised me that when two bulls fight, only the grass suffers. Maybe we can try to get along and not be just two bulls fighting all the time."

"You mean we can share?"

"Yeah, Mike. We can share."

Llewellyn opened the front door for Carlisle and offered a grin and this time it was the projectionist who placed his hand on the arm of the lawyer. The engaging grin and the gentle hand forced a sigh of surrender from the old lawyer. He was not used to either receiving or accepting such kindness from his lifelong adversary. But now, they were combatants no longer. As they entered the old Victorian house on Scuppernong Drive, they both realized that their personal war was over. They had nothing left to fight about and they had everything to share.

And so the summer had come and gone and autumn brought along crisper air, cloudless skies, and personal clarity to two old men who felt the love and death of two women. They now inherited from those same women two families that gave them both a shared purpose and a sense of belonging. Eventually, the soft gloaming of autumn evenings gave way to dark winter winds that blew a cutting cold across the Wisconsin landscape. But they held fast to their mutual agreement for the safekeeping of their families until the last of their days… and the grass did not suffer.

www.ingramcontent.com/pod-product-compliance
Lightning Source LLC
LaVergne TN
LVHW041619060526
838200LV00040B/1347